INFERNAL

T. Joseph Browder

This is a work of fiction. Names, characters, places, and incidents are products of the author's imagination or are used fictitiously. Any resemblance to persons, living or dead, events or locales, is entirely coincidental.

Cover Art by T. Joseph Browder
ISBN 1-50-753867-8

For my Dad
Who never stopped believing

INFERNAL

PART ONE

THUNDERSNOW

Chapter 1

Richard Farris forced the storm door open against several feet of snow and was almost bowled over as Charlie fled the house. Greedy fingers of wind tore at his face making his eyes water while icy teeth nibbled his ears. Charlie, a one-hundred and eighty pound St. Bernard in desperate need of making his toilet, bounded away through drifts that rose to his shoulders, unaffected by the cold.

Ignoring the snow shovel standing sentry by the door, Richard slogged through the remnants of the drift that had been blocking the door and headed for the garage fifty yards away. Halfway there the sidewalk beneath his feet had been scoured clean of all but a thin layer of ice by fickle winds. He stopped. Under a fast moving sky where storm clouds and sunlight battled for domination he turned a slow circle, surveying the property with wonder.

The landscape appeared as if painted by Dali. Icicles clung to every surface, windblown into tortured shapes that defied gravity, some pulled almost horizontal as if God had tilted the earth as they'd formed. Several trees in the side yard had lost branches. They lay in supplication on the snowy ground, a drift of twisted appendages. A sixty foot pine that had stood on the property for as long as Richard could remember was now bent double; its trunk cracked and splintered wide, the jagged rent covered in a sheet of ice. An insufficient bandage for a fatal wound. Juniper bushes lining the edge of the property paid homage to a line of diamonds, refracting intermittent sunlight in multi-colored hues.

Richard whistled at the beautiful destruction.

Light tore through the sky like a flashbulb. A rumble, more felt than heard, followed. Reminded that Northwestern Kansas was experiencing but a brief respite from the storm that had been ravaging its amber waves of grain for the last three days, Richard returned to the task at hand.

He bulled through snow that was thigh deep in places, arrived at the garage, and delivered a kick to the door that freed it from a rime of ice clinging to the sill. Once inside he flicked the light switch. The act, more habit than common sense, rewarded him only with darkness and served to remind him why he'd come here in the first place.

The storm had moved down out of the Colorado Rockies earlier in the week. On the first day it had brought snow, heavy and fast accumulating. The National Weather Service had issued a Severe Winter Storm Warning for the states of Colorado and Kansas. Local television stations posted school closings and event cancellations. Overnight the skies dumped three feet of snow on Cheyenne County while temperatures plummeted into the teens.

The second day brought a warming trend from the south. The snow turned to sleet and ice and there were reports of *Thundersnow*, a rare and awesome spectacle of nature possible in this part of the country when there was a cold front with warmer air aloft. Lightning touched down in numerous locations leaving rural areas without power and prompting the Governor to declare a state of emergency. Winds increased as that day turned to night, howling up to sixty miles an hour, downing tree limbs and power lines. Reports of weather related accidents crowded the airways:

An ambulance transporting a woman who'd suffered a stroke slid into the front of a jewelry store at better than forty miles an hour, killing the driver and lodging the bus in a gaudy display of gold and diamonds.

An elderly man traveling east on Route 36 lost control of his car in near whiteout conditions and rolled into a ditch. Unable to release his seatbelt, he drowned, his last gasps filling his lungs with mud and muck.

A young couple with a newborn had set their house ablaze with an outdated floor furnace. There had been no survivors.

Just past four a.m., long after Richard had grown weary of reports of death and destruction and gone to bed, the power plant in St. Francis sustained a massive lightning strike. Turbines blew as 30,000 amps of electricity traveling at nearly the speed of light coursed through the station. Backup generators overloaded. Transformers within two miles of the plant showered sparks on the ground below like celebratory fountains. Four Kansas counties, as well as two in Nebraska and Colorado, went dark.

Richard, awakened in typical fashion by Charlie trying to lick the flesh from his face with a tongue the size of a man's palm—and breath that would stop an enraged bear dead in its tracks—found that he too was without power. The house was bitter cold; the fire stoked the evening before reduced to dim embers. Shivering from the cold, as well as the image of him and the dog frozen solid in the house in reflection of Jack Nicholson at the end of the film version of *The Shining*, Richard threw on some clothes and made his way outside.

The sky resembled a rumpled grey blanket. Clouds continued to bunch up overhead, gaining ground on an embattled sun and promising fresh snowfall. Occasional rumbles of distant thunder vibrated his nerve endings as Richard pulled the Mag-lite he kept by the garage door from its charger and clicked it on.

To the left, beneath shelves of motor oil, anti-freeze, and various and sundry hand tools, was Richard's prize possession. A black 1970 Ford Mustang Mach One in near mint condition. Richard had purchased the vehicle for cash the prior spring, drove it every day, even made up excuses to get behind the wheel. High fuel costs be damned. For Richard, the car was the ultimate expression of the freedom he'd been denied for over ten years. For that reason alone he'd hated to garage it even in the face of the storm.

His palms itched to get behind the wheel.

"Not today, sweetheart," he sighed.

To the right was a pallet of Iams Eukanuba and an old dresser that he might one day refinish but used to store power tools and loose hardware in the meantime. Ahead of this were three fifty-gallon drums of fuel, an old fashioned hand-crank rotary siphon, and the object of Richard current interest; a *Generac* electric start portable generator.

Portable being a relative term, the unit took up a large amount of space in the two car garage. At over four feet in length and almost three wide the large orange and black machine would generate 17,500 watts of power to the house and garage for over eight hours on a single tank of fuel. The fact that it sounded like a Mack truck idling in a bathroom was irrelevant.

Richard checked the fuel level and gauges. Satisfied that all was well he pressed the starter. The engine roared to life without hesitation. Fluorescent lights mounted on the ceiling blinked and clicked as their ballasts warmed. The garage was soon bathed in their cold but reliable glow. His reflection peered back at him from the Mustang's windshield. He needed a shave. Reddish two day old growth crept across his chin and up his cheeks, skirting an inch-long scar beneath his left eye before reaching his blonde, brush-cut hair. A matter of convenience rather than style. He was thirty-nine years old last May but the bitter cold made his often battered body feel closer to fifty.

As he turned to leave the garage, he tripped and fell over the dog.

Richard had no desire to have fifty pound bags of dog food torn apart and spread about the garage. So thinking, he'd made a point of teaching Charlie to wait outside whenever he found it necessary to come in here. This lack of obedience was unusual for the dog.

"What do you think you're doing?" Richard said, his voice muffled by the roar of the generator and the fact that he was face down on the floor.

Charlie didn't answer. Just put his cold nose against the back of Richard's neck. Richard swatted at the offending nose, missed, and pushed himself to his knees.

"Out! You know you're not allowed..." he began, then noticed a blue something dangling from the corner of Charlie's mouth.

"What's this?" Richard asked. The dog relinquished the object at Richard's urging.

Richard examined it.

It was a mitten. About the size a child would wear.

There was blood on it.

"Where'd you get this?" Richard asked.

Charlie sat. Whined.

The blood on the mitten was fresh.

"You found someone out there?"

Charlie stood. Pranced a little, and then shot out the door. He paused outside, looked back, and barked.

Richard followed.

Charlie paused every so often to look back, ensuring that Richard was still following as he led him towards a stand of trees and brush several hundred yards from the garage on the back corner of the property.

Richard's pants were soaked through with snow in minutes, his legs numb before he'd made half the trek. The temperature was dropping rapidly, the wind gusting. While he'd been in the garage clouds had claimed victory over the sun. The sky was now a dark and angry shade of grey.

Richard dipped his chin into his collar against the cold. His cheeks and ears were burning. He yearned for a scarf or a ski mask.

"There better be someone out here," he grumbled.

He meant nothing of the sort. If someone were out in this weather, incapable of getting to shelter on their own and relying on a dog to raise assistance, they were in real trouble. Better that Charlie had found nothing more interesting than an odd mitten left in the thicket by a forgetful child.

But there was an air of urgency in Charlie's antics.

And fresh blood on the mitten.

Lightning crossed the heavens in a whip stroke. Thunder roared in reply. Richard increased his pace, closing on the tree line. Charlie waited beneath an old pine that sheltered smaller vegetation. He was whining again, his agitation showing in the sweep of his tail. Then he disappeared into the foliage like a shadow before the sun.

Richard brushed limbs aside and pushed into the scrub. There was a depression here, about twenty feet across and clear of all but a light dusting of snow and some branches that had succumbed to the weight of the ice. Densely intertwined tree limbs had caught and held most of the storm's fury as efficiently as a canopy. That couldn't last, though. He could hear the groaning and occasional pop of stressed timber overhead.

It was warmer here, too, out of all but the strongest gusts of wind. Richard had played here as a boy. It had at various times been redoubt against invading Apaches, a Vietnam jungle, and the bridge of a starship. An old tree, fallen long before Richard's birth, had served as barricade, backstop, and once, the plank of an old pirate ship. It now sheltered a child sized form curled on one side, all too quiet and still on the cold, hard ground. Charlie sniffed around the hood of the pink parka the child wore. Pink that was stained with a wide swath of blood from the middle of the back to the hemline.

"Oh, Jesus," Richard said.

He knelt, rolled the girl onto her back and pulled back her hood. Black hair spilled out framing the face not of a child but a woman in her twenties. Her skin was bronze; a natural, year-round tan. Her nose was somewhat flat, a trademark of people of Pacific Island descent. She was petite, but not, as Richard had feared, a young girl. The fading light and her position—as well as his own expectations—had conspired to deceive his senses.

"Hey," Richard coaxed, placing his fingers to the woman's throat. He was rewarded with a pulse, thready and weak but there all the same. She didn't respond, however, and Richard thought fast, unsure of her injuries and uncertain if carrying her was the best course of action.

Several small branches broke free from the canopy above, tumbling to earth carrying large clots of snow behind them. One landed on Richard's shoulder with a wet plop. A stroboscopic burst of light followed closely by thunder decided him. He gathered the woman into his arms and, Charlie leading the way, carried her back to the house.

Chapter 2

The woman was resting in the bedroom. Richard sat in the living room leafing through a decade old copy of McGraw Hill's *Current Medical Diagnosis and Treatment* he'd plucked from the bookshelf in the hallway. A fire warmed his toes while a comforter took care of the rest of his body. The storm raged and railed against the windows like a living thing trying to get inside.

He'd have preferred a more recent edition of the *CMDT*, or even better, access to *WebMD*, but the internet was down. The repeater towers used by his provider had either fallen in the face of the storm or the wind, sleet, and lightning were disrupting the signal.

Getting the woman into the house had been a chore unto itself. The sleet had come again before they were halfway to the house; hard, tiny spicules that lashed his face as if trying to drive him back into the shelter of the copse. He'd crushed his nose and mouth against the hood of the woman's parka—her hair smelled of lavender—squinting against the sleet and relying more on the tip of Charlie's upraised tail ahead to guide him than his own sense of direction. He'd then had to lay her on the ice-covered woodpile beside the back door before he could wrestle it open against the wind driven snow. Maneuvering her through a kitchen in the midst of renovation had been no joy either but at least it had been warmer.

Once in the bedroom he'd laid her on the bed and tried the telephone. It was, not surprisingly, out. His cell phone was dead as well, displaying its moronic NO SIGNAL message as soon as he'd touched the screen. His last hope, an HP Pavilion laptop that was his link to the outside world, was also down. The wireless assistant tried to do its duty, the little ball on the screen bounced back and forth between the icons for his computer and the Earth for several minutes before the machine informed him no network connections were available.

With no real medical assistance forthcoming, Richard steeled himself against the knowledge that he was the woman's only chance for survival. Until he could raise the EMT's or get her to a hospital—

forty miles away, may as well be on the moon in this weather, he thought—he and Charlie were the only hope she had.

Asking God for a little help and begging the woman's pardon for what he knew he had to do, Richard returned to the woman's side and gently unzipped her parka.

The sweater she wore beneath was lilac; a fisherman's knit. The right side turned to crimson just below the ribcage. A ragged hole had been torn into it. Blood oozed from a rent in the flesh beneath.

"Sweet Jesus," Richard said. Charlie, standing sentinel duty close by, wuffed in agreement. Richard had seen this kind of wound before. The woman had been shot.

Richard retrieved the first-aid kit and several towels from the bathroom and set to work. He cut the sweater open from the *v* at the neck to the waist and then laid it open to reveal her stomach. The wound, a puckered hole just above the waistline of her jeans, was a little over a half inch in diameter. Blood filled the hollow of her stomach and her navel. Richard gently rolled the woman towards him and found its twin somewhat higher on her back. It too was trickling blood, painting the mattress pad red like an artist creating a fresh blooming rose. He lay her back down guessing she'd been hit by a single round; what was called a through and through. From the amount of blood he decided it had to have happened within the last hour. She'd have bled out if it had been much longer.

"Sorry about this," Richard said, not knowing if the woman could hear him or not. He slit the ruined sweater and parka down the sleeves and removed them and the remaining mitten. Then cut first down one leg of her jeans, then the other, and slid the jeans from beneath her. Her panties were sodden with blood so he cut them free as well, averting his eyes and placing a towel over her modesty. He removed her bra in the same fashion, adding it to the pile of bloody clothing on the floor.

Charlie whined from his position at the foot of the bed as Richard covered the woman's breasts.

"I know, boy," he told the dog, embarrassed despite his intentions. "I don't like it either. But there's nothing else we can do."

Richard swabbed the woman's belly free of blood with saline solution from the first-aid kit. No fresh blood came from the wound.

He didn't know if that meant she had stopped bleeding or if the new position caused it to flow from her back. He swabbed the wound with Chlorhexadine solution—despite centuries of misinformation he knew that hydrogen peroxide is more useful for removing blood from clothing than for treating injuries—and taped Telfa pads into place over it. He rolled the woman over and repeated the process. There *was* still some bleeding there, a slow trickle, and he'd had to swab the area clean three times before applying the Chlorhexadine and bandages. He prayed that the bleeding would stop. And that whatever internal injuries she'd sustained were minor.

He wished for a sphygmomanometer or one of those neat little electronic blood pressure cuffs as he checked her pulse—he had some experience with the device and knew how to use them and what the numbers meant. Her pulse was stronger than it had been in the copse but still not as strong as he'd have liked. He then took her temperature. It was one hundred and four. A high number, but he had no idea if that was her body's natural reaction to the wound itself or if it signaled impending infection. He decided to check it every hour or so in any event. If her temperature rose any higher he'd have to take some other kind of action.

He dug through his dresser and found an old t-shirt and sleep pants he no longer wore. They were too big for the woman but sufficient under the circumstances. He carefully dressed her, then added a pair of thick woolen socks that bunched around her ankles. He then made the bed with fresh sheets, removing the soiled mattress pad and rolling the woman gently from side to side as he worked around her. Charlie wuffed his approval as Richard added not one but two comforters.

His task complete for the time being, Richard turned his attention to the clothing the woman had been wearing. A quick search of her pants and parka turned up nothing. No wallet or identification of any kind. The pockets held nothing but lint and, in the front pocket of the blue jeans, a crumpled cherry Starburst wrapper.

Richard sat on the edge of the bed, running his hand across his crew cut.

"I don't know what else I can do, boy," he told the dog.

Charlie came forward and nudged Richard's hand with his nose. Richard stroked his great furry head, drawing comfort from the act. Animals that choose to spend their lives with humans can at times be their greatest source of strength and succor.

"There's just so much I don't know."

Charlie whined in commiseration and laid his head on Richard's knee.

"Where did she come from?" he asked. "Who did this to her? Do they know where she is now? Will they be coming for her?"

The dog remained silent save the contented whisking of the floor with his tail.

"Is she going to die?"

Charlie looked up into his eyes and fixed him with solemn regard. The dog seemed to be telling him that that might very well be up to him.

"Coffee," Richard said, apropos of nothing. "And research," he added.

He rose from the bed to make the one and approach the other when the woman's arm lashed out. She grasped his wrist.

"The focal point!" she screamed. "Has it opened?"

Charlie startled, let out a low *woof*, and rounded the bed to the Richard's side.

"What?" Richard asked. Her grip was stronger than expected, her hand hot and dry on his wrist. He shook his arm free and placed his hand on her forehead. She was burning up with fever.

"The key," she told him, lifting her head and locking gazes with him. Her eyes were brown, a lighter shade than most, but clear and bright, not hazy and unfocused with delirium. "We must find the key! We have to stop them!"

"I don't know what you mean," he began, but she had already succumbed to exhaustion. Her head rolled back onto the pillow, her jaw slackened. She was asleep, or unconscious, in seconds.

"Well that explains everything," Richard remarked.

He took the woman's temperature again, surprised to find that it had dropped a degree despite the heat radiating off her. Charlie looked on, approving of the gentle way his human cared for the new human in his life. Some humans were good, while others were bad.

His human was good, though that hadn't always been the case. The new human, the *female* human, was also good. He also knew in the way that dogs know things that she was in great danger. They were *all* in great danger.

Satisfied that he had done all that he could and that the woman was in no immediate jeopardy, Richard again set off to make his morning coffee. He paused at the door, looking back at Charlie holding firm by the bed.

"You coming?"

Charlie lay down on the floor. A sentry for the wounded.

"Okay," Richard said. "She probably needs you more than I do right now, anyway."

The kitchen was by far the coldest room in the house. Three brand new windows looked out on the storm, slick white polyvinyl frames gleaming in the light from the overhead fixture, the brightest surface in a room that had been stripped and gutted of all but a central cooking island. No insulation stood against the creeping fingers of the wind, only exterior wallboard and aluminum siding shielded the two-by-four framing and bare floors from the elements. It was like standing inside the ribcage of some great, long dead beast.

The new flooring, insulation, and wallboard—and a light oak paneling that he thought would look nice in a kitchen—all awaited in the utility room. Those tasks, he thought as he rummaged in the crowded cabinet beneath the island searching out the coffee and filters, his breath streaming out before him like a banner, would have to wait. The door between the kitchen and living room was sufficient to keep the worst of the cold from the rest of the house but he doubted it would provide an adequate barrier against the sound of a saw or hammer. His charge, whoever she was, would doubtless benefit more from peace and quiet than the noise of construction.

His coffee perking cheerily away Richard returned to the living room. He rebuilt last night's fire, retrieved a steaming mug of the now finished brew—hazelnut, his favorite—and settled in with some texts from the bookshelf. He was asleep in minutes.

A dream of iron bars and angry, caged men dissolved as something cold nudged Richard's hand. He'd slumped lower in his chair as he slept and now sat up, dislodging the CMDT and a text on practical home remedies from his lap. They fell to the floor with successive thumps. Charlie stood at his side. He issued a thin, anxious whine as his human reasserted himself in the present.

"What is it, boy?"

The dog turned away and padded into the bedroom. Tossing aside the comforter, Richard followed.

He was just inside the door and noted that the woman appeared to be resting peacefully. Her chest rose and fell slowly beneath the blankets. One fist was tucked under her chin in a gesture that Richard found both child-like and charming. Then he heard it. A low, almost subaudible buzzing. It seemed to be coming from the pile of ruined clothing at the foot of the bed.

"Damn," Richard muttered, simultaneously recognizing the sound of a cell phone set to vibrate and berating himself for not checking the woman's clothes more thoroughly. He'd searched the side pockets of the parka but had missed a small zippered one on the sleeve. He unzipped it and found a slim black cell phone.

It was about the size of a credit card though thicker, unmarked, and of a make and model he was unfamiliar with. It slid open under his thumbs, stilling the vibrator and revealing a *qwerty* style keypad. Once rotated, the top revealed a screen that read: ENTER CODE:

Richard thumbed in four nines; the default code for his, and, so far as he knew, every cell phone in existence. The screen reset to ENTER CODE:

He keyed in four zero's with the same result.

He tried several four letter combinations and random entries, but nothing coaxed a response from the device. The screen reset each time, mocking white letters on a black background. Richard sensed the phone held the secret of the woman's identity and the answers to at least some of his questions and suppressed the urge to throw the uncooperative device into the fireplace. Instead, he closed it and slipped it into his pocket.

He looked at Charlie.

Charlie looked back. If he could have shrugged, Richard thought he would have.

"Crap," Richard said, his hopes of enlightenment dashed.

He turned to the woman, still sleeping and oblivious to the world around her.

"Who *are* you?" he asked.

She offered no response. Richard gathered the woman's clothing from the floor. After searching them to make sure he hadn't missed anything else, he washed the blood from her underclothes. The jeans, parka, and sweater were beyond repair and he threw them in the trash.

The wind outside caressed the house like a lover as he left the room.

Charlie, still standing sentry, returned to his place at the side of the bed and lay on the floor.

Chapter 3

Charlie maintained his vigil beside the bed, dozing off and on, aware enough to respond if he sensed any sign of distress from the human female while dreaming doggy dreams of chasing rabbits, rolling in endless fields of honeysuckle and jasmine, and huge piles of meaty bones just for him.

The night had passed taking the storm with it. The cold front had moved off to the northeast and was currently dumping snow on Nebraska and southern Iowa, leaving a warm front in its wake that, as the sun rose, melted snow and ice from roofs and gutters, tree branches and power lines—those that had managed to stay aloft—the soft rataplan of runoff echoing pleasantly in Charlie's sensitive ears. Kansas would recover as it had countless times in the aftermath of severe thunderstorms and tornadoes that visited the state each year in succession.

Charlie's human had gone outside after rising from the couch in the living room where he'd slept the night before. The power had gone out again—Charlie knew this because the low hum that usually travelled inside the walls and out through the square, wall mounted boxes he wasn't allowed to paw at or even lick, had stopped—and his human had gone out to where the food came from to start it up again. Presumably it needed to be fed occasionally too.

Charlie lifted his head as the woman on the bed made a soft sound and shifted her position. She was sleeping now, healing. Her hurt place was getting better. His human had tended it with care before going outside, removing the funny white cloth he'd placed on it, all full of blood and bad smelling liquid, and replacing it with new cloth that would catch any more that might come out. Charlie didn't use a cloth when he had a hurt. He licked it—if he could reach it—until it went away. He would lick the woman's hurt if his human would let him but he understood that humans did not always do things the right way.

A new sound, low and powerful, came from outside the house. Charlie stood and cocked his head to one side, trying to identify it. It was like the sound the big black horse he and his human sometimes rode in made. Charlie liked riding in the big black horse, even if it was not an alive thing and made funny smells when they weren't moving. When they *were* moving the wind blew in Charlie's face and he could smell and taste many things. Humans, trees, grass, other dogs; all of it riding the wind that blew back Charlie's ears and sometimes made his eyes water. Riding in the big black horse made Charlie happy.

This horse sounded different. This horse sounded *wrong*.

Charlie padded into the living room trying to smell the horse as the hum in the walls started up again and the lights came on. A big *whoosh* like a huge bird passed over the house and the bedroom and living room windows crashed in, followed by a flash and a boom that lifted the dog off his feet and tossed him in the corner like a rag doll.

Richard had awakened that morning with a stiff neck from sleeping on the couch. There was an old trundle bed in the attic but he hadn't wanted to be that far away should his charge regain consciousness—likely terrified and confused—and navigating the steel frame bed and mattress set down the narrow stairs seemed more trouble than it was worth.

The power had gone out again. He'd left a light burning on the end table in case he needed to move swiftly from the living room to the bedroom—he'd tripped over some of Charlie's rawhide bones and larger toys in the dark before and had no desire to do so again—and the soft glow of the bulb had been absent when he scrubbed the sleep from his eyes and tossed back the comforter. He wasn't surprised by the power loss. The generator only held enough fuel for about eight hours. He should have topped the tank off the evening before but hadn't wanted to make another trip out into the storm.

The woman had been sleeping peacefully when he'd checked on her. She mumbled a few soft nothings as he changed her bandage—almost no blood this time and the wound had crusted around the edges; a sure sign it was healing—and checked her temperature. It was an even one-hundred Better by far than the evening before. He didn't think she was out of the woods yet but believed she'd recover with time and more appropriate medical attention.

That taken care of, he'd patted Charlie on the head and praised him for being a good sentry:

"Hospitals should hire you, you know that?" he told the dog. "Maybe they'd even pay you. You could help out with the bills around here."

He'd then let Charlie out to tend to his toilet before tending to his own and pulling on clothes suitable for the weather.

He'd checked his phones and laptop before going out. The lines were still down. He puzzled over the call or message that had come into the woman's cell phone while his was still inoperable. He'd checked it after the failed attempt to access hers and found the same NO SIGNAL message. He decided she was on another, stronger network, but the question remained in the back of his mind, joining the long list of other unanswered questions already in residence.

The sun bedazzled his eyes as he stepped out the back door. It gleamed from every surface, coruscating from the icy coating on the garage, winking from the wreck of the pine tree to the ice shrouded bushes lining the property and shimmering from the rapidly melting snow at his feet. It was like standing at the center of an immense jewel.

The thermometer hanging by the back door read forty-four degrees. If the temperature stayed this high throughout the day the snow would be all but gone by noon. He could have the woman in town by sunset, relinquishing her to proper medical personnel who could tend her much better than he.

There was bound to be police involvement. One didn't turn up at a local hospital with a shooting victim and simply walk away. An investigation would follow and he would be questioned, perhaps detained. In the end, however, the woman would regain consciousness and give a statement that would exonerate him of wrong-doing. He wasn't looking forward to the situation but despite one notable run-in with the wrong side of the law in the past, Richard still had faith in the system.

In the garage Richard used the old rotary siphon to pump fuel from a fifty-five gallon drum to the generator. The engine roared with a touch of a button and the overheads blinked to life in short sequence. Richard was cleaning the siphon with a shop towel when something droned by his ear with the sound of an angry insect. The Mustang's windshield starred, a craze of cracks blooming on the passenger side like a small rose.

Richard jerked his head towards the door and saw a man in what looked like military arctic gear leveling a long barreled pistol at him. He was grinning like a hyena and lining up for another shot. He wouldn't miss a second time.

Richard lashed out with the only weapon he had on hand. The siphon hose wasn't long enough to cover the distance between them, and wasn't much of a weapon in any event, but the fuel that flew from the end of the hose splattered the intruder's face burning his eyes on contact and spoiling his aim. The round intended for Richard's heart spanged through the Mustang's grill and lodged in the engine block instead.

In times of stress and insurmountable danger most people's first instinct, hardwired into the brain by evolution, is to flee. Having lived in an environment where there was nowhere to run when danger arose, Richard turned to fight. He lowered his head and barreled into the intruder before he could adjust his aim and fire off another shot.

The headlong plunge carried them both out the door, air *whoofing* from the intruder's lungs as they sprawled in the ice and slush in the back yard. Landing atop his opponent Richard delivered blow after blow to the man's face, neck, and abdomen.

Unprepared for the ferocity of Richard's counter-attack the intruder was momentarily stunned by the assault. He was three inches taller than Richard's five-foot eleven frame and out-weighed him seventy pounds, however. He had little trouble muscling his way out from under Richard and locking him in a leg hold around the waist before rolling him over as easily as a mean spirited child might flip a turtle on the roadside. His gun had flown into the snow when Richard struck him so he wrapped his hands around Richard's throat and squeezed.

Richard grasped at the man's hands, found a weakness at the pinky finger, and twisted it up and back. The finger snapped with the sound of a small branch breaking. The intruder grunted and pulled away only to deliver a stunning blow to the side of Richard's head. He grasped Richard's neck, closing his airway again.

The world swam away, the brilliant blue sky above dimming. Richard looked into the eyes of his attacker and saw no mercy there; only that hyena's grin as he choked the life from a complete stranger.

His heart crashed in his chest as Richard pulled at the hands that bound his throat like iron bands, pushed at the chin of the man grinning his lunatic grin, and threw a blow to the neck that was shrugged off as one would shrug off the sting of an insignificant insect. Spots bloomed before his eyes, his vision darkened. His brain was shutting down his peripheral nervous system in an attempt to preserve oxygen.

Richard groped in the ice and slush around him. Found something thin and hard and brought it up against the side of the intruder's face. The chunk of ice shattered harmlessly against his forehead.

He reached out again, fumbled through ice, snow, and mud, seeking something solid, something *useful*. He seized a round, semi-solid something and brought it up, this time into the intruder's face, crushing it into that maniacal grin and upwards into his nose. The partially frozen dog turd ground against the man's teeth, filled his mouth and nostrils, smeared across his forehead. He made a *gaak* sound, released Richard, and spat, his hands flying to his own throat as if he were the one now being strangled.

Richard dragged in a breath of the sweetest air he'd ever drawn. His throat burned, his lungs ached. His heart sped in his chest like a team of galloping horses. He thrust the sputtering man backwards and gained his knees, taking in great whoops of air as he did so.

The intruder, soldier, whatever he may be, was on his knees, head bent, trying to hawk dogshit from his nose and mouth. Richard punched him in his ear with everything he had, aiming for a spot just beyond the man's head. The blow toppled the intruder onto his side. He grunted and rolled onto his back, eyes watering from gasoline, pain, and the smell of feces. The lunatic grin was gone, replaced by a grimace of revulsion. Richard punched him in the nose. Twice. The first blow broke cartilage and bone. The second sent a spray of blood and feces from his nostrils. The man howled, striking out at Richard's legs as he gained his feet. Richard kicked the hand away and kicked him in the jaw as if he were punting from the fifty-yard line. There was a satisfying crunch and the man lay still.

A dim, dark part of Richard's mind hoped he had killed him.

Richard spied the intruder's pistol, an H& K USP9 fitted with an Abraxas Titanium suppressor lying a few feet away. He picked it up and unthreaded the suppressor, lightening the weapon's weight and making it easier to conceal. He slipped the suppressor into a pocket on his parka. The pistol he kept in his hand.

He approached the intruder with caution. He seemed to be unconscious but it could be a ploy to get Richard into range so he could renew his efforts to kill him. Richard was debating searching the man for more weapons and identification—and maybe pumping a round from the 9mm into the man's head to ensure there'd be no further trouble with the bastard—when he heard commotion from within the house.

Charlie, barking in agitation. Voices raised in alarm.

He headed for the back door at a run, thought better of it, and ran around the side of the house. He slid to a halt as he took in the M1114 HMMWV parked in the dooryard, doors open, engine idling. One look at the light grey on white camouflage told him that it was no civilian 'Hummer' model. The protective covers for the Central Tire Inflation System and the worn airlift hooks on the hood were clues. The M249 light machine gun pintle-mounted above the cab was a dead giveaway.

The Marines—or someone very much like them—had landed in Richard Farris's front yard.

He approached the front door with caution. The storm door leaned drunkenly against the porch wall, the closing mechanism broken. The interior door yawned inwards, the frame splintered where the deadbolt and latch had torn through the wood.

He crossed the foyer and entered the living room in a crouch. He could hear Charlie, somewhere off to the left, his barks reduced to muffled growls. Someone in there—not the woman, the voice was too deep—was screaming. The tang of cordite filled the air.

Something crunched underfoot and Richard looked down. Broken glass littered the floor, the sofa, and end tables. Several dragon figurines he had collected were knocked over or shattered. Tiny black spheres peppered the room. He picked one up, rolling it between his finger and thumb. It was hard rubber; a projectile from a sting grenade. From the looks of the room more than one had been launched through the windows.

He was considering his position and next move when a fat man jerked backwards through the bedroom doorway, tugging on something and whining. He too wore arctic gear but it was tight and ill-fitting. As he retreated further, oblivious to Richard's presence, Richard could see what he was tugging at.

Charlie was worrying at the fat man's arm. The sleeve of his parka was shredded below the elbow and blood poured out in freshets. Charlie's teeth were clamped down like a steel trap above his wrist. As Richard watched the dog planted his back legs and shook the arm like a rag. There was a snapping, crunching sound from the man's wrist and he *shrieked.*

Good boy, Richard thought.

The fat man was almost in the middle of the living room, his shrieks reduced to sobs as Charlie continued his assault on his arm.

"Get it off me!" he screamed.

A second man entered from the bedroom. This one was slender, with greasy black hair and a thin mustache that made Richard think of Snidely Whiplash from the old Rocky and Bullwinkle cartoons. He carried a USP9 identical to the one Richard had taken off of the Hyena and was lining it up on the dog growling fiercely a few feet away.

"Hold still, Doc," he said, his voice calm amidst the melee. "I got him."

Richard didn't hesitate. He shot Snidely Whiplash through the knee. Blood and bone sprayed out like a macabre party favor and Snidely went down, clutching his knee and bawling like a newborn calf.

Charlie and his captive both turned at the noise, the fat man's eyes widening at the sight of the gun now trained on him.

"Let him go, Charlie," Richard said, rising.

Charlie obeyed, releasing the man's arm and backing off a step. A warning growl continued, deep in his throat.

"Good boy," Richard said, and closed on Snidely Whiplash, now holding his knee and mewling pitifully. He kicked the man's weapon out of reach. He spared a quick glance into the bedroom. The woman was still on the bed, unconscious or sleeping. The sheets and blankets had been pulled up around her in a sort of makeshift gurney. They'd been preparing to move her somewhere—likely the HumVee—when they'd been interrupted by one very large, very angry St. Bernard.

No one else appeared to be in the bedroom. The bathroom door was closed. Someone *could* be in there but Richard doubted it. The struggle with Charlie and the subsequent gunshot would have drawn them out. He scanned the living room and what he could see of the front yard. There was no one else in evidence.

He didn't like that the kitchen door was closed. Anyone could come through that door without warning.

"How many of you are there?" Richard asked the fat man.

"Don't tell him anything," Snidely Whiplash said through clenched teeth.

"Shut up," Richard said. "Or you'll need *two* new knees."

To the fat man: "How many?"

"Three here," the fat man replied, sobbing, "four more in the helicopter."

Helicopter? Richard thought. *What have I gotten myself into here?*

"You're dead, Doc," Snidely said from the floor. "Jefferson's gonna kill you."

"Charlie," Richard said. The dog turned to Snidely, a warning growl building in his throat. The man winced away.

"Okay, okay," he whined.

"Doc, is it?" Richard asked. The fat man nodded. "I'm going to ask you some questions. Now we don't have time for pleasantries so I'm just going to shoot you, maybe in the leg, maybe somewhere more vital, every time you refuse to answer. Or if I think you're lying. Do you understand?"

Doc gaped at him. He was sweating. It matted his hair and ran down his face making him look greasy and unkempt. Blood from his arm pattered to the floor. Richard leveled the gun at his knee in warning.

"Yes!" he cried. "I understand!"

"Good," Richard said. "Who are you people?"

"We're a retrieval team. Sent to bring back the woman."

"Who sent you?"

"BanaTech."

"What is BanaTech?"

"A research firm. They specialize in biotech and physics research."

Richard processed this. Biotech companies were a dime a dozen. He'd never heard of BanaTech but could name a dozen other such companies off the top of his head. To his knowledge most were small companies that studied plants and animals looking to bring new medicines to the market. The larger ones, it was rumored, worked hand in hand with the government cooking up bioweapons for military application. He'd never heard of one that also dabbled in physics.

"What are they researching?"

"I don't know. We're just part of the internal security team. Please, my *arm*."

"Why do they want the woman?"

"She stole critical information. They want it back. *Please*. I don't know any more."

The fat man was crying now. Tears rolled down his cheeks, mingling with sweat and blood. The damage to his arm had to be causing him considerable pain. These men had broken into his home, tried to kill him and his dog, and tried to kidnap an injured woman to whom he'd given shelter. Richard felt no pity for the man.

"Where's the helicopter?"

"*Please*," the man mewled.

Richard raised his gun to the man's face. "I won't ask again."

"It's supposed to circle the area and wait for our signal, then escort us to the extraction point."

"Why are you with this team?"

The last question seemed to baffle the man. "What?"

"Snidely over here," Richard said, gesturing with his free hand at the man on the floor clutching the remains of his knee to his chest, "and the man outside are military types. You're not. You're fat, your clothes don't fit, and, quite frankly, you're singing like a canary when you should be keeping your mouth shut. So why are you with this team?"

Richard never got his answer. He'd been keeping an eye on Charlie and the man he was guarding out of the corner of his eye. Snidely didn't move, he didn't hear what was coming. But Charlie did. He whipped his head towards the kitchen door as if spying a squirrel darting across the room.

Richard fell back, pushing off with his feet. Broken glass ground into his back but the slugs that arced across the room as the Hyena burst through the kitchen door blindly firing an MP-9 machine pistol missed him altogether. Fate, circumstance, or just good old-fashioned luck also spared Doc and Charlie from the onslaught. The man Richard thought of as Snidely Whiplash wasn't so fortunate. One of the slugs took him just above the ridge of the nose, opening the back of his head and depositing his brain on the wall in a garish smear.

Richard propelled himself backwards with his legs and returned fire. His awkward position and frantic motion conspired against him and he missed his target. When the slide of the USP9 locked back on an empty chamber he rolled on his shoulders and dove out the front door. Charlie, having sense enough to know when he was outmatched, came through the door behind him.

"Run!" Richard yelled at the dog. Charlie obeyed, heading around the house out of the line of fire. Richard gained his feet as bullets splintered the doorframe and burst through the open door seeking flesh to rip and rend.

His thoughts—running a million miles a second—took him to the HumVee. He thought he could gain the vehicle despite the barrage of bullets coming from the house. It was armored and could handle the snowmelt and ice with ease. It doubtless had GPS and a transmitter, making it vulnerable to the BanaTech helicopter lurking about, but the light machine gun should be sufficient for staving off attack unless they were carrying a rocket launcher or other heavy ordinance. That option, however, meant abandoning Charlie and the woman. He dismissed the thought and followed the dog around the side of the house at a run.

His best course of action, he decided, was to enter the house through the rear and get behind the intruder who was no doubt following him and the dog. With his weapon empty he'd have to be swift, stealthy, and decisive. He couldn't allow the man another chance to kill him.

He rounded the back corner of the house, leapt a still frozen bush and spied Charlie heading into the bowels of the garage.

Good boy, he thought. *Hide in there until I come for you.*

He was several feet from the open back door when the Hyena appeared in it. He'd intuited Richard's hasty plan and reversed his own course to meet him head on. His face was distorted by swelling and bruises. His nose was bleeding and misshapen. His jaw hung at a strange angle where Richard's kick had broken it. The injury didn't stop him from grinning like a cat that had cornered a hapless mouse, however, and Richard could see specks of dogshit amidst the blood and saliva between his front teeth. With less than five feet separating them there was nowhere for Richard to go. The Hyena lifted the machine pistol into a firing position. At this range, he couldn't miss.

When there's no way out of a situation, the only thing to do is go further in. Richard increased his speed and flung himself at his attacker.

The brazen move didn't work this time. The Hyena sidestepped Richard's lunge, pulling the pistol's trigger as he did so. The first round went astray but the second and third rounds found flesh. One pierced Richard's right shoulder, the other traced a line of fire across his left ear. Several more rounds buzzed through empty air above Richard's head.

The Hyena's aim had been too high, the wounds would not kill. They had been sufficient enough to halt his forward progress, however, and Richard crumpled to the ground, a mass of pain and burning.

The Hyena stepped forward to deliver a coup de grace shot to Richard's head. Richard looked up into the face of his murderer. There was still no mercy there. Only glee, and a sort of insane light dancing merrily behind his eyes as his finger tightened on the trigger.

Chapter 4

Furious barking erupted from the garage as one-hundred and ninety pounds of enraged St. Bernard charged the man Richard thought of as the Hyena. The Hyena's attention shifted to the dog, as well as his aim. Charlie was close. Ten or fifteen yards away at most, but it was too far. He'd be cut down before he reached his target.

"No!" Richard yelled. Despite the pain in his shoulder and ear he lunged to his feet. The Hyena's aim shifted again to cover the more immediate threat.

Instead of pulling the trigger the man jerked forward as if slapped from behind. The arm holding the machine pistol dropped to his side as a look of confusion overtook his face. He lurched again, took a loping step towards Richard and then fell forward. Richard took a step back to avoid the heavy body.

Charlie, his charge halted, woofed querulously and padded to Richard's side. Richard stroked the big dog's head absently, staring down at the man in wonder. Two holes had appeared in the man's back amidst the white and grey pattern of his arctic gear.

Motion at the back door caught Richard's attention. The woman stood there, pale and drawn. She was a vision in sweat pants, an old flannel shirt, and bare feet; a silenced handgun—likely taken from Snidely Whiplash, Richard thought—was gripped tightly in one fist.

"Prime," she said. "Last...hope." Then she crumpled to the ground.

Richard went to her side and knelt. Charlie tagged along but stayed out of the way. He checked her pulse—again weak and thready—then lifted her head. Her eyes were open but unfocused. She was conscious, but only just. Richard pried the weapon from her hand before lifting her into his arms. His shoulder protested with a wave of pain that threatened to loose his hold. He fought it and pulled her to his chest where she rested her head in the crook of his neck like an exhausted child.

Intending to return the woman to the bedroom Richard started into the house. The roar of an engine out front halted him. He'd forgotten the Doctor. He'd escaped the Hyena's wild burst of gunfire and was now in the HumVee attempting to flee. No doubt calling in the helicopter with reinforcements as well.

Richard maneuvered his burden through the kitchen and into the living room, ignoring broken glass grinding beneath his heels as he moved to the couch where he deposited the woman gently.

"Hurry," she said, and offered the gun still clutched in her hand. Richard could hear the roar of the HumVee's powerful engine but the sound wasn't moving away from the house. The vehicle was either stuck in the ice and snow or not in gear. Either way he had a chance to stop the Doctor from fleeing and maybe get some answers.

"Stay," Richard told Charlie and took the proffered weapon. He then turned and bolted through the shattered door. The porch was in ruins, its support columns pockmarked with bullet holes. Richard had replaced the old wooden columns with steel framed supports just over a month ago and fleetingly wondered if they had deflected rounds meant to take his life.

As his feet hit concrete in front of the house he could see the Doctor inside the HumVee, slapping at the steering wheel with his right arm and frantically trying to coax the vehicle into motion. The tires weren't spinning despite the throaty roar of eight cylinders. In his haste he'd neglected to shift the vehicle into gear. Richard covered the ground between the house and the HumVee at a full out run. It wouldn't take the man long to figure out his mistake and Richard would lose the opportunity to question him.

The Doctor saw Richard coming and began rooting around the immediate area of the driver's seat, searching for a weapon. Richard yanked open the driver's side door and thrust the woman's gun forward into the Doctor's face. Then thought better of it and jammed it into the man's crotch.

"Think about it, Doc," he said. "You're already down one arm. That's gonna make jerking off a lot less fun. This'll make it impossible."

"Please, God," the man whimpered.

"I doubt he's listening right now considering what you and your friends have done here. Now get out."

"No," a voice called from the porch. It was the woman. She was leaning against one of the porch supports, her face pale and drawn. She'd walked through the glass in the living room and her feet were cut and bleeding. Charlie stood at her side, looking from her to Richard as if to say *I tried to stop her.*

"We have to go," she said. "Now. The others will be coming."

"Shove over then," Richard told the Doctor and pushed against his mangled left arm. The man wailed in pain but got moving towards the passenger seat.

"No," Richard prodded with the gun. "Get in the back." The Doctor did as he was told, trailing blood as he went. He'd pass out from hemorrhagic shock soon if something wasn't done about it but Richard had neither the time nor the inclination to help him.

Richard got behind the wheel, put the vehicle in gear, and drove as close to the porch as possible. He leaned over and threw open the passenger door. Charlie jumped in first, climbing into the back seat.

"Watch him," Richard told the dog. "If he moves, eat his other arm."

Charlie snorted and bared his teeth at the doctor, licking his chops. The Doctor whimpered and cringed away.

Richard ran around the HumVee and helped the woman into the passenger seat. It was clear she was running on adrenaline and pure determination, on the verge of total collapse. Richard didn't know how much longer she'd be conscious or what shape she'd be in when this—whatever this was—was over. He belted her in and turned towards the house.

"No!" the woman said. "We have to go!"

"One second," Richard responded. "There's something I need in there." He handed her the gun. "I'll be right back."

He ran into the house and located a false panel in the living room wall that disguised the attic stairs. A firm push at the top of the panel released the pressure latch and the door swung open. He reached under the fourth riser and slid another latch aside with his fingers. The stair opened on hinges to reveal a small cavity. He reached in, removed a heavy backpack, and turned back to the living room.

He surveyed the parts of the house he could see. This had been his home since birth. His life was here. His history. He'd been a boy here. Become a man here. Despite his absence for more than a decade, it had stood firm. A symbol of family, strength, and peace.

Knowing he would never see it again, he turned his back on it and walked out.

Richard tossed the backpack on the floorboard of the HumVee, handed the handgun to the woman, and got in. He put the vehicle in gear and backed across the yard, the tires slipping briefly on the snow. He made a reverse u-turn at the entrance of the driveway before turning onto the main road. It was covered in snow-melt and icy, and though not specifically designed for use in these conditions, the HumVee handled it well. He accelerated to fifty miles an hour before the rear end of the vehicle started to shimmy, then backed off to forty-five.

"Would someone...," he began, but the woman, half turned in her seat, cut him off by raising the pistol and aiming it at the Doctor's face.

"Give me your RLP," she said.

"I...I don't have it," he stammered. "Jefferson had the only device. We followed him..."

"Bullshit!" she said. "No one comes through without a portable. They're probably tracking it right now. Now give it to me or so help me God I'll blow your brains all over the back of this car and find it myself."

"Hold on a minute..."Richard said, negotiating the turn onto Highway 36.

"Sophia, please!" the Doctor whined.

"...let's just calm down here." Richard continued. "What is an RLP, and would someone please tell me what the *hell* is going on?"

"I'm sorry, Richard," Sophia said, her finger tightening on the trigger, "there isn't time." To the Doctor she said: "Last chance."

As the tension in the HumVee rose, time stretched like a rubber band pulled taut. Richard noticed several things all at once.

Charlie, visible in the rearview, had been watching the exchange between the Doctor and Sophia with great interest. As the Doctor reached for a pocket on the sleeve of his beleaguered arm, the dog raised his head, his attention drawn to something beyond the man's shoulder. Sophia—he had her name now, at least—was turned halfway round in her seat. She still trained the gun on the Doctor and was reaching out with her free hand to receive whatever it was she'd demanded. Richard himself had taken his eyes from the road and was looking at her in wonder. He'd rescued her from the mouth of the storm and tended her wounds, assuming her a victim. The violence of the past ten minutes made him question that assumption.

A shadow grew outside the vehicle, slim and swift. Richard looked to Sophia, perhaps to ask if she too were felt that time had slowed to a crawl, perhaps to ask again what the hell was going on. Perhaps to just babble incoherently at the madness that had invaded his life. Before he could utter a sound the window behind Sophia crazed and her face began to stretch outwards. Her eyes bulged from overpressure as her forehead expanded and finally burst like a balloon, showering Richard in blood and gore. Charlie yelped from the back seat and time snapped back into place as the burst of .50 caliber rounds fired from the EC635 light combat helicopter that had been stalking them since they'd turned onto the highway found their way inside the lightly armored vehicle.

Richard grasped the wheel to prevent a rollover and floored the accelerator. He wiped blood and bits of bone from his brow, spit a wad of something he didn't want to think about from his mouth, and squinted through the shattered windshield. The helicopter, black and threatening against the clear blue sky, raced ahead of the vehicle, turned, and hovered in place. Richard noted side-mounted M2 Browning machine guns and something far more ominous pod mounted beneath the nose.

A line of fire traced a path from the pod to the HumVee. Richard pulled the wheel hard to the left but couldn't avoid the missile that had been fired from the BanaTech helicopter.

It struck the vehicle broadside, just ahead of the rear tire. The Doctor was pulled apart by explosive force and Richard's world went topsy-turvy as the HumVee was tossed into the air. It flipped over three times before crashing to earth upside down in the middle of the road.

"Hit it again," the Hyena ordered.

He was aboard the EC635, bruised, bleeding, and highly pissed off. His nose was broken, his spine burning where the rounds had slammed into his body armor. He stank of dog feces. To top it all off, his words were garbled from trying to speak without moving his broken jaw.

"Mr. Jefferson, sir," one of the two pilots responded, "they're gone. That was a Hellfire II missile with a thermobaric charge that incinerates anything in the immediate area."

"I said hit it again," the Hyena/Jefferson growled. "That bitch shot me. Twice."

The pilots looked at each other and shrugged. A second missile traced a line of fire from the helicopter to the HumVee, striking the exposed undercarriage. Flames and shrapnel shot into the air as the vehicle was reduced to a burning shell. Jefferson found it painful, but satisfying, to smile.

"Good deal," Jefferson said and patted the pilot who'd fired the missile on the shoulder. "Now let's get back to that house. I want some answers and we have a little housekeeping to attend to."

The helicopter turned south and headed away.

PART TWO

THE MIRROR AND THE KEY

Chapter 5

Time stretched like a rubber band or the elastic in an old pair of socks. Richard gripped the wheel as slugs tore through windows sending up sprays of glass like raindrops on a pond. He turned to the woman—*Sophia, at least I have her name now*—and her face expanded, the left eye bulging until her head burst like over-ripened fruit. He could feel her all over him. Taste her in his mouth. An enormous black insect shot past the vehicle, blocked the road in front of him, and hovered ominously. It spat fire and Richard grabbed for something, *anything*, to hold on to as the world shifted and spun around him, throwing him up. Out. Into a cold white void where he knew no more.

A knock at the door interrupted the dream and Richard lurched erect. The left hip still hurt when he stood suddenly but six months had healed the dislocated shoulder, broken wrist, multiple gunshot wounds, and the burns on his hands and face.

He still went by the name Richard. The document manufacturers in San Francisco's red light district had assured him it was better to keep his first name; he was unlikely to hesitate or fail to respond to Richard as he might have been to Stan or Ralph. His last name, or so his California driver's license, his passport, bank accounts and bills all assured him, was McGee. He found the new name amusing. His favorite novels starred a character named McGee.

He'd fallen asleep working at his computer again. The desk was littered with chip bags, candy wrappers, and empty Sobe bottles; the debris of yet another night spent digging through search engine after search engine for any trace of a company called BanaTech. Yanked from an uneasy slumber by the knock at the door he'd unwittingly swept the haphazard pile of notes he would later compile and add to the gigabytes of information that he already had stored in an external terabyte drive to the floor.

What time is it?

He glanced at the gadget bar on his computer desktop. Just after nine a.m., Saturday.

The knock came again. More insistent this time. He reached under the desk and removed an H&K P30 from a magnetic mount. It was one of many weapons scattered throughout the Santa Monica bungalow he'd been renting for the last three months. There were two .40 caliber Beretta PX4 Storm's in the bedroom; one on each side of the bed. A 9mm 92FS by the same manufacturer was concealed in a false wall panel just outside the bedroom. The kitchen contained three Smith & Wesson .40 caliber M&P compacts; one in the cutlery drawer, one magnet mounted inside the hutch, and one under the kitchen cabinets.

Three more weapons were concealed in the living room. Aside from the H&K he now held in his hand, the leftmost cushion of the couch covered a .454 caliber Taurus Raging Bull while a potted Areca palm housed a 9mm Glock 19 within its decorative planter.

The real firepower, however, was concealed in the attic trap door in the front hall. One pull on the cord and the ladder unfolded revealing two .380 ACP Ingram Mac 11A1s, one clipped to either side of the risers. Each could deliver 1200 rounds per minute at 980 feet per second. In short, controlled bursts they could prove deadlier than the rest of Richard's arsenal combined.

Wait, Richard told himself, fingering the slide release on the P30. *Just think a minute.*

The dream clung like the silken strands of a spider's web. Awakening in cold, confusion, and pain. Upside down in a snow bank, the strap of his backpack gripped in one hand. Staggering out onto the road to survey the flaming pothole that had been the HumVee.

Charlie, he'd thought miserably. *I'm so sorry.*

The white Cadillac that had slowed, stopped. The skinny, twenty something youth with black hair that had emerged, eyes wide and jaw agape.

"Oh, snap!" the young man had said for lack of anything else that would convey his astonishment at the flaming wreckage, Richard's burned and broken visage, or both.

Richard had pulled an pistol—the same one he now held in his hand—from the backpack and pointed it at the boy.

"I need your car."

"Seriously?" the boy said. His eyes widened even further and Richard wondered crazily if they would fall from their sockets and dangle loosely around his chin.

"Seriously," Richard answered.

"For real, for real?" the boy asked.

Richard briefly thought he might have to shoot the obviously intoxicated youth in the leg to make his point. Instead he said:

"For real, for real."

The kid had shrugged, plunged his hands in the pockets of a woefully inadequate windbreaker, and said:

"These things happen."

Before turning the car in a westerly direction Richard had fished a banded pack of one-hundred dollar bills from the backpack and tossed it to the kid standing outside the car.

"It's cold out here," he'd told the boy. "Get a heavier coat."

The last vestiges of the dream/memory slipped away and the present reasserted itself.

The knock at the door came again, this time accompanied by a small, feminine voice:

"Mr. McGee. It's Samantha. I have your cookies."

Richard blew out a breath. *Of course*. This morning was the delivery date for Girl Scout cookies. He'd ordered three boxes of Somoas and a box of Tagalongs from the neighbor's toe-headed nine year-old daughter last month. It crossed his mind that he almost answered the door with a handgun. His endless hours spent vetting the Internet for information on the incident in Kansas six months ago was crumbling the thin line between vigilance and paranoia.

"Great," he said to the room. "Now I'm blowing third graders away over caramel and peanut butter cookies."

Richard bent, replaced the gun on its mount, and dug through the debris on his desk until he came up with his wallet. He padded to the front door and after a cursory look through the peephole, unbolted it. Samantha Peterson, resplendent in her green scout uniform, shoulder length blonde hair braided into pigtails, grinned up at him.

"Hiya, Sammy," Richard said, returning her smile.

"Hi there, Mr. McGee," she answered, reaching into the green shoulder bag she carried in one hand. "I've got your cookies."

"So I heard," he said, his eyes never left her hand as she withdrew it from the bag. *Paranoia,* he warned himself as she handed over nothing more dangerous than four boxes of cookies. "So what's the damage?"

"Eighteen dollars," she said.

"Hmm," Richard said, digging through his wallet and handing over a bill. "All I have is a twenty. You can have the change. Call it a tip."

"We're not allowed to accept tips, Mr. McGee," she told him solemnly.

"A donation, then," he said.

"Sorry, Mr. McGee," she said. "All donations have to be sent directly to the council office. My Daddy will have change, though. Can I bring it right back to you?"

"Sure thing, kiddo," Richard said. "No hurry."

"Bet," she said, and then spun off in the direction of her house, pigtails bouncing off her shoulders as she ran. Her innocence and *joie de vivre* reminded him of another girl in another place. *That* child's life had been stolen from her by a sick and twisted pedophile named Patrick McCormack. Richard had tried, but had been unable to save her. He *had* avenged her, though the decision to do so had cost him ten years of his life.

Richard closed and re-bolted the door, swallowing a lump in his throat at the memory. It had been twelve years since the disappearance of Katie Marsh. Her body had never been found.

Back at his desk Richard began picking up the notes he'd scattered. He'd spent hundreds of hours accumulating information on companies researching both biotechnology and physics, specifically one named BanaTech—and anyone named Sophia or Jefferson connected with such an entity. He'd sifted through thousands of companies specializing in either biotech or physics but had found a mere handful that dabbled in both. Most of those were owned or controlled by the government which made accessing their personnel files a daunting and dangerous task.

He'd realized the need for stealth in his data mining and had turned to the Internet to learn how to use multiple proxies to mask his ISP address and encrypt his files and hard drives. Had he not, his activity might have been discovered and traced back to his location bringing the very people who had wrought violence and murder in Kansas the previous winter crashing through his windows and knocking down his front door. He'd discovered he had a knack for writing code. It was a small leap from setting up secure browsing protocols to learning how to find and exploit back doors to servers. An even smaller step to learning to install algorithms, or worms, which alerted him to information matching his search criteria.

He'd found little of use with these methods. Of a company named BanaTech, he'd found no trace. There wasn't now, and never had been, any such entity.

There were dozens of employees at various research companies named Sophia or Jefferson. He'd even found two women named Sophia Jefferson working for two separate research firms; one in Ohio, the other in Australia. Neither them nor any of the other employees he'd found had matched the description of the woman or the walking juggernaut of destruction he was familiar with.

He'd fared somewhat better with the public search engines like *Yahoo!*, *Google*, and *Bing*. While achieving the same results related to BanaTech he'd yielded reams of information on Richard Farris. According to public information his former self was dead, the result of bad wiring to a faulty generator that had overheated and exploded. The resulting fire had spread to the house and, encouraged by building material and the lack of response by emergency personnel due to the weather, had burnt it to the ground. One charred body had been pulled from the wreckage. Despite positive identification being impossible due to the condition of the remains it was presumed to be Richard Farris. Who else would have been in his home in the midst of a snowstorm?

There had been no mention of intruders or the resulting firefight.

A curious incident several miles away wherein an intoxicated youth had discovered the burning wreckage of a vehicle containing two unidentified human bodies and one of a dog had not been linked to the fire at the Farris house. There had likewise been no mention of a carjacking—the vehicle had probably been stolen in the first place,

Richard surmised—or the banded stack of one-hundred dollar bills Richard had given the youth in compensation.

A soft beep issued from Richard's computer signaling that one of his search algorithms had returned a new result. The machine had entered sleep mode and was now dark, requiring Richard to enter the sixty-four character password he had set up to access the hard drive. He entered the code carefully. One incorrect character and his hard drive would crash, wiping its contents so thoroughly a scanning electron microscope wouldn't be able to retrieve any useful data from it.

"Sonofabitch," Richard muttered as the screen lit up and he moused over the new data.

It was an article recently posted on the Wall Street Journal's web page. A research firm in the field of biotechnology and physics had incorporated itself and was seeking funding for several projects. The founder, Doctor Stephen Bana, had been working privately but since going public had named his venture BanaTech. His Chief Financial officer, the article said, was listed as one Alex Jefferson.

It now made sense to Richard that his searches had turned up nothing on Dr. Bana in the past. He'd searched for Bana as a possible name but had come up with tens of thousands of results, none of which corresponded to any of the other keywords in his queries. The man had been working privately and private researchers were rarely noted in the press unless they published articles related to their work. Stephen Bana had obviously not done so.

What didn't make sense was that this was a fledgling company, only just incorporated. Yet the man Richard had known as Doc had alluded that BanaTech was a huge corporation. Their gear and hardware, much of it military, pointed to a company with vast resources and near infinite power.

Another curiosity was the listing of Alex Jefferson as CFO. Richard had gotten the feeling that Jefferson, if it was the same Jefferson he'd been unfortunate enough to meet last winter, held a security position rather than a corporate title.

Richard was pondering these inconsistencies when there was a knock at the door.

Samantha, no doubt. With his change.

"Coming, Sammy," he called. He put his computer back to sleep with the tap of a button and reached for the H&K beneath the desk.

Vigilance, he asked himself, *or paranoia*?

Deciding upon the latter he padded to the front door empty handed. *Semper vigilans be damned*, he thought. *Nine year-old cookie pushers pose no threat to me whatsoever*. So thinking, Richard opened the door with the cheery smile he reserved for children and small animals.

"Hey, Sammy," he began, and was so stunned when Sophia pushed her way past him and entered the hall that had he brought the weapon with him he'd have forgotten how to use it.

"We have to go, Richard," she said. She wore khaki BDU's over a black, long sleeve shirt. A tactical holster housing a Glock 17 rode her right thigh. A 3 magazine 9mm pouch at her waist completed the ensemble. "Right now. If I can find you, so can they."

Richard felt his heart skip a beat, a momentary pause, and then thump in his chest like a horse kicking at a stall door.

"Don't just stand there with your mouth hanging open," Sophia said sternly. "We have a long way to go and not a lot of time."

"Let's *go*." She grasped his arm and propelled him into the living room. "*Move!*"

Chapter 6

"Do you have weapons?" Sophia demanded.

"What?" Richard blinked, still stunned by the apparition before him.

"Do you have any weapons?"

She dragged him into the living room, clutching his arm and guiding him like a small child. He'd been dumbstruck by her sudden appearance. She looked like Sophia in every way except one. She wasn't pale from exhaustion and injury. She was vibrant, alive. *Energetic*. And she carried with her an air of urgency that demanded he take action.

Richard shrugged her off, pulled his desk chair to one side as he knelt and pulled back an area rug. Underneath was a grate concealing a void where a floor furnace, removed decades before, had been. He lifted the grate and pulled a duffel bag from the space. His original pack—he'd called it his bug out pack; as in, in case he had to bug out fast—had been so badly beaten and burned during the incident in Kansas that he'd replaced it. The duffel was larger and could accommodate far more than the fifty thousand in cash and the single handgun his old pack had contained. At present it held extra clips and ammo for several guns, twenty thousand in cash, a small copper box, and a first aid kit.

"In the bedroom," he said, pointing over his left shoulder, "Attached to the bottom of the nightstands on each side of the bed."

Sophia moved to collect the firearms hidden there as Richard collected the others from the living room and kitchen. He placed each in the duffel. They met up in the hall where he hesitated before handing the duffel over to Sophia.

Who *was* this woman? He'd watched the Sophia he knew die. Not a Hollywood death that was vague and undefined, allowing a character to return in a plot twist the audience would (hopefully) never see coming. But a brutal, definitive death that left no room for doubt. Her head had *exploded* for Christ's sake.

Still, it *was* Sophia. She looked the same. Sounded the same. Even *smelled* the same. As she'd dragged him from the entry hall he'd caught a hint of lavender scented shampoo. The look of determination and urgency on her face mirrored the expression she'd worn when questioning the man he'd known as 'Doc' in the HumVee before the world had turned upside down. Despite all logic and what he knew to be reality instinct told him that this was the same woman. He decided, for now at least, to trust her.

He handed Sophia the duffel and pressed what appeared to be just another section of the wall with the palm of his hand. A concealed latch sprung and a panel opened. Inside was a touchpad for a home security system and a Beretta 92FS. He took the gun and left the panel open.

He crossed to the entryway and was pulling down the trap door to the attic when someone knocked on the door. Richard startled. Sophia, who'd been eyeing the contents of the duffel with approval, froze. The ladder slid down its track and thumped on the floor.

"Mr. McGee?" Samantha Peterson called.

Richard looked and saw with dismay that the front door was hanging open a few inches. When Sophia had pushed her way into the house neither of them had thought to close it.

The door swung inward as Samantha, as unmindful of propriety as any nine year old, pushed it open.

"Oh, hi, Mr. McGee," Samantha smiled her usual sunny smile. The smile faded as she took in the scene: Richard looking guilty, as if caught in the act of doing something he shouldn't; Sophia, a duffel full of handguns and ammo gaping at her feet.

"Uh," Samantha continued, a small frown of confusion creasing her brow, "I have your change." She held out Richard's two dollars, eyeing him with suspicion.

"Thanks, Sammy," Richard said.

As he reached for the money two things happened at once. A low hum, the sound of a cell phone set to vibrate, came from somewhere on Sophia and a black SUV screeched to a halt at the curb. Four men in assault garb emblazoned with the yellow FBI logo poured out before the vehicle had come to a complete stop.

"They've found us," Sophia said.

Before the words were out of her mouth Richard kicked the front door shut and threw the bolt. He scooped Sammy from the floor with an arm around her waist, grabbed a Mac 11 from its mount with his free hand, and headed for the back of the house. Sophia snatched the duffel from the floor and followed.

"There'll be another 'round the back!" she called out. As if to emphasize this point, there was a loud crash from the back of the house.

Richard, a struggling and squalling Samantha in arm, altered course into the bedroom.

"That door is 22 gauge steel set into a 24 gauge steel frame with composite locking blocks," Richard explained. He spoke to reassure Sophia, to calm the child, and to keep his own mind clear. He set Samantha on the floor extended his finger in a 'stay put' gesture, then started pulling up the carpet along the outside wall. To her credit, Samantha obeyed, sniffling back her tears and quieting immediately. "Not steel *clad*, mind you. Steel wrapped. So is the front. It's one of the reasons I rented this place. They'll be a while trying to get in through there."

What he didn't say was what he feared they would try next.

Under the carpet was a trap door leading to a crawlspace beneath the house. Realizing Richard's intent, Sophia moved to help him wrestle it out of its frame. Once open, Richard swept Samantha into the opening. She squawked as her rump hit earth three feet below. Sophia followed, duffel in tow, and Richard nose-dived in behind her.

The sound of breaking glass came from above the trio and Richard yelled "Cover your ears!" and did so himself.

Flashes of light followed by percussive blasts filled the house. As the thunderous noise died away Richard rolled, located Samantha and Sophia near the outside wall of the foundation, and quickly appraised them. Sophia had covered her ears and opened her mouth to reduce overpressure. Samantha, not understanding Richard's warning, had not. Eyes wide with pain, blood trickling from one ear—*probably a burst eardrum*, Richard thought—the young girl screamed so hard that no sound came except hoarse exhalations of air. Richard grabbed her by the shoulders and shook her gently.

"Sammy," Richard said. "Sammy." He knew she couldn't hear him and so moved his mouth carefully to form the words. "Sammy, you have to be quiet. *Shh,*" he said, gesturing with a finger across his lips.

Though tears coursed down her cheeks and her body quaked like a rag doll, she seemed to understand. She quieted, her breathing now coming in hitches and gasps that tapered off slowly.

Christ, Richard thought, *she must be more terrified than she's ever been in her life.* And yet she followed his lead having no reason to trust him whatsoever. He impulsively hugged her.

Gunfire erupted in the kitchen. A wide burst designed to maim or kill anyone hiding within. A similar burst came from the living room.

Richard turned to Sophia and pointed out the vent cover for the crawlspace.

"That lets out into the neighbor's yard through a three foot privet hedge. Take Sam and get her through the hedge. There's a privacy fence at the back of the property. Just reach over the gate and pull the latch. Sammy's house is three doors down and they never lock the patio doors. Get her home safe. I'll slow these guys down and catch up to you."

"I can't leave here without you," Sophia said. "You have no idea how important you are."

"Lady," Richard hissed, digging in the duffel for clips, "the only thing I give a shit about right now is getting this little girl home. She didn't ask for any of this. Now you move your ass!"

Anger, so quick Richard almost missed it, flashed across Sophia's face. She scooted to the vent and kicked it open with her heels. Richard slapped a clip home in the belly of the Mac 11 as woman and child slipped through the breach, then turned back to the opening above his head.

And waited. He wanted to give Sophia and Sammy as much time as possible before making his next move. It bothered him that the men invading his home wore federal garb. Could the entity he knew as BanaTech, officially nonexistent until less than an hour ago, have enough power to have infiltrated and corrupted the Federal Bureau of Investigation? Or was it merely a ruse to appear as law enforcement officers to any onlookers? Were these BanaTech security forces? Or innocent cops just following orders?

He prayed it was the former.

There were footsteps throughout the house. Stealthy creaking and groaning; the sound of men in heavy boots searching. He could hear what sounded like two sets from the kitchen area and two more from the living room. He held his breath as the floorboards at the threshold of the bedroom gave out a soft squeak. Fine dust drifted down from spaces between the hardwood.

"I have a breach in the bedroom," a soft voice came to him from the doorway. The low voice of a man speaking into a throat mic. "I think they're under—"

Richard popped up through the opening like an armed jack-in-the-box and leveled the Ingram a few inches above the floor. He fired in a short arc centered on the doorway. The man just inside the door took a round through the shin, toppling him backwards. A second man, just outside the room, took a round in the arch of his foot, his boot filling with blood as he screamed and lurched back. Richard heard him crash to the floor outside the bedroom.

Richard sprang out of the hole and rolled to the side of the bed while chaos erupted around him. Someone yelled: "The bedroom!" Someone else yelled: "Go!" A third and closer voice screamed: "I'm hit, *I'M HIT!*"

Gunfire erupted from the doorway. Two more men had taken up position there and were firing wildly into the room. Lead filled the air. Plaster and woodchips flew from the walls, trim, and crown molding. One round tore through the mattress mere inches from Richard's head.

He made himself as small as possible and crawled for a section of wall at the side of the bed. Overturning the nightstand, he pulled down and outwards on a slightly discolored section of baseboard revealing a timer and a host of wiring.

After the incident in Kansas Richard had lived with a recurring sense of impending doom. That two day period—it boggled the imagination that so much had happened in so little time—had turned him away from the road he had chosen to follow after his incarceration: The sedate, if not somewhat reclusive, *normal* life he had so desired during ten years in the company of murderers, rapists, and thieves. Prison, he had soon learned, is a timeless, soulless void in which one does not mature, grow, or experience even the simplest of life's pleasures. It is, instead, a venomous atmosphere rife with hatred, hostility, and petty indifference to the needs of any living being. One cannot *live* in such a place. Only exist. He had vowed to do everything in his power to prevent a return to such an existence.

It had taken less than forty-eight hours to turn Richard away from his chosen path and set him back on one of a multitude of roads that terminate in confinement or death, each of those roads littered with violence and paranoia.

"A.P.P.A." a fellow inmate had once told him. "Absolute paranoia is perfect awareness." He'd then added, "Just because you're paranoid doesn't mean someone isn't out to get you."

Richard had since decided that the lower end of paranoia was vigilance. With that in mind he'd prepared a little surprise should BanaTech's security forces again invade his home. He'd wired two other panels similar to this one in the bungalow's kitchen and living room. All three were synchronized. Setting the timer on this unit to three seconds activated all three. Richard curled himself into a fetal position, opened his mouth, squeezed his eyes shut, and covered his ears.

His heart beat just twice before the thirty-six CTS 9590 sting ball multi-effect grenades he'd purchased over the Internet with false law enforcement ID went off. The near simultaneous explosions sent over 3500 .31 caliber rubber balls racing outward at tremendous velocity, accompanied by a 101 millisecond burst of light at 6-8 million candela and a 175 decibel ear shattering blast. The six man retrieval team sent by BanaTech was instantly incapacitated.

Richard didn't escape the melee unscathed. Several of the rubber balls had peppered his back, arms and legs. The effect of the flashbang portion of the grenades was minimal since he'd been prepared for it. Abandoning the Ingram, he rolled over twice, not bothering to survey the inside of a room he'd never see again, and dropped into the crawlspace beneath the house.

The duffel was undisturbed. He pulled the first weapon his hand touched from the bag, zipped the duffel shut, and pulled it behind him as he duck-walked to the vent and outside through the privet hedge. He pulled the duffel over his shoulder as he stood erect. There were groans and sounds of pain coming from the bedroom window to his left. Its glass littered the side yard like little gems gleaming in the sun. The windows that hadn't been broken by the assault team had coughed out their glass when Richard's nasty little surprise went off.

From his position between the two houses Richard could see his neighbors coming out onto their porches. Into their yards. Into the street. All curious, attracted by the action at Richard's house.

Ignoring them Richard headed for the back of his neighbor's house. He'd made it to the gate when Sophia came dashing through the opening at a sprint.

"Sammy?" he said.

"Fine," she answered, pulling him towards back of the property as sirens took up a mournful song in the distance. "Safe. But her father is *pissed*. And headed this way with a shotgun."

"Damn," Richard said. He reversed direction towards his own back yard in response. A small grass alleyway separated his house from the next and he pulled Sophia towards it. A twin of the black SUV that had pulled up in front sat catty corner to his back porch, doors open, engine idling.

"The SUV," they both said in concert.

They raced for the vehicle as gunfire erupted from the back of the house.

Lead tore up clods of earth and foliage, tree bark splintered and flew. The shots went wide and missed the SUV. Richard dove into the passenger seat and pulled the door shut. He raised his head enough to peer out the window as Sophia slammed the driver's door closed and threw the vehicle into reverse.

Jefferson stood on the back porch, grinning his mad hyena grin and lining up a shot with a Colt Defense M4 Carbine. He looked different, somehow. It took Richard a millisecond—about the time it took Jefferson to squeeze his finger around the trigger of the weapon—to realize that the difference was the man's nose. His eyes still had that dancing light of madness in them; the face was still rugged and creased. He was still larger than life and twice as intimidating. But his nose was flatter, squashed down and bent to the left. BanaTech's doctors had been unable to restore it to its former aquiline form after Richard had shattered it. Richard's grin at the realization rivaled that of his adversary.

Sophia tromped the accelerator and the SUV lurched backwards. Jefferson's round sailed over the hood and into a tree lining the opposite side of the alley. The vehicle shot down the narrow passage in reverse, gaining speed and blowing by a startled Norman Peterson who was indeed toting a shotgun. The rear doors of the vehicle, still open, missed bowling him off his feet by inches. He wisely dove for cover.

As the SUV hit the entrance of the alley at high speed Sophia made a left hand turn in reverse. Richard spotted Jefferson limping into the alley from his back yard hoping for another shot. Jefferson, Richard guessed, had not been spared the multiple impacts of high velocity pellets from the sting grenades. His grin grew larger. A horn blared and the sound of anguished brakes filled the air as the SUV slammed to a halt narrowly avoiding a nasty collision with a Chevy travelling on the main thoroughfare. Sophia slammed the vehicle into drive and tromped the accelerator. The rear doors of the SUV chunked shut with the change of direction.

"Go left. Left!" Richard yelled.

"Why?" Sophia asked, but complied.

Richard dug in the duffel bag until his fingers found what he was looking for. Curious neighbors, startled by the appearance of the vehicle, dove out of the street where they had been gathering to discuss the melee at the McGee house.

"Here!" Richard yelled as the vehicle approached the front of his house. "Stop!"

The SUV squealed to a halt.

Richard popped open the passenger door, stood on the running board, and leaned over the roof of the SUV. Neighbors screamed and ran as he put five .454 caliber rounds from the Taurus through the engine block of the assault team's remaining vehicle.

"Go! Go! Drive!" Richard yelled, ducking back into the vehicle. He wore a lunatic grin of his own as the SUV sped away. "That ought to slow them down."

"Don't bet on it," Sophia said sharply, glancing away from the road as she blew through the quiet residential neighborhood at well over sixty miles an hour. “They have resources you can’t even imagine.”

“Who *are* they?”

Sophia tore twin paths through peonies and nicely manicured fescue as she cut a corner too fast and accelerated. The route she was following, Richard noticed, would take them to the Interstate.

“The security arm of BanaTech,” she said. “They may look like the military, or the FBI, or even the OSS. And they’ll have the ID to back it. But they’re really just Jefferson’s goons and they do whatever he tells them.”

OSS? Richard thought. He said: “What do they want from me?”

Sophia said nothing. Simply merged the SUV onto the Interstate and reduced speed to the legal limit. The Saturday morning traffic was light by California standards. There were only a dozen or so other cars heading north. Richard knew it would get much busier as the lunch hour approached.

“What do they want with me?” Richard repeated.

Sophia remained silent.

Impatience leads to frustration and anger. Richard had learned this as a prisoner of the state of Kansas. A man doing time, where there is little to do but wait for the next meal, the next yard period, the next day that brings you closer to the day they finally let you back into the real world, can easily implode under the weight of all that anger. An intelligent man will seek to fill all that time spent waiting with card games, television, conversation with other inmates—though that holds its own perils—or, in Richard’s case, education. He’d first studied religion, then philosophy, then human psychology. What he’d taken away from the experience was patience. All things reveal themselves in due course. When Sophia didn’t answer his question the second time he decided to let it go. For now.

A semi with the Mayflower logo emblazoned on the trailer passed them. It was running at least ten miles an hour over the legal limit.

“I know you have a lot of questions and I promise you’ll get your answers,” Sophia said shortly. “But we don’t have time for that. Not here. Not now.”

"When then?"

"Soon," Sophia replied. "When we get a little distance between them and us. For now I need you to navigate. Can you do that?"

Richard sighed and answered: "Of course. Where are we going?"

Sophia fetched a slim black object out of her hip pocket and handed it to Richard.

The device appeared to be a cell phone, a clone of the one he had retrieved from the other Sophia's belongings as she lay wounded in his home in Kansas. He started to mention this, then thought better of it. Trust can be built quickly in times of duress but months of vigilance born of years of paranoia advised caution. He thumbed the slide open and got the idiot glow of the login screen.

"It wants a password," he said.

"Sophia six three," she said, "no caps or spaces."

Richard entered the eight characters, pondering their significance. He was rewarded with a topographical map of the county with several blinking dots.

"The steady blue dot is us," Sophia told him. "What we need is the closest steady red dot. It's a touch screen, so just touch it and it will tell us how to get there."

Richard did so. The image shrank then expanded to a smaller section of the county complete with roads and city names. Other lines that seemed irrelevant crossed the screen at odd angles. Richard ignored them as a yellow route between the icon representing the SUV and the red dot lit up.

"Okay," he said. "It says there's one of those things, whatever they are, about three miles from here. You need to take the next exit and backtrack one-half mile on the feeder road until you come to a street marked 'J' avenue."

"There should be a counter at the bottom left corner of the screen. What does it say?"

"Four minutes, thirty-eight seconds. Counting down."

"Shit," Sophia muttered and tromped on the gas. They shot past the Mayflower truck that had passed them just moments ago, blowing the speed limit by a good twenty miles an hour.

"Hey!" Richard exclaimed, "What the hell?"

The exit they wanted was less than a quarter mile ahead. Sophia cut the semi off to the accompaniment of barking airbrakes and the loud wail of the truck's air horn and took the exit at close to eighty miles an hour. She turned onto the feeder road at perilous speed, kept the accelerator glued to the floorboard, and sped back in the direction they'd come from, albeit on a different road.

"Jesus," Richard said. The truck they'd just cut off had jackknifed on the interstate and now blocked both lanes. Traffic was slowing to a halt behind it. "Take it easy. You could kill someone that way."

"You just keep an eye on that counter," Sophia said as the SUV passed one hundred miles an hour.

"There's 'L' avenue," Richard pointed out as they blew past the marker. "And there's 'K.'"

He started to tell her she should slow down or they'd miss the turn when Sophia abruptly turned off the feeder road, the tires of the SUV leaving the ground as they bounded over a shallow drainage ditch and headed out over barren ground at an angle.

The vehicle bucked and jerked. Richard hit his head on the roof as they slipped into, and then out of, an arroyo. Then they were on 'J' avenue and the ride smoothed out once more.

"That'll save some time," Sophia said and winked at him.

"Hmmph," Richard pulled the seatbelt over his shoulder and snapped it into place. Sophia had already locked hers down. Sparse vegetation and telephone poles flashed by the windows.

"How are we doing on time?" she asked.

"Two minutes, fifteen seconds," he said. The screen changed; Richard assumed the satellite feeding information to the receiver was updating their location as they approached their destination. Details on the screen steadily became more defined.

"Uh-oh. According to this your red dot is less than a mile away, just up there," Richard gestured towards the windshield. "It's in the middle of a network of arroyos. There's nothing else out there at all."

"There's something out there, all right," Sophia said. "And we need to find it."

"But what could—" Richard began, and the device began to vibrate in his hand.

"Damn!" Sophia said. "They've found us."

Richard's stared hard at the device. The image had zoomed out again. A second blue dot was moving rapidly across the screen on an intercept course heedless of roads or vegetation and much too fast to be anything but airborne. Richard craned his neck up and back and spied the black dot of what he feared to be a helicopter on the horizon.

"If you're going to do something, now would be a good time," he said.

In answer, Sophia drove off the road and dropped into an arroyo with a crash that again sent Richard's head into the roof. She braked, took a right hand fork in the wash, and accelerated as the walls of the arroyo narrowed on both sides. Richard watched the ominous shape of a Blackhawk helicopter flash by overhead.

"Which way?" Sophia demanded.

"Back," Richard said. "To the left. We're moving away from it."

The arroyo branched again. This time Sophia took the left-hand wash. It deepened and the walls were now above the roof of the vehicle.

"That's better," Richard said. "Less than a thousand yards if we can stay on this course. Whatever this is it better be good."

The arroyo took a left-hand swing and widened out, the bottom turning from a semi-smooth surface to buckboard. The two of them were bounced around like corn kernels popping in a pan, their seatbelts the only thing saving them from flying out of their seats. Richard lost track of the number of times his head hit the roof. They were again swinging away from their target.

"We've got forty seconds," Richard said. "We're going to miss it. No! We have to go right!"

Sophia slammed on the brakes fetching Richard up hard against the shoulder restraint. She then reversed and pulled a perfect three point turn. They'd passed a side tributary about twenty yards back. It had looked too narrow for the SUV to get through.

She took the turn anyway, peeling the side view mirrors off their mounts along with a goodish amount of paint from the door panels. A large clod of earth broke free and fell into Richard's open window. Dirt and dust filled his mouth and nose. He spat it out.

The arroyo widened, the walls dropping away at the same time. It looked as if they would crest the slope and be in the clear when the helicopter dropped in front of them, cutting off their route.

Richard recognized the Sikorsky MH-60L Direct Action Penetrator from his research. He ducked instinctively as manned miniguns depending from each door thundered to life. The ground between the helicopter and SUV began to churn

Sophia didn't flinch. She sped towards the helicopter. At the last second she swung the vehicle left past the field of fire and under the helicopter. The craft rose to avoid the onrushing SUV, then nosed down and to the right to follow. The unexpected maneuver had spoiled the door gunner's aim.

"Where is it?" Sophia cried. "That won't work a second time!"

Richard looked at the device and saw only the red dot. They were here, wherever here was. He saw nothing through the windshield save the faint silver-blue shimmer of a desert mirage some fifty feet to the right of the vehicle.

"We're right on top of it, but there's nothing here!"

"There!" Sophia pointed at the mirage. She hauled the wheel to the right and tromped the accelerator. The mirage seemed to shrink from the size of a large barn that of a small house but did not recede before the vehicle as had every mirage Richard had ever seen before.

"Damn it!" Sophia smacked her hand on the steering wheel. "It's closing!"

The earth behind the fleeing SUV began to churn as the Sikorsky lined up and began another run on the vehicle. In seconds slugs would find their way inside and begin chewing through steel, vinyl, and upholstery before shredding Richard and Sophia's flesh, bones, and vital organs. Richard steeled himself for the onslaught while a quiet, rational part of his mind told him that the mirage now looming in front of them looked more like a curtain of heat waves rising from the ground.

Then they were in the mirage and everything Richard knew to be the truth was in doubt.

Nausea passed through Richard and day turned to night as if some celestial switch had been thrown and the sun had winked out of existence. Water, cold and invigorating splashed against the side of his face. As his eyes tried to adjust to the sudden darkness twin lights loomed in the windshield, grew larger, and then wailed at him with the sound of an air horn as they swerved to avoid a collision.

The sound of the California desert rushing past the window fell away, replaced by the thrumming sound of pouring rain, wet tires on pavement, and the burst of not too distant thunder. More light loomed before him and a shriek of brakes added their voice to the cacophony.

He was thrown left, then right, then left again as his mind tried to sort through the onslaught of new information that *could not be.* More lights, onrushing objects, and protesting sounds of rubber against asphalt. Then the world did a one-eighty as Sophia slewed the SUV around in the direction of traffic flow and pulled to the side of the Interstate.

Though impossible, on Richard's right and seen through the downpour of a nighttime summer thunderstorm was the six-hundred and thirty-four foot steel archway—resembling a single sheen rainbow that led not to a pot of gold but was the Gateway to the West—on the bank of the Mississippi River. To his left reared a building that appeared to be ablaze but was not; the artificial inferno the result of a clever computer program controlling thousands of LED's that covered one entire side of the Millennium Hotel.

Before him lay Interstate 70-North. Eight lanes of traffic going to and fro as is normal for a bustling city. Richard took a deep breath as what just happened to him began to set in.

Sophia smiled at him from the driver's seat.

"Welcome to St. Louis."

Chapter 7

"You drugged me," Richard said. He'd thrown open the passenger door after Sophia's sliding stop, leaned out, and vomited. Little came up. Some Doritos mixed with Sobe green tea and part of a honey bun, the majority of which ended up on the SUV's running board instead of the asphalt. A sour taste like burning rubber and rotting meat flooded his mouth. A headache was taking hold at his temples. "You drugged me and drove me half-way across the country. That's the only explanation."

He sat erect and closed the door against the sight of partially digested food mixing with rain water. Sophia pulled the vehicle back onto the Interstate, heading east and keeping pace with traffic around her.

"Sure I did," Sophia said. "And I managed to time it so you'd regain consciousness as I was going the wrong way on one of the most dangerous sections of Interstate in the country. Wake up, Richard. We just traveled across four states and nine hours in milliseconds and you're reaching for an explanation that fits what you think you know about reality."

"Why don't you explain it to me then?" Richard said. The headache was building. It grasped his head like a steel clamp, slowly tightening. He felt his brain would burst and squirt out his ears. The pain was doing nothing for his temper. "You can start with who the hell you are."

"I'm Sophia Bledell. Until recently I was a field researcher for BanaTech Industries."

"You maybe have a twin sister?" he said through clenched teeth. "One that uses your name on occasion?"

"No," Sophia said. As they passed through East St. Louis the traffic thinned. Sophia reduced speed to the legal limit as they left the urban sprawl behind. The thunderstorm they'd emerged into continued to rage around them. Bright stroboscopic flashes lit up the night like a madman with a flash gun. Thunder roared in response like applause. "That was also Sophia Bledell. She was my Mirror."

Richard's headache built to a crescendo. He could feel his brain pushing against the back of his eyes as if to pop them out to lie on his cheeks like macabre party favors. Then, with one final blast of pain, it was gone.

"Jesus!" Richard screamed, grasping his head in his hands.

"That'll be easier next time. It's a neural response to passing through the Rips. Most people feel nothing. Maybe a little tingle, like the hairs stirring on the back of your neck. It's worse for Primes but only the first few times."

Several of the words Sophia used stuck out in Richard's mind. *Rips. Primes. Mirrors.* She'd used the words as if they were nouns, as if she were speaking another language. He'd understood nothing of what she'd just said and little of what had just happened. Understanding a situation is tantamount to resolving it. He'd been plunged into a nightmare and this woman held the answers to the ever-spiraling madness that was consuming his life.

"Look," he told her, "I will accept, *for now*, that you didn't dope me up and that we really did just travel across space and time with the help of a souped-up cell phone through this whaddyacallit…"

"A Rip," she interrupted.

"…and," he continued, "I will accept that I didn't see your head torn apart and your body blasted beyond recognition back in Kansas though I know damn well I did."

"You did. And you didn't."

Richard sighed. This was getting him nowhere fast.

"Please," he said. "Just start at the beginning."

"Very well," Sophia said. "But I can only tell you what I understand. I'm a researcher, not a tech, so I'm a little spotty on the physics of the Rips and how the RLPs work. I'm a little better versed on the history of BanaTech though, so that's where I'll start.

"About two-hundred and fifty years ago from your perspective," Sophia began, "A physicist named Steven Bana discovered strange energy fields popping up around the globe. They appeared to be natural phenomena, usually occurring along the Earth's lines of magnetic flux wherever they crossed certain ley lines. This was interesting because ley lines, or vortices, are supposed to be nothing more than the alignment of points of geographical interest.

Given the density of historic and prehistoric sites on any given land mass, if you draw a straight line between any two points on that map you're bound to hit several of them. That means ley lines are trivial coincidence rather than intentional or natural artifact. However, the greatest concentration of these energy fields form along these intersections. Using satellite imagery and spectrographic analysis Dr. Bana began studying these phenomena and discovered…"

"Wait," Richard interrupted. "You said two-hundred and fifty years ago. That would be the late 1700's. Satellites didn't exist back then, let alone the technology required for spectrographic analysis."

"I said two-hundred and fifty years ago *from your perspective*," Sophia said. She paused; grasping, Richard thought, for an explanation for the hole he just shot in her narrative. After a moment, she said:

"Imagine where your science and technology would be if a little event called the Dark Ages had not occurred or had been significantly shortened. For over eight hundred years scientific study was anathema, suppressed in the name of God and religion. Knowledge of what we call chemistry, biology, and physics was outlawed; its practitioners called witches and burned at the stake. Or worse. A society that doesn't have a gap that large in its technological learning curve would be far more advanced than yours is now, don't you think?"

Richard nodded, grudgingly conceding the point. Sophia continued:

"Dr. Bana theorized that these energy fields, which occur most frequently at these intersections but may also occur in the wake of severe weather patterns just as tornadoes develop on the back side of a thunderstorm, were conduits. Wormholes if you will. Rips in the fabric of reality."

"Rips leading where?" Richard asked, playing along.

"Some, like the one we just traveled through, lead to other points in the immediate space-time vicinity. Those are the localized Rips. The ones that show up in red on the RLP. That's shorthand for the souped-up cell phone, as you called it. The Rip Locator and Plotter. And don't give me any guff about the cheesy name. Dr. Bana may have been a genius when it came to physics but he had no imagination whatsoever when it came to naming his inventions."

Despite himself, Richard smiled.

"Localized Rips are more numerous, though not very stable. They come and go with no recognizable pattern and their destinations are difficult for the computers that map the Rips to predict. That's how we ended up in the middle of on-coming traffic. We might just as well have ended up on the top of Mount Everest or on the bottom of the ocean."

"And you risked it anyway?" Richard asked, incredulous.

"You'd have preferred I let that gunship catch us?" Sophia shot back.

Richard said nothing.

"And stop interrupting me. This is hard enough to explain as it is.

"At first Bana kept his discoveries to himself. One, he was in that mode reserved for any genius with an IQ of 240 that takes them over completely. They don't eat or sleep for days on end and they think of nothing outside the parameters of what they're working on. Two, he knew that most of his conclusions would be met with scorn and ridicule and he'd be laughed right out of the scientific community, if not locked up in a mental hospital somewhere.

"His theories were varied and wild. They explained away ghosts and hauntings as incidents of thin spots in the fabric of reality. Windows that allow the witness, albeit briefly, to perceive occurrences from another time and place. The knocking in the middle of the night was simply a sound that traveled through the window to be heard by someone on the other side. The vision of Aunt Agnes on the stairs really *is* Aunt Agnes on the stairs, just viewed from another perspective in the Multi-verse."

"The *what?*" Richard exclaimed, ignoring her admonition not to interrupt. "Are you talking about parallel dimensions? Alternate realities?"

"No." Sophia sighed. "And yes. Those are terms coined by science-fiction writers to lend credence to their stories. The common reaction to such terms is disbelief, the very reaction Dr. Bana was concerned with. The proper term is the Multi-verse, which is something else entirely."

"A hypothetical infinite number of multiple possible universes," Richard quoted, "including the universe we consistently perceive, that together comprises everything that exists: Space, time, matter, energy, and the laws and constants that describe them. That's high school physics."

"Except it's not hypothetical," Sophia said. "Not a theory.

Richard digested this as they passed a sign announcing that they'd just crossed into the state of Illinois. The east and westbound lanes of the Interstate separated and trees encroached upon the blacktop, crowding the highway like sentinels charged with keeping trespassers at bay.

"Another of Bana's theories," Sophia said, "was that déjà vu' is not an anomaly of memory. Nor, as is commonly believed, is it an overlap between the neurological systems responsible for storing long-term and short-term memory. According to Bana, the sensation we refer to as déjà vu' is nothing more than a person slipping through a Rip and entering another Earth in the Multi-verse, one where time is moving at a slightly slower rate, causing the person to relive an event they've already experienced."

"How is that possible? Wouldn't someone entering a Rip realize that something has just happened?" Richard said.

"In some cases people *do* realize something has happened. But except for the occasional case where a man falls asleep in his bathtub in New Orleans and wakes up in a hot tub in Albuquerque, or where a mother and daughter step into their kitchen in Atlanta and end up at a frat party in Manitoba, they don't experience anything significant enough to alert them to it. They may feel some disorientation, perhaps a rash of gooseflesh, but when nothing else seems out of place and one has no concept of events outside of what they perceive to be reality, the incident is soon forgotten. Chalked up to megrims and vapors.

"I wouldn't know," Richard said. "I've never experienced déjà vu'.

"That's because you're a Prime," Sophia said.

"You've mentioned that twice now. What's a Prime?" Richard said.

"A Prime is exactly what it sounds like: A number divisible only by one and itself. In other words, there is only you in the Multi-verse. No Mirrors."

Sophia went on before Richard could interrupt.

"Most of us exist across the Multi-verse. We have copies, or Mirrors, on any Earth that supports human life and has an adequate society base with a similar history. We are virtually the same person, living similar lives, doing similar things. I have black hair on my world, black hair in the next world, and so on and so on. Each is unaware of the existence of the other but usually like-minded, so we have the same basic traits and characteristics."

"There are more of you?" Richard said.

"Absolutely. One-hundred and twenty-three that I know of, not counting the Mirror of me that was murdered on your world."

Richard put his head in his hands and groaned. The headache had not returned, he was simply trying to sort through the impossible information he was receiving. "How is that even possible?" he asked. "If these Rips are everywhere and there are Mirrors all across the Multi-verse people would be bumping into themselves at every turn. The Multi-verse would have been exposed ages ago."

"It doesn't work that way," Sophia said. "It seems there's some sort of natural mechanism in place that prevents that from happening. If a person slips through a Rip in one Universe, their Mirror slips through a similar Rip in their Universe at the same time.

"There *are* numerous Rips out there. So many that the Quantum-Crays have a hard time predicting their exit points despite their awesome computing power and speed. But for some unknown reason Rips seem to shut down or shy away from people and other life forms. It's as if they're of intelligent design and are trying to prevent one world from contaminating the next.

"Incidents of spontaneous cross-over do occur but ninety-nine percent of the time it takes an active force of will to enter a Rip. Dr. Bana theorized that Rips are not just natural anomalies but that they serve a purpose. They may be some sort of pressure relief valve. Existing to keep the tremendous energies that bind the Multi-verse from overloading and creating permanent Rips that would allow separate Universe's to collide and contaminate each other."

"Why would that be a problem? You said the individual Universe's are virtually identical."

Sophia shot Richard an incredulous look and passed a slow moving Oldsmobile before continuing. "I said they were similar."

"You're familiar with computers, so imagine that the Multi-verse is laid out like sectors on a hard drive. These sectors are laid out in a circular pattern, in rings if you will, sort of like the grooves on an old vinyl album. Each sector represents a different Universe. If you travel to a neighboring Universe, say the next sector over, you might notice only a few differences. Money printed with blue ink instead of green. Landmarks you're familiar with altered. Your wristwatch might be a few minutes off. Or you might not notice anything at all.

"As you move to sectors further inward or outward on the disc the changes begin to be dramatic. Worlds torn apart by war. Worlds with red grass or purple skies. Worlds with species of animals you've never seen before.

"Now, imagine that your hard drive is the size of the solar system. That's a lot of sectors. Now make your hard drive a sphere, with not just one layer of sectors, but countless layers radiating outward from the center. If you travel far enough away from your point of origin you'll find worlds where water flows uphill, where there are two moons instead of one, or where giant crabs are the dominant life form because physics and time as you know them are not absolutes. They are relative to the Universe they exist in. Anything you can imagine exists somewhere, in some Universe."

"So in some other Universe there are ants frying little boys under a magnifying glass?"

"Absolutely."

"That's insane," Richard said, envisioning dinosaurs roaming the Kansas flatlands, giant carnivorous vines draping skyscrapers in New York City, millions of people choking on huge clouds of toxic atmosphere from uninhabitable worlds.

"Insane or not, that's the reality of the Multi-verse. That much we know for certain. But consider this: Dr. Bana further theorized that there may not be a single Multi-verse but a likewise infinite series of Multi-verses that are held apart from one another by this force that binds our own Multi-verse together."

"And?" Richard prompted.

"So what happens," Sophia said, "if that force, that *machine*, breaks down and Universes begin colliding with one another?"

The question was rhetorical. It would mean the end of everything.

Sophia signaled for the right hand lane and pulled into it, reducing her speed.

"What's wrong?" Richard asked, alarmed. He looked around the vehicle and saw nothing but rain and the headlights of oncoming traffic.

Sophia gestured ahead of them to an exit ramp for a rest area.

"I have to use the facilities. Check the RLP and see if there are any bogeys about. They'll show up as black dots and the device will buzz like crazy."

Sophia pulled into the space closest to the low building housing the restrooms. The door chunked shut as she stepped out into the still pouring rain, muffling the sound and leaving Richard alone with his thoughts.

He plucked the RLP from the dash where it had ended up while he was enjoying his breakfast for the second time. She'd given him a lot to think about in a short period of time. He didn't fully accept her version of how they'd happened to end up in St. Louis after being in California mere moments before. He'd been disoriented after the events in the desert. Then came the nausea, vomiting, and the headache. Those reactions were consistent with awakening from drug-induced slumber by any number of sedatives. The symptoms had lasted mere minutes, however, and that was inconsistent with any drug he knew of, though there were bound to be many sedatives out there he was unfamiliar with.

There were other inconsistencies to consider as well. Sophia had earlier spoken of the military, the FBI, and the *OSS*. Not the CIA, as the Office for Strategic Services had been renamed in 1947.

Perhaps the biggest inconsistency was Sophia herself. He'd seen the woman murdered before his eyes. His rational mind had tried to tell him that this was her sister. A twin. A double made up to gain his confidence. But he could *feel* that that was wrong. This *was* the same woman. Healthier to be sure but he knew it in the way that you know that it's your bed you're waking up in after a bad dream, even before you open your eyes. Sophia Bledell had lived, died, and now lived again.

Her words, "*You're reaching for an explanation that fits what you think you know about reality,*" had struck a chord within him. Something more basic than gut instinct. Something within his nervous system, perhaps even on a cellular level.

Very well, he thought. *Let's say she's on the level. That the Multi-verse exists as she describes it and that travel through it is not only possible but rather easy. What does it mean? Why am I involved in all of this? What does BanaTech want from me?*

I could get out of this car right now and walk away. I have cash and weapons. I can start over again. Try to figure this out in my own way. My own time.

He couldn't do that and he knew it. Curiosity is a powerful motivator. Sure, it had killed the cat, but hadn't satisfaction brought the inquisitive feline back? He had to know more. Sophia had the answers, even if they were the sort that made him wonder if he was, in reality, sitting in the corner of a padded cell drooling on a urine and sweat stained straight jacket while the real world carried on around him. Not a soul caring that his gears had gone way past slipping and were now stripped beyond repair. He couldn't walk away from this until he had more answers.

He thumbed the cover of the RLP back exposing the *qwerty* style keyboard, keyed in sophia63 at the prompt, and waited for the screen to resolve itself. It did so immediately showing a still blue dot at their location. There were no other dots on the screen, blue or otherwise. No bogeys, as Sophia had called them.

Richard marveled at the technology required to support such a device. If what Sophia had told him were true there would have to be thousands of satellites in orbit around thousands of worlds to stream data to just this one small screen. Could all that be done in the two-hundred and fifty year time frame Sophia had suggested? He thought it could. Man's first satellite, Sputnik 1, orbited the earth in 1957. He knew that the United States Space Surveillance Network had tracked over 26,000 man-made objects orbiting the earth in the 50 or so years since. Most were of U.S. or Russian origin but many belonged to large corporations with enough power and money to launch such vehicles into space.

How did the data travel between separate locations in the Multi-verse? Were there Rips in orbit around the planet that allowed some form of data transmission? How did BanaTech track active Rips and plot their destinations? The questions were endless and mind numbing.

She'd mentioned something called a Quantum-Cray. Was she referring to quantum based computing? If so, scientists on her world—*if* it was her world and not the world of another Sophia—had perfected something that scientists on his world had yet to only theorize. The computing power of such a device—and she had used the plural when she'd referred to it—would be astronomical.

When the device rang in his hand, sounding much like a 70's era telephone, Richard was so startled he almost dropped it. The screen dissolved and a message appeared:

INCOMING CALL

He thought better of answering it. It could be anyone. A wrong number. Someone trying to sell life insurance. Or a ruse by BanaTech security forces to learn Sophia's location.

He decided to chance it. BanaTech hadn't needed to call on the two previous occasions they'd found them and he just might learn something. He slid the cover on the RLP closed, righted it, opened the second slider and hit the TALK button.

"McGee's whorehouse," he said. "You pay, we play."

There was a moment of startled silence from the other end, then:

"Farris, you bastard," a voice rasped. "Where is that traitorous bitch you're consorting with?"

"Why, Mr. Jefferson," Richard said with mock delight. "Is that you? How kind of you to call! I'm sorry, but Ms. Bledell had some personal business to attend to and can't come to the phone right now. May I take a message?"

"I'll get you, Farris. You, that bitch, *and* the Key."

"And my little dog, too?" Richard quipped.

There was a snarl from the other end of the line before Jefferson broke the connection.

Sophia exited the building in front of the vehicle and Richard, smiling inwardly, watched her make her way through the slowing rain. The drumming on the roof had become a soft rat-a-plan no louder than fingers tapping on a keyboard. As she made her way to the SUV Richard noticed something that had previously escaped his attention. Directly in front of him on the dash, in raised decorative letters, was the legend 'Tucker.' He glanced at the steering wheel. It had the familiar blue oval in the center of the ring but the script there read 'Tucker' also.

Richard was aware of only one Tucker Motor Company, an arm of the Tucker Corporation owned by Preston Thomas Tucker. That entity had gone out of business in 1950 after a lengthy SEC investigation into allegations of fraud and misappropriation of funds. Neither Tucker nor any of the others named in the indictment had been convicted of any crimes and it was believed in some circles that the entire investigation and resulting trial had been an effort on the part of other automotive companies to shut Tucker down. If so, it had worked. Under other circumstances the Tucker Corporation might have prevailed to become one of the leading manufacturers of aircraft and automobiles in the world.

More inconsistencies, he mused. Was this further evidence supporting Sophia's story? Or stage dressing designed to inspire his belief in the Multi-verse?

Again: *To what end?*

"Your boyfriend called," Richard told Sophia as she pulled the door shut behind her and wiped rainwater from her face.

"What?" she said, alarm in her voice. "Who?"

"He didn't leave his name," Richard said. "It was a brief conversation, mostly threats and insults. But I'm pretty sure it was Jefferson."

"Give me that," she ordered.

Richard surrendered the RLP and Sophia slid open the keyboard, her fingers flying over its surface with practiced precision.

"No," she said to no one at all, "the Great Lakes are too far. There has to be something closer. There! That's it!"

Without another word Sophia dropped the RLP in Richard's lap, reversed out of the parking slot, and shot out of the rest area.

"Hey," Richard said. "You want to slow down? We don't want to tangle with the local authorities. Not with all this hardware we're toting around."

Sophia reduced her speed but only to turn the vehicle and cross an overpass that led to the westbound lane of Interstate 70.

"Wait," Richard said. "We're going *back*?"

"We have to get to Granite City," Sophia said. "In Missouri."

"What's so special about Granite City?"

"Horseshoe Lake," she said, maneuvering the vehicle down the ramp and onto the Interstate. She accelerated to eighty miles an hour. Sentinel trees crowding back against the breakdown lane looked on disapprovingly. "There's a Rip forming there."

"Oh, now wait a minute," Richard said, aware in some deep recess of his mind that he was now accepting the idea of Rip travel if little else. "I'm not too keen on the idea of going through another one of those things. That last one almost killed me."

"It won't be as bad this time," Sophia assured him. "A few more trips and you'll hardly feel anything. Besides, we don't have a choice. That call means that Jefferson knows exactly where we are and that he's coming."

Richard picked up the RLP and examined the screen.

"I don't see any bogeys," he said. What he did see was the last screen Sophia had accessed. Sure enough, there was a lake outlined on the map that resembled a horseshoe. On the East side of the lake was a blinking green blip, growing steadier by the moment.

"It doesn't matter," Sophia said. "You will soon enough. He's tracking the RLP."

"Then turn it off!" Richard said, dropping the device back into his lap as if it had suddenly grown hot. As if he could stop Jefferson and his goons from tracking them if the RLP weren't in his hand.

"Can't," Sophia said.

"Then pull its battery."

"It doesn't *have* a battery. Look, these things are all networked. The RLPs, the satellites, the Quantum-Crays on the Homeworld. They draw their power from the same source that powers the Rips and binds the Multi-verse. I don't know exactly how it works. I told you, I'm a researcher, not a tech. We could destroy the thing.

Smash it to bits and walk away, just as my Mirror must have done back in Kansas. But that would leave us stranded here with no way out and Jefferson would find us eventually, just as I found you."

"Which led him to me," Richard said sourly.

Sophia shot him a sharp look.

"The point is," Sophia continued, "we need the RLP. We can't retrieve the Key without it and without the Key, the Multi-verse is lost. You'll just have to take my word for that. I don't have time to explain it now. We only have seventeen minutes before the Rip closes."

Richard sighed. He didn't like it, but every argument he had against her story felt wrong. As if he were reaching for something solid to hold onto in an earthquake. *Sometimes*, a voice in his head spoke up, *the only way out is to go further in.*

"Drive faster then."

Chapter 8

"Tell me more about Primes," Richard said.

The SUV blew through the night like a breeze through the gutters, splashing up twin fantails as the tires cut through pooling rain on the surface of the Interstate. Sophia kept their speed around one-hundred miles an hour. Any faster would have been to court death by hydroplaning into the sentinel trees crowding the macadam.

"We know a lot about the Primes," Sophia said, "but most of it is just general knowledge. What we don't know is much more interesting,"

"Such as?" Richard prompted.

"You have no Mirrors," she said. "I've already told you that. We don't know why. Thousands of hours of computer time over four decades have been devoted to answering that question. Aside from a consistent number of Primes existing throughout the Multi-verse at any given time, the QCs—that's what we call the Quantum-Crays—can't come up with a reason."

"A consistent number?" Richard asked.

"Yes. No matter what happens where, there are always one-hundred and forty-four thousand Primes. One of you dies, another is born. Instantaneously. We have no idea why, or what that specific number represents."

The number rang a bell in the back of Richard's mind. Something from a history book, he thought. Or maybe the Bible. He couldn't quite grasp the memory, however. It squirted away from his conscious mind like mercury from grasping fingertips.

"Theories abound, of course. That you're a mistake of nature, a fluke that time and evolution will weed out. Or that you're alien to the Multi-verse and therefore outside of its natural processes. Neither of those theories pans out, though. A mistake of nature wouldn't be so consistent. Evolution would have eradicated the Primes long ago if that were the case. You're still here, therefore you're supposed to be. And you're certainly not aliens. Not unless Dr. Bana is correct and there are a multitude of Multi-verses. And even then, how can something be from outside the whole?"

"It's good to know I'm not a little grey guy with bug eyes in disguise," Richard said.

"Don't be so flippant," Sophia said. "They're out there."

"You're kidding," Richard said.

"I'm not. The general rule is, we don't bother them and they don't bother us. It's irrelevant, though. You're not one of them."

"Then what am I?"

"The leading theory is that you're a part of the mechanism that holds the Multi-verse in balance."

"How does that work?"

"We don't know," Sophia said.

"Well what *do* you know?" Richard said, exasperation evident in his tone.

"For starters," Sophia said, "you're all mules."

"What?"

"Mules," Sophia said. "Sterile. So far as the QCs can deduce not a single Prime, male or female, has ever reproduced. It's one of the many parameters for finding you. If a person has a Mirror, or has had a child, they can't be Prime."

Richard digested that information. Like any other adult male he'd had thoughts of what it would be like to father children. He'd never felt driven to do so as had so many other men he knew. Just the errant thoughts and passing fancy of an idle mind. He'd taken the usual risks as a teenager, unprotected sex, passing the point of caring whether he had protection or not when the play got too hot for such considerations. He remembered two weeks of fear and agony when a girl he'd thought he'd loved in high school had been late after an encounter in the woods behind his Kansas home. Reflecting on it now he realized just how unimportant having children was to him. He'd chalked it up to his long incarceration and the idea of raising children at his age being undesirable. Now he wondered if he'd known, somewhere deep inside, that he'd never be a father at all.

The trouble with such thinking, he realized, was what psychologists referred to as the hindsight bias. One has a tendency to judge new information as being more predictable than it was before it was revealed.

"You're also exceptionally intelligent," Sophia said.

"I wouldn't go that far," Richard said with genuine modesty.

"No, really," Sophia said. "When was the last time you had a hard time grasping a new concept? Deducing a new fact? Don't things seem to come to you clearly and easily when others around you are trying much harder to see the big picture? Weren't you always in the accelerated learning classes in school? Outperforming your classmates and even some of your instructors? Didn't you hold yourself back at times so as not to embarrass the other kids or be bullied by those that didn't have your gifts and were jealous?

Richard nodded. He'd never considered it but supposed it was true.

"You picked up computer operation and information technology at a rate far beyond others who have spent years in school trying to gain a tenth of what you seemed to know instinctively."

"I'm just good with machines," he said.

"No." Sophia said. "You're good with *everything*. You were good with sports before you decided it was a waste of your time. There isn't a hobby or pastime you've tried that you weren't good at before you got bored with it. Cars. Music. Art. Cards. Shall I go on?"

"No," he said, embarrassed.

"And it was *you* who tracked down a child killer when every law enforcement agency in Kansas failed to do so."

"I saw him take her!" Richard protested.

He remembered the day. The steel blue clarity of it. He'd gone out for a drive that morning for no particular reason other than the urge to feel cool air blowing on his face, to have control of a powerful machine, to be in motion. A shady spot under an old elm tree on a little traveled side street outside a housing development had appealed to him so he'd parked there. Sat back. Listened to a mix CD of 80's rock music.

A short while later a blonde girl of about eight or nine wearing beige Capri pants and a pretty pink blouse had ridden by on a bicycle. She turned the corner at the end of the block and vanished from sight behind a line of poplar trees.

A light breeze played through the trees. Branches caressed each other, their leaves whispering some secret tree language

A rusty yellow sedan had followed the girl slowly enough to get his attention. It somehow looked threatening. Menacing.

The hair on Richard's arms had stood up and he kept a close eye on the vehicle until it turned the corner in the opposite direction as the girl, disappearing behind a similar line of trees. He dismissed the uncomfortable feeling the sedan had aroused in him.

A few minutes later the girl pedaled by again, her hair trailing out behind her like a banner in the breeze. Circling the block, Richard assumed. No doubt fulfilling a similar urge to feel the wind in her face and be in motion.

No rusty yellow sedan had followed.

Richard had been drowsing, marking the girl's passage as she made another, then yet another trip around the block. It was her fifth time past his vehicle and his eyes were closed, his mind drifting the currents of not quite sleeping. His ears registered the *ticka-ticka-ticka* of the playing card clothes pinned to the frame of the bicycle so that it struck the spokes as the rear tire turned. As the sound of the playing card faded a new sound invaded Richards senses. An engine accelerating. Richard opened his eyes.

As the girl entered the intersection to make her turn the yellow sedan entered from Richard's left, accelerating to a joggers pace. The bumper clipped the rear tire of the bicycle sending it scooting out from under the girl. She hit the hood of the sedan with an audible squawk.

Richard was stunned. The slow motion collision had been intentional. What he saw next made the hairs at the base of his neck stand on end.

The driver's door of the sedan opened and a portly man in his early forties, hair graying at the temples, got out and hurried to the front of the vehicle. The girl had slid off the hood of the car and was sitting in front of the bumper holding her leg and crying.

"I'm sorry, honey," Richard heard the man say over the whispering trees. "Let me get you to a hospital."

With that the man scooped the girl into his arms, hurried back to the car with her, and deposited her in the passenger seat. Richard could see the man's mouth moving, but could hear nothing through the rolled up windows of the car. He didn't need to hear the thumping noises and screams from the child as the man slammed her face into the dashboard once, twice, three times. It could have been Richard's imagination but he thought he saw tiny spicules of blood fly from the girl's nose on the third blow.

Richard started his car, cursing the slow starter of the second hand Cougar's engine. By the time the engine roared to life the yellow sedan had pulled out of the intersection, grinding the pink Schwinn the girl had been riding under its tires as it roared away.

Despite leaving twin trails of rubber where he'd been parked, Richard lost sight of his quarry before he reached the intersection. He turned right, narrowly avoiding the battered Schwinn and frantically searching the road ahead for any sign of the sedan. He saw nothing save empty asphalt, parked cars, and trees writhing in the air currents. At the next intersection he cast his eyes left and right, praying for a glimpse of yellow.

Nothing.

He'd driven around the area for another twenty minutes before admitting to himself that the abductor and the little girl were long gone. He'd then driven straight to the police station and reported what he'd seen to the authorities.

"You were in the right place at the right time," Sophia said. "That's happens to you a lot, doesn't it?"

"How do you know so damn much about me?" Richard asked.

"We have detailed files on you and every other known Prime in the Multi-verse."

"Then you know that the description I gave police led them to a postal employee named Patrick McCormack. There was ample evidence he'd taken the girl. Both on the car and in his home. Pink paint transfer on his bumper. Her blood on the dashboard. Her torn and blood stained clothes were found in his basement."

"They never found her body though, did they?" Sophia said.

"No," Richard said, remembering the frustration the police had expressed at their inability to find Katie Marsh's body. The grief of her parents. His own rage when the judge presiding over the case had had no legal choice but to declare all evidence inadmissible due to a clerical error that had broken the chain of custody, setting a dangerous pedophile loose to rape and murder another innocent child.

"And when they let him go, you killed him."

"I *avenged* her," Richard hissed. "She was so tiny. So *innocent*. She'd never hurt anyone in her life. Just a pretty little girl who'd wanted to spend the morning outside on her bicycle, feeling the wind in her hair. That's all. Just to enjoy the weather and go for a ride. And that son of a bitch, that *monster*, took her. Did unspeakable things to her and then just threw her away." Richard stopped when he realized he was ranting, tears coursing down his cheeks like small streams of grief and rage.

"Do you regret it?" Sophia asked. "Killing him, I mean."

Richard considered what it had cost him in the end. Ten years of his life in a hell of man's creation. The toll it had taken on his parents and how they, now long in their graves, had had to live with the knowledge that their son, too, was capable of unspeakable acts of violence. How he'd been branded a murderer and was therefore untrustworthy in all aspects of life.

"Not for a second," he said.

"And that's *why you*."

"What?" Richard said, confused.

Sophia said: "You've been asking yourself since you first found my Mirror: *Why me?* That's your answer. Your confidence, your *certainty*, that killing Patrick McCormack was the just thing to do. Despite the social taboos and legal consequences you killed a man—quite brutally, I understand—who would have preyed on more children, destroyed more innocent lives, maimed and broken more families. You're a crusader, Richard. With an innate sense of right and wrong and gifts granted you by the Multi-verse that don't extend to the rest of us."

"That's ridiculous," Richard said. "You make me sound like the Batman."

"No," Sophia said. "Not the Batman, or any other comic book superhero. You're a Prime; human and flawed to be sure, but, like all Primes, something *more*.

"That's why Sophia Nineteen sought you out. And that is why you're needed now."

Richard digested this as Sophia exited the Interstate and turned onto tree sheltered, one-lane asphalt that was more path than road. A sign reading *Granite Lake* loomed large at the side of the road and then disappeared in the rearview as they passed it. A quarter mile later they topped a rise that gave a view of the lake that would have been magnificent in the daylight.

"What does the RLP give as the location of the Rip?" Sophia asked.

"No need," Richard answered. "I can see it. Down by the shore on the left, about three feet out over the water."

The Rip seemed to be casting a light of its own through the after-storm gloom. Blue and shimmery, like a sheer curtain stirred by the wind.

"I'll have to take your word for it," Sophia said, continuing down the other side of the rise. The intervening trees blocked the Rip from Richard's sight.

"What do you mean?" Richard said.

"Your awareness of Rips," Sophia said, "Your exposure to their energy by traveling through one has awakened a part of your subconscious that allows you to see them. It's another of your gifts. One us non-Primes don't share."

"You saw the one in California," Richard argued.

"I saw the refraction of sunlight and the effect the energy of the Rip had on the surrounding terrain. You're seeing the Rip itself."

"Great," Richard said. "Where's SG-1 when you need them?"

"Who?"

"Never mind."

Sophia maneuvered the SUV around a curve and into a turnout. A split-rail fence barricaded the asphalt from a steep wooded drop leading to the shoreline. The cool blue glow of the Rip a mere fifty yards away drew Richard's gaze like a moth to lamplight.

"We're on foot from here," Sophia said, checking the RLP. "We should be okay," she added, "there's no sign of bogeys."

Richard collected his duffel and exited the vehicle.

Headlights approaching from the rear lit them up. Richard's hand slipped into his duffel and grasped the butt of a Beretta PX4.

"Easy," Sophia cautioned from inside the SUV. "It isn't them."

The vehicle, a tan Landcruiser with a top mounted light bar pulled in behind their SUV—effectively blocking their route should he choose to duck back inside and flee, Richard noted—and rolled to a stop. A spotlight blinded Richard as it first panned him, then the SUV. Sophia got out and stood in the V formed by the open driver's door and the carriage.

The spot cut off and the driver got out of the Landcruiser. He wore an ankle length rain slicker, open at the front, revealing a khaki uniform and deputy sheriff's badge. His hand eased onto the butt of the Glock he wore on his belt. Raindrops glistened as they hit the Stratton protector fastened over his Stetson, keeping the felt and a pair of gold acorns corded to the brim dry.

"Morning folks," he said. "Would you mind stepping over here where I can see you a little better? And could you maybe keep your hands where I can see them?"

Richard dropped the duffel on the ground and stepped towards the back of the SUV, his hands out to his side and his mind awhirl. If the cop found the weapons—and he undoubtedly would if he searched the vehicle—they were sunk. This little adventure of theirs would come to a screeching halt right here by one of the prettiest little lakes in Missouri.

Beyond what that would mean for the Multi-verse, or this particular world, it surely meant Richard was going back to prison for a lengthy stay and Sophia would be arrested and charged, her belongings confiscated. She'd be trapped here, without access to an RLP. Fair game for Jefferson's men. There was no choice in Richard's mind. They somehow had to get the drop on this guy, lock him in his vehicle, and make their escape through the Rip.

"Is there a problem, officer?" Sophia asked as she joined Richard on his side of the SUV.

"Well, ma'am, there very well may be," the deputy replied.

"What we have here are what you might call suspicious circumstances. Now I'm sure you all are just a nice couple come down to the lake this morning to do a little sight-seeing, or maybe do a little necking on the beach. But," he said, tilting his head to the sky, "it's a might early yet and the weather just don't seem right for that sort of thing."

Richard noted that though the deputy had given the impression of looking upwards, his eyes had never left the two of them.

"And when I ran your plate a few minutes ago," the deputy continued, scratching at the five o'clock shadow on his jaw line, "the DMV database told me that that tag doesn't exist. Not here in Missouri, or anywhere else for that matter.

"It could just be a mix up. I could've entered the wrong tag number *both* times I ran it, or the computers at the DMV could be having a little hiccup. These things happen. But I figure just to ensure public safety we ought to wait right here for my friends to show up—they'll be along any moment—and we'll sort this all out together. You all wouldn't mind that now would you?"

"I don't think that's necessary, officer." Sophia, arms crossed at her breast up to this point, dropped them to her side, her hands creeping towards the small of her back.

"Please don't do that, ma'am." the deputy thumbed open his holster and pulled the Glock halfway free. "That right there could be interpreted as an offensive move. One that I'd have to defend myself against. As you're no doubt just trying to scratch an itch that's suddenly started gnawing at the middle of your back it'd be a shame to make this situation uglier than it has to be."

Sophia returned her arms to her side as Richard stared at her, wondering at what she'd been about to do.

"Now ma'am," the deputy said, "I'd be happy to let you scratch that itch to your heart's content if you'd just turn around and lift your shirt. You do that, and let me see that there's nothing back there for me to worry about, and you can scratch away."

"No," Sophia said. "It's fine. It's gone now."

"Well, ma'am," the deputy said and sighed. He shifted his balance almost imperceptibly, widening his stance. "Now that we're on this road I really have to insist that you show me anyway."

Things happened very fast after that.

As Sophia turned she cast Richard a glance that said *It's now or never,* confirming that she did indeed have a weapon concealed at the small of her back. Richard set himself. He would lunge forward as the officer, distracted at the sight of whatever she had back there, drew the Glock fully from his holster. Richard would force the deputy's arm up and back, and wrest the handgun from him. By then Sophia would have her own weapon drawn and they could cuff the deputy inside his vehicle and make their escape before his backup arrived.

None of that happened.

As Sophia turned the deputy's Glock was already clearing its holster. Just as the front sight cleared leather the right side of his head dissolved into a mist of blood and shattered bone. His once immaculate Stetson flipped through the air twice before landing on the tarmac several feet away. A second silent shot plowed through his chest before his body hit the ground.

"What?" Richard said in confusion as Sophia tackled him. He landed on his side, facing the fallen officer. Rain trickled down the deputy's face mixing with the blood pooling on the asphalt.

A weapon on full auto opened up, throwing chunks of asphalt into the air around Richard and Sophia, filling the night with the discordant applause of gunfire. The deputy's body took two more rounds, as if he wasn't already dead enough.

Adrenaline surged through Richard's body. He rolled and lunged forward, all but carrying Sophia with him to the relative safety behind the Landcruiser. The vehicle took multiple hits as they crouched there, metal spanging and spronging before the automatic fire let up and all was still again save the lone cry of a startled bird and the still falling rain.

"You said there were no bogeys," Richard hissed through his teeth.

"There weren't," Sophia protested. "Jefferson must have sent someone through without an RLP. This Rip has been stable long enough for him to have done that. Maybe he's getting desperate, sending teams through to any stable Rips in this vicinity to keep us on this world."

"I don't think it's a team," Richard said, thinking furiously. "Unless there are only two of them. The muzzle flash from the shots *and* the automatic fire came from the same position. But why shoot the deputy and not me? Or you? We were as exposed as he was."

"Something blocking his shot, maybe?" Sophia said. "Rocks or trees or something?"

"Maybe. It doesn't matter." Richard said. "We're not safe here. If it were me I wouldn't be just sitting out there hoping one of us pops our head up before more cops show up. I'd be circling, looking for a way to flank us. Catch us in a crossfire if there *are* two of them."

He pulled the handgun she'd been concealing at the small of her back from her waistband and handed it to her.

"I'm going for the SUV. If anyone fires on me target the muzzle flash." He then rose from his crouch and, keeping as low as possible, dashed for the SUV.

Weapons fire thundered through the early morning gloaming. Muzzle flash lit up the scene from a new, closer position, confirming that the shooter was indeed on the move. The rear window of the SUV vanished in a tinkling of glass and the liftgate bloomed holes like tiny flowers. The sharp bark of Sophia's weapon answered, stilling the automatic fire as the BanaTech henchman ducked for cover.

Richard gained the SUV, its passenger and driver's doors still hanging open, the engine still idling. He dug through the duffel as Sophia exhausted her ammunition and brought out the Beretta PX4 and its twin. Disengaging both safeties he stood, the bulk of his body blocked from where he thought the weapons fire had come from, and loosed a two handed volley of .40 caliber rounds in that direction.

"Move!" he yelled to Sophia.

It was pure Hollywood, he knew, but he wasn't trying to hit anything. He hoped only to lay down cover fire so Sophia could make it to the SUV unscathed.

The gambit worked. As Sophia reached his side Richard dropped into a crouch, ejecting the spent clips on both weapons and replacing them with fresh ones from the duffel.

"What now?" she asked; trading the spent weapon for one of Richard's. Richard replaced the clip in the spent weapon before dropping it in the duffel and held on to the other PX4.

"We keep moving," he said.

Richard reached into the SUV and dropped the transmission into Drive. The vehicle crept forward under its own power and then began picking up speed. Richard and Sophia kept pace alongside. Gunfire erupted; lead tanging against the rear and side of the vehicle.

Twenty yards from the split-rail fence dividing the lookout from the dropoff Richard realized that the SUV didn't have enough momentum to break through.

"You have the RLP?" he asked.

"Here," Sophia said, patting her hip pocket as she trotted to keep up.

"Good," Richard tossed her into the open door of the SUV. She let out a squawk as first the duffel and then his body landed atop her. His feet still sticking out the open door, Richard reached over Sophia and rammed the accelerator to the floorboard with his hand.

"Pull 'em in!" Richard yelled. Sophia tucked and rolled into the passenger side foot well as Richard bent his knees and crawled forward. The SUV crashed through the split rail fence, both doors slamming shut as wood splintered and flew. Now airborne, the vehicle crashed into brush on the other side, bouncing Sophia and Richard around the interior.

Forty yards in, the uncontrolled vehicle clipped a pine tree, crumpling the left front fender and dissolving the headlight in a spray of plastic and glass. The SUV slewed around sideways, tearing a larger swath through the underbrush before fetching up against larger trees. Rattled by the successive collisions, Richard shook his head to clear it.

Sophia was already on the move. She climbed up and over Richard, dragging the duffel behind her, heading for the rear of the vehicle. Richard saw the wisdom in not exiting through the driver's door where they would be exposed to the shooter if he'd made it to the top of the rise above them and followed.

"You're bleeding," Sophia told him as they paused in the cargo area. He thumbed a warm trickle from his nose, vaguely remembered his face slamming into the steering wheel during the jaunt down the slope.

"So are you."

She touched a stinging spot on the side of her head, came away with blood, and shrugged:

"We're gonna bleed a lot more if we don't get out of here."

He smiled, brought up the pistol he'd managed to hold on to during their roller coaster descent and dove/rolled out the empty back window of the SUV. A broken branch gave him an ugly scratch across the forehead as he landed and he took up a position behind the vehicle, aiming the Beretta uphill. Sophia tossed out the duffel and followed suit, the underbrush sparing her countenance. There was no gunfire from above.

"Can you still see the Rip?" Sophia said.

"It's there," Richard pointed to a spot just out over the water, visible through the trees. "About twenty yards away. It's smaller now."

"Then let's go."

A lone sniper stood atop an outcropping of rock above the shoreline. Watching. Waiting. He raised a sniper rifle mounted with a scope and sighted in the couple zigging and zagging through the trees. He followed as they reached the open terrain of the shoreline, his finger tightening on the trigger as the male turned to check their back trail. Holding his fire, the sniper continued to follow their progress as they waded out into the water.

Several feet from shore, without flash or fanfare, the couple vanished into thin air. The sniper lowered his rifle and retrieved a two-way radio from the leg pocket of his BDU's. He raised the walkie to his mouth.

"It's done," he said. "They're on their way."

He looked on a while longer, noted red and blue flashers approaching from the east, then faded from the outcropping and vanished into the trees.

Chapter 9

Color.

Not color, but *color*. A chiaroscuro so rich and vibrant that Richard could feel it. *Taste* it. It traveled around him, through him, wrapped him in a warm embrace. He'd never seen anything like it, though he knew this sensation was far beyond anything as simple as sight. His senses were inadequate to convey the raw power of what he was experiencing. This sensation, this *immersion* in energy, was being communicated by senses he was unaware he possessed. It felt like bliss. Like touching the divine.

And then it was gone.

Replaced by a wave of pain through his head that staggered him. He dropped to one knee on cold, wet earth.

"Are you alright?" Sophia asked, grasping his arm.

"Dear God," Richard said, shaking his head. The pain cleared as quickly as it had come he regained his feet. "What was that?"

"I told you the pain would diminish with each subsequent trip through the Rips," Sophia said.

"Not *that*," Richard said. "There was something else. Something *in* the Rip. As we traveled through it."

"You experienced the lights?" Sophia looked startled. "On only your second trip through? Impressive."

"It was much more than light," Richard said. "It was…" He had no words for what he had experienced. Only a sense of longing and loss. He wanted to return. Go back through the Rip and be wrapped in that ecstasy for eternity. "Well, you know."

"No," Sophia said, her voice tinged with something like bitterness. "I don't. Us non-Primes don't experience the lights. We can only imagine them based on what's been reported by those of you who do. Rip travel is instantaneous for us. We have no sense of anything between worlds."

"I'm sorry," Richard said, meaning it. "It was…amazing."

He'd dropped the duffel as they'd emerged from the Rip. He retrieved it as Sophia checked their location on the RLP.

"I think we're in the clear for now," she said, dismissing whatever irritation she'd felt towards his experience of something she would never know. "The Rip closed behind us and there's no sign of bogeys."

"There was no sign of them back in Missouri either," Richard reminded her as he looked around to get his own fix on their location, "but someone shot that deputy and I doubt it was—*Oh my God!"*

His gaze had been drawn by what he had at first taken for stars in the night sky. What he saw instead was a brilliant band of glittering diamonds arcing bridge-like across the heavens. A bluish mist filled the space between the gems casting an unearthly glow against the landscape.

"Pretty, isn't it?" Sophia said.

"What is it?" Richard said with awe.

"It's an accretion disc. We're on E-372, the three-hundred and seventy-second Earth catalogued by BanaTech."

Sophia started walking in an easterly direction. Richard tore his eyes from the beauty in the sky and followed. Everywhere he looked he saw barren landscape and devastation. The air was still. Stale. It was harder to breathe here, as if they were ascending a mountain where the atmosphere was thinner than it was at sea level. Nothing moved. No insects flitted about them. No small, unseen animals scurried at their passing. No reptiles slithered amongst the rocks or the damp reddish soil.

"Several decades ago on this Earth's timeline," Sophia said, her words coming on labored breath "On December 21, 2012, a rogue meteor struck the moon shattering it like a Faberge egg dropped by a clumsy child. The resulting meteor storm wiped out the cities and most of the human population. Widespread wildfires, residual radiation, and the loss of tidal pull on the planet—critical in maintaining climatic balance—took the rest. What you see there," she said, gesturing towards the gem laden sky, "Are lunar remnants that were either too small or too far away from Earth's magnetic field to succumb to gravity. Instead of falling to Earth they formed a planetary ring."

"Radiation from the moon?" Richard asked. "I thought the moon was an Earth remnant formed by a massive meteor impact during Earth's formation."

"So far as we know it is," Sophia said, "The radiation didn't come from the moon fragments but rather the meteor that struck it. The press at the time dubbed it, aptly I think, the Hammer. It was expected to strike the moon but have little effect otherwise. Unfortunately, it was made up of materials far denser than expected and had absorbed high levels of radiation somewhere along its journey through space. The radiation caused cancer and widespread mutations in wildlife and the few who survived what the media termed Hammerfall. Forty years ago this would have been an interesting place to visit. New species and mutations of old ones were popping up all the time. There are reports from teams that investigated this world for years after the event telling of housecats the size of lions, with six or more legs and a dozen eyes. Sea creatures that would dwarf the Blue Whale, the largest animal ever known to live on this planet.

"Now," she said with a sweep of her arm, "it's just a dead world. There may be some microbes still present in the soil, some phytoplankton still surviving somewhere in the thick muck that used to be lakes and oceans, but nothing more complex can survive here for long."

"What about us?"

"We should be okay at the lower elevations," Sophia said. "For a day or so anyway. There's sufficient oxygen here to prevent asphyxiation by hypoxia—the build-up of carbon dioxide in the blood—but if we stay here too long we're susceptible to pulmonary or cerebral edema, fluid in the lungs or brain, similar to what someone experiencing acute altitude sickness suffers."

"The radiation?" Richard prompted.

"Radiation from the Hammer had an extremely short half-life in a nitrogen/oxygen rich environment. Say twenty years or so. As long as we don't go digging around in any impact craters and unearth an intact fragment our exposure should be minimal."

"Where are we going?" Richard said.

Sophia stopped, placing her hands on her thighs and breathing deep of the thin, stale air.

"There's an old research station about a day's walk from here. BanaTech hasn't sent any teams here for years but if we're in luck there may still be some supplies lying around. BanaTech outfits its teams well in case of unforeseen emergencies. When they pull out, they tend to leave whatever they don't need behind."

Retrieving an elastic band from one of the voluminous pockets of her BDU vest she pulled her long, dark hair back and banded it into a ponytail before continuing on.

"We'll be needing water soon," she said. "We're losing vapor from our lungs at a higher rate than normal. If we don't drink regularly dehydration will set in."

"I think I'm already halfway there," Richard said. "The ground is damp. There must be water under here somewhere. Maybe we could dig…?"

"We'd risk radiation poisoning or worse," Sophia said. "The water on this planet was contaminated by the Hammer. Then the fires burned everything. And there are all the manmade pollutants to think of. Chemicals released into the atmosphere that came down as acid rain, toxic and radioactive waste that flowed freely with no one to clean up when the containment vessels failed. I'm not that thirsty yet."

They continued on. Richard eyed the landscape, his brain telling him that *something* must still be alive on this rock. He couldn't comprehend an Earth in any part of the Multi-verse without life. His eyes told a different story, however. As unbelievable as it seemed, *this* Earth was a barren rock. He may as well have been on Mars.

"Where are we, anyway?" he asked. "Geographically. Relative to my Earth."

"The RLP indicated a location corresponding to Central America," Sophia said. "This would be a lush jungle on your world."

"Jesus," Richard muttered.

After a time the sun rose. The gems in the sky dimmed but did not lose their uncanny glow. Sunlight filtered through the accretion disc changing the sky to a sickly green that made Richard think of Kansas skies just before a tornado.

They plodded along under the disconcerting sky. Speaking required too much effort so they kept it to a minimum. Richard noted that the air became somewhat warmer but there was little in the way of wind. The stillness, save the scritch and scratch of their footsteps upon the earth, was maddening.

Sophia periodically checked their position on the RLP.

The color of the soil deepened to brown, then to black. Whatever had caused the moisture in the soil throughout most of the day—*an old riverbed, maybe*, Richard thought—was now gone. The earth here was dry. Blistered and cracked. Richard wondered if this was what St. Patrick had experienced on his journey across a blighted and burned Ireland.

He been staring at a formation on the horizon for several miles before he realized that unlike the terrain they'd been passing through, with distant outcroppings of rocks and natural pediments, this shape was far too regular. Boxy at the bottom and narrowing at the top. This…*structure*…was manmade.

"What is that?" he said when he'd worked enough saliva into his dry throat to speak.

"Oxwitik," Sophia said, checking the RLP. "On your Earth it's known as Copán. That's where the research station is. If there's anything left of it."

"Why there?" Richard asked. The knowledge that their destination was in sight re-invigorated his tired and aching lungs. The hope that there was untainted water there made him salivate.

"BanaTech started sending teams here a decade after Hammerfall," Sophia said. She, too, felt somewhat refreshed after miles of trudging along, her head down, seeing little more than her mud-caked boots leaving tracks in the soil. "They knew this planet was doomed but were interested in the *mechanism* of it. The major cities were already gone, smashed or burned. Some of the smaller ones and their outlying areas were still intact, though, and there were pockets of survivors living in these. Some banded together. Despite sickness and mutation they made a go of it. Eventually though, they'd meet another pocket of survivors—another tribe, if you will—and there would be conflict. War. What the Hammer started, man finished."

"And BanaTech just sat back and watched?" Richard said. "They did nothing to help any of those people?"

"Revealing themselves would have put the entire program at risk," Sophia said. "Besides, benevolence isn't exactly one of BanaTech's priorities."

"What is, then?"

"The complete and total domination of the Multi-verse."

Richard laughed. His amusement trailed away when he saw that Sophia had stopped and was staring at him with a stone-cold expression on her face.

"It's no joke, Richard," she said. "These people are to the Multi-verse what Adolph Hitler was to your world in the nineteen thirties. Only worse. They have thrived for over two-hundred years, raping and pillaging worlds for resources and building an empire that spans almost a thousand worlds while destroying anyone and anything that stands in their way. Do you think the lives of a few thousand people on a dying planet mean anything to them at all?"

Richard swallowed, the small amount of saliva in his mouth turning the consistency of mud. The enormity of what she was suggesting, the brutal indifference it implied, was overwhelming.

"I suppose not," he said.

Sophia began walking towards the edifice in the distance again. Richard readjusted the duffel's weight on his shoulder and followed.

"This location was remote enough," Sophia continued, "that BanaTech could remain hidden while still performing their research. They used satellites and drones for remote surveillance and would have had vehicles at their disposal for work that required them to be on-site."

"How would they have gotten all that equipment here?" Richard asked. "They certainly didn't scrounge it up once they got here."

"No," Sophia said. "There was no need for that. The Rips are dimensionless. For reasons unknown the event horizon normally appears at right around sixty-two feet, or a ten foot diameter. However, you can push a city bus through a Rip only a few inches across with the same result."

"That would explain a lot of disappearances," Richard said, "from aircraft to ships at sea."

"Exactly," Sophia said. "As I've already pointed out, Rips tend to form along ley lines and natural magnetic vortices, the same ley lines and vortices the Mayans, Egyptians and other ancient cultures built their monuments in conjunction with."

"Which means travel to and from this area would be relatively easy," Richard said.

"Relatively, yes," Sophia said. "Team members would still have to wait for a Rip the QCs predicted would terminate in the right location, but a lot can be moved through a Rip of sufficient duration."

And the area would be easily defensible given the terrain, Richard thought.

As they walked, Richard mulled over BanaTech's motives. An audacious endeavor, Richard thought, attempting to take over the Multi-verse. But he thought he could see how it could be done.

Baby steps at first: Take over the home world. The Rips could be used to acquire the resources needed, primarily money, then weapons on a massive scale. Rip onto a neighboring Earth, take what you need, then rip out before anyone there could put a stop to it. Subvert the local political structure back at home with the bounty and then, when enough politicians were in your corner, take the rest by force. Which made BanaTech a political and military complex as well as industrial.

He was simplifying things, he knew. It would have taken decades to acquire the resources needed to fund the research and development of the QCs and the RLPs. Then more time to place the satellite network, both at home and on other worlds, that linked the entire operation together. All while moving quietly behind the scenes to gather allies and build an indomitable power base that would stand against any and all adversaries.

Once that structure was in place, however, once an entire world had been turned to BanaTech's purposes, other worlds could be taken. Rip in, repeat the subterfuge and political maneuvering, and another world would be under BanaTech control before the populace became the wiser. Another planet to draw resources, technology, and military might from.

Over two-hundred years and a thousand worlds, Sophia had said. A lump formed in Richard's throat at the thought. His stomach rolled over and he wanted to puke.

Sophia stumbled. Richard thrust out a supporting arm before she could fall.

"Sorry," she said. Her voice grated through dry vocal cords.

"It's okay," Richard said. He was having a hard time speaking as well. He'd been so lost in his deliberations he'd barely registered the passage of time. His thirst was now a clamoring need, his throat as rough as leather. As he looked around at the terrain his head spun. "We can rest a while if you need to."

"No," she said. "If we stop we may never get moving again." Slowly at first, then picking up momentum, Sophia struck out towards the necropolis once again.

They'd covered a lot of ground. Approaching the ancient ruins from the east Richard could make out individual features of the vast complex. Three massive pyramidal structures stood on the left, with smaller buildings and edifice beyond. To the right was a wide opening into the city that led to the ceremonial plaza.

During his incarceration Richard had watched a National Geographic series on the Maya and their cities. The documentary had centered on the better-known finds at Chichén Itzá, Tikal, and Palenque, but there had been a short segment on Copán. He recalled vigorous vegetation throughout the city. Trees and shrubs, bushes and greenery of every sort that thrived in South America, all meticulously maintained and trimmed to appeal to the tourists. He remembered thinking that he'd hate to have been the one responsible for all that maintenance.

There were no vast grassy fields now. No trees to trim. No shrubs to cut back. No need to protect the city from the encroaching jungle just outside its perimeter. The vegetation was gone and nothing remained to indicate that it had ever grown here at all. It struck him as odd. They'd spent the day walking through what had once been a tropical forest but there was no evidence of it in sight. Long before Richard had been born his grandfather had cut down an oak tree on the property that had been split open by lightning during a thunderstorm. The stump from that oak had remained throughout Richard's adolescence and adulthood, slowly eroding away but not decaying entirely. It had been over fifty years since that tree had been removed, and, to Richard's knowledge, the stump was still there. Richard looked out across the vast, empty expanse. Why had none remained here?

He thought to ask Sophia about it, but his parched throat deterred him. He shelved the question for later.

His mind began to wander. The events of the past twenty-four hours—*Dear God, has it only been a day?*—played through his mind, mixed with the events in Kansas last winter. There was no particular order to his musings. His thoughts wandered from the jarring arrival in Kansas City, Missouri, to a fist-fight he'd had his first week in prison. From the abduction of Katie Marsh to his first kiss outside the middle school he'd attended as an adolescent. The subconscious is a fitful and incongruent beast. Left to its own devices, without conscious guidance, it may wander back alleys opening doors onto long buried memories best left to rest. Suffering the effects of dehydration and oxygen deprivation, Richard's conscious mind retreated into a dark corner to spare him the fatigue and pain his body was enduring. He dreamed on his feet.

Patrick McCormack had reacted with hostility when Richard knocked on his front door a week after being set free.

"Fuck you want?" he growled, reaching down and locking the wood framed storm door between them. This was not the chubby but well dressed man Richard had seen in the courtroom. Clean-shaven, hair neatly parted in the middle, tie knotted perfectly at the throat of an expensive Calvin Klein dress shirt. The picture of innocence. Wrongly accused and graciously—but timidly—enduring the gaffe.

This was a new image. Wild, unkempt hair that hadn't seen a comb in days. Spotty growths of whiskers on the throat and chin that had been plucked and picked to the point of irritation. A yellow stained t-shirt—the debris of many meals embedded in the fabric—above piss stained undershorts that had been worn so long they gapped about the legs. McCormack stank of alcohol, rotting food, and urine. *This* was a man who'd been exposed for what he was: A snake, a reptile. A walking, talking, predator so far devolved that he'd soon be hunting another victim.

Any hesitation Richard might have felt at what he'd planned, what his mind had chewed upon since this piece of filth had been released into an unsuspecting world a mere week ago, fled him at that moment.

"Ain't you caused me enough problems?" Patrick whined.

"Not enough by far," Richard said and promptly shot his arm through the thin fiberglass screen separating them. He caught hold of

McCormack's hair before he could reel back out of reach and pulled. The older man crashed headlong through the door landing face first on the porch.

McCormack screamed a shrill, old woman's scream that pierced Richard's ears like a hatpin. McCormack lived at the far end of a rural route and there wasn't another house for a quarter mile. No one would hear his cry at twice the volume. Such an innocent bray from this unrepentant monster, however, enraged Richard further. He kicked the man in the stomach, cutting the sound off like someone throwing a switch.

Richard pulled a Colt .45 from the small of his back and pointed it at the man's head. He'd intended to simply shoot the man. Execute him where he lay and be done with it. No fuss, no fanfare, and very little evidence. He'd driven out to the property on two previous occasions. Watching, waiting. Simmering in his need for justice. His compulsion to avenge little Katie Marsh—and there had been others, hadn't there? Six other girls of the same age and body type gone missing from this and surrounding counties in the last three years—and prevent this animal's sick hunger from destroying any more lives.

He'd seen the tornado shelter McCormack claimed to have been digging several hundred yards from the house. Knew the police had keyed on it during their investigation, thinking the five-foot deep pit and pile of earth surrounding it—a shovel standing upright in the extracted dirt like a tombstone—might be a grave. A thorough examination of the property with a Self-Contained Sub-surface Penetrating Radar System, however, had revealed the excavation was just what McCormack claimed it was. Wherever McCormack disposed of his victims, it wasn't anywhere on his property. The dig, however, gave Richard an idea.

"Get up," Richard said. He gave the man a not so soft nudge in the ribs with his foot. "Now." He didn't move fast enough to suit Richard so he helped him along. He grabbed the man's greasy hair at the nape of the neck and pulled him erect. McCormack screamed again. This time, Richard let him.

He hauled him around the side of the house to the pit, McCormack wailing and blubbering the entire way, asserting his innocence and pleading for mercy. Richard would have none of it. The protestations only served to fuel the fury that had kept Richard awake every night since a simple clerical error had loosed this fiend from custody. He let go of McCormack at the edge of the concavity and gave him a kick in the rump, adding a footprint to the stains already spreading there. McCormack sqwawked and tumbled into the pit.

"You gonna bury me alive?" he wailed, getting to his knees. Snot ran down his face, mixing with dirt from the fall and bits of food that had dried there. Tears coursed through similar residue on his cheeks. "*Oh God, please, NO!*"

Richard squatted beside the hole, lining the Colt up with McCormack's nose.

"Not quite," Richard said. "We're gonna have a little chat and I want you immobile while we have it." He gestured at the mounded earth surrounding the pit with the Colt. "Pull the dirt in around yourself."

"Fuck you!" McCormack cried. "I ain't burying myself! You can just go on and shoot me!"

"I can." Richard nodded. "I'll start at your feet and work my way up, avoiding anything vital." He turned the gun over in his hands, inspecting its smooth finish. "I have seven rounds in this magazine," he continued, "and one in the chamber. I also have two spare magazines in my pocket. That's a total of twenty-two. You'll probably pass out from the pain after the first few rounds but I have all day. I can wait for you to wake up before I start shooting again."

McCormack whimpered, then began pulling the dirt in around himself.

"I ain't done nothin'," he sniveled as he worked, "this ain't right." The hole began to fill up. Earth first surrounded, then covered McCormack's ankles.

"Where are the bodies?" Richard asked.

"I don't know nothin' 'bout no bodies!" McCormack protested. "I didn't kill that girl! I ain't some sicko!"

"And all the evidence found in your basement was planted, right?"

"Tha's right!" McCormack howled. "Them cops, tryin' so hard to find someone to pin it on. And *you*! Runnin' 'round shootin' your mouth off that you'd seen *me* take her! Seen *my* car! For all I know *you* killed her and planted all that stuff in my house! Just tryin' to cover up your own…"

Richard belted him across the temple with the Colt. Had the earth in the hole not already been up to McCormack's knees he'd have fallen flat on his back. Instead, he swayed back like a drunkard. A thin line of blood ran down his temple and dripped off his chin.

Richard stood and started shoveling dirt in the hole around the semi-conscious man, packing it down to ensure he remained erect. He had filled the hole to the man's shoulders before McCormack spoke again.

"You gonna kill me, ain't ya?" His voice was softer now, resigned.

"Tell me where you hid the bodies and we'll discuss it."

McCormack laughed softly as Richard continued to shovel. He was almost level with the ground now, though a substantial pile of dirt remained. His father had told him that when shoveling there was always more dirt left than hole. Just like evil, there was always far more than the world they lived in could contain.

"They was sweet, you know," McCormack said, almost whispering. He met Richard's eyes and smiled at some memory Richard didn't want to understand. There was something behind his eyes. Something muddy and dark, yet shining and capering madly with glee.

This, Richard thought, *is the beast that must be vanquished. The evil light that must be banished from the All.*

He shook his head to clear it. He didn't know where the thought had come from. Had never had such a thought before.

"I did 'em up real good," McCormack continued. His voice had changed, become thicker. Slurred now with more than alcohol or the addled tongue of someone impaired by a blow to the head. "Spread them sweet little legs and tore the innocence right out of 'em. Defiled them. *And* the All."

He was talking nonsense. Richard's hopes of locating the bodies of McCormack's victims and helping the families find some sort of closure, some sort of peace in their lives, was fading fast.

"You go on keep her," McCormack said. "You do what you have to do. I'll just move along somewhere's else. I ain't tellin' you shit."

After a time, Richard gave up asking for the remains of the girls McCormack had brutalized. McCormack remained unresponsive as Richard leveled the ground around his neck, tucked the Colt into the small of his back, and walked to the small shed several yards away. He uttered neither word nor sound as Richard wheeled out McCormack's John Deere riding mower and settled into the seat. He neither balked nor objected as Richard started the mower and swung it in his direction.

Just before he passed from view McCormack shot Richard a baleful glare of utter hatred so fierce it raised goosebumps on his forearms. Then the deck of the mower bumped up and over McCormack's head and three spinning blades tore into it. Blood, brain, and bone shot from under the mower's deck in a circular pattern.

Richard shut off the mower and walked away avoiding the mess. He went home and slept peacefully for the first time in weeks.

A staying hand on his arm pulled Richard back to reality. His throat hurt and his head spun. He blinked his eyes several times, clearing the past from them and reasserting himself in the present.

"We're here," Sophia croaked.

They stood in the central plaza at Copán, surrounded by stelae adorned with the stylized faces of brooding kings and fantastical creatures. An ancient ball-court and stepped pyramid structures loomed to their left, other monuments and altars to their right. A smaller pyramid, perhaps forty feet in height and three times that at the base, dominated the plaza. Sophia pointed towards the edifice.

"That's where we need to go," she said, and promptly collapsed.

Chapter 10

This is becoming a habit, Richard thought. Unable to rouse Sophia from her faint—*blackout*?—Richard picked her up and cradled her to his chest like a small child. Her hair smelled of lavender over the stale odor of this dead Earth. Just as her Mirror's had back in Kansas. His senses told him this was the same woman, though he'd watched her Mirror die and knew it was not so.

He carried her, despite his own fatigue and waning strength, adding her weight to that of the duffel strapped across his shoulder. He'd considered leaving it behind but had discarded the notion. There were things in there besides the weapons and ammo that he might find useful before this journey was over. *If* it were ever over.

The edifice Sophia had pointed to was a pyramid at least five times his height. Stepped blocks so large a grown man would find them difficult to scale led to the top. It may have once served as a ceremonial altar but had more likely been a tomb for one or more of Copan's many kings.

As he approached he noted an incongruity in the worn, hand chiseled stone. A steel, man-sized door was set into the base of the pyramid. To the right of this was an illuminated keypad glowing green in the waning evening light.

He gently lay Sophia on the ground and examined the alpha-numeric pad. It resembled a telephone keypad with CLEAR and ENTER where the asterisk and pound symbols would be. He tapped sophia63 into the pad and hit enter. A negative buzz issued from a speaker set beneath the keypad. The door remained closed.

"Worth a try," he muttered.

Sophia made a noise at his feet. Richard leaned over and she breathed in his ear:

"RLP."

Of course. BanaTech wouldn't send people through the Rips without some way of accessing research facilities and bases like this one. The RLPs looked like common cell phones, but were, in fact, uplinks to the satellites BanaTech had in place around worlds they either controlled or had interest in. The RLPs themselves were password protected which eliminated the need to further protect any data they or the Quantum Crays back on the Homeworld contained.

"Sorry," Richard murmured as he fished around in the pockets of Sophia's BDU for the RLP. She gave him a weak smile and her eyelids fluttered shut.

Once he had the device in hand Richard hesitated to use it. Sophia had told him that the QCs could track the RLPs anywhere. It was a safe bet BanaTech already knew where they were and it was only a matter of time before a Rip opened that brought Jefferson and his goons screaming down on their heads like the meteor that had destroyed this world decades ago. But there was little choice. If he couldn't get the door open and find water inside they were going to die.

Richard opened the slider. At the prompt he typed in Sophia's password. The screen cleared and showed their present location as a blue dot on the GPS map of the ruins. Back on his version of Earth he'd noted a Help tab on the main menu. He scrolled to it and hit enter.

The screen dissolved to a list of options. He ignored these and typed PASSCODE into the search bar. A long list of locations scrolled down the screen. There were hundreds of entries under that keyword. He thought for a moment, hit CANCEL, and was returned to the help prompt. He typed in the keywords: PASSCODE, **X**-372, and OXWITIC.

The RLP listed four options: MAIN COMPOUND, LABS, ARMORY, and FPG. The armory and FPG listings were marked RESTRICTED.

He keyed on MAIN COMPOUND and received a ten-digit code that he keyed into the pad beside the steel door. The door sank into the ground without pause and a light flickered on inside revealing an airlock.

Richard pocketed the RLP, gathered Sophia in his arms, and carried her inside. The door rose behind them. He heard a whirring and a thunk followed by a soft chime. A door in front of them rose into the ceiling and a sweet smelling blast of oxygen rich air enveloped them.

Richard breathed deep and Sophia stirred in his arms.

"I can stand," Sophia said. Richard set her on her feet and, after a wobbly moment, she stood on her own.

"Water?" Richard said. His throat felt like sandpaper.

"You bet," Sophia said.

She motioned for the RLP and Richard handed it over. Her fingers worked the tiny keypad much faster than his clumsy pecking.

"Here," Sophia held up the RLP and showed him a section of floor plan for the installation. "The dining hall is our best bet. It's one level down. This is all maintenance and garages up here."

Sophia led him down the corridor. Lights activated by motion sensors blinked to life as they progressed. Richard's vision was becoming shiny around the edges as if the fluorescents overhead were putting out too much light. His thirst had become a need that was driving out all other consideration.

When they reached a door marked SL 2-8 Sophia straight-armed the bar that held it shut and pushed through, descending the staircase beyond without waiting for the overheads to fully illuminate.

One level down was a door marked LIVING QUARTERS.

If it's locked, Richard thought, *I'll tear the damn thing off its hinges*.

It wasn't locked. Sophia opened the door and then stopped. Richard caught up with her and saw a wondrous sight. On the wall opposite the door was a pair of drinking fountains, one set higher than the other. Their brushed chrome surfaces gleamed invitingly.

They looked at each other and grinned like children. Then they burst through the door.

"This is amazing," Richard said forty minutes later.

They were seated at a table in the dining hall, a vast space that could easily accommodate a hundred people. The lights in the food prep and serving areas had blinked on as they'd entered but the dining area remained unlit. Either the motion sensors were rigged to conserve energy or there was a bank of light switches they hadn't found. The result was eerily thrown shadows and murky corners where anything could be waiting. Watching.

After drinking their fill at the water fountains—Sophia had vomited up her first greedy gulps despite Richard's warning to drink slowly—they had discovered hunger. Richard had had nothing to eat since Sophia had barged through his front door a day and a half ago. He had no idea when she might have last eaten.

The dining hall, several hundred yards down the corridor and past dozens of living units, was their next stop. In a pantry tucked away behind the food prep area Sophia had found hundreds of foil wrapped packages marked MEALS READY TO EAT. They had both taken double handfuls at random. Richard had torn through two helpings of roast beef and Sophia was busily scooping the eggs from three different packages into her mouth.

Sophia said: "I never thought green eggs could taste so good."

Richard tore open a ration of beef stew, dumped it on a plate, and dug in.

"Or meat that's probably older than I am,"

Sophia chuckled and then froze, staring at a shadowy spot behind Richard's left shoulder.

"What is it?" Richard said.

"Nothing," Sophia blinked. "Just my eyes playing tricks on me. For a second there the tables behind you looked like spiders. *Big* spiders."

"Visual matrixing," Richard said. "When you see a mass of shadows and shapes your brain doesn't understand it imposes familiar images onto them in an attempt to make sense out of chaos. It works the same way with sound. The hum of the compressors and pumps on the refrigerators in here are unfamiliar to me so I've been hearing whispering. Auditory matrixing. Like when you hear someone call your name while you're running a vacuum cleaner but no one is there. It gets worse when you're tired."

"I passed tired about twelve hours ago," Sophia said. "I'm wasted."

"So am I. We need sleep, but is it a good idea to sleep here? On this base?"

"We're going to have to risk it," Sophia said. "I've reached my limit. I was sleeping on my feet out there. I'm not sure if I blacked out because of oxygen deprivation, dehydration, or just plain old exhaustion."

"What about Jefferson?" Richard asked.

"He already knows where we are," Sophia replied. "and is probably just waiting on a Rip that will bring him and his men close enough to the compound to launch an assault. That could be hours or days from now—or minutes. The QCs are pretty good at predicting the duration of a Rip once it has formed, as well as where it will terminate, but not so good at predicting when one will form in the first place. Jefferson could be cooling his heels for a while."

She yawned, her red-rimmed eyes watering. Observing this, Richard yawned hugely himself. The nature of human physiology.

"We also have access to the computers here," Sophia continued, "That gives us an advantage. BanaTech can't sever that as long as we're on site, nor can they sever our link to the satellites without blinding themselves as well. So we'll see them coming if they show up before we can bug out.

"How are your computer algorithm skills?"

"Pretty good actually," Richard said. "Why?"

"If you can re-write the password protocols we can change all the codes and lock the facility down. They can't attack us if they can't get in. How long would it take?"

"Not very long. Forty minutes, maybe an hour. Providing I can get past the internal firewalls and gain administrative access."

"Not a problem. I'm in research, remember?" Sophia smiled. "I have access to those codes."

"Then let's do it," Richard said, "while I still have the energy to stay awake."

It took better than two hours. By the end of it Richard could barely hold his head up. He'd nodded off a time or two, awakened to find his forehead resting on the keyboard, holding down keys and entering nonsense strings into commands he'd been trying to write.

The facility was made up of eight sublevels. The computer mainframe was located on sublevel seven above an entire level of cooling towers and air handlers for the facility. Sublevel three was comprised of more housing units *sans* dining hall. These larger, single living units were presumably for the brass rather than the three and four bed units for the grunts upstairs. Levels four and five housed laboratories covering everything from human physiology and biochemistry to electronics.

All of Level six was restricted. Access was via elevator only, and then only with a special code Sophia did not possess. The level was marked FPG: RESTRICTED. Richard asked Sophia what *that* was all about as they descended to sublevel seven.

"Later," she replied, her voice hoarse. Given her bloodshot eyes and the fact that she had to lean on a rail in the elevator just to stay on her feet, Richard let it pass.

The facility was massive. Sublevels four, five, and six ranged out over a square mile beneath the surface of the planet.

"How did they accomplish all this?" Richard had asked.

"The Mayans built Oxwitic atop existing ruins. That city had been built atop the remains of another. BanaTech's Corps of Engineers only had to remove what they didn't need from existing tunnels and seal off the rest. The entire operation took months instead of the years it might have taken to excavate it all at once."

Scanning the mainframe Richard discovered there were five access points to the facility. In addition to the door they had entered through there were two ramp entrances concealed beneath cleverly disguised doors that accessed the motor pool, one large enough to move small aircraft through. Another, larger door was concealed within Copan's cemetery group far to the west of the city where the Maya had disposed of their dead. This door led to an elevator shaft that serviced level six exclusively.

Shuttered twin shafts leading directly to sublevel eight were the fifth and final access point. They were simple vent shafts, one drew fresh air in from the surface, the other vented stale air out from the facility. At the bottom of each two-hundred foot shaft was a twenty-four foot fan spinning at eighteen-hundred RPMs. Anyone attempting to enter through either shaft would likely find out what fruit feels like in a Cuisinart. Still, Richard re-wrote the access codes to the shutters. Better safe than sorry.

The computer was more advanced than Richard had anticipated, the language far more complex than anything he'd worked with before. Still, the root of all code came down to math. He applied his skills—and quite a bit of instinct—to bend the machine to his will.

He ultimately managed to not only lock the facility down but also activated a perimeter defense system consisting of forty-eight Browning M2 quad-mounted guns on pop-up gimbals. Each would pour .50 caliber rounds into anything larger than a dog that moved within twenty-five hundred yards of the facility. Richard had no qualms about activating a lethal system on a dead world where the only thing moving would be BanaTech's security forces.

Last, Richard locked out any changes to the system without his own personal password. Then he and Sophia returned to level three where unmade but inviting bunks and much needed sleep awaited.

The dreamer seldom realizes he's dreaming. Or that more can be observed when the subconscious is running the show. Things misunderstood, things overlooked.

They was sweet, you know, Patrick McCormack said. Buried in the ground up to his neck there was little need for pretense. The innocent man he'd tried to portray had fled. The evil that lived in his heart had stepped up to be heard.

As he slept a deep but restless sleep in an ancient Mayan ruin on an Earth that had been murdered by a meteor decades before, Richard remembered the clear, strong voice that had spoken up in his head as he stood over Patrick McCormack, a Colt .45 pointed at the child killer's head. It was his voice, of course, the voice he heard whenever deep in thought. But there was something more there too.

Something righteous.

"This is the beast that must be vanquished. The evil light that must be banished from the All."

At the time, Richard had chalked the unbidden thought up to the many sleepless nights he'd had since the McCormack trial had concluded so disastrously, to the adrenaline surging through his body since the realization that justice would require kidnapping and murder.

The All? He asked himself now, as in the dream time slowed and his perceptions sharpened.

McCormack was speaking again. Richard cast his attention back to the talking dead.

...tore the innocence right out of 'em. Defiled them. And *the All.*

Something was pushing its way up out of McCormack. Up out of the ground he was buried in. A shadow perhaps, or a shade. Except the afternoon sun was directly overhead and still the shadow emerged where none should be.

Sinuous arms reached up out of the soil. Elbows rested near McCormack's neck, then pushed downwards. A dark shape rose from within McCormack, shaking its head as if to free itself from the confines of its human host. McCormack spoke, and the shadow spoke with him.

You go on keep her, McCormack and the shadow said in unison. *You do what you have to do. I'll just move along somewhere's else. I ain't tellin' you shit.*

Keep her? Richard thought. *Or keeper?*

The apparition ceased struggling to free itself from McCormack. It had no definition to speak of, was still a shadowy form without substance. To Richard's heightened dream sense it now seemed bored. It crossed its arms and began drumming its fingers on the soil as if waiting impatiently for Richard to act.

Just before the front axle of the riding mower passed over McCormack, before the machine's blades cut into his skull ridding the world of his miserable existence, the shadow rose fully from the earth. It touched Richard's shoulder as it passed. Gooseflesh broke out on his arms and he shuddered as one word rang out in his mind.

Infernal.

Chapter 11

In another Universe, nearly a mile beneath the surface of a planet known simply as Earth 01, Alex Jefferson strode through a series of twisted corridors. Anger burned within his six-foot two inch, two-hundred and twenty pound frame. Anger that Farris had bested him and then slipped away. Anger that the traitorous Bledell woman had stolen the Key right out from under his nose and spirited it away.

Decades had been spent researching and locating the Key. Without it, nearly a half-century of experimentation and untold billions of dollars would be wasted. The Focal Point Project would never reach fruition and the Elder's plans would fail. Finding another Key would be impossible.

The current Key *must* be located. But how does one find an object hidden on an uncharted Earth in an infinite series of Earths? It was like looking for a needle in a stack of needles.

Jefferson turned a corner and entered a cavernous space filled with towering computer servers, crowded banks of monitors, and control consoles. A dozen or more technicians bustled about the room engaging in technical conversation, checking this monitor and that, recording various data on the touch pads they carried for transfer to this or that device. It was like walking into the control room at NASA just minutes before a launch. This was BanaTech's communications room. From here one could communicate with any of the hundreds of security and research teams in the field, access any of the nearly ninety-thousand satellites in orbit around the hundreds of Earths BanaTech had interest in or controlled, or even interface with the forty-seven Quantum Crays buried in super-cooled chambers another half mile beneath the complex.

The Quantum Crays were a marvel of bioelectrical engineering. While BanaTech owed its rise to power and global domination to the discovery of the Rips and the subsequent use of them, it owed its continuing existence and expansion onto other Earths to the QCs. Each of the massive devices had an individual intelligence, a distinctive *personality* that gave rise to multiple perspectives. While unnecessary for common computing problems this trait allowed for collaboration and competition among the QCs, an essential element in consensus decision making. Though the QCs did not always unilaterally agree on the outcome of any given situation, their collective intelligence enabled them to *predict* results with astounding accuracy.

Jefferson strode towards a secure room at the back of the area noting the looks of alarm and trepidation on the faces of the technicians that saw him. He smiled inwardly at the reaction. He was an imposing figure, he knew. His broken jaw had healed, but his nose had remained crooked, giving an already predatory countenance a brutal appearance. These mousy little techs *should* scurry away before him like mice from a sinking ship.

He pulled a keycard from his pocket and swiped it through a security lock on the door. The door beeped and opened before him.

"Where are they?" he growled at the lone man seated in the room.

"On E-372," the tall, thin man whose security card identified him as Robert Wilson replied. "The Oxwitic facility."

He was unphased by Jefferson's aggressiveness. The two had known each other for years, since before Wilson had come up through the ranks of the Security Service. They'd fought side by side for most of a decade before the Elder had, at the QCs suggestion, placed Wilson as the head of the Communications Division, making his security clearance second only to Jefferson's. Though he looked ungainly, Jefferson knew he was a skilled martial artist and could kill with his bare hands if necessary. His prowess with firearms and bladed weapons was equally impressive.

"We've been getting some strange readings from level six ever since they got there," Wilson added, "but they're up on level three right now. Sleeping."

"The new tracking and communications system is working well then?" Jefferson said.

"It's had its share of glitches," Wilson said, "but it *is* working. I have a team in the vicinity and despite Farris changing the facility's access codes I can have them retrieved at any time. Are you issuing an order?"

"I am," Jefferson said, "but it's not to retrieve Farris or the traitor. They are to be followed, assisted if necessary, but nothing more. They are in no way to be made aware that they are being tracked."

"That's the standing order, sir," Wilson prompted, awaiting an update.

"You're certain you can track them once they've left the grid?" Jefferson asked.

"Absolutely, sir. Testing has confirmed that they can be tracked and retrieved from worlds with no BanaTech satellites or Rip tracing technology. Essentially, there are *no* versions of Earth that are off the grid anymore."

"Very well," Jefferson said. "The order is that when the time comes, Farris is no longer to be retrieved at all. Once the Key has been located, he is to be terminated."

Richard knew something was wrong the moment he entered level six. The air here was thicker. Stale. As if the recycling units weren't running efficiently. An electrical tang like burnt wiring filled his nostrils. Beneath that was another odor. Sweet, yet pungent. The smell of fresh roses tinged with an unpleasant hint of blood.

The hallway was long and full of jumping shadows. The overhead fluorescents had come to life as Richard stepped off the elevator but before he'd taken more than a few steps they'd begun to blink erratically. The result was unnerving. Shadows leapt before the light like living things and the simultaneous ticking of warming and cooling ballasts gave an audible impression of light-footed creatures slyly cavorting just beyond his senses.

The elevator doors slid closed behind him leaving him alone, his imagination at the mercy of faulty wiring and the vestiges of a nightmare.

He'd slept no more than seven hours before the unfamiliar name

Infernal

rang in his ears, jolting him from much needed sleep. In the seconds before his waking mind had fully asserted itself he'd felt power in the name. An ageless, boundless power that sent ripples of gooseflesh up his back and arms and across his skull. He'd been touched by the divine on his second jaunt through a Rip. Now he knew he'd also been touched by its opposite number. The effect was humbling. It made him feel small and powerless.

He'd shaken off the feeling and gone to check on Sophia. They'd chosen adjoining rooms on level three leaving the doors between open in case one of them needed the other. The rooms were small but each contained a bed, a small desk, and a wardrobe. Out of curiosity Richard had peeked in the wardrobe in his room. It was empty, as was the desk, save for a fountain pen bearing the logo of a bank he'd never heard of. *At least one thing is the same everywhere,* Richard mused. Money, it would seem, makes every world go around.

Sophia had been snoring softly, curled on her side, one arm slung over her head and the other tucked under her chin. If she were dreaming it wasn't the sort of dream that had wakened Richard.

He smiled. Despite the military style BDU's she wore and the Beretta lying inches from her outstretched hand she looked very much like a child. Small and defenseless. Trusting. *This* Sophia, he decided, would come to no harm. Not as long as he was alive to protect her.

Leaving her to slumber a while longer Richard had decided to do some exploring. This was BanaTech turf and there was knowledge to be gained by poking around in it.

He'd retrieved the pen he'd found in his room—*Community Bank of the Commonwealth* it said in bold red and blue letters—and an old receipt from his wallet and jotted his intentions down. Leaving the note in the middle of the desk where Sophia wouldn't miss it he went back to his room. He collected one of the handguns from his duffel, checked the loads, and tucked it into the small of his back. Only a fool poked around on the enemy's turf, abandoned or not, without some way of protecting himself. Then he headed for the elevators.

Seized by curiosity from the moment he'd read the legend FPG: RESTRICTED—a curiosity only heightened by Sophia's earlier deflection of the subject—Richard had deleted the access restrictions to all levels within the facility while reprogramming the computers. At the time he told himself he'd done so because they would want access to the armory, also on the restricted list, before they departed. If

BanaTech hadn't removed the weapons before they'd abandoned the base they'd be able to re-arm. Their current supply of weapons and ammunition was rapidly dwindling.

Curiosity might be a great cat that greedily devours others. Richard could almost feel it perched on his shoulder, its warm tail wrapped around his neck, whiskers brushing his ear as it purred to him that what was on level six could reveal the answers to all his questions. Questions about himself. About BanaTech. And, if it were more than just a specter in a bad dream, the *Infernal.*

He'd descended to level six, the doors obediently parting before him.

Blood and roses, he now thought as the overheads continued to flicker. *Or maybe rotten fruit.* The parts of the facility he'd encountered thus far had smelled antiseptic; like bleach or ammonia. Cleansers in the kitchen. The hot smell of working electronics in the computer room. This level smelled different, as if an animal had crawled into the ductwork and died, its decaying corpse releasing the gasses of decomposition into the air to circulate on this level and this level alone.

He swallowed and could taste the odor.

"Lovely," he said aloud. His voice echoed back to him from the end of the corridor.

The hallway ended in a T-junction. He strode toward it, shaking off his unease.

Three words were painted on the cream colored wall at the end of the corridor:

FPG

CONTROL

ZeVATRON

The first word was painted red, the second yellow, and the last blue. Each had corresponding solid lines painted on the floor indicating direction, much like he'd seen in hospitals and other large institutions.

The word ZeVATRON sparked a memory. Something he'd read about gluons and other subatomic particles, but he was focused on the first word: FPG. He turned right, following the red line, recalling that there had been red lines in prison. Warnings that one was approaching the perimeter fence. Crossing *that* line into the so-called no man's land was a good way to get shot.

The floor sloped downwards here, the walls widening out until he was walking a corridor he estimated to be three times as wide and twenty feet deeper that the one before. He felt as if he were shrinking. He cast a look back over his shoulder. In the flickering fluorescents the corridor he'd just left looked tiny. Impassable. It reminded him of the perceptual door trick from *Willy Wonka and the Chocolate Factory*.

Something stirred the hair at the nape of his neck. Brushed down his arm and raised the hair there as if a cold hand had touched him. He looked above, certain he'd see an air vent that had kicked on. He saw nothing but smooth white ceiling panels. He shifted his eyes to the right certain he'd seen motion there, but there were only shadows thrown by malfunctioning light fixtures.

The corridor curved to the left. Richard continued following the red line much as Dorothy had followed the Yellow Brick Road, trusting it to take him not to the Emerald City but to the FPG, whatever that was. The hallway continued to curve before straightening out and ending in a solid steel door.

The door was featureless, made of polished stainless steel about fifty feet wide and twenty feet tall. A single almost invisible seam ran down the center. Richard approached it and ran his finger along the closure. He didn't think he could get as much as a sheet of paper in there. He looked around and saw no controls. No lighted keypad, no computer interface. Nothing he recognized that would gain him entry to whatever lay beyond.

He doubted that waving his arms and shouting "Open sesame!" would have any effect.

The light shifted again and he saw motion behind him in the reflective surface of the door. Heard footfalls coming closer. He spun, drawing the H&K. Then sighed, dropping the weapon to his side.

"You'll never get in that way," Sophia said. "That door is twenty inches thick with another ten inches of porcelain lining the other side."

"What the hell is in there?" Richard said, tucking the gun back into his waistband.

"A failed experiment," Sophia answered. "One in a long line of failed experiments. And the reason for all of this. The reason *you're* involved in all of this.

"The Focal Point Generator."

They retraced their steps and were approaching the T-junction when a shadow passed them accompanied by a sound. Richard reacted. This was no mere shadow thrown by flickering lights. It had form. Richard could almost make out an arm moving towards a mass that might have been a head, followed by a soft expulsion of air like a cough.

"Ignore them," Sophia said. "They're not there."

"*Something* was there," Richard said. "That was *not* visual matrixing."

"No," Sophia said. "It wasn't. It was a time rift."

"A what?"

"A time rift," she repeated. "Remember I told you that Dr. Bana theorized that most hauntings could be explained by thin spots in the fabric of reality? Windows onto other places and times?"

"Yes," Richard said.

"That's what's happening. We're seeing things that happened here in the past. Or maybe in the future if those spiders I saw upstairs were real. The experiments BanaTech carried out in this complex had devastating consequences. Not just here but all along this planet's natural timeline. A literal hole was ripped in time. Though the effects should have been confined to the generator room it's obvious that they're leaking out and spreading. It seems to only be affecting this level for now but it won't be safe to stay here much longer. If we're caught in one of these rifts there's no guessing what could happen."

Richard digested this as they passed through the T-junction.

"This way to the ZeVatron," he quipped as they passed the legend painted on the wall.

"What?" Sophia said.

"An old P.T. Barnum ruse," Richard said.

"The circus guy?" Sophia said.

"Yes." Richard answered. "But before that he ran circus sideshows. In one of his most successful he put up signs that read 'This way to the EGRESS.' Since egress is nothing more than another word for exit..." he trailed off. Stopped walking. A look of shock came over him.

"What is it?" Sophia said, alarmed. She looked around for another apparition but saw nothing out of place.

"ZeVatron?" Richard said. "Dear God, they built a *ZeVatron*?"

"I suppose," Sophia said. "That's what they call the machine under this complex, anyway. I'm not familiar with the technical aspects of it but I know it's a particle accelerator. What's the big deal?"

Stunned, Richard resumed walking.

"The big deal," he said, "is that it's not possible."

Recognizing that it would take some time before Richard fully realized that there was no such thing as impossible Sophia waited for him to work out his thoughts.

"On my Earth," Richard said, "a European organization named CERN wanted to prove the existence of the so-called God particle, a hypothetical Higgs boson they believed was responsible for giving particles mass. It was the only particle science had yet to prove the existence of. To that end they built an unimaginably powerful particle accelerator called the Large Hadron Collider.

"There were protests about the huge amounts of money it cost. The possibility of an accident. The damage so much power could do in or near the 17-mile toroidal ring that would be used to accelerate the particles. The biggest fear was that they would inadvertently tear a hole in the fabric of space-time or open a black hole under Switzerland that would destroy the planet. None of that happened but that's not my point.

"My point," he continued, "is that the Large Hadron Collider is a TeVatron. That means it can accelerate and cause the collision of particles in multiples of TeV, or a trillion electronvolts. One TeV roughly equals the kinetic energy of a mosquito in flight.

"A *ZeVatron* would be a collider with the ability to accelerate particles in multiples of ZeV. That's a *sextillion* electronvolts. Or a one followed by twenty-one zeros. That sort of particle acceleration only occurs in galactic jets where new solar systems are born. It's not something man is meant to control."

Sophia appraised Richard as they approached a door marked CONTROL ROOM.

"They've done it here," she said. "and on at least seven other Earths that I know of. It's a critical part of the Focal Point Generator. But it has had its consequences."

As she spoke Sophia thumbed a keypad on the wall. Since Richard had removed all access restrictions the door obediently slid open revealing a room twenty feet on a side. The space was crowded with control panels displaying flashing lights of every shape and color. The room was lit up like a carnival midway. Calliope music would have completed the scene but the only sound was the hum of electricity and the whirring of hard drives running unfathomable programs. To Richard it sounded like the stridulation of locusts.

A window of thick glass six feet high and fourteen feet wide dominated the far wall of the room. In the vast space beyond it looked to Richard as if it were snowing. He approached the window and realized he wasn't seeing snow but some other white substance slowly swirling about a space he estimated to be twenty yards across and as much as fifty yards high.

The window, situated near bottom of the space, revealed that the curved ceiling and floor were round, the walls tapered in at the bottom like an egg standing on its small end. At the center of the floor, amidst a conglomeration of unidentifiable machinery was a chair similar to those he'd seen in dentist's offices. Except this chair had wrist and ankle restraints—and there was a man seated in it.

He was screaming.

Chapter 12

"There's someone in there!"

Richard dropped his gaze to the hundreds of switches and dials on the boards in front of him frantically searching for some way, *any* way, to get into that room. The man strapped into the chair was in agony, his arms and legs rigid against the restraints that bound him. His head was thrown back, jaw agape, lips peeled back in a rictus grin so severe that the flesh at the corners of his mouth had split open spilling blood down his cheeks and across his chin. Richard could see muscles corded with strain and bulging veins in the man's throat, fists and forearms.

Richard located a covered button marked *Emergency Airlock Release*, flipped up the cover and was about to depress the button beneath when Sophia grabbed his wrist.

"You can't help him!"

Richard looked at her as if she were crazy. The man was trapped and in pain. Another victim of BanaTech's insatiable lust for power. He *had* to help him. Nothing could be more important. He shook free of her restraining hand and reached for the release button again.

"Richard!" Sophia screamed. "*Stop!*"

It was as if she'd slapped him. He stayed his hand and looked at her. *Really* looked at her for the first time since entering the room. Her eyes were wide, desperate. *Terrified.*

"If you release that lock," Sophia said, "the time rift will spread unchecked and we'll die or be trapped here forever."

"What are you talking about?" Richard moved his hand away from the button and Sophia closed the cover on it.

"That's Michael Manus in there," Sophia said, a look of great sadness on her face. "He is...*was* a friend of mine. He's stuck in a time rift that formed when they tried to create an artificial Rip. He's been there for fifteen years."

Richard looked back to the man in the room still fighting the restraints binding him, still silently screaming out in endless torment.

"Jesus," he said.

"When the focal point formed," Sophia said softly, "at the precise moment Michael was pulled in, *every Mirror of Michael Manus on every Earth died.* Each and every one of them suffered a severe cerebral aneurysm."

Richard was silent for a moment, letting the vastness of what Sophia had told him sink in. *Every* version. On *every* Earth. Millions, possibly *billions* of lives wiped out in an instant.

"Can the Focal Point Generator be shut down?" he asked.

"They tried," Sophia answered. "They cut power to the ZeVatron. To the inducer coils and other machinery you see arrayed in there. There was no effect. Once in place the field is self-sustaining. He's just stuck in there. Forever."

A thought crossed Richard's mind, horrible yet unavoidable.

"They should have killed him then."

Sophia barked a bitter laugh.

"They tried that too. Nothing outside the field seems to affect anything *inside* it. And once you're inside it, you're stuck. That whitish grey stuff you see floating around in there? There are no air currents or eddies in there. That stuff has been drifting around in the same endless pattern since it was pulled into the focal point fifteen years ago.

Richard leaned closer to the window, squinting at the substance he'd at first mistaken for snow. "What is it?"

Sophia sighed. "There were four techs in that chamber when they powered on the FPG. They were all supposed to be safe from the effects of the focal point. And they were, until the field began behaving outside the parameters of what had been predicted. When shutting it down failed Jefferson refused to open the doors and let the techs out. What you're seeing is the remains of those four people. Jefferson burned the room and everyone in it."

"This focal point," Richard said as they made their way back up the main corridor to the elevators. "You said it's spreading. How?"

His curiosity about the Focal Point Generator had not fully been sated but he'd already seen far more than he wanted to here. With the knowledge that there was absolutely nothing that could be done for

Michael Manus he only wanted to get back to level three and retrieve his duffel before heading to the kitchen for foodstuffs. Then they would explore the armory in hopes of re-arming before finding a way off this awful base.

"The walls of the generator room," Sophia said, "are made up of twenty inches of stainless steel and ten inches of porcelain embedded with layers of copper mesh at two inch intervals. A Faraday cage of sorts. You're familiar with Faraday cages?"

"An enclosure formed by conducting material that blocks incoming electrical fields," Richard said, nodding. "They block radio waves, cell phone signals, just about any external electromagnetic radiation."

"Correct," Sophia said. "What they can't block is static or slowly varying electromagnetic fields like those generated by the rotation of the Earth. Or those of The Source."

"The Source?" Richard said.

"It's what we call the energy field that powers the Rips, our RLPs, the QCs...just about every instrument BanaTech has ever developed. We can't define it. Don't know where it comes from or even exactly what it is. All we know is that it's there, *everywhere*, flowing through everything animate or inanimate. Even the empty depths of space. Dr. Bana found a way to tap into it, to focus it and use it. It's the foundation for all BanaTech technology."

As they reached the elevator Richard stretched his arm out towards the UP button and then jerked it back as a shadowy hand emerged from the stuttering light and pushed the button. Though the door in front of them remained closed they heard a faint *ding* followed by the rumble of elevator doors opening. Richard shivered as an indistinct figure passed them before disappearing through the still closed doors. He looked at Sophia and they exchanged a *did you see that?* look.

"Anyway," Sophia continued nervously as Richard pushed the button in the present, "the generator room is like a Faraday cage in reverse. It was designed to keep electromagnetic fields from leaking out instead of in. But it can't completely block the EM field generated by The Source and the rift is slowly leaking out into the present."

A chime sounded and they boarded the elevator. There were no apparitions here and, as the car rose, the unpleasant sensation of something being wrong that Richard had felt since he'd stepped onto level six began to fade.

"BanaTech," Sophia continued, "has monitored the focal point from the home world for over a decade. It's growing. The very edges of it have spilled out onto level six causing the phantoms and strange electrical disturbances you experienced. In time it will encompass the entire base, the continent, and then the world. Eventually, though no one can guess how long, the entire solar system will be overtaken. Then the Universe as a whole."

Richard tried to imagine an entire Universe where time had no meaning. Forward, backward, nil—all subject to the various eddies of electromagnetic radiation surging throughout the cosmos. Black holes first sucking up, and then spewing planets and galaxies back out. Ancient planets growing young and then being pulled back into the galactic jets that had formed them. Solar systems where planets didn't revolve around their suns, meteors and comets didn't pass by or crash into planets, all still and frozen in temporal stasis. He couldn't quite wrap his mind around the concept.

"You don't fuck with the infinite," Richard muttered.

"What's that?" Sophia said.

"Something I read in a book," Richard said. "Stephen King, I think."

"I don't read fiction," Sophia said. "Reality is disturbing enough."

"So what's the point of all this?" Richard asked as they arrived on level three and the doors opened onto the living quarters. "Why build the generator in the first place?"

Richard, his attention on Sophia and the anticipated answer to his question, did not see the shape outside the elevator as he began to exit the carriage. He let out a bark of surprise as Sophia roughly pulled him back inside.

"It's spreading," she hissed, flattening herself against the back wall of the car.

Richard looked into the hall. A thrill ran up his spine and across his skull as if the hair there had been ruffled by a breeze.

There was a spider in the hall. Its head was the size of a beach ball, its abdomen three times that. Legs the thickness of Richard's wrist and as long as his body scraped the floor and wall opposite the elevator as the spider busily worked at a spot near the ceiling. Chips fell from ceiling tiles as a spinneret the size of the faucet in Richard's kitchen ticked against the floor.

"Fiddleback," Richard whispered, noting the violin shaped marking on the dorsal side of the spider's cephalothorax.

Sophia dug her fingers into Richard's arm as the spider turned whip fast to face them. Richard shrank back. The ceiling tile the spider had been working on fell to the floor with a *flumph.* Richard saw himself reflected in eight black orbs as the spider reared back planting its legs for attack and *hissed* at them like an angry cat. It launched itself forward.

Then ceased to exist as its head crossed the threshold of the elevator.

There was no sound. No pop. No thunder. No slow fade as there had been with the phantoms on level six. The spider had been there, as real and solid as Richard and Sophia—and now it was gone.

Richard stood, pulling Sophia up with him. Without realizing it he had crouched down at the back of the elevator, tucking himself into a near fetal position to make as small a target of himself as possible. Sophia had done likewise, clutching his arm to her chest in absolute terror. He'd have bruises in the shape of her fingers for a week.

When his heart stopped booming in his ears and his blood pressure returned to a more or less normal level he took several deep, cleansing breaths and looked outside the elevator.

"I think it's safe now," he said.

Sophia, hyperventilating at the appearance of an arachnid the size of a golf cart, trembled visibly. Her legs were weak, unsteady.

"How can you be sure?" she asked. "Those things could be everywhere."

"Mmm. I don't think so," Richard said, pointing out into the corridor. "Look."

Sophia looked where he indicated. The ceiling tiles and far wall were unmarked. No crumbs or larger pieces littered the floor.

"Whatever time that thing came from," Richard said, "it must have gone back there. There's no evidence that it was ever here."

"Then let's get our things," Sophia said, "and get the hell off this level."

Richard and Sophia made their way to the living quarters, nervously scanning the corridor ahead and behind for signs of more untold horrors,

Time, Richard thought as they crept along, *is an artificial construct of the basal ganglia at the base of the human brain, useful for cataloging events that take place in that person's life. It's the mind's way of telling a chronological story. Events can conceivably occur in any order. Forward. Backward. Simultaneously, or not at all. Hence: Time does not exist.*

"That spider sure existed, though," he muttered aloud.

"What?" Sophia startled, looking in all directions at the mention of a spider.

"Never mind," Richard said as he entered the adjoining rooms they had shared and retrieved his duffel. "Just thinking out loud."

"You might want to think faster," Sophia said from the doorway, a nervous edge in her voice. "Our little trip down to level six must have set something in motion. "We've got more company out here."

Richard slung the duffel over his shoulder and poked his head out into the corridor. Sophia had backed up against the opposite wall. Her gaze was fixed on a diaphanous figure moving towards her. It was no spider, but just *what* it was Richard couldn't say.

It was a wild conglomeration of bird and beast taller than the corridor. Its head was covered in a great plume of feathers that reached up to, and passed through, the ceiling. Two legs covered in large brown spots continued up the torso where they disappeared under what appeared to be some ornate, feathered material. Two arms emerged from a great bulk of feathers that covered both shoulders and descended down the back like a cloak. The left arm faded out of existence just below the elbow while the right ended in a hand that clutched what looked like a staff topped off the head of some great cat;

a cheetah perhaps. As it moved closer Richard stepped out into the hall for a better look.

"Don't let it touch you!" Sophia hissed.

Richard stopped, heeding her warning.

The figure paused at the sound of Sophia's voice. The mass of plumage atop its head turned in her direction. The figure jerked backwards as if in surprise. Richard heard no sound but knew the figure spoke when he saw the jaw working. Then it continued on past the elevators before turning and disappearing into a solid wall.

"What *was* that?" Sophia said.

Richard took her elbow and guided her towards the elevators.

"I think he was Mayan," Richard said. "Probably of some importance considering the ceremonial garb. You said Oxwitic was built atop the ruins of other Mayan cities. This must have been one of the old tunnels your corps of engineers widened out for use."

"He *saw* me," Sophia said as they entered the elevator

"It seems he did." Richard pushed the button for level one. "You probably gave him a good scare. The Mayans were deeply steeped in superstition. If he saw you the way we saw him, he probably thought you were some sort of ghost or bad omen."

"This is bad, Richard," Sophia said. "If the spider was from the future of this world—and believe me there's nothing like it in any of the research I've done—and that Mayan was from the past, then the focal point is expanding faster than anyone predicted. Time is overlapping, becoming muddled. If we don't get out soon we could be trapped here."

The hardened woman Richard had fought side by side with was gone, replaced by a scared little girl seeking reassurance that the nightmare she was experiencing was not real. That the noise she heard under her bed was nothing more than a creaking floorboard, the shape in her closet a pile of toys and not some monster come to claim her soul.

The elevator stopped on level one and the doors rolled open. Richard stuck his head out and scanned the hall. No spiders. No Mayans or other phantoms out of time. They may have left all that behind on level three, risen past the edges of the time rift where what he thought of as present time was firmly in place. On the other hand, a six tentacle beast from hell could be lurking just out of sight down the corridor.

"We'll have to risk it," he said. "We need weapons, water, and some form of transportation. Since there's no way of knowing when a Rip within reach will open up we'll also need some way to carry oxygen with us. The atmosphere out there won't sustain us for long."

Sophia took a deep breath, visibly shaking off the fear that had crept over her. She pulled the Beretta from her waist, checked the loads, and chambered a round. Here was the Sophia Richard knew. The outcast. The rebel. The researcher turned warrior.

"Follow me," she said. "I know the way."

Chapter 13

They encountered no more anomalies as they ascended to level one. No more ghostly apparitions or phantoms out of time. No more nightmare creatures from God knows *what* time and place. The armory, located in a secure room near the motor pool, offered a plethora of supplies. Row upon row of weapons and ammunition both familiar and exotic. Sophia pointed out a Lauer MMS152, a pistol-sized weapon that emitted an electrostatic charge in the 30,000 amp range. It had an effective range of 50 meters.

"A lightning gun," Richard mused, thinking of the unpredictable nature of electricity. "Not for me, I think."

He chose to stay with the familiar. He selected 400 rounds of ammunition for the PX4 Storm and M&P compact, and another 400 rounds for the H&K P30 and Beretta 92FS. He considered replacing the .454 Casull lost in the California melee but decided to forego that powerful but unwieldy weapon in favor of the lighter, fully automatic H&K MP7.

"There are forty round magazines for that," Sophia said.

Richard nodded and said: "I'll take a dozen."

Spying a rack of clothing and tactical gear Richard decided to trade out the filthy jeans and flannel shirt he'd been wearing since California as well as his worn and battered duffel bag. His back to Sophia, he stripped down and slid into a set of beige BDU's before selecting a Voodoo Tactical "REAPER" Long Range Reconnaissance Patrol Pack from the rack.

Guns, a first-aid kit, a small folding knife, and a four by two inch ornate felt lined copper box he'd held on to since Kansas also went into REAPER. He left the thirty-five thousand or so in cash he'd been carrying since California on the floor. Away from his own Earth he doubted it would be of much use. He topped the pack off with the new ammunition.

"What's that?" Sophia nodded at a small copper box as Richard slipped it into a side pocket of the pack.

"Nostalgia," Richard said. "My mother collected trinket boxes. This one was her favorite."

Sophia shrugged and filled a similar LRRP with M.R.E.s, water, space blankets, flashlights, nylon rope, a fire kit, multi-tool, and a first-aid kit. She added Richard's Beretta and selected a compact pistol with an ankle holster as a back-up, and tactical knife in a wrist sheath.

"Nice MOLLE," Richard said. The term was pronounced *molly* and referred to what is commonly known as modular, lightweight, load-carrying equipment. A military *bug out* pack.

"I think that's about it," Richard said.

He appreciatively eyed some of the larger weapons he recognized: Colt M16A4 rifles, GE M134 7.62x51mm mini-guns, Browning .50 caliber HMG's. All too wieldy to be practical. They would have to rely on the small arms and well over a thousand rounds of ammunition they'd chosen to carry.

Richard let out a low whistle as they entered the motorpool. The space was vast, a thousand meters on a side and at least a hundred meters from floor to gantry ceiling. At the far end was an enormous set of doors that opened onto a ramp suitable for rolling out aircraft. Richard counted no less than a dozen drones of both the Predator surveillance/reconnaissance and Reaper hunter/killer types, as well as sixteen helicopters of various design and purpose.

At the near end of the chamber, just off the Officer Of the Day's office, was a smaller set of doors the size of residential double garage doors. Inside these, lined up like terracotta warriors, were rows of military vehicles: APCs, Breachers, M35 diesel flatbeds, LAVs, and half-tracks. None of these were suitable for their purposes.

At the head of the line were three light-duty HumVees. All had keys in the ignition and extra fuel cans—all full, Richard noted—and had been retrofitted with OnBoard advanced Oxygen Generating Systems to function in a low oxygen atmosphere.

There was a brief moment of concern about the defensive measures Richard had activated. Driving into the optical sensor range of any of the Browning M-2 quad mounts littered about the facility would be certain suicide. The idea of returning to level 7 to shut the system off was no less disquieting. The solution was less than dramatic. The OODs office contained safety overrides for the perimeter defenses. The system could be interrupted for fifteen-minute intervals or powered down indefinitely.

Richard chose to power the system down. Defending themselves against a raid by BanaTech forces was one thing. He had no compunctions about killing anyone who threatened his or Sophia's life. Leaving the system on to target the unwary, even the enemy, was, in Richard's opinion, nothing short of murder.

"They'll know we've gone anyway," Sophia agreed, referring to the tracking capability inherent to the RLPs.

The wall nearest the exit held a rack of Portable Oxygen Generating Systems, complete with masks and shoulder straps. Sophia strapped one over her face as Richard familiarized himself with the HumVee's controls and fired up the OBOG. He gave her a thumbs-up when he was ready and she hit the control panel that opened the doors. As the doors rolled aside the night sky appeared at the top of a long ramp, resplendent with the glittery, gem-like accretion disc casting bluish-green incandescence across the heavens.

Sophia opened the passenger door—there was a slight *whoosh* of air as the positive pressure built up by the OBOG escaped—and got in the vehicle. She removed the POG and tossed it and another she'd removed from the rack onto the back floorboard with both REAPER packs.

"You never know," she responded to Richard's raised eyebrows.

Richard guided the HumVee up the ramp and out into the night.

The vehicle bounced through another ancient wash sending the RLP flying from Sophia's hands to clatter across the dash. She reached out and scooped it up before it could drop to the floorboard.

"You could slow down," she said.

"I may have to," Richard said, easing off the accelerator.

Instead of driving around aimlessly hoping for a Rip to form that would take them off this version of Earth, they'd decided on a Northeasterly course that would follow the most prominent ley line in South America. The fact that this particular line traversed much of

South America before crossing the Atlantic Ocean and terminating at what Richard knew of as the Bermuda Triangle, one of ten so-called vile vortices on the planet, was not lost on him.

The terrain had become much rougher since they'd passed the outer limits of the subterranean toroidal ring used to accelerate particles for the ZeVatron. According to the odometer, they'd crossed thirty miles of open ground without any signs of decaying plant life or structures other than Oxwitic itself.

Once outside the area effected by the magnetic field, things changed. They passed long dead trees, their tortured branches reaching for an uncaring sky. Bounced through dusty washes and riverbeds, dry for decades, without a single sign of life or vegetation. Skirted a crumbling structure, its roof gone, stone walls toppled outward as if a bomb had gone off inside. Richard slowed to a crawl maneuvering through and around the larger obstructions. If not for the four High-Intensity Discharge floodlights mounted to the roof of the cab they'd have been nearly blind despite the luminescence cast by the accretion disc overhead.

Sophia, with nothing to do except watch the disturbingly surreal landscape the HumVee ground through spoke up: "Earlier, before the spider, you asked why BanaTech would want to build something as dangerous as the Focal Point Generator. It's simple logistics."

"I'm not sure I follow," Richard said.

"Standard military management," Sophia said. "Maintaining communications is the most crucial element of military strategy. Second is the ability to maintain supply lines. Military supplies follow a linear demand relationship. As you add troops to an area, more food, weapons, and ammunition are needed for those troops. As you add vehicles, you need more fuel and parts for those vehicles. An armed force without resources and transportation is defenseless.

"BanaTech's greatest advantage over any world that resists invasion through political subterfuge is that they can send virtually unlimited forces through a Rip and gain a military foothold on that world."

"There are worlds that have resisted BanaTech?" Richard asked, maneuvering the HumVee through a line of desiccated trees and into a clearing that may have once been a small village.

"Of course," Sophia said. "Jefferson's biggest problem with the Rips is that he can't control them. He can rip his forces onto a world but due to the random nature of the Rips themselves his forces might land on that world's version of Antarctica or some other location hundreds or even thousands of miles from where he needs them. There are worlds where he hasn't been able to get sufficient resources to the proper locations and the political chicanery was exposed or fell apart before BanaTech could assume control. There are other worlds that are more technologically advanced than the Homeworld, worlds where scientists were aware of the Rips but just hadn't learned how to exploit them yet. In those cases war broke out, with BanaTech usually coming out on top."

"Usually?" Richard said.

"There have been a handful of worlds Jefferson has failed to take," Sophia said. "In those cases there is a last resort."

Richard waited, slowing the HumVee as he approached a steep decline into what had once been a mighty river.

"The satellites BanaTech uses for communication and control are all armed with fusion-boosted nuclear fission devices of sufficient yield to reduce any Earth to smoking rubble three times over."

"Jesus," Richard said. He turned the vehicle parallel to the waterway, following it until he could find a safer place to cross.

"It's Jefferson's worst case scenario," Sophia said, "and one he's loathe to execute."

Richard cast a doubtful expression her way before returning his eyes to the landscape.

"It's true," Sophia said. "Oh, he could give a tin shit about the people. They're only useful to him if he can enlist them in his cause. He's a master manipulator and not above forced conscription if that fails but it's the resources he's after: The raw materials as well as the science and technology. If he has to burn an entire world he loses all that. The ability to create an artificial Rip and target its exit point further tips the scales in BanaTech's favor."

"So if he could create a Rip," Richard said, braking the vehicle as Sophia's RLP began humming in her hand, "and target, say, the Oval Office in Washington, D.C., he could put a stop to any insurrection attempts before they even got started."

"Or directly subvert the government from the top," Sophia added, "saving him time and resources."

Sophia slid open the cover on the RLP, silencing it. She studied the screen while Richard waited.

"Can you get into that riverbed?" she asked.

"Not here," Richard said. "The bank is too steep. We'd end up wrecking on the bottom and be on foot from there. I've been looking for a place to cross for the last ten minutes."

"Keep looking," Sophia said. "There's a Rip forming about forty miles from here and it's centered in that channel. The Quantum Crays predict it will be open for the next three hours."

"What if we're driving into the arms of Jefferson's goons? You said they've just been waiting for the chance to rip in here and take us."

"It's possible but unlikely," Sophia said. "You *can* travel through the Rips in both directions but the odds that this particular Rip terminates on a world where they're ready to attack from are astronomical. The RLP should give us warning if they come through the Rip before we get there."

"Like it warned us Jefferson's men were lurking around back in Missouri?" Richard said sarcastically.

"I still don't know what that was all about," Sophia said. "I've never known of anyone to go through a Rip without an RLP before. They'd be stranded without some means of communication with the Homeworld. It's just too dangerous."

"Then either Jefferson is past the point of caring about whether or not his troops get home," Richard said, "or he's found some way to mask the RLPs. Either way, I guess we take our chances." He pressed the accelerator resuming their course.

"Oxwitic was the second attempt at creating an artificial Rip," Sophia said, continuing the conversation. "The first took place on the Homeworld with disastrous results. I'm not well versed on the subject but as I understand it the science behind the Rips is supposed to be pretty straightforward. X amount of power plus Y amount of matter—in this case a particle stream of protons or anti-protons whose gluons bind to form a bosun—equals a loop of virtual quarks. These quarks are injected into a quantum field and more power is added until a field of quantum and temporal flux is achieved. The Rips naturally form inside this field. Unfortunately, it's not that straightforward in application. Jefferson's techs were able to create the quark loops but once they were injected into the quantum field the computers lost control. The resulting explosion took out several hundred square miles and killed over two thousand people."

"Shit," Richard said.

Sophia couldn't tell if it was in response to the loss of life on the BanaTech Homeworld or the massive pile of debris he was forced to detour the vehicle around.

"Despite the tragedy," she continued, "the first attempt wasn't for naught. Analysis revealed two flaws in the FPG design. One, they were tapping into The Source for power. That kind of unknown and unregulated power was too much for the TeVatron they were using to stream particles. They needed a higher energy particle accelerator and a way to regulate the power to it. Two, the QCs, though designed to be thinking machines, lacked something."

"The Rips *appear* to be a naturally occurring phenomenon but at the same time there seems to be intelligence behind them, some indefinable and illogical—almost *human* element—that defines when and where they occur. Armed with this new knowledge Jefferson ordered the experiments forward. He moved them off world where there'd be no chance of repeating the first disaster in a critical location and ordered his science team to find a way to integrate a human intelligence into the equation."

"Oxwitic," Richard said. "But something went horribly wrong there, too."

"Exactly," Sophia agreed. "They solved the power problems. Built the ZeVatron and ran through all the tests to ensure there'd be no explosion this time. They even found someone willing to be plugged in to all that energy to attempt Rip formation."

"Michael Manus."

"That's right. He was one of the original designers of the FPG who survived the first test by virtue of having the flu on the day of the test. He was also the one who analyzed the data and discovered that the QCs operate too logically to adjust to the myriad of ephemeral and intangible decisions that had to be made.

"No," Sophia corrected herself, "decision is the wrong word. The calculations *are* decisions, but they have to be made with human interaction. Human feeling. A certain…"

"*Je ne sais quoi*," Richard offered, referring to the French phrase for an indefinable quality.

"Right!" Sophia said, pleased that Richard understood.

"But Michael miscalculated too. Introducing a human intelligence into the machine wasn't enough. He couldn't control the forces inside the FPG either. He must have made some mental wrong turn, some bad virtual decision, because instead of a Rip he opened a temporal rift that encapsulated him, protecting him from any outside influence like Jefferson burning the room but also trapping him forever like a computer hard drive stuck in a nested *goto* loop."

"A computer crash," Richard said. "A blue screen with no escape button or reboot option."

"A fair analogy," Sophia said.

Richard had edged the HumVee past the debris along the riverbank—the remains of a fishing community, he'd concluded—and had moved the vehicle closer to the bank where the terrain was smoother.

"Well, lookee here!" he exclaimed.

Sophia did. The remains of a long concrete ramp partially blocked by smaller debris led down to the riverbed.

"Must have been a boat ramp," Sophia said. "Probably got a lot of use back when this river was flowing. Do you think we can use it?"

"I think so," Richard said. "It's blocked towards the bottom but I can't tell from here what's blocking it. Some old flotsam and jetsam would be my guess. We should be able to punch through. How are we doing on time?"

"We're okay," Sophia said, checking the RLP. "We still have two hours and we're only thirty miles away."

With that Richard guided the HumVee down the ramp crunching over small rocks, planks and old tree limbs that turned to dust when the tires rolled over them. Halfway down the headlights revealed the remains of an old tugboat heeled over to one side, its bow pockmarked with rust-eaten holes.

"Uh-oh," Richard said.

"Can we go around?"

"Maybe."

Richard eased the vehicle forward, the tugboat rising above them as they descended. Near the bottom of the ramp it towered over them, the size of a small house. Richard could feel it looming over the HumVee like some great beast playing possum, a predator awaiting its prey before pouncing with enormous rusty iron claws.

Swallowing a lump in his throat Richard edged past the derelict, the vehicle's tires kissing empty space at the edge of the ramp. If they rolled too far they would bottom out on that side, tires spinning uselessly. Worse, they could roll off the ramp and turn turtle in the riverbed. Either way the vehicle would be useless. On foot they couldn't make the Rip in time and they didn't carry enough water and oxygen to make it back to Oxwitic to wait for another.

There was a screeching, metal rending sound as the HumVee brushed the side of the tugboat. Brittle aged iron and steel gave way and the bow of the vessel disintegrated showering Richard's side of the vehicle with debris. He bore down on the accelerator to clear the cascading avalanche of wreckage before it could bury them, launching them off the end of the boat ramp and into the riverbed with a resounding crash.

Chapter 14

Richard ran his tongue around the inside of his mouth to make certain all his teeth were present and accounted for and that he hadn't bitten his tongue off during the violent impact.

"That was close," Sophia said, shaken.

A quick scan of the HumVee's interior assured Richard all systems were functioning properly.

"*Too* close," he said, turning to the left to illuminate their path with the floodlights.

The riverbed was armored with round stones, some larger than others but none impassable. Tree branches and silt deposits were strewn here and there along with other unidentifiable debris, likely manmade, but nothing as large as the remains of the still settling wreckage near the bottom of the boat ramp.

"It may be a bit rough," Richard said, "but it should be easier going than a dead jungle. If you don't mind a bit of jostling I'm going to push on a little faster."

"Jostle away."

He did, pushing the vehicle to just under thirty miles an hour, appreciating the military grade shocks and struts.

"I assume," Richard said after he'd adjusted to the constant shuddering and vibration of traversing a dry riverbed, "the FPG project didn't end with the debacle at Oxwitic."

"Of course not," Sophia said. "Analysis of the data revealed that though Manus had failed to open a Rip they were on the right track. They had just chosen the wrong subject. What they needed was someone who *experienced* the Rips rather than just passed through them. Someone who had a greater knowledge of what goes on inside them. Jefferson had the project moved to another world, had another ZeVatron built, and pushed on. This time he chose someone who more closely fit the needs of the project."

"He used a Prime," Richard intuited.

"Correct," Sophia said.

"But if all Primes are like me, all *crusaders* as you put it, why would one work for Jefferson? I've only met the man twice and I know the Multi-verse would be better off without him."

"Because all Primes are *not* like you," Sophia replied. "One of the things we know about Primes is that most of you die young. A mere handful actually encounter the Rips or become aware of the existence of the Multi-verse. That awareness seems to be some kind of trigger. As if knowledge or experience of the Rips allows you to live longer and fuller lives. As is you've been *touched*."

"And the others?" Richard asked.

"Most don't make it to adulthood. They die in bizarre accidents or tragic series of events. Or they develop cancer in late adolescence and quickly succumb. It's as if there's a design in place. As if you're being used by some force beyond the natural world. A few of you are useful and therefore survive. The others are not and are discarded like empty soup cans."

"Then how is it I've lived to such a ripe old age?" Richard asked. "I never encountered a Rip before and wasn't aware of the existence of the Multi-verse until a few days ago."

"I don't know," Sophia said. "Maybe you encountered a Rip without knowing it, experienced something you didn't recognize as abnormal. All I know is that something happened to you before you reached adulthood, something significant. Otherwise you wouldn't be here now."

"I think I would remember a thing like that," Richard said.

And now, as he thought about it, perhaps he did.

In grade school, Richard's route home took him past a ramshackle house that had been vacant far longer than he'd been alive. According to local legend—mostly the imaginings and fabrications of pre-adolescent minds—the property had been the home of Randolph and Helena Williams, founders and benefactors of the small town where Richard had grown up.

As the story went, Randolph was a native of a small town in Ohio, the eldest son of an oil executive and heir to a vast fortune. In early 1936 at the age of seventeen, Randolph left his parents lavish home and his inheritance behind. There was speculation that he'd gotten himself into some sort of legal trouble in Ohio, trouble that even his wealthy parents could not shield him from, and he'd fled before he could be arrested by authorities. Another line went that he'd had a falling out with his father about his place in the family hierarchy and had struck out to make his own fortune.

For several years he'd traveled the Midwest before settling in Northwestern Kansas.

As the United States entered the war in Europe and many men his age found themselves embroiled in tooth and nail battle with Hitler's Nazi machine overseas, Randolph Williams found oil on the vast acreage he'd purchased near the Colorado border. Later that year he met Helena Clafton, the fourteen year-old daughter of a derrick man. They were wed within a month.

Shortly thereafter Randolph built his young wife her dream home. Three stories and fifteen rooms on six acres unsullied by the growing sprawl of the nearby town or by anything as noisome and unwelcome—to Randolph at least—as neighbors.

After the war that had engulfed the world had come to its climactic and horrific close, Randolph William's fortunes reversed. The once seemingly inexhaustible wealth of oil being pulled from the Kansas soil dried up taking the itinerant workers and the large population of those who had come to serve their needs with it. The town, once spread over a twenty-five square mile section of the state like butter on a slice of bread, faded away to a mere shadow of its former self as residents sought their futures in larger cities like Kansas City, Topeka, and Wichita.

His oil company all but bankrupt and his fortunes depleted Williams retreated with his wife to their six-acre home. Some said he went mad at the failure of his business. Some said it was his wife's failure to give him an heir. In either case he became reclusive. It was only when his mother informed local authorities that she'd not heard from her son or his wife in over six months that their bodies were found.

Helena's head rested on a silver tray in the center of the table in the dining room. Her left arm was on a red padded velvet bench in the foyer, the index finger forced and tied so that it pointed to the dining room table as if to ensure that whoever came into the house would find the delectable taste treat left there. Her right arm was similarly positioned and nailed to a wall near the back door of the house. The rest of her was in the kitchen amidst huge dried swashes of blood, a meat cleaver, two saws and a pocketknife.

The county sheriff found Randolph in an upstairs bedroom with a large bottle of sulfuric acid used for opening drains and a Smith and Wesson .44 caliber revolver he'd kept on display in his study. He'd quaffed better than half the bottle of drain cleaner before blowing his brains out in a garish smear across the headboard.

In 1964 a wealthy young couple had bought the property, then consisting of a mere acre of land bordered on three sides by farmland and fronted by what would one day become US 36. Undeterred by the legends of the house and its former occupants they set about renovations. While excavating a hole for a swimming pool the decades old remains of at least thirteen pre-adolescent girls were discovered.

The couple fled less than a month later claiming odd noises and screams that persisted throughout the night, strange lights that darted about from room to room no matter the time of day, and—the final straw for them—punches and scratches from unseen hands on their arms and across their backs.

They claimed the house itself was alive and wanted no one in it.

No one remembered the name of the young couple much less cared. The *story* was Randolph Williams and the atrocities he'd committed there. It was then, and always would be, the Williams house.

The property had not sold again.

The house and remaining outbuildings were taken by a tornado that tore through the area in 2005 finally laying to rest anything that might be wandering about the property and going bump in the night.

It was a cool autumn evening in late October of 1982 Richard was thinking about as he maneuvered the HumVee through the riverbed and around drifts of deadwood that resembled the bones of long dead and unimaginable great beasts. On *that* night the Williams house had still been standing, though dilapidated and in a complete state of disrepair.

And, if one believed local lore, still very much alive.

Richard passed the property twice a day on his way to and from school for seven years. Despite hearing of the Williams murder-suicide and the murders of the young girls, as well as the purported haunting, he'd never given the house a second thought in the light of day. Even at night, as he lay ready to sleep, the stories passed along by his classmates on the playground failed to conjure images of dismembered apparitions screaming out their sorrow and rage in the confines of the house.

On that evening just a few nights shy of Halloween, as the sun fell slowly towards the horizon casting a purplish goodnight kiss upon the earth, something had changed.

It was almost eight o'clock. Baseball practice had run late. Their coach, in a bad mood as he seemed to be most of the time, had made them run laps until they'd all been dogging it—breathing heavily, their tongues swollen in their mouths for want of water. He could have called his father for a ride but even at that young age Richard had preferred to be alone with his thoughts. To walk in the twilight and feel the late evening breeze cool his hot face.

As he passed the Williams house he noticed the once pristine white walls with glorious blue trim were now faded into monochromatic shades of grey. The porch balusters were cracked, the paint peeling. Broken windows stared from all three floors like sightless, soulless eyes—and Richard heard a beckoning voice from deep inside the decaying walls:

Richard.

He stopped and looked at the house. Truly seeing it for the first time.

Riiichard.

The house seemed to *loom*. As if while he'd been passing it had moved closer to the road.

"Ha, ha, funny," he said, thinking one of his classmates, a member of the baseball team perhaps, was playing a prank on him. Except all his friends called him Rick. And his enemies—everyone had a few—called him *Dick*. Always with emphasis in case others should miss that they were referencing male genitalia. Only his parents, teachers, and other adults called him Richard.

Without realizing it he'd moved up the broken and overgrown brick walkway, between the rusted iron bars of the wrought iron fence, past two long dead cherry trees that lined the walk, and had placed one foot on the front porch steps. His weight on the aged wood made it creak in protest, startling him from his fugue.

Riiichaaard.

Then he was in the parlor, the front door open in the foyer behind him, casting the last of the days light tepidly through the opening. The room smelled of mold and mildew, the same smell he remembered from breaking open rotten logs to see what creatures—millipedes and spiders, mostly—lived inside. Underneath that smell was something else. Something dead. Something rotting. Something that made him think of a rancid woodchuck he'd found in the woods behind his house the summer before.

Riiichaaarrrd!

The voice was most certainly in his head. What he saw when he next came to his senses in the dining room had to be as well.

The room should have been dark but was not. Light as bright as candle flame seemed to come from everywhere and nowhere. Shadows clung to the walls and covered the ceiling and floor as if hiding great secrets. There was no usable furniture left in the old house, yet, in the center of the room stood a polished mahogany dining table complete with eight high-backed chairs and an intricate, pristine white lace tablecloth.

On a footed silver tray with ornate handles in the center of the table rested a woman's head. It sat upright in a pool of blood crawling with flies and maggots. Her cheeks were poofed out as if she were holding her breath, the skin a ghastly shade of green. Her eyes were shut but had swollen behind purple-black eyelids until they threatened to burst through the thin tissue. Her mouth was open, the tongue swollen to the point that it stuck out and lay upon the silver tray as if she were licking it.

Really *dogging it*, Richard thought absurdly.

The eyelids popped open. Maggots squirted out from around the sightless, clouded grey eyes. The mouth opened even wider and the woman screamed:

RIIICHAAARRRDDD!!!

Maggots spewed from the wide open maw, twisting and writhing upon themselves, bursting open in a torrent of flies. Richard wheeled and fled into the night.

He looked back just once. Through the dining room window he saw a turbulent flash of light, a mélange of color so beautiful and violent as to stop him in his tracks and take the breath from his lungs.

At the window, in front of this cacophony of color, stood a dark figure. It seemed to gesture to him. To come back. Step into the light. See what wonders it beheld.

Sensibly, Richard kept running.

By the time he'd covered the distance between the Williams house and his own Richard had convinced himself the entire incident had been the byproduct of exhaustion—the long baseball practice followed by the extra laps. By the following morning he'd put the event out of his mind and had never given it another thought. Until now.

What was in that house? What foul and

Infernal

thing had stood in the window, beckoning him to return?

Had that luminescence glimpsed briefly as terror drove him fleet of foot away from the property, that light he now thought so similar to the radiance of the Rips, been a Rip forming? Was that when he was exposed? What if he had entered it then, as the shadow had beckoned? At the tender age of thirteen. What course would his life had taken then?

And what if he'd *never* entered that house? Hadn't fallen into that trancelike state and stepped across the dooryard, through the foyer, and into that wretched room full of shadow and horror? Would he have been considered useless by whatever intelligent design drove the Multi-verse? Deemed unnecessary and thrown away like an old pair of socks? The thought that he might be a mere pawn on some celestial chessboard was appalling.

Have I no control over my life now at all?

Have I ever?

If the Infernal is on one side of the board, who, or what *is on the other?*

"Years ago," Sophia interrupted Richard's train of thought bringing him back to the moment, "Jefferson began a campaign to wipe out every Prime in existence. The QCs had kept a list of potential Primes for decades based on public records like birth and death certificates, education records, reproductive status, and other data that fits their algorithm. Hell, I think they even use credit reports. He took that information, which includes descriptions, home worlds and addresses, and began hunting. He got a lot of you, maybe as many as a thousand."

"Christ!" Richard said.

"But every time a Prime was killed another was born and he soon realized his efforts were fruitless. So he switched gears and began tracking Primes. Once they were old enough, he'd expose them to the Rips and subvert their thinking to match his own. In some cases coercion was necessary. In most cases it was not. He gets them when they're young, ten or twelve at the oldest. A young mind can be easily molded by an older, more experienced one."

"He brainwashes them," Richard said.

"Yes. And for every Prime like you Jefferson has a dozen more ready to do his bidding. Finding one to volunteer for the FPG project was relatively easy."

"What went wrong that time?" Richard asked.

"You really are perceptive, aren't you?" Sophia said with something like admiration.

"Not really, no," Richard said. "Achieving control of an artificial Rip would be like handing Jefferson the keys to the Multi-verse. Since he hasn't ripped in to kill us, he doesn't yet have that ability. Hence, he hasn't perfected the Focal Point Generator. Simple deductive reasoning."

"Well put, Sherlock." Sophia said. "You're right, though. The experiment failed again. The Prime who volunteered for the project came within a hair's breadth of opening a Rip but something went wrong. He, the FPG, and a control room full of techs vanished into thin air. No trace of them has ever been found. That set the program back for years. For a time Jefferson was forced to resume his original method of incursion, political subversion prior to civilian subjugation. Failing that, all out war.

"In the end the data from that second failed attempt revealed another clue. The Quantum Crays alone can't open a Rip. Pairing the computers with a non-Prime won't work either. The combination of a Prime and the machines should have worked but didn't. Not in that test or the two similar tests that followed."

"Why am I not surprised that Jefferson never gives up?" Richard said sourly.

"A fellow researcher, an acquaintance of mine, came up with the answer," Sophia said. "A prodigious savant."

"A prodigy?" Richard asked.

"Not exactly," Sophia said. "A prodigious savant is someone with a particular skill level far beyond that of a prodigy. They usually suffer from some sort of cognitive disability like Autism or Asperger's Syndrome. The most common trait is seemingly limitless mnemonic skill. Many also have eidetic or photographic memories. Prodigious savants are extremely rare. Less than one hundred cases have been discovered on any one Earth in the last century. It's possible that less than five thousand are alive throughout the Multi-verse.

"My acquaintance," Sophia's voice grew softer as if it pained her to continue, "had a daughter with Autism. The child had difficulty communicating with others and connecting emotionally with anyone, even those closest to her. She had to have help with day-to-day things like eating and dressing. Her mother was under incredible stress all the time. The child was clumsy, a common characteristic of Autism. She fell and hurt herself numerous times but never cried out in pain. Perhaps she didn't feel it or just didn't know how to express it. Raising the child required constant care and attention, a demanding task for anyone let alone a working, single mother.

"In spite of all that the child was a prodigious savant. Anything related to numbers or math the girl could solve with ease in a matter of seconds—even high function calculations that took the QCs hours to solve. It was if her seven-year old, rack-thin body contained the computing power of thousands of Quantum Crays.

"The child's ability with numbers and all manner of abstract problem solving led her mother to posit that the artificial Rips could not only be successfully formed but directed as Jefferson desired. *If* a Prime with the same abilities as her daughter could be found.

"Wait." Richard said, incredulous. "Are you telling me that the Key we're searching for is a *child*?

"I am. An eight-year old girl with severe Autism to be exact. Her name is Elianna."

"And the Sophia I met back in Kansas, your Mirror, stole the Key—this *Elianna*—from BanaTech?"

"Yes," Sophia said, "but stole is hardly the right word. Absconded with is more like it."

"I don't understand," Richard admitted.

"Jefferson was not about to scour the Multi-verse for a Prime that fit his needs. Not when he had one right at his fingertips. He planned to abduct the child from the very researcher who had discovered the solution to powering the Focal Point Generator. When she learned of his plan, she took the child and ran.

"Richard," Sophia shifted in her seat and looked at him. "Elianna is my Mirror's daughter."

Chapter 15

Twenty minutes later, his backside feeling as if he'd been riding a mechanical bull in some roadside bar, Richard cleared an enormous wash of driftwood and debris in the riverbed and let the HumVee slow to a stop. They'd traveled in silence since Sophia's revelation that her Mirror was Elianna's mother. Richard had questions, many of them. Sophia seemed to recognize his need to get his thoughts in order before they discussed the matter further. He was grateful for her empathy but now they had another problem.

"This is your idea of 'centered in the channel'?" he asked.

He'd seen the glow of the Rip before navigating around the deadfall. It was mostly trees and stone but he'd seen shapes intertwined in the wreckage that may have once been vehicles or boats. Closer inspection might reveal other things, things that had once been alive and walking.

"Where's the Rip?" Sophia asked.

Richard remembered that Sophia could not see the Rips and there was no heat haze on this version of Earth to refract the energy into a visual range she *could* see.

"There." Richard pointed up and left through the windshield. "About fifty feet up.

Sophia whistled softly.

The spot Richard pointed at looked like the open maw of some long dead beast, a rictus grin of uprooted trees, stones, and mangled manmade objects. At some point in the planet's history, perhaps due to a nearby meteor strike, this area had flooded and then drained rapidly. The riverbank had been washed away as the receding waters carried what looked like miles of dense jungle vegetation and everything else in its path to this low spot. Looking downriver revealed that the deadfall went on as far as the HumVee's lights illuminated.

"We won't make it up that in one piece," Sophia warned.

"Unless you have a way to bring the Rip to us," Richard said, "we don't have a choice."

"Can we get to it from above?" Sophia asked. "Drive around this and find a way back up to the top?"

“We could drive for miles and not find a way out of here,” Richard said. “Do we have time for that?”

Sophia glanced at the RLP and shook her head. “This Rip is closing in less than ten minutes.”

“And we don’t have the fuel or oxygen to wait for another to open,” Richard said, ending the discussion by retrieving the POGS from the back floorboard. He handed one to Sophia and strapped the other in place on his head.

“We climb,” he said, his voice muffled by the vinyl and rubber headgear.

The deadfall looked even more treacherous up close. A jumble of long dead palm trees resembling matchsticks swept from a table by an uncaring hand. Rocks were mixed in—some the size of delivery trucks—and unrecognizable masses of twisted metal. Richard spied one semi-intact structure that might have been the remains of a radio or electrical transmission tower.

He placed his foot on the root ball of a smaller palm at the base of the pile intending to step onto a man-sized rock from there. The cluster of roots disintegrated under his weight and his foot plunged through. He lost his balance and fell forwards, the weight of the pack on his back driving him headlong into the deadfall. More wood turned to dust as he crashed into it. There was a groaning, shifting sound from above.

Richard glanced up and saw several rocks, one the size of a small dog, tumbling toward him. His pack saved him from the worst of them but he realized his misstep was about to bring the entire deadfall crashing down upon him. He’d be buried alive.

There was pressure at his ankles and then he was heaved backwards, his shirt rucked up and stones scratched his belly. The faceplate of the POGS snagged on something and was jerked from his head, only the hose between it and the canister clipped to his waist preventing its loss.

Stale air rushed into Richard’s lungs. It tasted of ash and pumice.

The deadfall continued to cascade down around him with a tortured, rending sound. There were snaps and crashes, thuds, and long, tortured moans. An old Jeep previously entwined in a huge snarl of trees like a toy car in a child's fist shot out of a tangle of debris. It left most of its rusting front end on a large boulder it glanced off of and flipped end over end twice before crashing into the roof of the HumVee.

Sophia let go of Richard's ankles and grabbed the carrying strap at the top of his pack. She heaved him to his feet and yelled, "Run!"

They ran. The HumVee, its roof dented in and rust from the old Jeep still pattering down its sides didn't seem to offer much shelter so they made for the opposite bank of the riverbed. Once there Richard grasped for the dangling POGS mask, desperate to replace the dead smell of this world with that of stale, canned air.

"Christ, Richard," Sophia gasped into her own POGS, her hands on her thighs as her heart rate slowed, "that was stupid."

The mournful, almost human wailing sound of the deadfall settling gradually tapered off. With no breeze to clear it the fine debris of its collapse hung in the air casting a haze like that left by a recent forest fire over everything.

"Agreed," Richard said. "Stupid, but not without merit."

He pointed to the opposite side of the riverbed.

Sophia peered through the haze and saw a huge concavity where moments before there had been a twisted pile of wreckage. The avalanche had cleared the rotted wood and twisted metal leaving only the rocks, boulders, and large sections of concrete shot through with rebar behind. Richard's hasty attempt to climb the deadfall had created a virtual staircase of stone and dense rubble.

"It would seem God not only watches over drunks and small children," Richard said, "but Primes as well."

"Is it close enough to the Rip for us to get through?" Sophia asked.

"I think so," Richard said, squinting through the haze at the Rip above them.

"Then we better get going." She'd pulled the RLP from a pocket and examined it. "The aperture of the Rip has already started to close."

Despite fine layers of dust and fragments of wood chips and metal clinging to the stones the climb was easier than Richard expected. There was one uneasy moment when a section of concrete shifted beneath his feet threatening to topple him. His hold on a rock above saved him a nasty trip down the deadfall to the riverbed thirty feet below. Sophia, lighter and more agile, had elected to go first and was a good twelve feet above him when he shouted through his POGS:

"Stop there! On that ledge."

She waited patiently as he moved into position beside her.

"It's about four feet over," he said, pointing into what appeared to her to be empty space.

She looked down. There was nothing beneath the area he indicated but a fifty-foot drop into mangled wreckage.

"We'll have to jump for it," he said. "It's closing fast." He didn't tell her that the pulsating red and blue disc had shrunk to a mere two feet in diameter.

"If I miss…" Sophia began.

"You told me that a Rip of any size will carry an object through to the other side, right?"

"So long as enough of its mass crosses the event horizon, yes," Sophia said.

"Then I suggest you go now."

"Richard," she warned, "mass exits the Rips at the same velocity it enters."

He hadn't considered this.

"Tuck and roll, then," he said. "And hope this one exits over a California King with lots of pillows."

Without another word Sophia turned and leapt into space. Richard breathed a sigh of relief when she vanished, consumed by the multi-colored brilliance of the Rip.

"Here goes nothing," Richard said, inwardly praying that he wasn't leaping into a volcano on another version of Earth. Or worse. He took a deep breath, steeled himself, and jumped.

Peace.

Not the peace between two men who've long been at odds and recently settled their differences but *Peace*. Eternal contentment and satisfaction. This was beyond love and compassion, beyond human gratification. This was a warm, all encompassing sensation Richard had never felt before or even knew existed.

Once again he saw/felt/tasted the colors of the Rip, was wrapped in them as if he were part of them and they a part of him. They flowed into him and through him, guiding him. For the first time he felt a glimmer of something else, a stray and tangent thought that perhaps, in time, he could guide the Rips as well.

Then all too quickly he was out of the Rip, plunging downward. He curled as well as he could but the ground rose up and met his back with tremendous force, expelling the breath from his lungs with a *whoosh.*

He dragged the POGS from his face as if the oxygen it provided was what prevented his lungs from expanding. Tried to breathe but couldn't get anything in.

Diaphragm spasm, he thought. *Known as getting the wind knocked out of you. The paralysis is temporary so just relax.*

Within a minute the spasm subsided and he drew in a great gulping lungful of acrid but breathable air. When his breathing returned to normal he got to his knees and looked around.

There was little light and a lot of noise here. Thunderous explosions followed by concussions that threatened to knock him back to the ground. He looked frantically about for Sophia but saw only a dark wasteland briefly lit up by stroboscopic bursts of light from above. The earth was soaked with rain and gunfire erupted from seemingly everywhere around him. He made out long strands of razor-wire before him and large steel obstacles reminiscent of enormous jacks from a knucklebones game. The air was thick with the smell of cordite and spent explosives.

My God, he thought, *we've ripped into the middle of a war!*

He could hear voices shouting in the distance. The repeating pop of automatic weapons fire made it difficult to pin down direction, impossible to discern the language being spoken. A huge explosion went off to his left and the shouting turned to screams.

His confusion was mounting. As was his anxiety at not being able to locate Sophia.

Where the hell is this? He thought. *And when*?

He started to rise, thinking the razor wire in front of him might border a foxhole and that it would be a good idea to get to cover when something roared overhead. He looked up, tracking the sound through the smoke and haze of spent gunpowder. A P-51D Mustang shot through the sky followed closely by three others. Each spat .50 caliber death at the earth from six M2 Browning machine guns.

"Oh my Christ!" he heard himself yell.

There was a splash of wet footfalls behind him. As he turned to run he heard a perfectly clear though oddly accented voice yell:

"I got this one!"

Then a rifle butt slammed into the back of his head and he heard no more.

Richard came to in a seated position, his arms and legs bound to a chair. He had time to think of Michael Manus, bound in eternal agony to a chair on another world before a hood was pulled from his head. Light stabbed into his eyes. He squinted and shook his head to clear his vision. His vision only doubled, then trebled.

"I'd take it easy there, boy," a voice told him. His mind struggled to place the same sort of accent he'd heard before being butt-stroked. "You took a hell of a knock and may well be concussed."

His vision returned; a single, blurry line of sight. Richard looked around. He was in a room with concrete walls surrounded by men. One stood at his right shoulder. He had the look of a man who was awaiting an order to kill. Another was seated at a table before him. Sophia was bound to a chair beside him, watching. Blood welled from a cut above one eye but she looked otherwise unharmed. That eye would blacken beautifully. If they lived long enough.

"I see you didn't give up without a fight," Richard chuckled weakly.

She gave him a curt smile and nodded towards the man behind the table.

Richard's vision cleared fully and he took in the items on the table. Their packs, weapons, supplies. His mother's copper trinket box.

He took in the man seated at the table. He expected the black uniform but not the man himself. He was obviously in his sixties, thin of face and sporting a neatly trimmed beard that descended to his chest. Despite the soft, not unkind voice he'd addressed Richard with moments before his eyes had hardness in them. This man had both seen and dealt death. But the eyes were not cruel as was often the case with seasoned killers. The man was no thug or murderer. Whatever his cause he felt it was just.

Whoever he was, he *wasn't*, as Richard had feared, Jefferson. And he did not appear to be one of his men. The uniform was black but looked to be cotton and not a synthetic material like rayon or polyester. It was cut simply as if stitched by hand. Not at all like the fitted attire Jefferson and his men had worn when last they had met. The insignia on the man's arm and chest bore a stylized devil's head over crossed swords which was not, to Richard's limited knowledge, of BanaTech design.

Relieved that they were not at the mercy of BanaTech forces though fully aware they were still in danger, Richard's curiosity was piqued.

"And who might you be?" He asked the man.

"You shut your damn mouth, Westie," a voice from the left said.

"No!" Sophia protested as the man delivered an open handed but powerful blow to Richard's head.

There was a blast of pain and the room went blurry again. "We'll ask the goldarn questions here!"

Though his ears were ringing Richard placed the accent. North American. The rural southeast. Tennessee or West Virginia, maybe.

"That will be enough, Johnse," the man behind the table said mildly. "I can answer his question and then maybe he'll answer one of mine."

"I am Brigadier General William Anderson Hatfield, sir," the man said to Richard, "serving under the President of these here Eastern United States. Now who might you be and what are you doing on the West Virginia side of the Tug?

Chapter 16

Richard's mind raced. The bearded man's revelation sent fact, fiction, and what he knew to be history reeling around in his mind like bumper cars in a dodgem game.

William Anderson Hatfield, aka "Devil Anse'" Hatfield, sat behind a large table not twenty feet in front of Richard. One side of a feudal coin that bore Randolph "Ol Ran'l" McCoy's face on the other. The imposing figure was dressed in a military uniform he had never worn on Richard's Earth, holding a rank he had never held, fighting a war that had never been fought—*had he said Eastern United States?*—with weapons that would not have existed on Richard's Earth for another fifty years.

The bunker suddenly shook under the impact of aerial bombardment reminding Richard of the four P-51D Mustangs he'd seen tearing through the sky. Dust sifted down from massive concrete blocks overhead. All eyes in the room looked up, waiting perhaps, for those enormous stones to buckle, fall, and crush them all.

The Hatfield-McCoy feud had started on Richard's Earth in 1878 over the supposed theft of a McCoy hog by Floyd Hatfield. The matter had been taken to the courts but the local Justice of the Peace, Anderson "Preacher Anse'" Hatfield, had ruled in the Hatfield's favor based on the testimony of Bill Stanton, a relative of both families.

Bill Stanton was later killed by two McCoy brothers.

Though Stanton's murder was the first recorded incident of violence between the two families the feud likely had its origins in the murder of Randolph's brother, Asa Harmon McCoy.

The Hatfield's hailed from West Virginia, near the Tug Fork of the Big Sandy River straddling the West Virginia-Kentucky border, while Randolph and the McCoy clan had moved across the border into Kentucky years earlier. Both clans supported the Confederacy during the Civil War but Asa McCoy had chosen to fight for the Union. Jim Vance, the uncle of Devil Anse' Hatfield had taken exception to this betrayal and was widely believed to have murdered Asa in 1865.

The feud escalated after Anse's eldest son Johnse began a relationship with Ran'l McCoy's eldest daughter, Roseanna. When

Roseanna left her family to live with Johnse and the Hatfield's in West Virginia both families had rejected any notion of marriage. Roseanna, pregnant by that time, returned home to Kentucky. Disowned by her father and abandoned by Johnse Roseanna grew ill and lost the child. It's believed she committed suicide after Johnse married her cousin, Nancy McCoy, in 1881.

During the Pike County, Kentucky Election Day celebration in 1882 a fight broke out between the two families. Ellison Hatfield, brother of Anse', was killed by three of Roseanna McCoy's young brothers: Tolbert, Pharmer, and Bud. Ellison was stabbed repeatedly and shot. The trio was immediately arrested but Hatfield and a large posse took the McCoy brothers by force from constables before they could reach safe haven. Devil Anse' tied Roseanna's brothers to pawpaw bushes and each was shot numerous times.

The feud reached its peak in 1888 during the New Year's Night Massacre. Several members of the Hatfield clan surrounded the McCoy cabin and opened fire on the sleeping family. The cabin was then torched in an effort to drive Randolph McCoy into the open. He made a break for it and escaped but two of his children were shot. His wife was beaten and left for dead.

Later that year a posse arrested Wall Hatfield and eight others. They were taken to Kentucky where they were tried and found guilty of the murder of Randolph McCoy's young daughter Alifair, shot and killed during the New Year's Massacre. Seven received life in prison. The eighth, Ellison "Cottontop" Mounts, was executed by hanging.

By 1891 the feud had made headlines across the country. Another dozen deaths had occurred between the two families since the New Year's Night Massacre prompting the Governor of West Virginia, Jacob Beeson Jackson, to threaten sending his militia into Kentucky to end the violence. To prevent what would most certainly have resulted in a second civil war Samuel Bolivar Buckner, the Governor of Kentucky, sent his Adjutant General Samuel Ewing Hill to West Virginia to investigate the Hatfield-McCoy hostilities. His investigation resulted in another eleven deaths with nearly the same number of wounded.

Arrests and trials related to the massacre continued until 1901. A truce was not officially declared between the two families until 2003.

What happened on this Earth? Richard wondered. Had Samuel Hill's investigation into the Hatfield-McCoy feud sparked a larger conflict? Had Governor Jackson made good on his threat and sent his militia into Kentucky? Was that the spark that lit the tinder? And how was this war being fought with military technology that wouldn't exist on Richard's earth until well into the next century?

Something Sophia had said to him days earlier came to mind: *"Imagine where your science and technology would be if a little event called the Dark Ages had not occurred or had been significantly shortened. A society that doesn't have a gap that large in its technological learning curve would be far more advanced than yours is now, don't you think?"*

The aircraft and fortifications he'd seen on the battlefield were from his World War II era. On his Earth that war ended with the dropping of two nuclear bombs. Richard cringed at the thought.

"We're travelers," Sophia spoke up when the dust settled and the sound of detonations overhead faded. "From abroad."

"Dear lady," Hatfield said, a note of warning in his voice, "I was addressing the gentleman. Please be quiet."

"We're travelers," Richard repeated, following Sophia's cue. "The lady is Sophia Bledell. I'm Richard Farris. We're travelers, nothing more."

"Well armed travelers," Hatfield said with a grin, gesturing towards the cache of weapons laid out on the table. The two men behind Sophia and Richard laughed. "What do simple travelers need with such an arsenal?"

Richard opened his mouth to say that only a fool would travel abroad in war time without weapons but Sophia interrupted him: "Those are not our weapons. We picked them up along the way."

"Aren't you the impertinent one?" Hatfield cast his gaze on Sophia. "Dressed as a man and not as a woman, your tongue running as if it's hinged in the middle and wagging on both ends." He picked up the RLP and turned it over in his hands, his eyes narrowing at Sophia. "These weapons match your attire. You're either a liar or a thief. I hold no truck with either. I'll ask you once more to shut your mouth, young lady. Open it again and I'll have you gagged and removed."

Sophia shot Hatfield a baleful glare but said no more. Unmoved by the hate in her eyes Anse' returned his attention to Richard.

"You were about to say, Mr. Farris?" He prompted.

"The weapons are ours," Richard admitted, sensing the futility of denying the obvious. "They're for our protection."

"Protection from whom?" The man Hatfield had called Johnse spoke up as he crossed the room to stand at his father's side. His voice conveyed disbelief.

"We are fugitives of a sort. Falsely accused," Richard said, choosing his words carefully. "The weapons are to protect us from our pursuers."

"Ah." Hatfield said simply.

He toyed with the RLP but had not managed to trigger its screen or discover the slider. Richard wondered what would happen if the device suddenly activated, warning of an impending Rip opening or the presence of BanaTech forces.

"How did you manage to cross over a quarter mile of fortifications and end up in the middle of the largest battlefield in Logan County unseen and without injury?" Hatfield asked.

"We crawled," Richard said. Nothing else came to mind.

"They do look like they been crawlin' through shit, sir," the man behind Sophia said. He slapped a none-too-gentle hand on her shoulder releasing a plume of dust and dirt from a rockslide on another world. She winced as he leaned in and sniffed her hair. "Smell like it, too."

He and the man behind Richard laughed at this. Even Johnse cracked a smile. Hatfield's expression remained set in stone.

"What is this?" he asked, still examining the RLP. "An explosive of some sort?"

The room fell silent. The men in the room stepped back from Richard and Sophia. Johnse, Richard noted, did not leave the elder Hatfield's side.

"It seems a bit small," Hatfield continued, "but it could contain enough explosive to kill anything within in, say, six feet."

"It's not a bomb," Richard said.

The room had gone quiet. Even the aerial bombardment had stopped for the moment. *The quiet before the storm,* Richard thought. He'd seen situations like this in prison. Two groups of men would talk at first. Then argue. Then all would grow still. That stillness, that *silence,* was dangerous. It was the silence of fear and paranoia. It usually ended when the killing started.

"It's a communication device," Richard said. "It operates much like your two-way radios..."

"Richard, no!" Sophia cried. "Don't tell them anything!"

Hatfield was on his feet and around the table much faster than Richard would have thought possible for a man of his apparent age. He slammed the RLP down on the tabletop and descended on Sophia like a man possessed.

"No!" Sophia cried, this time in fear as Hatfield pulled something from his pocket and pushed it towards her face. She jerked her head away but he grasped the back of her neck, wadded the handkerchief he'd pulled from his trouser pocket, and forced it into her mouth.

"Tie it!" He barked at the man behind Sophia. The soldier obeyed with obvious relish, pulling the length of cord he'd pulled from his own pocket so tight it cut into her cheeks.

"Damn women." Hatfield grunted and returned to his seat. "The Devil split their tails and tongues with the same stroke." To the men behind Richard he said: "Take her to a holding cell. Johnse"—he turned to his second—"go with them. See that no harm befalls her."

"You want I should leave you alone?" Johnse asked. "With him?"

"Do as I say," Hatfield said. "I'll be fine. Mr. Farris and I are going to continue our conversation."

"Yes sir." Johnse fired off a smart salute.

Sophia was cut from the chair, her arms re-tied behind her. Richard caught a brief look from her—one meant only for him—just before she was escorted from the room. It was a look of intent, of cold calculation. The look said she'd *wanted* to be removed. Had she played on Hatfield's misogyny to achieve that end? He'd seen a similar look on her face once before, back in Missouri. Just before everything erupted in gunfire and bloodshed.

"Don't be concerned for the welfare of your companion," Hatfield said, misinterpreting the alarm on Richard's face as the door to the bunker clanged shut behind him. "I do not condone the mistreatment of prisoners under my command no matter their gender. Ms. Bledell will come to no harm. Johnse is a good boy. He will see that she is not abused."

Hatfield stood and turned away from the table. His shoulders, square and strong before, now slumped with age and exhaustion He stared at the blank wall behind the table as if looking through a picture window onto the vast landscape of his own mind. Richard wondered if he liked what he saw there. The confident Brigadier General who'd so aggressively had a woman bound, gagged, and removed from his presence only moments before was gone. In his place was a tired old man who now spoke to Richard as if speaking to an old acquaintance.

"Are you a religious man, Mr. Farris?" Hatfield's voice was bereft of the strong authority it had held since the hood had been removed from Richard's head.

The change of subject, like the change in demeanor, so threw Richard that he was uncertain how to respond.

"Come now." Hatfield turned back to the table and eased himself back into the chair. Arthritis, Richard thought, excruciatingly painful in an era with no advanced medicine. Likely hidden from those under his command. "I realize the question impolitic. Impolite, even. But please indulge me. I have found that one can best judge a man based on his relationship with God."

"I suppose I am," Richard answered, recalling that on his Earth Anse' Hatfield had been a devoutly religious man and had, on more than one occasion, accused the McCoy clan of being godless heathens. "To a degree."

"To a degree?" Hatfield repeated.

Richard chose his words carefully. He was treading on dangerous ground here. If Hatfield *were* basing his decision on whether or not to release them on Richard's answer to the seemingly irrelevant question, if he were indeed judging him based on his religious views, then Richard's response carried the weight of both his and Sophia's lives.

He was being *interrogated*, he realized. No more and no less. He wasn't being waterboarded—*not yet anyway*, he thought with a chill—but he couldn't help feeling that Hatfield was after more here than Richard's views on God.

Stall, he told himself. *Play his little game and give Sophia time to work out whatever plans she has. But do* not *let this man know what we're doing here.*

Believing that the older man would recognize a lie immediately he decided to be honest. "Where I come from," he said, "there are many forms of religion. With many followers, each subscribing to his own belief system in his own way without a lot of interference from others."

"There are Christians, here," Hatfield said. "Baptists, Presbyterians; the list goes on. As well as Catholics, Jews, and, I believe, even a new group who refer to themselves as Jehovah's Witnesses."

"It's much more diverse in my…country," Richard said. He'd almost used the word *time*. As weary as Hatfield now seemed Richard was not fooled. Historically Anse' Hatfield had been a shrewd and cunning man who would not have missed the slip. "There are dozens, perhaps even hundreds of recognized religious groups all claiming to be the one true religion of God."

"Sounds confusing." Hatfield brushed dust from his lapel in a lazy gesture. Smoothed his beard. "To which of these groups do you subscribe?"

"None of them," Richard said.

The old man scowled. "You're an atheist, then?"

"Not at all," Richard said. "I believe in God. I spent over a decade studying the subject. There is too much proof of His existence for any rational man to deny Him. It's organized religion I have problems with."

Hatfield's eyebrows shot up at that, his lazy expression replaced by one of keen interest. "Please explain."

Richard thought for a moment, deciding how best to put into words feelings he hadn't spoken of for the majority of his life. Despite being raised Methodist and taught never to question the Word of God or His methods he had always had questions. Why had God created the Earth and populated it with human beings? Was He lonely? Bored? And why allow the existence of evil? Why tolerate something that would, bit by bit and piece by piece, destroy that which He had so lovingly created? Were the firmaments of Heaven so familiar and dull to Him that He required a bit of sport for distraction?

He'd sought the answers while incarcerated, absorbing everything he could on the subject of God and religion. His research had led to no solid answers but he'd drawn one simple conclusion: "We, as human beings," he said, "are missing a big piece of the puzzle."

"I'm not sure I understand," Hatfield said.

"The major religions—not the little cults that pop up from day to day assuring our imminent destruction based on the dream or nightmare of some nut job or another—all agree that there is a God and that He is good. They also agree that there is an evil force, commonly called Satan, and that he is bad. Satan is to be avoided, God is to be obeyed, and this is how we should do it. That's where the trouble starts. The how we should do it part.

"We base that part of the equation on various versions of the Bible, commonly the King James version. Problem is, the New Testament of the King James Version was finished in 1611, a full millennium and a half after the death of Christ. That was the *third* English translation of the original Greek text, translated by *forty-seven* different scholars who were directed to ensure that the text conformed to the ecclesiology of the Christian church *as it was understood at that time*. The Old Testament had already been translated from ancient Hebrew texts, some dating as far back as the year 1500 BC, and there is an entire set of texts called the Apocrypha that were considered too profound or sacred for the masses that were left out of most versions of the Bible altogether.

"Therefore, the modern Bible is a text conceived of and written by human beings based on other texts handed down throughout the ages that have been re-interpreted and re-translated countless times by other human beings."

"Which means…?" Hatfield prompted.

"The texts that our religions are based on have been changed by *thousands* of hands over thousands of years, by human beings who, by their very nature, can't help but introduce their own personal interpretation of how the texts fit our needs into their work."

"Meaning," Hatfield said, "that while having the same essential structure as the original Word of God, whichever version of the Bible you're basing your beliefs on has been changed so much as to have little significance."

"I wouldn't say the texts are insignificant," Richard said. "I would say that much has been lost or is missing, dismissed as being of spurious origin or considered apocryphal in nature. Whatever the reason, the answer to the riddle of God, his reason for creating us and his plans for humanity, have been lost to us."

"You do not believe in faith, then?" Hatfield asked. "That God has intentionally left out the answers as a test of our devotion?"

Richard found himself admiring a man who would undoubtedly order both Sophia and himself imprisoned or executed. Despite his advanced age and physical infirmity his mind was sharp, his intellect keen. On another Earth, under different circumstances, Richard felt the two could have had a rewarding friendship.

"I believe in faith," Richard answered. "Faith in the Father and in His love for his creations. Faith in His promise that we will ultimately sit by his side in glory. But I don't believe He set down his Word to cause confusion among us, to spawn religious group after religious group with different ideations, philosophies, and values. Those who steadfastly believe that theirs is the only true interpretation of His Word and will commit acts of violence to prove it. Those who will happily break His firmest commandment—thou shalt not kill—over and over again in His name.

"No," Richard continued after considering the events of the past few days, "I don't believe this conundrum is a matter of faith. Nor do I believe it to be of God's design. I believe some vital piece of information has been left out, intentionally or by chance. And without it, we are all lost."

There was a knock at the heavy iron door and it opened with a groan. Johnse stepped through closing the portal behind him with a resounding *clang*.

"The device has arrived, sir," he said, firing off a smart salute.

"Enough of that, Johnse." Hatfield rose from behind the table. "Mr. Farris here knows we are kin." To Richard, he said, "You are a fascinating man, Mr. Farris, if a bit of a fanatic. I'd like nothing more than to discuss your delusions further but I have to see to the arming of the nuclear device your friends at BanaTech delivered to me just now."

The look of shock on Richard's face must have been as clear as a neon sign at night. He lurched forward in his chair, straining against his bonds. He'd been had. Hatfield not only knew about BanaTech and Jefferson but knew about the Rips and the Multi-verse as well. His ignorance of the RLP and its function, their dialogue, the unexpected questions, the tired disposition and the old man's apparent frailty—it had all been a ruse. Subterfuge. Both to stall for time, as Richard had thought *he* was doing, and to get him to open up on some level, any level, so that Hatfield could get a sense of why they were being pursued by BanaTech.

Richard felt as if one of the aerial bombs earlier had loosened a block of concrete and it had just now dropped on his head.

"You son of a bitch!" he cried.

"Ah, now he understands." Hatfield smiled. "And you thought our conversation was simply the result of a tired old man's curiosity. No, Mr. Farris. I know exactly who you and your friend are and from whence you came. I simply wanted to know why Alex Jefferson is so interested in what he claims are mere rogue operatives. So interested, in fact, that bulletins demanding your arrest have been sent to every known Earth in the Multi-verse. What is it, Mr. Farris, that makes you so dangerous to them?"

Richard shot him a look of such hatred, such *venom,* that Johnse took a protective step towards his father. Hatfield, awaiting an answer, appeared unmoved by the display of hostility.

"They're afraid that I can destroy them all," Richard snarled.

"Really," Hatfield replied, drawing the word out. "One man with the power to bring down BanaTech and all its forces? As dangerous as I think you and your little friend may be, I hardly think you're capable of that."

"My first thought when you turned up so nicely on my doorstep was to hand you over as ordered. After all, we're supposed to be friends here BanaTech and I. Our arrangement to stamp out the McCoy's once and for all and regain control of the West is my first priority. It also crossed my mind to simply let you walk away. Rip through to the next Earth or wherever it is you're going and get on with your business. Your affairs are not mine and if you are a thorn in BanaTech's heel what is that to me? But a man should never bargain from a bad position."

Hatfield motioned to Johnse who promptly cut the ropes binding Richard to the chair. Even if he'd wanted to fight—and he found that in that moment he did—he would not have been capable. His hands and feet had lost all circulation, making even the simple act of standing difficult.

"When this is all over and Pikeville is reduced to ashy ruins your friends at BanaTech will undoubtedly seek to gain control of the restored United States," Hatfield continued. "That means that my men and I will have to be disposed of. I had thought to fight them but our weapons are no match for theirs and after three long years of war we are tired.

"You and Ms. Bledell offer a unique opportunity." Hatfield watched as Johnse bound Richard's hands behind his back. "While I'm still unclear as to why you pose such a threat to Jefferson he may be willing to offer safe passage off this war torn planet to the person that can deliver you to him."

Richard stumbled across the bunker, his feet unresponsive and awash with the fire of blood returning to sleeping nerve endings. Still angered by how easily he'd been manipulated and deceived one thought resonated through his mind as the bunker door clanged shut behind him and he was led down a long hall with minimal lighting.

Devil Anse' Hatfield and Alex Jefferson may well have many surprises in store for each other.

Chapter 17

An old trick from the early nineteenth century might work here, Richard thought as Johnse Hatfield bound his arms behind his back with a length of thick hemp. Forged steel handcuffs were not widely used in the early twentieth century. And forget zip-ties; those plastics had yet to be invented.

As Johnse looped rope around Richard's wrists making two tight figure eights and tying a knot in the center, Richard tightened the muscles in his forearms while pushing outwards. In his haste to do his father's bidding and set about destroying their enemies Johnse didn't notice. The move gave Richard enough slack to rotate his wrists and move his fingers freely.

Johnse handed Richard off to a subordinate—the same man who had nearly concussed him with a blow to the back of the head earlier. Blood flow returned to Richards's fingers, the nerves rejoicing by sending wave after wave of painful impulses tingling up his forearms. His hands felt as if hungry ants were devouring them. His feet felt little better.

"Put him in with the woman," Johnse told the man. "And Thomas," he warned as the man grabbed Richard's arm in an iron grip, his fingertips digging into the bicep like the teeth of a bear trap, "No rough stuff. The General wants both of them alive."

"'Course, Major," Thomas responded dully, digging his fingers even deeper into Richard's muscle. When Johnse turned and walked away Thomas yanked Richard forward so roughly he nearly lost his footing.

Richard feigned more pain and weakness than he actually felt and let himself be dragged along the hall. Behind his back he flexed his fingers to hasten the reawakening of nerve endings. Once his hands felt more like his own and less like gloves half filled with sand he ran his thumbs over the knot in his bindings searching for a weakness. He was bound with a common whipping knot. A bight, or loop, had been laid under the center mass of the cinch and the end of the rope pulled through it. If he could work his thumb under the whipping and find the bight he could work the end loose enough to free himself.

Thomas yanked him hard to the left and down a side hallway. The cinderblock walls were cracked, intermittent piles of dirt and debris shaken loose by repeated bombardment littered the floor. At the end of the hall Thomas pushed him into a room fifteen feet to a side with a desk facing a barred cell at the far end. Sophia sat on one of two bunks inside the cell, her hair hanging in her face. She looked up as they entered. The gag had been removed from her mouth but Richard saw a fresh set of bruises on the left side of her jaw.

Richard cast his captor a look of pure malice.

"She's feisty, that one," Thomas said cheerily before shoving Richard face first into the bars. He retrieved a set of keys from the desk. "Stomped Tater's foot real good and tried to run off. Me an' Johnse had to chase her a bit but I caught up to her and convinced her to settle down."

Thomas unlocked the cell and shoved Richard inside, slamming the gate before Richard could cause him any trouble.

"I reckon she'll settle down a might more when Tater gets back from the infirmary. Smashed his toes all to hell and broke one or two of 'em for certain. He's gonna want to repay that favor."

Richard said nothing to the grinning man. Only stared at him through the bars as he pocketed the keys and headed back to the hall.

"Y'all sleep tight, now," he said, and with that he was gone.

Richard worked his thumb under the bight in his bindings and loosened it from the cinch, creating enough slack to work his wrists free. He let the rope drop to the floor, turned to Sophia and crouched. He gently took her face in his hands.

"Was it worth it?" he asked softly.

She gave him a lopsided grin and pulled her hands from behind her back. She'd slipped her bonds as easily as he had. In one hand she held a set of keys similar to the ones their jailer had just pocketed.

"Tater's in quite a bit of pain." She spoke slowly. The left side of her face was swollen. It would be a lovely shade of purple by morning. "I don't think he's going to miss these for a while."

"You *are* a feisty one, aren't you?" Richard laughed softly.

"If we can get back to our weapons," Sophia said, "they just might find out how feisty I can be."

Free of the cell, Richard cautiously poked his head out into the hallway and looked down the corridor. No footfalls hurried towards him, no voices rang out in alarm. The hallway was deserted. He nodded to Sophia and stepped out. She followed closely behind.

"So what did the General want to talk about?" She asked in a low voice.

"Religion, of all things," Richard said. Their feet rasped noisily on the gritty floor as they approached a junction in the hall.

"Why religion?" Sophia asked.

"It was a feint to see if I'd slip up and reveal who we are," Richard told her. "To get a sense of what we're about. Hatfield *knows* about the Rips and the Multi-verse. He's working with Jefferson. BanaTech is here and has been for a long time. They want control of this world and they're using the Hatfield-McCoy feud to get it."

Richard took a look out into the adjoining corridor. Seeing no one he started forward. Sophia pulled him back.

"This is bad, Richard," she hissed. "*Very* bad. If Hatfield is in BanaTech's pocket he'll hand us over to Jefferson or have us executed."

"No he won't," Richard said. "He wants to use us as a bargaining chip to get off this Earth. But we have bigger problems. Hatfield is going to nuke Pikesville."

"*What?* Where the hell did they get nuclear weapons?"

"*Shhh,*" Richard admonished, taking Sophia by the shoulders. "Either BanaTech gave them nuclear technology or stole it from another country on this Earth for them. It doesn't matter. Hatfield has a device and he and his son are on their way to arm it. We need to grab our gear and put a stop to this before they kill thousands."

Richard took another look into the junction, still saw no one, and stepped around the corner. Sophia followed but only to halt him again.

"Richard. Wait. You don't understand. Jefferson is a master manipulator. He's taken dozens of worlds without firing a single shot or losing a single operative because he knows how to play both ends against the middle and come out on top every time. If he's given

Hatfield a nuclear device to destroy Pikesville then you can bet he gave McCoy one to destroy Logan county. That way BanaTech and whoever they have in Washington, D.C.—and you can be certain they have someone—are the only ones left standing when the dust settles."

"Jesus Christ," Richard muttered. "He'll kill tens of thousands. *Hundreds* of thousands, maybe."

"As long as he wins whatever is left of this Earth in the end," Sophia said solemnly, "he won't care."

"I thought maybe we could stop one device," Richard said, "but two?"

"We can't worry about *either* device, Richard. I know you want to save these people—I do, too—but we have to think about the bigger picture. If we don't find the Key and stop BanaTech from opening a permanent focal point the entire Multi-verse could be lost. Not just these two cities on this one Earth but *every* city on *every* Earth could be thrown into chaos."

Richard sighed. People were going to die here. He knew it and was powerless to stop it. It pained him to turn his back on this Earth and allow Jefferson's plans to play out unopposed. He knew in his heart, however, that Sophia was right. There was much more at stake here than two little cities on one little Earth.

With a sigh of regret Richard dismissed the notion of interfering with BanaTech's designs for this world and turned his attention towards getting the two of them out of here before the bombs went off.

The hallways were empty. He expected at least a sentry or roving guard but there was no one. He and Sophia made the interrogation room where they'd first been held without incident.

"Where'd they all go?" Sophia wondered.

"I don't know." Richard opened the heavy steel door slowly. Rusty hinges wailed in protest. He and Sophia froze, expecting to hear someone charging their position. No one came. They stepped inside the room and left the door hanging ajar.

"Maybe Devil Anse' is out there rallying his troops with a rousing speech like Mel Gibson in *Braveheart*."

"Like who?" Sophia asked.

"Never mind."

Their gear was still laid out on the table. They each began grabbing up supplies and stowing it in their REAPERS. Richard elected to keep a PX4 Storm and H&K MP7 at the ready while Sophia returned the Gerber Mark II to its wrist sheath and reholstered the Springfield XD(M) compact at her ankle. She kept the Beretta 92FS within easy reach. Extra ammo went into various pockets of their BDU's.

Richard checked a side pocket of his LRRP—his mother's trinket box was still there—while Sophia opened the slider on the RLP and entered her password.

"Is it still working?" Richard asked, remembering the way Hatfield had slammed it down onto the table in his rage at Sophia.

"It's fine," she said. "These things are built to take a beating. Short of intentionally destroying it with a hammer or a rock there's little that can damage them."

As Richard watched she worked the keypad of the device. Screens changed, maximized, minimized again, and flashed by faster than Richard could follow.

"Lexington," Sophia muttered as she scanned the results of her search. "No, too far. Lima, Ohio. *Way* too far. Wait. Here. Charleston. There's a Rip opening there now. We have four hours. We can make that."

"Charleston?" Richard asked. "South Carolina? We can't make that in four hours. Not without one of those Mustangs I saw flying around out there."

"Charleston, West Virginia," Sophia corrected. "It's about thirth-five miles from here."

"We'll have to find the motor pool." Richard said. "Steal a Jeep."

"There's no need to steal," Hatfield interrupted from the doorway. He had a Colt .45 leveled at Richard's head. Johnse, the man named Thomas, and three others that Richard could see were crowded outside the door of the interrogation room, all armed to the teeth. "We'll go in mine."

The convoy of Jeeps and troop transports numbering in the dozens headed northeast towards Charleston at a brisk pace. Richard and Sophia—again stripped of their REAPERs, firearms, and the RLP before being led unbound to a troop transport—rode out the pocked and pitted roads in the back of a covered two and a half ton GMC Jimmy.

"I have no quarrel with you," Hatfield had told them before they clambered into the back of the vehicle. "I rather like the idea of you running around mucking about in Jefferson's affairs."

Richard thought what he really liked was the distraction their continued existence would provide from what Hatfield and his men were doing but he remained silent.

"Jefferson is pure evil," Hatfield said. "He gave McCoy the same weapon he gave us. Our spotters saw 'em loading it up just as we were loading ours. We're evacuating everyone who would leave."

Sophia shot Richard an *I told you so* look as Hatfield continued:

"I've been manipulated and lied to and do not cotton to such. Your choice is simple. You come along, play nice, and when we get to Charleston I'll return your gear and weapons and you're free to go. Or"—he smiled a crocodile's smile—"you can cause me and mine trouble and I'll leave you by the side of the road to die in what's coming."

"Fair enough," Richard replied.

As the truck pulled away from the base he'd seen a chilling sight through the open back of the vehicle—an airstrip lie within sight of the convoy. Sitting on it was a B-29 Superfortress, her four powerful Wright R-3350 Duplex Cyclone engines spooling up to operating temperatures. The nose of the aircraft bore the name ENOLA GAY. He briefly wondered if a similar aircraft bearing the name BOCKSCAR was spooling up on an airstrip to the west.

Richard had been lost in thought since spotting the B-29 and the deadly cargo he knew it carried. The collision of time and events here on this Earth, the sheer anachronistic mayhem evident in Hatfield's existence in a time when aircraft and nuclear technology should have been half a century in the planet's future drove home a simple point:

If the Focal Point Generator goes online and the Rips all open simultaneously technology and history will collide with unimaginable results throughout the Multi-verse. The natural order will be thrown into chaos. Nothing and no one will survive.

Again: *Why am I here? What is my role in all this?*

The truck hit a large pothole that sent them and the lone guard Hatfield had placed in the back of the truck scrambling for leather straps that hung in intervals above their heads.

The soldier, a youth of about seventeen, had looked pale and panic stricken since they'd climbed into the Jimmy. He constantly cast his gaze out of the rear of the vehicle in the direction of Logan County, sheer terror evident on his features.

"Relax, kid," Richard told him. "If any of this holds to history that bomb detonates a fraction of its fissionable material and will only affect a five mile radius. We're well beyond that."

The soldier looked at him as if he were speaking a foreign language.

"Just don't look at it when it goes off," Richard cautioned. "You'll go blind."

The boy's eyes widened further until Richard feared they would fall from their sockets. Then the youth pinched his eyes shut and bowed his head, muttering a prayer under his breath.

Far to the south, two planes separated by a mere thirty-nine miles dropped twin packages of death on the unsuspecting populace below. Pikesville went up first; more than a square mile of that fair city ceased to exist nanoseconds before nuclear fire swept out engulfing another four square miles in the blink of an eye. Logan County felt Asa McCoy's wrath within seconds of Pikesville's destruction. Those outside the blast areas later reported that it sounded as if God himself, grown weary of the Hatfield's and McCoy's and their petty feud, had stomped twice upon the earth in rapid succession, ending the conflict forever.

Nineteen miles northeast of Logan County, Devil Anse' Hatfield's convoy motored on. Those who could see the twin pillars of destruction rising from what had once been their beloved land were struck dumb by the sight. Those who could not scrambled for position so that they could. A few moments later a warm rush of air buffeted the column.

Richard, his heart heavy with grief for the thousands of lives that had winked out in an instant, did not look.

Chapter 18

Sophia moved closer to Richard on the bench and laid her head on his shoulder. Consolation? Commiseration? He didn't know but appreciated the gesture.

The boy soldier had somehow managed to fall asleep. *Battle fatigue*, Richard thought. *And maybe, just maybe, relief.*

They sat like that, silently, as the truck bounced over roads that had seen their share of wear and tear from a war that was now, in one final act, over.

After a few miles, Richard spoke up: "Jehovah's Witnesses."

"What?" Sophia straightened up on the bench but did not move from his side.

"Hatfield mentioned a new religion that had sprung up recently. The Jehovah's Witnesses," Richard explained. "We were discussing religion and faith. Or rather, I was; and what I think are holes in Christian doctrine. Things left out. Things misinterpreted or missed. But that's not what I'm thinking. Jehovah's Witnesses on my Earth have been around for decades and believe that a literal number of their ranks are marked to ascend to heaven. No more, no less. The rest of their number will live eternally in a paradise on earth. That number is one-hundred and forty-four thousand."

Sophia pondered this a moment. "So you think you and the other Primes may be linked to these Jehovah's Witnesses?"

"No," Richard answered. "Hatfield's reference to them just helped me remember something I didn't before. The number one-hundred and forty-four thousand is mentioned several times throughout the Bible but more specifically in the book of Revelation. In chapter seven the apostle John speaks of the Sealed of Heaven. In verse two he speaks of an angel ascending from the East with the seal of the living God. This angel commands another four angels, each standing at one of the four corners of the earth and holding back the wind, not to harm the earth or sea until the servants of God have been sealed. He gives the exact number; one-hundred and forty-four thousand, and further breaks that number down into twelve thousand from each of the twelve tribes of the children of Israel.

"The book of Revelation is steeped in vivid imagery and symbolism and according to modern doctrine the list is highly stylized. As is the number itself."

"What do you mean by stylized?" Sophia asked.

"The number twelve represented completeness to the Israelites. By squaring it and multiplying it by a thousand it represents, symbolically, a more vast number. Just as Jesus Christ told Peter to forgive his brother seven times seventy times in Matthew 18:21-22. He wasn't telling Peter to forgive his brother four-hundred and ninety times and then punch him in the face. He used a symbolic number to tell Peter to *always* forgive his brother no matter how many times he offended him."

"All right," Sophia said as the truck bounced through a particularly bad stretch of road. "I understand."

"John then goes on," Richard continued, "in verse nine I believe, to describe a great multitude which no one could number, of all nations, tribes, peoples, and tongues, who are standing before the throne and before the Lamb. Those who, according to verse fourteen, have come out of the great tribulation and washed their robes and made them white in the blood of the Lamb. In other words, this multitude, *and not the one-hundred and forty-four thousand*, are the redeemed who will ascend to Heaven."

"So who are the one-hundred and forty-four thousand?" Sophia asked.

"That's where the waters become murky," Richard said. "There's no further mention of them or their role in the apocalypse until chapter fourteen where John speaks of the Lamb standing on Mount Sion with the one-hundred and forty-four thousand. All bear His Father's seal on their foreheads and are singing a song that none could learn. They are described as being without guile. Virgins redeemed from among men and without fault before the Throne of God. According to verse four they follow the Lamb wherever he goes."

"*Virgins?*" Sophia said.

"Obviously more imagery, "Richard said. "The word virgin represents a moral purity of spirit, if not of body."

"And what is their role?" Sophia said. "Christ's personal vanguard?"

Richard shot her a sour look. "Again, the text is unclear. It is commonly believed that after the Rapture, once God's church is in Heaven and the rest of the redeemed are under His protection, they are to be His voice in a world marked by rampant sin and darkened by the reign of the Antichrist. They are *sealed.* This means they have the special protection of God from all of the divine judgments as well as the Antichrist. The seal is supposed to defend them during the tribulation as God pours out His wrath against those who would stand in rebellion against Him, allowing them to faithfully proclaim the gospel of Christ in the face of persecution inflicted on them by God's enemies."

"And you think this is the role of the Primes throughout the Multi-verse?" Sophia asked. "Ministers of God during the apocalypse?"

"I don't know," Richard admitted. He brushed his hand across his head and sighed. "The number may just be a coincidence, though it's a rather specific one I think. I've believed for a very long time that the Bible is only a glimpse of what we call God and his methods. A quick-start guide and not the complete manual. In the face of what I now know about the Rips, the Source, and the Multi-verse, it's hard to grasp that everything we're supposed to have faith in and live by is in there.

"Besides," he added, "you said that BanaTech has been trying to work out the meaning of a constant number of Primes for centuries, all to no avail. It's hard to believe I could have figured it out in a matter of days."

"Don't sell yourself short," Sophia said as the Jimmy hit another pot hole—this one the size of a six-pack cooler—that threatened to throw the both of them and the now startled awake soldier to the floor of the truck. The youth grumbled a bit, reset himself on the bench, and went back to sleep. "You Primes are known for leaps of intuition that rival that of the Quantum Crays. It's one of the reasons Jefferson has enlisted so many of you in his cause."

"Then I'll have to hope I'm wrong," Richard said, "because there is no mention whatsoever in any Biblical text I'm familiar with of what the one-hundred and forty-four thousand are up to while everyone else is waiting around for the apocalypse.

And because of the phrase 'doúlos tou theoú.'

"Which means?" Sophia prompted.

"Modern translations of the New Testament repeatedly use the English phrase 'servant of God' as opposed to the original Greek phrase 'doúlos tou theoú.' I suppose it was the translator's way of sanitizing the text and removing a distasteful phrase with dark historic attachments."

"Okay, then, what *exactly* does it mean?" Sophia asked.

"Slave of God."

"This," Hatfield said, extending his hand to Richard, "is where we part company."

The column had come to a halt several miles outside of Charleston. Richard steeled himself for whatever was to come. Would Hatfield live up to his end of the bargain? Or were he and Sophia to be executed by the side of the road?

The third option—that they would be handed over to Jefferson—seemed improbable. Given that Jefferson had betrayed Hatfield and tried to kill him and his men right alongside Asa McCoy and his followers, and that Hatfield now had an RLP in his possession and intended to use it to flee the planet, it seemed unlikely Jefferson would be invited to whatever party was about to commence.

The fact that as the convoy stopped the soldier that accompanied them did not cover them with his weapon and instead helped Sophia to her feet was encouraging.

Richard took Hatfield's hand and shook it. He did not know why. The man had just murdered thousands and was now running from the scene like a punk from a street cop. Perhaps it was the look in his eyes. Haunted. Mournful. Richard thought that Hatfield would hear those thousand voices that had had no time to scream every night for the rest of his life.

"I have done a terrible thing," Hatfield said as if reading Richard's mind.

"You have." Richard released his hand. "And you'll have to live with it. But by letting us go you may save far more lives than you took here today."

"I hope you're right," Hatfield said.

Johnse, at his father's side with the RLP in hand, gestured towards the front of the convoy. "The Rip is about a mile from here. Don't try to follow us. Don't try to come through. We'll be waiting until it closes. If we see you, we'll shoot." With that he pocketed the RLP and he and his father turned away.

"Wait!" Sophia cried. "You can't take the RLP! We'll be stranded without it!"

Hatfield turned back. Whatever moment had passed between he and Richard was gone, as was the remorse he'd worn like a mask as they'd spoken.

"Be that as it may young lady, we *are* taking the device. There are no guarantees that the next world will be any better than this one."

"It will be of no use to you," Sophia pleaded. "It times out every sixty minutes and you don't have the code to reset it."

Richard groaned inwardly. He'd been happy to let the convoy go on its way before the RLP timed out, giving them time to clear the area before Hatfield realized he'd been duped. By the time he and his men had returned to this spot to find them and get the code out of them he and Sophia would be long gone and the Rip would have closed. Hatfield and his soldiers would be stranded here on this world with a useless RLP where maybe, just maybe, justice would be served.

Johnse turned back at Sophia's outburst, a cunning grin on his face. "SOPHIA63, right? The code you typed in back at the bunker? You should check your surroundings a little more often, ma'am. You never know who might be skulking around outside a door with a pair of binoculars."

"You son of a bitch!" Sophia shrieked, and would have launched herself at Johnse if Richard hadn't stopped her. Guns previously pointed at the ground were now leveled at their heads.

"Young lady," Hatfield said in the exasperated tone one usually reserves for idiots and small children, "you would do well to have more confidence in your man. He is far more resourceful than you give him credit for."

As the Hatfield's returned to their vehicle at the head of the column Richard struggled to restrain Sophia.

"He's killing us all!" she shouted, trying to twist from his grasp. "We have to stop him!"

"It's all right," Richard said. "It'll be okay."

The last truck in the convoy passed them. Soldiers peered out in bewilderment as Sophia turned her anger on Richard and punched him on the jaw. He staggered back and she began pummeling his face, his arms, and his chest. The blows, save the first, were mostly ineffectual.

"Shit!" he yelled. "Would you stop it?"

"I will *not* stop it!" She screamed with tears of frustration and rage in her eyes. She lowered her fists and swiped angrily at her wet eyes. "Without the RLP we're stuck on this Earth. No way to get home. No way to find the Key. We were the last hope for the Multi-verse, Richard. *You* were the last hope. Now there's nothing to prevent BanaTech from finding the Key and opening the focal point."

Richard sighed and crossed the road to where their REAPERs and weapons had been dropped by one of Hatfield's men. He picked up his pack, dusted the dirt off, and shouldered it.

"Let's go," he said. "It's not safe here."

Sophia scowled but said nothing as she retrieved her pack and weapons. Richard headed off the road in an easterly direction, into the wind and away from any fallout from the devastated cities behind them.

"Wait," Sophia called from the middle of the road, gesturing to the north, the direction Hatfield and his men had gone. "Aren't we going to go after them? Get the RLP back on the other side?"

"You heard him," Richard said over his shoulder. "We go through that Rip and they'll shoot us. I don't think they'll be aiming for our legs."

Sophia hurried to catch up to him. They entered a stand of maple trees that were just losing their color and went on as far as the eye could see.

"We can't just let them go," Sophia argued. "We have to get the RLP back."

"We can't make that Rip before it closes."

"God*damn* it, Richard!" She grabbed the strap of his REAPER and tugged him to a halt. "We're screwed. Can't you see that? *Everything* is screwed. Aren't you in the least bit concerned?"

"We're alive," he said simply. "That counts for something."

He turned away and continued on through the woods.

Not a word passed between them as they continued to the east. Richard felt rage coming off Sophia in waves. Her mind was no doubt reeling, alternating between devising some way to get the RLP back and her anger at Richard for being so damn nonchalant about the whole thing. At times it was obvious she was restraining herself from kicking him or launching into another frenzy of screaming and punching.

They crossed one stream and then another, their waterproof boots sloshing up water and leaving short-lived mini rainbows in their wake. The sky to the south, when they could see it through the foliage, was an angry shade of red. Lightning flashed between and around the tops of twin mushroom clouds above Tennessee and West Virginia.

An hour and a half later, once he was certain the Rip near Charleston had closed, Richard stopped and shrugged off his pack. He unzipped the side pocket and took out his mother's copper trinket box.

"Feeling nostalgic?" Sophia asked. The question dripped with sarcasm.

Richard ignored her and worked the latch on the box. It sprang open and he removed a slim black object from within. Grinning, he held it up where Sophia could see it.

"How...where..." she gasped, her eyes widening in astonishment.

"This belonged to your Mirror." He held up the RLP. "At the time I didn't know why I put it in here. As it turns out, this box makes a nice little Faraday cage. Any idea what the code is?"

Sophia's jaw was hanging open. She snapped her mouth shut with an audible click.

"You...*bastard*," she said and advanced on him. He thought she might take another poke at his jaw but instead she threw her arms around him and hugged him. She smelled awful but her body was warm and a feeling of desire thrilled through Richard.

At that very moment he understood what it was he was fighting to save.

Sophia pulled away from him, a startled look on her face. Perhaps she too had felt the pure and innocent wave of warmth and love that had washed over him

Sophia placed her hands on her hips and spoke in a scolding tone like a mother speaking to an unruly child. "Why the hell did you wait so long to tell me?"

"It didn't seem important until we lost the other RLP. And then I wanted to be sure Hatfield and his men were through the Rip before I opened the box."

"Why should that matter?" she said.

"It was the last card I had to play with Hatfield. I had hoped the RLP he took would time out before he reached the Rip but after he let us go. Once he realized the RLP was useless without the code he'd have spent hours searching for us and the Rip would have closed, trapping him and his men here forever. Your antics back there on the road foiled that little plan. At that point, if he hadn't already had the code to the other RLP, I would have given it to him. It was either that or risk them using violence to get it out of us."

"And you knew you had this RLP to fall back on." It was a statement, not a question.

"So did Hatfield." Richard said. Sophia's eyebrows went up and he continued. "It was what he said about me being more resourceful than you gave me credit for. He would have opened the box. It was right there on the table in front of him and the latch isn't all that complicated. He knew I had another RLP and for some reason decided to keep quiet about it. He could just as well have taken it along with the other."

"That still doesn't explain why you waited two hours to let me in on your little secret." Sophia was still fuming.

"I wanted that RLP—*your* RLP—off this world before I exposed it to the Source. BanaTech couldn't track it in the trinket box and had probably written it off as being destroyed, either by your Mirror or in that little dust up back at my house in Kansas. Whatever the case they may no longer be actively tracking it. Instead they're tracking an RLP on another world in the hands of someone who is *not* looking for the Key."

A slow smile spread across Sophia's face. "They won't know where we are or where we're going."

"Finally," Richard said, "she sees the light."

Chapter 19

"Try SOPHIA19," Sophia suggested.

Richard typed the code in at the prompt. The screen reset to ENTER CODE.

"Nope," he said. "What else have you got?"

"I don't *have* anything else," she said, her shoulders dropping. "We always use our first name followed by our designation code. It's practically SOP."

"Given that *this* Sophia snatched her child and fled the BanaTech homeworld to avert a Multi-universal apocalypse," Richard replied," don't you find it conceivable that she might have decided to forego standard operating procedures?"

"If she did, then she could have come up with anything. Any random word, number, or combination of both. We could stand out here inputting codes for a thousand years and not stumble over it." Sophia's newfound optimism, so great that Richard had seen it on her face and heard it in her voice, slowly began trickling away like air from a tire with a nail in it.

"Unlikely," Richard said. "Random codes are easy to forget. If you write it down then anyone who finds it can access whatever it is you're trying to protect, so most people use words or phrases that are familiar to them. A birthday, phone number, or the name of a pet. *You* are her Mirror. You told me that Mirrors live similar lives and are similarly like-minded. You should be able to figure out her password."

"You're right, of course." Sophia sighed. "Give it to me and I'll try."

"Try while we're moving." Richard handed her the device. "I don't think it's safe here."

They moved on, not talking, keeping to an easterly course through the foothills of West Virginia. The going was easy despite being in a heavily wooded area. Dense vegetation overhead—a multitude of maple, elm, and oak leaves—kept the sunlight at bay. Only the occasional bright shaft broke through the canopy to reach the ground below and spark undergrowth.

A light but constant breeze played through the trees, stirring leaves of red and gold together in a sound like the whispers of conspirators. Leaves fell sporadically in swirls of crimson and amber. The only sounds were their footfalls, Sophia's irregular tapping on the RLP, and zephyrs cavorting amongst tree branches.

The air was crisp and redolent with the rich smells of loam, decomposing wood, and flourishing wildlife. Pollution on this Earth, Richard reminded himself, would mostly be contained to larger cities, mill towns, and areas boasting large factories. Out here in the sticks all was fresh and clean. The smell sparked melancholy memories of playing as a child in the scrub behind his home in Kansas. He was startled to realize he was homesick.

"Got it!" Sophia cried. A bird squalled from overhead as if scolding her for the outburst. Richard stopped and turned to her, a questioning look on his face. "It's ELIANNA," she continued, excited. "I should have known. I wasted time running through names important to *me* when I should have been thinking about what was most important to *her*."

"Very good," Richard said, smiling. "You're officially a hacker now."

"Ha," Sophia deadpanned, her fingers moving across the device. "Damn." Her excitement vanished. "I was afraid of that."

"What is it?" Richard asked.

"The nearest Rip is in Kowloon."

"Kowloon?" Richard repeated. "*As in China*?"

"Yes." Sophia sighed with frustration. "I knew this might happen."

Richard reached for the RLP and she handed it over. He flipped through screen after screen from their present location to ever widening views of West Virginia, the United States, and then the entire North American continent. There was nothing to indicate the presence of a Rip. No indication that one would be forming.

"I don't understand," Richard said.

"It's the nuke," Sophia explained. "I told you that the Rips tend to shy away from people not intentionally entering them as if there's intelligence behind them. It's the same for catastrophic events. When the nukes went off the Rips here all closed. We've seen it before. A year or so ago on E-88 the Yellowstone caldera erupted. The entire planet was affected and Rips didn't form there for months."

"A cosmic safety valve." Richard imagined a Rip opening in the middle of a volcanic eruption, channeling pyroclastic ash and magma to the heart of a large city on another unsuspecting Earth. "Probably a good thing."

"Except that in this case it strands us here," Sophia said.

"For how long?" Richard asked.

"It could be days," she answered. "Or only hours. There are a lot of variables. Wind speed and direction of radioactive fallout. The rate of decay of the fissionable material used to detonate the devices. Resultant emission levels. The list goes on. We just have to wait it out."

"We can't wait here." Richard handed the RLP back to Sophia. "We're still too close. If the wind shifts we'll likely get a dose of radiation ourselves. We should keep heading east and hope a Rip opens in that direction before too long."

"There is one consolation," Sophia said. "With the Rips closed on this continent, Jefferson won't be sending anyone after us anytime soon. And if the one near Charleston closed after the detonation Hatfield and his boys are stuck here too."

"All the more reason to move," Richard said.

Sophia slipped the RLP into the sleeve pocket of her BDU—the better to feel the vibration of the device when and if the proximity alarm went off—and they started off again. The bird overhead chirped at them again, a farewell perhaps, Richard thought as he stepped over a fallen tree branch as thick as his leg. A vole, grey and sleek, startled by the sudden intrusion of man in its habitat streaked away from the branch, a bit of fruit or tasty root still hanging from its mouth.

Richard felt for the animal. He too had been disturbed into headlong flight. One moment he was living in Kansas trying to build a life from the rubble of his murder trial and subsequent incarceration; the next he was hiding out in California trying to make sense of what had happened in Kansas. Who had tried to kill him there and make off with the mysterious woman? And why?

He'd gotten the answers to those questions, as fantastic and unbelievable as they were. But those answers had led to more questions. A number of which still remained unanswered.

He briefly wondered why, in moments of uncertainty, someone couldn't just come along and give him the answers.

"What am I doing here?" he asked the wind, the trees, the very Multi-verse at large.

The Multi-verse remained silent. It was Sophia who said: "What do you mean?"

"I mean, what am *I* doing here? Why am I not at home, reading a book with my feet up in front of the fire? Petting my dog or remodeling my kitchen? Here we are, running around blind, with no idea whatsoever where your Mirror hid the Key or how to find her. We could rip onto a thousand worlds, search every one of them from pole to pole, and be no better off than we are now. It sounds like a good premise for a TV show but it's not very productive."

He stopped and turned to Sophia, frustration evident on his features.

"Why does BanaTech think that I can find the Key? Why are *you* so damn convinced that I can save the Multi-verse? So I'm a Prime. What does that mean? That I'm better at math and sports? That I can see the Rips? So what? I'm not a hero and certainly not some savior. I'm just a guy from Kansas who lost his temper and acted when the system chose to protect a predator instead of the innocent life it was created to defend."

"You're forgetting," Sophia replied, "that out of all the people in the Multi-verse, all the *Primes* in the Multi-verse, my Mirror came to *you*, Richard. That has to mean something. BanaTech obviously thinks so. What's more, the Quantum Crays think so too and they're rarely wrong."

Richard started walking again. "Did it ever occur to you, BanaTech, or your high and mighty Quantum Crays that your Mirror just happened to choose a random Rip that coincidentally terminated in the back yard of a Prime? That I'm here because of a capricious act of nature?"

"Impossible," Sophia said, keeping pace with him.

Richard snorted. "I've seen a lot of things I thought were impossible recently."

"The Rip my Mirror used to get to your home in Kansas wasn't predicted by the Quantum Crays. It didn't behave the way normal Rips behave and only lasted long enough for her to exit before collapsing. The QCs have only ever recorded an event like it once before. That Rip wasn't a capricious act of nature, as you put it. It didn't occur naturally. It was *created*."

"How is that possible?" Richard stopped and faced her. "I thought that attempting to create an artificial Rip would cause chaos throughout the Multi-verse. Have untold consequences on countless Earths."

"We don't *know* how it's possible." Sophia said. "Nor do we know who or what created it or why they would do so to help my Mirror. We only know that it happened. That someone, or *something*, has the power to open a Rip of specific duration for a specific purpose."

"And BanaTech wants this power," Richard said. It was not a question.

"It's one of their goals, yes."

He started walking again, mulling over this new information. The trees were thinning out. The underbrush grew thicker wherever sunlight broke through the canopy. He pushed through a knee high grouping of young hemlock trees.

Another power with the ability to create a focal point and open artificial Rips at will was certainly a threat to BanaTech's scheme. Who or, as Sophia had put it, *what* could have that power? Was this entity, whatever it was, benign in its purpose? Or were its goals similar to those of BanaTech and simply achieved in a different way? Did he and Sophia have an ally in all of this? Or was that just wishful thinking?

And why, he wondered, breaking into a field of milkweed and daisies, use that power on only two occasions?

"You said the QCs recorded a similar artificial Rip only once before. When was it?"

"The night my Mirror fled the Homeworld with the Key," Sophia said. "She'd been causing Jefferson trouble since she learned he planned to use Elianna to control the Focal Point Generator. It was her idea to use an autistic Prime but she knew the risks associated with attempting to open a Rip and refused to risk the safety of her own daughter. Jefferson feared she might try to abduct the child so he took Elianna from her and housed her with a surrogate. Elianna became even more reticent than usual and stopped eating so they gave her back to my Mirror and held them both under armed guard. Then the Monk appeared in her room and took them."

"The Monk?" Richard said.

"That's what they called him. He was wearing robes and a cowl. The tech monitoring the room never saw his face. One second my Mirror and Elianna were alone in the room, the next there was this guy standing there talking to them. No one saw the Rip, the cameras in the room wouldn't have picked it up, but everyone knew what had happened. The tech raised the alarm but by the time they got into the room the three of them were vanishing into the back wall. One of the guards got off a shot, swears my Mirror was hit in the side, but no one wanted to fire blindly into the Rip for fear of hitting the Key."

"Oh, he hit her alright," Richard said. "I patched her up myself. If I hadn't found her as soon as I had she'd have probably bled out in a matter of hours."

Sophia frowned. "That doesn't make sense. If the wound was that bad someone else must have tended to it before you did."

"No," Richard said. "She hadn't been treated. The wound was fresh when I found her. No dressing and no sign it had ever been cleaned."

"That's just not possible, Richard," Sophia said.

"Why isn't it?" Richard asked, thinking that these days the line between the possible and impossible was diminishing rapidly.

"Because the time between my Mirror vanishing from her quarters on the Homeworld and reappearing in your back yard wasn't a matter of minutes or even hours. It was four *days*."

Night came and with it an abundance of stars. They glittered across the Eastern sky, cold and uncaring to the plight of wanderers below. To the southwest the sky raged, red and angry as if the very air were afire. Richard knew the effect would last for many nights to come. Even after it faded, for a time, those looking in that direction in the evenings would see the most stunning sunsets they'd ever witnessed. In the midst of total annihilation, there is still beauty to behold.

He and Sophia had been walking a little more than six hours. Richard estimated they'd made twelve miles from where they'd been left at the side of the road and were now roughly fifty miles from Logan County

They'd shifted their course to a more northerly direction. To throw off Hatfield if he and his men were set on tracking them down for answers as to why their ticket off this Earth had been cancelled, and to stay closer to the inhabited areas skirting Charleston. They were both tired and needed rest. They were more likely to find shelter closer to a city.

The phrase 'doúlos tou theoú' kept running through Richard's mind. *Slave of God.*

Is that what it is to be a Prime? A slave? To God or something like Him?

He didn't feel like a slave, exactly. More like a 19th century conscript shanghaied in a waterfront bar. Drugged and pressed unwillingly into service by a master Crimp. Forced to serve aboard ship until voyage's end under penalty of imprisonment or death.

Many a conscript had chosen to face the cold and unforgiving sea rather than serve, he recalled. Jumped ship and risked drowning rather than swab a deck or hoist a sail at another man's behest. Some had made it home, he presumed. He knew that most had not.

Could I abandon this voyage—this quest—if I wanted to?

Or would something out there stop me? Force me to walk some numinous plank?

His thoughts were broken when Sophia touched his arm.

"Look," she whispered.

He'd been so lost in thought he hadn't noticed they'd left the treeline and were walking on cultivated ground. A field that had recently been harvested, threshed, and winnowed for rest through the coming winter.

A large barn stood on the far side of the field fifty yards from where they stood. Beyond that a small house; its windows dark. Either the landowner was out for the evening or, more likely, had gone to bed with the sunset.

"It's big enough to have a loft," Sophia said. "We'd be out of sight and have plenty of warning if anyone comes looking for us."

Of course, Richard thought. *She's been thinking of Hatfield too.*

"Some MREs and some sleep, then," Richard said, striking out for the barn.

Richard awoke to the soft sound of new snow falling on a still night.

It had been cool that day. The fauna they'd passed indicated it was early fall on this Earth, with temperatures, he guessed, in the high fifties. While it wasn't something he'd thought about at the time there had been no indication that temperatures would drop low enough for it to snow overnight. Nor did he think their elevation was sufficient enough for such a thing.

He wasn't cold. The barn was comfortable enough that they hadn't felt the need for cover. He had, in fact, shed his bulky BDU ripstop choosing to sleep in his A-shirt. He'd laid the ripstop beneath him to ward off the needlelike prick of the straw.

He looked around for the source of the sound. While it was dark in this far corner of the loft he could make out Sophia lying on her side to his right, breathing deeply but not quite snoring. One hand was curled innocently under her cheek, the other across her waist. Her nose crinkled briefly as if she'd smelled something or got a tickle, then smoothed again.

To Richard's left, a good eight feet away, was the edge of the loft and a twelve-foot drop to the barn floor below.

He heard nothing amiss save that light, airy tinkling sound. Saw nothing out of place from his supine position. Slowly, so as not to awaken Sophia, he pulled himself erect and crept to the edge of the loft for a better look at the floor below.

A light framed the side door of the barn. Not the yellow light of a candle or lamp but a light soft and white like the pure glow of an LED. *Would they even have those on this Earth yet*? Richard wondered. *Wouldn't they still be using incandescents*?

He started to go back and rouse Sophia, certain they'd been discovered, and then thought better of it.

With no Rips on this continent if they *had* been discovered it was either Hatfield and his men or simply the landowner. He doubted Hatfield had a tracker with sufficient skill to pursue them in the dark. *If* they were out there searching for him and Sophia they'd have likely camped at sunset, intending to pick up the trail at first light.

If it was the landowner he could maybe convince the man or woman that they meant no harm and were simply seeking shelter for the night. And that they would now be on their way. A task better suited to a lone, unarmed caller than to two trespassers armed to the teeth.

So thinking Richard disarmed himself, climbed down the ladder, and crossed to the door. The light grew no brighter as he approached. No voices rose in alarm from outside. He expected to hear *something*; the shuffling of feet, low voices, a cautious "Who goes there?" There was no sound save his footfalls on the floorboards and the faint whisper of snow falling on velvet.

He paused. The glow cast itself a few feet inside the half open door, across his boots and over his shins. It neither warmed nor cooled his legs. It simply was.

This was certainly not right.

It didn't feel wrong, either.

Richard opened the door slowly, not wanting to take a bullet if whoever was outside was of the 'shoot first and ask questions later' variety.

The light, pure and white, did not increase or wink out. No bullets crashed into the doorframe. No new sounds arose. With a single look back and up towards the corner of the loft where Sophia still slept Richard cautiously stepped out into the radiance. His jaw dropped.

There was no snow. Neither on the ground nor falling from the sky.

A girl about eight years old stood before him, her face downcast as if she were studying the ground. The incandescence seemed to be coming from her. She wore a white dress that rippled out to the side as if it were being blown by the wind though there was no such wind present. The same non-wind blew the purest blonde hair Richard had ever seen about the child's head and face obscuring her features.

Above her shoulders and down her sides a pair of wings folded tight against her body. Tiny, delicate feathers of the purest white stirred in the breeze that wasn't there. Her arms were at her sides, hands clasped in front holding a clutch of roses. Petals of the deepest red fluttered to the ground in stark contrast to the white visage of the girl.

Behind the child rose a staircase so high Richard had to crane his neck back to see all of it. Steps of cut granite ascended to a point far beyond his sight, the top obscured by the same clean radiance that surrounded the child.

The girl lifted her face to Richard and the non-wind blew her hair aside. Eyes as blue as the deepest sea pierced him and he gasped as he recognized the face of young Katie Marsh.

Dear God, Richard thought, *I must be dreaming.*

"What is a dream," the child spoke in a voice very much like the sound of snow falling in stillness, "but reality from another perspective?"

Neither a confirmation nor a denial, Richard noted.

"Who are you?" Richard said.

"You know who I am," the girl replied.

"Are you Katie Marsh? Are you her spirit?"

"I am she," the child said simply. "And I am others. I am Erelah. I am of the All."

There it was again. That phrase. The All.

He'd thought it himself, back in Kansas at McCormack's house. At the time he'd taken it for an errant thought brought about by the stress of confronting the child murderer and his intent to kill him:

This is the beast that must be vanquished. The evil light that must be banished from the ALL.

Then McCormack himself, or whatever had taken up residence inside him, had spoken of it: "Defiled them" he had said, referring to his victims, "*And* the All."

Once is happenstance. Twice is coincidence. Three times…there was something to this. Something beyond Sophia, Banatech, and the Rips. Beyond anything he'd experienced thus far. Something he intuited this child, ghost, whatever she was, could not or would not explain.

Just what is the All, he asked himself, *and what does it mean*?

"Why are you here?" Richard asked aloud.

"You called me," the child answered.

Richard thought about it but could not remember doing any such thing.

"And where does that go?" Richard asked, indicating the staircase behind her.

"Everywhere," the girl replied. "And nowhere."

"That's helpful," Richard muttered.

"You must choose a path, Richard Farris," the child said.

"A path?" he said.

"To what lies ahead," the girl said indicating the staircase, "or what lies behind." Though she nodded in Sophia's direction Richard felt she meant his old life back in Kansas.

"I can go back?" he asked. "End all this and just have my old life back?"

"Every living thing has a choice," the girl said. "Every choice has its consequences."

Meaning, he thought, that if he gave up this pursuit of the Key and returned to his Earth BanaTech might well create a focal point, threatening chaos throughout the Multi-verse.

Some choice.

"I need answers," Richard said, more to himself than to Erelah.

"Then go," the child said and pointed over her shoulder.

"Can't you tell me what I need to know?" Richard said.

"I am but a gatekeeper," said the child, "it is only the Seraph, pure of dignity and light, who can lead you to the Messenger."

With that the girl was gone. She didn't fade out or vanish with a flourish. No sudden gust of wind sprang up. One moment she was there and the next she was not. Rose petals littered the ground where she'd stood. The staircase remained, the steady white radiance from the top beckoning.

Richard glanced back towards the barn and the sleeping Sophia.

No harm will come to her, the child's voice spoke up in his mind.

Richard mounted the stairs.

He had no idea how long he ascended. It felt like hours though it remained dark and the sun did not rise on this part of the world as it should have. His legs ached from the climb. His lungs burned with the effort.

Everyone should have one of these, he thought at one point. *Beats the Treadclimber by about a million miles.*

He felt no fear of falling though by this time he had to be thousands of feet above the surface of the planet. He had no urge to go to the edge of the wide steps and look down either. He didn't suffer acrophobia—great heights didn't bother him at all—but he had no desire to step to the edge and see the world spread out below him like the view from an airplane window either.

He expected high altitude winds of the force that threaten to blow urban climbers, known as *builderers*, from the faces of buildings but there was nothing save a faint breeze of fresh air coming from above. He expected the air to thin making breathing difficult and ascending impossible but his lungs remained full of oxygen and, though somewhat labored from exertion, his breathing was the same as it had been on the ground.

One thing *did* change. The further he ascended, the closer he got to the soft glow coming from what had to be the apex, the more color he could see coming from it. The pattern was familiar, a swirling mix of every color imaginable. And a few that couldn't be.

At the top of the stairs was a Rip. A big one. By far the largest Rip Richard had encountered.

As he mounted the final step, Richard bathed in the luminescence. It had an almost imperceptible *feel* to it. As if he were being lightly caressed by the hands of many lovers. That much light should have blinded him but did not. The sheer beauty of it should have driven him mad but he remained conscious and sound of mind.

The Rip beckoned.

Like Alice through the looking glass, Richard stepped forward.

PART THREE

OF DOGS AND DRAGONS

Chapter 20

The Elder sat alone in his tower looking out upon the perfect world. He wore no satin robes as one might expect of the most powerful man in the Multi-verse. Sat upon no gilded throne. At eighty-one years of age he had no need of impractical embellishments and instead sat in a simple armchair wearing black denim pants and a sweatshirt that bore the logo of a college football team from another Earth. He had no interest in sports of any kind. Only found the idea of a buckeye wearing a cap and a shit-eating grin amusing.

The world outside the window—technically labeled Earth-01 but more commonly known as the Homeworld—was bleak and grey; crisscrossed with long-untraveled highways, crumbling buildings in an advanced state of decay, and ugly black scars from multiple high-intensity power discharges. Dark thunderclouds filled the horizon. A constant barrage of lightning reached from cloud to cloud and sky to ground as if Mother Nature were lashing out in fury at what had been done to her. Sunlight had not touched the blasted surface of the planet in the Elder's lifetime.

It was of no consequence. The surviving population had moved underground over a century ago. Eight billion souls lived, worked, and played in the series of tunnels that reached around the planet to a depth of four miles. Power was supplied by a series of solar collectors parked high above the dense clouds, each transmitting its load to enormous batteries spread around the globe. The raw energy was then piped to underground depots that converted it to usable electricity. Food was plentiful. Vast hydroponics bays large enough to house small forests supplied vegetables while cattle, pork, and poultry were raised on the many ranches scattered beneath the surface. All other necessary provisions were ripped in from other planets. Water was abundant, drawn from rivers, lakes, and streams above and heavily filtered.

Only a handful of people ever ventured to the surface. Why would they? There was nothing to see save an endless expanse of aging concrete, glass, and steel. Still, it *was* the perfect world. His predecessors had seen to that.

It began with the first Elder, a man of vision who had immediately seen the potential of the Rips. He'd supported the brilliant but clearly insane Steven Bana, both emotionally and financially, while quietly working behind Bana's back to build his fledgling tech company into the most powerful corporate entity on the planet. It had taken decades for Bana to decipher the mechanics of the Rips and make travel through them safe enough to forward his benefactor's plans but once the system was perfected the first Elder had moved swiftly, seizing control of the Homeworld through political reform and military means.

Then the purges began.

Eliminating crime and criminals was the first order of business. The justice system was simplified; laws enacted that left only two means of punishment for offenders. For misdemeanors such as shoplifting, drug abuse, or vagrancy, the mandatory minimum sentence was ten years indentured servitude to BanaTech. For felony crimes such as murder, rape, burglary or any other violent crime, the penalty was death. Courtrooms and juries were abolished. Arresting officers carried out judgment and sentencing—including execution—on the spot. *Ex post facto* rights were repealed making all new laws retroactive. Within months tens of millions of felons worldwide were summarily executed. Those on parole or discharged, their debt to society paid or not, had been hunted down and killed.

Addressing poverty was the next order of business.

With the sudden reduction in population and the constant flow of resources from other Earths there was no need for anyone on the Homeworld to be without means. The monetary system was eliminated. Cash and credit became obsolete. Those who were willing to work, to forward the goals of BanaTech, flourished. Those who refused, who chose indolence over industriousness, were convicted of vagrancy. Repeat offenders were executed.

Eradicating disease was the final order of business in the Elder's plan to create the perfect world. While this had proven impractical—a list of *known* genetic defects took hours for the Quantum Crays to generate and would have taken a century to screen for—major diseases such as Alzheimer's, Muscular Dystrophy, ALS, Down syndrome, and certain cancers were eliminated by controlling reproduction. The populace was screened *in toto* for genetic markers indicating a propensity towards defect. Those with the markers for such diseases were sterilized.

In other cases marriage and breeding were strictly controlled. Still, heart disease, cancer, congenital birth defects, and some chemical/mental disorders such as Autism were so prevalent they were impossible to completely eradicate. Incidences of these diseases were deemed inconsequential until they became problematic. The lame and the insane were dealt with swiftly, usually by euthanasia. Others were monitored and studied in the hopes of discovering a cure.

In his seventy-fifth year the first Elder recognized the need to pass his legacy on to a man of equal ideology and vision. He had the known Multi-verse—at that time less than a hundred worlds—scoured for a Mirror of himself who most closely fit his requirements. He took the young man under his tutelage and groomed him for the role he trusted no other to fulfill. In his eighty-ninth year, satisfied that the second Elder would continue where he had left off, the first Elder stepped into a Rip that the Quantum Crays predicted terminated in the vacuum of space.

The second Elder had nearly destroyed Earth-01.

Under the first Elder's rule the existence of the Multi-verse and BanaTech's exploitation of other versions of Earth had been a closely guarded secret. Few outside the Elder's inner circle of most trusted advisors knew the true breadth and scope of BanaTech's hegemony. The populace knew what they needed to know and little else. The second Elder viewed this as a mistake. He felt that a perfect world should be united in goal, if not in mind.

He'd expected some outcry. Though the populace had been ignorant of its government's true agenda and had been submissive to its reign for over half a century the knowledge that entire worlds were being harvested for resources was certain to raise some opposition. He was equally certain, however, that any dissenters would be rapidly identified and subdued.

It may have been his youth that led to this error in judgment. He'd been taken by the first Elder at the age of thirteen and educated for nearly fifteen years in Multi-verse theory, Rip travel, politics, and the use of military might to achieve BanaTech's goals. He had little practical experience in the administration of such power, however, and like the spoiled child who inherits a fortune but has no understanding of how that wealth was acquired, the second Elder nearly lost the legacy that had been left him in less than a decade.

The political structure of the Homeworld was akin to a monarchy. The many countries on all six populated continents had been demoted to Commonwealth status by the first Elder and united under one body of government, each with an appointed Regent. The Regents, all members of the inner circle and privy to BanaTech's secrets, were chosen for their ideologies and loyalty to the Elder. Their powers were illusory, however, their titles titular. Each held power over the various Commonwealth's on his or her continent but all six answered to the Elder.

Shortly after the first Elder handed over his empire the European Regent—a shrewd and cunning man named Vasily Ivanovich Alexeyev—angered by political impotence and enraged that neither he nor any other Regent had been promoted to the role of Elder, began undermining allegiance to the new Elder inside the European arm of BanaTech's military.

For two years Alexeyev gathered allies throughout Europe before daring to divulge his planned insurrection to his lifelong friend and the Regent of the South American continent, Valentina Mayte Vientena. Collaborating on two continents, Alexeyev and Vientena had only to wait for the opportunity to seize control of BanaTech, and thus the world.

The revolt was planned to coincide with the Elder's public revelation of BanaTech's true objectives. Disguised as public outrage at the atrocities committed on the other, innocent versions of Earth, the scheme almost worked. And surely would have if Alexeyev and Vientena hadn't underestimated the Elder. What he lacked in political experience he made up for with brutality. At the first hint of rebellion Europe and South America were all but obliterated by nuclear fire.

The Homeworld was plunged into nuclear winter. Billions died and the planet was forever scarred. Because its central operations and research arms were already housed in a warren of tunnels hundreds of miles long and several miles deep beneath the surface, BanaTech emerged victorious.

The Elder realized that once sown, the seeds of rebellion can never be fully eradicated. He quickly took steps to make sure any future attempts at insurrection died on the vine.

He swept away the few feeble vestiges of democracy that remained. Democracy was an illusion anyway, a fiction designed to give the masses the idea that they still had free will. Elections were suspended indefinitely. The population of Earth 01 was now under the direct control of BanaTech. Every man, woman, and child knew it; and they'd seen what happened to those who dared to oppose its corporate sovereignty.

The four remaining Regents were executed. Their staff and military attaches similarly culled. The inner circle was vetted for traitors. Those who fell under suspicion were killed, the others placed under close scrutiny for the rest of their lives. Nothing garners loyalty, the Elder believed, like a gun to the head.

The Elder also took steps to ensure that his misstep would not be repeated. He began searching for *his* successor at the age of fifty. His ten year old Mirror was rigorously trained in all facets of BanaTech operations beginning with a decade-long study of military tactics and strategy, plus five years of provisional rule as Elder before the second Elder, in homage to his predecessor, stepped through a Rip into oblivion at the age of eighty-three.

That third Elder, now looking out upon the scarred face of the perfect world, knew the void was out there waiting for him as well.

"*Not before you've completed your task, old man.*"

The voice, a thick and raspy whisper that would go unheard by anyone else even if he were in a room full of people came from behind him and off to the left.

Bernael, the Elder recognized the voice. A form of shadow and darkness who'd advised he and his predecessors for more than two centuries. He knew not from whence the creature or others like it came, nor exactly what they were. Only that they'd revealed themselves early in the first Elder's career and led him to Dr. Stephen Bana. Without the influence of these creatures, these *Infernal*, BanaTech would not exist.

When the voice came next it was directly in front of him though no one was there:

"*There is much to do yet before you've earned your rest.*"

"If you're referring to the Focal Point Generator, old friend, it will soon be online. Every version of Earth will be united and the perfect Multi-verse will be born." The Elder's voice, coarsened with age, nonetheless reflected the conviction of his obsession. As the first Elder had created the perfect Earth, he himself would create the perfect Multi-verse.

"*You have the Key, then?*" the thick voice asked.

"You know we do not," the Elder said. "You can read my thoughts as easily as I read the daily sector reports. Do not treat me as you would treat those who do not know what you are."

A shadow detached itself from the wall and rushed towards the Elder.

"*Do not dictate to us old man,*" it hissed with rage. "*It was* we *who guided your predecessors on this course,* we *who warned your Mirror of impending insurrection,* we *who instructed him to wait until their plot was in motion to stomp them out, thus ensuring BanaTech's domination of all life on this world.*"

"And it was no doubt you who fomented that failed revolution in the first place," the Elder responded without a hint of alarm at the creature's wrath. He stood, brushing the shadow aside as if it were no more than vapor. "Stop your posturing, Bernael. Why are you here?"

The shadow reassembled at the Elder's right shoulder, its tone that of a repentant child:

"*The Keeper,*" it said. "*He must be destroyed once the Key is retrieved.*"

"The order has already been given," the Elder said. "He has proven far too resourceful and clever for my taste. But what is your interest in the matter? Can he not be turned? As we have turned the others?"

"*Not this one,*" the shadow said, flickering out of existence only to appear at the Elder's left side. "*This one* is different."

"Different how?"

"*Question us no further, old man. It was not we who lost the Key. Not we who jeopardized all we have worked towards. Perhaps we should have let Alexeyev and Vientena have their victory. Perhaps they would not have failed us so miserably. Destroy the Keeper and you will be rewarded.*"

The shadow drifted over to the wall and melted into it.

The Elder remained silent as the shadow faded away and did not ask the question that had been disturbing him since the Key's unlikely escape nearly a year ago. Did not voice aloud his fear: *If the Infernal are the omnipotent creatures they claim to be how is it they allowed the Key to be lost in the first place?*

A finger of fear ran down his spine at the thought of a force more powerful than those born of the dark. He shrugged it off. It was much too late to change the course of things now.

He stepped over to a console and brought up the screen for military operations. A face appeared on the screen. A much younger version of his own.

"Sir?" Jefferson said.

"Where are Bledell and Farris now?"

"We believe they're still on E-514, sir."

"You *believe* they're still on E-514?" The Elder asked, his eyes narrowing in annoyance.

"We've been getting some strange readings from there since the nuclear devices detonated," Jefferson said, unabashed by the Elder's ire. "All voice communication with our agents has been disrupted by the electromagnetic pulse and we're relying completely on our satellites. Also, we're now tracking not one but *two* RLP signals."

"How is that possible?" the Elder asked. "I ordered our agents on the ground to go in without devices so that Farris would not be warned of their presence."

"That order was given and followed, sir," Jefferson answered. "We believe the second device belonged to Bledell's Mirror. We know she had one in her possession when she fled the Homeworld."

"An astonishing lapse in security," the Elder reminded him.

"Yes, sir," Jefferson said, accepting the reprimand. They'd been over this before and while the fault had not been Jefferson's, he was ultimately responsible for the actions—or inaction—of those under his command. "We think Farris found some way to cloak the second device and retained it. It went active several miles away from a Rip that had formed but closed when our nukes went off."

"Assessment?"

"Hatfield is alive, sir," Jefferson said. "I think he apprehended Farris and Bledell shortly after they ripped onto that world, disobeyed our order to alert us of their presence, and took their RLP so that he and his men could escape to another Earth. Signals from that device now indicate a search pattern closing on the location of the second device. I believe the second signal to be Farris and Bledell. Hatfield is trying to find them, probably to find out why the Rip closed early and cut off his retreat."

"Where are Farris and the woman now?"

"They're holed up in a barn, if you can believe that."

"I can believe a great many things, my young Tyro. A great many things." The soubriquet, meaning novice or beginner, irritated Jefferson and the Elder knew it. His successor felt that after nearly thirty years of tutelage the nickname given him as a young boy no longer applied. "How long until Hatfield finds them?"

"An hour, maybe less," Jefferson said. "If he were more familiar with our technology he'd turn on the proximity sensor and have their location in seconds but he hasn't stumbled across that feature. Yet."

"And how long before our communications are back up?"

"Maybe forty minutes, sir. The QCs are predicting that the Rips will reopen around the same time," Jefferson said, then added, "There is another problem though, sir." The Elder remained silent. Waiting.

"The QCs have reported another Enigma incident."

"Like the one that preceded the loss of the Key?" The Elder said.

"Yes, sir," Jefferson said. "The Enigma Rip opened several yards from what I believe to be Farris and the woman's location, remained open for several minutes, and then closed again. With all the electromagnetic interference we can't determine if anyone passed through the Rip from either side but the RLP in Farris' possession is recording life signs within its limited range."

"So they have not yet fled," the Elder surmised.

"It doesn't seem likely," Jefferson said.

"Do they have company then?" The Elder asked, thinking of the robed figure that had come through the first Enigma Rip, ferreting away the Bledell woman and the Key.

"Unknown."

"Very well, Tyro," the Elder said. "Our mission on E-514 is nearly complete. Our agents in their capitol will finalize the transfer of power from their government to ours in the wake of their dirty little civil war.

"Once the electromagnetic interference clears I want you and your men on site. Hatfield and his men have served their purpose and have now become a liability. Eliminate them. All of them"

"Sir," said Jefferson, grinning like a hyena approaching a helpless impala, relishing the idea of sending the traitorous Hatfield to his death, "that will be my pleasure."

Chapter 21

Richard stepped out of the Rip. He wasn't catapulted or thrown out—there was no sense of transition—just one step that began on one world and ended on another.

He was disappointed. There had been no light within the Rip, no soft and warm embrace. He'd sensed nothing of the presence, vast and unknown yet full of light and love, that he'd felt there before.

His disappointment fled when he took a look at the Earth around him.

He stood in a clearing surrounded by fields of honeysuckle and lavender that went on as far as he could see. Trees, perhaps aspen or spruce—they were too far away for him to be certain—stood in the distance where the earth rose into hills before ascending to mountains.

A multitude of dragonflies flitted about, lighting upon this flower, tasting the nectar of that. Some pursued damselflies that demurely resisted their advances. Sunlight caressed diaphanous wings and iridescent bodies, flashing green and blue, a living riot of color reminiscent of the Rips.

Fat thumb-sized bumblebees with fuzzy black and yellow bodies abounded. They too tasted the lavender but seemed to find the red, yellow, and purple honeysuckle blooms more to their liking. They buzzed and hummed a pleasant song as they met and passed each other: *Hi there. Hello. Just going about our business here.* Some flew off—to where Richard did not know—their legs weighted with so much golden pollen it was amazing they could gain the air at all.

The sky overhead was the bluest he'd ever seen, flawless. Marred by neither cloud nor jet contrail, as if God were a master glassmith and had blown a perfect sphere to place the Earth in.

Richard gasped in surprise when a dragonfly lit briefly upon his nose, then alit once more and circled his head twice before rejoining its brothers and sisters. The air he took in was sweet and fresh. It tasted of honey.

A glance back revealed that the Rip had closed behind him. It also occurred to him that he'd left the RLP behind. The ghost child at the stairs—*Elerah, of the All,* she'd told him—had said no harm would come to Sophia. At the time he'd taken it to mean he would be returned to her. Now he wasn't so certain.

A wave of anxiety washed over him. His felt his heart speed up as his brain dumped adrenaline into his nervous system in response. Acrid saliva flooded his mouth and sweat broke out on his arms as a chill raced down his spine.

He was alone here. With no weapons, no gear, and no support. Abandoned on an unfamiliar Earth with no apparent way back. The land around him was undeniably beautiful but he was conscious of the fact that beauty was often deceptive.

He took a deep breath, cleansing his lungs while reminding himself he had been *sent* here, not abandoned. Erelah had said only the Seraph could lead him to the Messenger. She—if it had truly been a she and not something else masquerading as that beautiful dead child—had given no indication as to who or what the Seraph was, or when and where he would find it.

Did she mean Seraphim? Richard wondered. In medieval Christian mythology Seraphim were beings of inextinguishable light, the caretakers of God's throne. The highest of the angelic choir, whose mere presence was so pure as to perfectly enlighten others and make direct communication with God's messengers possible.

He didn't know if Eralah had meant Seraphim or not, only that so far, nothing had presented itself. The Seraph may appear in minutes, hours, or even days. Whatever the case, anxiety would only be a hindrance here.

His best course of action, he decided, was to head for the distant treeline. There he could find water, shelter, and, if he were lucky and skilled enough, food.

He began walking, accompanied by curious dragonflies and milling bumblebees, a miniscule entourage, and began to feel better. Working muscles consume excess adrenaline. Steady, controlled breathing expels toxins and regulates the heart. He'd walked less than a half mile before he'd purged the anxiety from his system.

A barely perceptible ringing like distant sleigh bells caught his attention and he again focused on the fields around him. He saw no cause for the sound. Only flitting insects and lazily floating chaff kicked up by his passage. Dismissing the sound as auditory matrixing he moved on.

His thoughts turned to Eralah. And the All. Just what, exactly, was the All? If it was as the name implied the sum total of everything, then what was its purpose? Was it a sentient being, all knowing and all powerful? Or was it just a mechanism by which the Multi-verse existed? If it were all powerful then why this cat and mouse quest for the Key? Surely it could put a stop to BanaTech on its own, without help from him or any other Prime. Or did it only act through agents such as Erelah and himself?

He recalled a painting he'd once seen on an eighth grade field trip to the Wichita Art Museum. At first glance it was a simple painting of two men seated on opposite sides of a chess-board. When he'd looked closer he'd noted that one of the figures was bearded and adorned in white robes with gold trim; the other dressed in a black hood and cowl, his skin a deep purplish shade of red. The second figure was reaching over the chessboard as if to move one of the pieces, but instead of a hand he'd raised a cloven hoof.

Further examination revealed that the chessboard was littered with men, women, and children. All were covered in blood, some slaughtered and rent into pieces. Every face bore an expression of anguish and torment.

The painting had been titled *The Divine Game*. Nauseated, Richard had turned away.

Was that the meaning of all of this? Some twisted distraction for a pair of bored supreme entities? A cosmic game whose pieces were countless billions of living, breathing, flesh and blood beings? If so he wanted nothing to do with it.

Or was it something entirely different? Was the All simply a Creator? An artist's hand that had produced something magnificent, a Multi-verse of wonders, and then moved on to another work allowing what it had created to thrive or perish of its own volition?

You must choose a path, Eralah had told him.

Do I throw in the towel here? Richard asked himself. *Take all my toys, go home, and let the Multi-verse sort itself out? Or do I continue? Take up the mantle despite this all seeming so overwhelming, the odds so impossible, and try to defend those countless billions of lives?*

But how? He asked himself. And again: *Why me?*

That peculiar ringing came to him again. It increased in volume and then shot past his head. Pollen followed the sound like a contrail and he inhaled some of it. It made his sinuses tingle and he sneezed three times in rapid succession.

What is it? What is it? What is it? He heard whispered as his sinuses cleared.

He whipped his head around searching for the tinny, child-like voice and saw only the bees and dragonflies dancing amongst the honeysuckle. He sneezed again and heard childish laughter.

We make it sneeze, he heard, followed by a multitude of giggling voices mimicking *ah-choo, ah-choo, ah-choo!*

The giggling continued, the sleigh bell sound intensifying in magnitude if not in volume. Two more dragonflies buzzed Richard's head, ringing his head in the pollen-like substance. He sneezed uncontrollably for more than a minute.

His ears were ringing, his eyes watering and his nose running. Richard had had enough. These were no ordinary dragonflies and if this kept up he'd sneeze himself to death amidst a cacophony of mocking laughter.

A larger than average dragonfly rose up from a thatch of lavender in front of him, no doubt intent on buzzing his head and starting another sneezing fit. Richard batted it away before it could ring his head with pollen. It issued a tinny scream and fell to the ground. The laughter around him stopped.

Richard looked to the ground where the dragonfly had fallen and for a moment his heart—his very mind—stopped.

That's impossible. He saw wings, so light and finely purple they were almost indistinguishable from the lavender blooms surrounding him. These were attached to a tiny body of the palest, almost white green hue. Two arms and two legs were tangled in a pose reminiscent of the one he'd found the first Sophia in several months ago.

He bent and gingerly picked the creature up in the palm of his left hand, the motion triggering the rapid intake of many breaths from the lavender thatch surrounding him. He held the creature close to his face, inspecting it. The hairless body was no more than four inches long from the top of its head to the tips of its toes, but was perfectly humanoid otherwise.

Is she dead? Is she dead? Is she dead? he heard from the lavender. The voices were not angry, merely curious. He realized that despite their amusement at his sneezing, he had nothing to fear from these creatures.

"Don't be dead," he said, meaning it. *Wishing* it. His heart filled with remorse at the thought that he may have destroyed such a wonderful creature.

Be it his wish, his breath across the small form or some other cause, the faerie—for *that's what it is,* Richard thought with wonder—stirred in his palm. Two tiny eyes, wide-set but as pale purple as its wings, opened and looked into his eyes. The creature sat up and shook her wings, emitting a fine cloud of pollen—*no, not pollen,* Richard thought with delight, *faerie dust*—and he held the faerie farther away from his nose so he wouldn't start sneezing again. He felt the indentations her tiny feet made against his palm as she stood, shaking herself from head to toe, emitting that sleigh-bell like sound and showering his hand in glittery dust. A relieved *ahhhh* arose from the lavender. It was a sentiment Richard shared.

The faerie linked her hands demurely behind her back and looked up at Richard.

"We're sorry if we hurt you," she said in a voice so soft and pure Richard had to struggle to hear it over the buzzing of true insects. "*We've never seen anything like you before. Why do you not have wings?"*

"I…uh…" Richard said, unsure of what to say and struggling to believe what he was seeing, hearing and sensing around him. "I'm a man, a human being. We don't come with wings. And you didn't hurt me. I was afraid *I* had hurt *you*."

Several more faeries rose from the lavender and hovered around Richard. They were careful to keep their distance. Not out of fear, Richard thought—he didn't think these innocent creatures even knew what fear was—but to minimize the faerie dust.

Where are you going? one asked.

"Why do you have fur?" asked another.

"How did you get so big? Why do we make you sneeze? Are there more of you? Can you fly without wings? Why are you here?"

The questions, all of them at once and from dozens of sources melted together into an indistinguishable cacophony of curiosity.

"I'll try to answer all your questions," Richard said, holding up his right hand in a stopping gesture. "But one at a time."

The faerie in Richard's palm stomped her foot for attention. It felt like being tapped lightly with a pencil.

"Why do you venture to the foothills?" she asked.

"I'm looking for shelter," Richard said. "I don't know how long I'll be here, but while I am I'll need water. Maybe food, a place to sleep, and a fire."

"Fire? Fire? Fire!" The faeries sang out in unified alarm. As quickly as they'd appeared they sped off, trailing faerie dust and the sound of sleigh bells in their wake.

So they do *know fear,* Richard thought watching glittering faerie dust slowly fall onto the lavender. Closed buds opened where the dust touched them.

His palm was stomped again. The faerie he'd swatted from the air wanted his attention. She hadn't fled with the others and looked agitated. She pointed over her shoulder, in the direction of the foothills.

"You must not venture that way," she said.

"Why?" Richard asked.

"You are too big," she said, lifting off from his palm and heading away. She looked back past fluttering wings and sing-songed a warning: "*You will be eaten.*"

Eaten? Richard thought, alone again save the bees and the real dragonflies that had accompanied him since he'd set foot on this world. *Eaten by what?*

He couldn't imagine. So far he'd found nothing in these fields but insects and faeries. The Seraph had not yet shown itself. *Why* had Eralah sent him to this strange and wonderful Earth? Was it a trial? A test? *You will be eaten,* the faerie had warned. Richard squinted up at the clear blue sky realizing how exposed and vulnerable he was in this wide open space. He struck off again toward the forest hoping he could find a way around the foothills.

He'd made little more than a mile when a new sound invaded his senses. It was a far off foraging sound, perhaps a large animal moving amongst the honeysuckle. Whatever it was it wasn't the faeries returning to the area. It was too big for that.

And it was moving in his direction.

He scanned the fields behind him trying to home in on the noise. A quarter mile behind him he could make out a large brown smudge moving through the foliage. It wasn't trying to be stealthy, that was certain. As far away as it was it sounded like moose in a cornfield.

He could make out a large round head and big floppy ears. Kiting along behind the animal like a mast above the honeysuckle was a jaunty, hairy tail.

"I'll be damned," Richard said aloud.

The animal making a beeline toward him was a dog.

As if to confirm his suspicions, the animal let out a series of barks and began running directly towards him, rapidly closing the distance between them. Richard could now make out more details. It was indeed a dog—a damn big one.

You will be eaten, the faerie had warned.

Richard scanned the field. It wasn't uncommon for pack animals to distract their prey by letting one of their own be seen while the real threat snuck up from the side or behind, but he saw no signs of any other dogs. Dragonflies fled in droves before the lumbering beast making its way to him, though none seemed to be bothered elsewhere in the field.

It's barking—it paused every hundred yards or so to bark, presumably at him—didn't sound threatening in any event. It seemed almost...*joyous.*

And strangely familiar.

The dog was close enough for Richard to make out the breed. A St. Bernard. *What an odd coincidence*, Richard thought, when coincidence became astonishment. He recognized that gait, that jaunty tail. That funny brown smudge between the eyes and down the tip of the nose that he'd spent countless hours rubbing, much to the dog's delight.

Richard gasped aloud, his throat seizing and unbidden tears springing to his eyes as the big dog careened clumsily toward him at break-neck speed.

It was Charlie.

Chapter 22

The big dog reached Richard and leapt up, knocking him to the ground. They rolled over twice in the honeysuckle and grass while tears coursed down Richard's cheeks. His heart soared.

"Charlie?" Richard laughed, flat on his back with both hands full of fur as he grasped the dog. He was laughing and crying at the same time and didn't care.

He rubbed and petted the dog as Charlie nuzzled and squiggled against him, his great tongue lapping Richard's face. Charlie's enormous tail whisked bees, dragonflies, and foliage aside as if caught in a gale. "Is it really you, pal?"

The St. Bernard sat back on his haunches in answer, his enormous tail still busily whisking the earth, and let Richard have a good look at him. He sat up and took the big dog's ears in his hands. Looked into his big brown eyes. This was no Mirror dog, if there was such a thing. This was *his* Charlie, through and through.

"Son of a bitch, it *is* you!" Richard threw a hug so fierce around the dog that Charlie grunted.

"But how?" Richard asked, as if he hadn't seen more than his fair share of impossible in the past week. "Oh, shit, who cares?" he said and hugged his dog again.

"Jesus, Charlie," Richard said, finally sitting back and solemnly looking the dog directly in the eyes again. "I'm so sorry about Kansas. I let you down."

Not let Charlie down.

The voice so stunned Richard that he scooted away from the dog. It seemed to him later that he hadn't merely been surprised that Charlie had spoken, but that he'd spoken in the very voice Richard imagined he would have if he had been able to speak. A soft and easy, yet strong and thoughtful voice, like that of someone far more intelligent than they liked to let on.

Richard laughed hysterically. Rips, multiple Earths, ghosts, giant spiders, angels, and faeries. Sure. Why not talking dogs, too? *Resurrected* talking dogs, he corrected himself. He ran his hands through his hair and tried to find some semblance of sanity.

Richard upset?

Richard looked at Charlie as the dog sat beside him and nuzzled his ear.

"No, pal. I'm not upset. Just a little off-kilter." Richard absently pushed the cold nose away and scratched the dog behind one ear as if conversing with a dog were the most natural thing in the world. "How is it you can talk?"

Not talk, Richard heard. *Thought. Charlie and Richard think together because Charlie...* more.

Richard noted that Charlie indeed wasn't speaking *per se*. His lips weren't moving across his teeth like a CGI dog in a children's film. He really was hearing Charlie's thoughts. Or maybe he'd just gone mad and the dog, the faeries, and this Earth were simply figments of a psychotic imagination.

"What do you mean, *more*?"

Cannot explain more. *Must see. Charlie just is.*

Richard gave up on that line of inquiry in favor of the larger question. "Why are you here, Charlie? How?"

Charlie come to Richard. To make Richard understand the ALL.

"The All?" Richard asked. "What the hell is the All?"

No. Not All. **ALL.**

The thought was accompanied by a mental image of the word in ten-foot tall capital letters, glittering, gleaming, and gilded in gold.

Infernal is *ALL. Charlie and Richard ALL. Everything ALL.*

Richard considered that for a moment, trying to make sense of the information. And never mind that he was getting the information from a previously dead dog. If the ALL is everything; every person, every animal, every single thing down to the smallest particle of dust and photon of light, then what Charlie was really talking about was balance. There is no night without day, dark without light, and so on. The Infernal must be the evil counterbalance to the ALL. It must exist, else the ALL, as a presumably benevolent entity, could not.

Richard understand. Some.

"You heard what I was thinking?" Richard asked.

Yes. Charlie more.

"Then what am I thinking now?' Richard said.

The big dog's tail went from slowly whisking the ground to powerfully stroking it.

YES! Charlie love *milk-bone.* The dog's tail slowed. *Richard not* have *milk-bone.*

"Sorry, pal." Richard stroked the dog's back. "If the Infernal is just another manifestation of the ALL, what's the problem? Why doesn't the ALL just straighten all this out for Itself?

Cannot. God not straighten out Devil. Is same.

"But God banished Satan. Threw him down from the heavens."

Yes.

"Where he's been screwing around with man ever since," Richard finished.

Yes.

"Are you telling me that the ALL is God, and the Infernal Satan?"

No. Yes. Maybe. Charlie not know.

Richard worked his hands around to the dog's flank. Charlie sighed happily and rolled over, presenting Richard his belly. Richard obliged.

"The war between God and Satan has raged for millennia," Richard said. "God always comes out on top. What's different this time?"

Rips.

"Man found the Rips and started using them, so the ALL, Infernal, whatever, gets all pissy?"

Charlie snorted as if disgusted and rolled over, gaining his feet.

ALL not care about man. Man like termite. Pest. Serve purpose, but not important. In past, Infernal only influence man. Kill. Have greed. Make war. Until man ally with Infernal. Now Infernal threat to ALL.

"Man like termite," Richard repeated. "Termites are only unimportant until they start eating your house. Then they're a real problem. So what you're saying...sorry, *thinking*, is that before the Infernal were just running around mucking things up for man, influencing pedophiles like McCormack and serial killers like Bundy and Gein. Starting wars and putting lunatics like Stalin and Hitler in power."

That and more.

"But now they're not just working against man. They're working *with* him," Richard continued. "To upset the balance. To bring down the ALL."

Yes.

"You mean BanaTech."

Yes.

"How could a group of people, even a corporation as large and powerful as BanaTech, threaten something as powerful as the ALL?"

Not people. Just one.

"One man is going to upset the balance of the ALL?" Richard said, incredulous.

Open focal point. Rips converge. Chaos everywhere. Every Earth. Every planet. Every Universe. ALL cannot fix. Multi-verse be destroyed.

Richard looked around at the flowers, the insects, and the clear blue sky; the warm sunlight and the forest in the distance, its untouched trees giving off clean, fresh air. He thought of the faeries and the beauty surrounding him and wondered what other beauty and marvels this Earth might contain.

"This will all go away if the focal point is opened," he said, a statement, not a question. "Not just here, but everywhere."

Yes. Richard now understand.

"And I can somehow stop it."

Yes.

Richard groaned. "*How?*"

Richard Prime," Charlie responded. *Richard* Keeper.

He'd heard that word before. Over a decade before when he'd killed the pedophile McCormack. At the time he'd thought the man, or the thing inside him had said, 'Keep her,' but now he realized his mistake: "You go on, *Keeper*," McCormack had said. "I'll just move along somewhere's else."

Richard's thoughts moved past McCormack to the first Sophia, then back to his encounter at the Williams's house all those years ago. A grim, heavy *rightness* settle over him.

"There was never another path for me, was there?" He said to Charlie. "This has been my course all along."

Every living thing has choice, Charlie mimicked Eralah.

"And every choice has consequences," Richard finished.

There was no going back to his simple life in Kansas. Richard knew that now. He'd been born into this. Born *for* this.

Richard Keeper of ALL, Charlie said.

"Richard thinks that means he's a recruit in someone else's war," he grumbled. "How does a Keeper stop BanaTech from opening the focal point?"

Charlie lay down, resting his head in Richard's lap. *Charlie tired. Too much think. Richard go. See Messenger. Messenger tell Richard how destroy Key.*

"Destroy the Key!" Richard exclaimed. "You mean kill the child?"

Yes.

Richard pulled Charlie's head up until their eyes met.

"You listen to me, fur face," he said with every ounce of sincerity he could muster. "I will not kill a child. Not for you. Not for the Universe. Not for the ALL."

Then Multi-verse is lost.

"It most certainly is not," Richard said. "If I'm a Keeper as you say then I'll find some other way. I'll find the child and hide her. Fight to the death if necessary. But I *will not* kill her. I will find the Seraph and this Messenger, and then I'll figure something else out."

Richard already find Seraph, Charlie said and got up. *Richard must* see.

The big dog trotted away a few steps and then sat. A light of blinding intensity flashed out and Richard saw Charlie—his pet, his pal, his friend—transformed. The loveable, good-natured St. Bernard he'd lived with, played with, and shared meals with was still there. Massive head erect, tongue lolling as usual, that colossal tail whisking dragonflies senseless as it cut the air, but over this, or perhaps *beneath* it, there was something else. Like one image superimposed over another in a photograph. In that instant Richard saw the true Charlie. What he was now and perhaps had been all along.

The creature closely resembled a lion, if lions grew to be nine feet tall. It had eyes all over its body, across its broad and powerful chest, throughout a mane as thick as steel cables and down muscular legs tipped with claws the size of table legs. Six sets of wings sprouted from its expansive back rising above and to the sides of the creature. One set was folded at its ribcage, feathers the size of boat oars rustling in the light breeze. An enormous tail, also covered in eyes, rose from behind the creature. It busily whisked the air in time with Charlie's.

More, Richard heard Charlie's thought. And both dog and Seraphim winked in unison.

Richard swallowed the lump of awe that had formed in his throat before speaking. "*You* are the Seraph?"

The light faded away and with it the image of the Seraphim.

Charlie Seraphim, Richard heard as the dog trotted back to his side. Richard reached out, hesitated, and then stroked the brown smudge between the dog's eyes. Richard wasn't burned or electrocuted. The magnificent beast did not reappear. He felt nothing but Charlie beneath his trembling hand.

"Have you always been Seraphim?" Richard asked. "Even when it was just you and me back in Kansas? Before all of this? Before you…" the last word died in his throat, "died?"

No. Yes. Always Charlie but Seraph there. Seraph too big for always.

"You mean the Seraph has always been a part of you, but you're still just Charlie most of the time?"

Yes. Richard understand. Charlie tired now. Charlie go back soon.

"Go back?" Richard said, dismayed at the idea of losing his friend for a second time. "Go back where?"

Home. To ALL

"No." Tears of sadness clouded Richard's vision and he buried his face in the warm fur of Charlie's neck.

Charlie not belong here.

"I know," Richard said. And he did. He had all along.

Richard not belong here. Not yet. Charlie got to his feet. Color brighter than the sun cut through Richard's eyelids and he opened his eyes to see a Rip had formed a few yards away. Charlie said, *Come.*

A shadow fell over them and Richard looked up. He expected to see some sort of bird. What he saw instead made his breath catch in his throat.

A long, horned head passed no more than fifty feet overhead followed by a mottled grey underbelly sandwiched between four scaled and claw-tipped legs the size of large trees. A great black tail dozens of times longer than Charlie's trailed behind dipping and lifting in opposition to the powerful thrust of immense, leathery wings. The air around them was stirred as if by a helicopter leaving behind a scent of sulfur and brimstone.

"You have got to be fucking kidding me," Richard said.

The dragon turned its head mid-flight and cast the pair a baleful glare; its eyes full of hunger and venom. Teeth the size of a man's leg stuck out of the creature's mouth at odd angles as if it had too many of the razor-sharp tines growing in there. To Richard's relief the dragon did not slow or change its flight path. Simply turned its head away and continued on towards the foothills behind them.

"You will be eaten," Richard said, shivering at the memory of the faerie's warning. As he and Charlie made their way to the Rip he wondered why the dragon had passed them by.

Not hunt in fields. Richard heard, and would have sworn the dog was laughing. *Allergic to faerie dust.*

At the Rip Richard knelt and hugged his dog for what would likely be the last time. Tears welled up again and he wiped them away on his sleeve.

"You really can't come?" Richard asked.

Charlie finished. Richard go to Messenger. Richard understand then. Charlie must go home.

"Wherever you're going, I hope there are fields just like this one," Richard said gently, "teeming with rabbits for you to chase all day long."

And piles of bones just for Charlie?

"Yes. That, too."

Richard destroy Key.

"No, pal. I won't kill her."

Then Richard die.

“Maybe,” Richard said. “But the Key will not. Not by my hand.”

Charlie Richard’s friend.

“I know, boy,” Richard said, tears threatening again. “I’m your friend, too. I’ll miss you.”

Richard turned and stepped into the Rip. Sunlight flashed across his face and in his eyes blurring his vision. He again saw the Seraph with Charlie, full of fire and holy light. This time he felt the incandescence as well as saw it; a pure, cleansing radiance that filled him with peace and clarity.

Richard’s path was chosen. Purified by the Seraph, he was whisked into the Rip beyond which the Messenger awaited.

Chapter 23

One step, began on one Earth and ended on another.

Richard stepped out of the Rip blinking rapidly, his pupils dilating. The Earth he'd just left had been bright, the sun warm on his back. This Earth was dimly lit and cold, the air heavy with moisture. A steady wailing sound like wind pounding the eaves of a house in a storm rose and fell around him, punctuated with intermittent thuds and crashes like distant cannon fire.

He looked back. The Rip had stayed in place this time; it's bright and swirling colors further spoiling his vision. He looked away, closed his eyes, and waited for the brilliant afterimage to fade. When he opened his eyes again he was facing away from the Rip, looking into the heart of a maelstrom.

A wall of clouds so high he could not see their tops soared an eighth of a mile away. Within the wall tumultuous shades of black and grey raced around each other, crackling with energy and electrical discharges. He turned counterclockwise, his eyes following the motion. It continued on and around, much further than he could see. It was like getting an ant's eye view of a football stadium.

He recognized the phenomena. He'd just never seen one on such a vast scale.

A hurricane. I've ripped into the eye of a hurricane.

A bolt of lightning leapt from the eye wall to the ground throwing up great clods of earth and rock and leaving behind a crater big enough to bathe in. A clap of thunder so loud it hurt his ears followed. Though the discharge had been several hundred yards away Richard felt its raw power as a rumbling beneath his feet and took a few steps back further into the eye of the storm.

Biggest damn hurricane ever imagined, he thought.

He looked towards the Rip but not directly at it; he didn't want to spoil his vision again. He briefly entertained the notion of stepping back through; leaving this strange and dangerous world behind in favor of the safe and wondrous Earth he'd just left. But the answers he sought were here, or so he'd been led to believe.

He couldn't find it in his heart to believe that Charlie

Seraphim

had led him astray. Still, he'd best find his answers quickly, before the far wall of the eye reached him. A storm this size could generate winds of such immense power that nothing would survive.

Above the howl of the wind and rumble of continuous thunder Richard heard a new sound, a beckoning and familiar sound from long ago Sunday afternoons. It took Richard a moment to sort out what it was—*church bells*—and the direction it was coming from. It was coming from deeper within the eye.

He followed the sound into the gloaming. As he walked he noticed there were trees here, as well as grass and other vegetation. Not sparse and damaged as he would have expected in the lee of the prevailing wall of a storm this size, but thick and lush, as if untouched by more than an afternoon shower. He passed one sturdy oak that was over seventy-five feet tall. He was no botanist but thought an oak that size had to be at least a hundred years old.

How could all this have survived the storm? Or *did the eye somehow form around it?* He was no meteorologist, either, but did not think such a thing was possible. Not that impossible meant much anymore.

He pushed into a dense thicket of white and pink *Rosa Carolinae*, the North American pasture rose, and felt a pull against his pants legs and a sting in his right arm as straight, needle-like thorns scratched at him. He hissed and rubbed his hand across the wounds—two of them felt quite deep—but felt no blood under his fingers. The pain faded away quickly like the fragments of a dream upon waking.

Once through the thicket he could make out plain, rough-hewn stone walls surrounding a structure in the distance. The walls were a good twenty feet high and looked to be a third as thick. A massive arched door, a dozen feet tall, was centered in the wall immediately before him. Beyond, three windowless towers of equal height reached skyward. Each was topped with a simple slate roof. Like the walls that protected them the towers were plain stone without any adornments or embellishments.

He reached the door. Closer inspection revealed that the ten foot wide portal was made up of six slabs of thick, rough cut wood bound with iron. Richard lifted his arm to knock.

Nothing ventured, he thought, *nothing gained.*

Before he could curl his fingers to rap on the door he heard the sound of a large bolt retracting on the other side. The door swung smoothly inwards despite its obvious weight. The double-fist sized iron hinges must be oiled regularly, Richard thought, amazed when the door opened with barely a sound.

A man wearing a brown robe and hood stood inside.

The Monk, Richard thought. *Is* this *the Messenger?*

The man pulled back his hood revealing black hair gone silver at the temples and slate grey eyes. He smiled. "Welcome, brother. It has been too long since last we met."

Richard was speechless. The man before him greeted him like an old friend, and called him *brother* with a sincerity that ruled out casual acquaintance. Richard had never seen the man before in his life.

"Who *are* you?" He asked.

"I have had many names." The man swept out his left arm in a *come in* gesture. Richard passed through the gate and the man closed it behind him. He closed it easily, with one hand. *That thing is* really *well oiled,* Richard thought.

"I once lived as Kaelen O'Connell," the man continued. "Another time as Mitchell Bryer. I even spent one thoroughly enjoyable lifetime as an Indian actor named Rajesh Khanna."

He laughed and led Richard away from the wall toward the two-story stone building it protected. The structure was three sided, like a triangle set inside a square. At each point of the triangle rose one of the towers Richard had spied above the wall. Like the towers, the building was plain and unadorned but had small openings every five feet or so. He estimated their size at two feet by three. He could see flickering light through some of them; behind others darkness held reign.

They approached the entrance to the building, a twin of the gate in the wall. Two steps before they reached it the door swung open as silently as had the gate. Two men in robes stepped out and took up position on either side, their faces shrouded under their hoods.

"Thank you," the man said to the pair and led Richard into a large hall.

Unlike the outside of the building—*is this a monastery or a fortress?* Richard wondered—the inside was lavishly adorned with tapestries, rugs, and fine, ornate furniture. Where drapery didn't cover the walls they bore hand-painted frescoes of angels and demons in battle, seraphim, cherubim, and celestial beings Richard did not recognize. All the frescoes were good, the labor of many hours. Some were exquisite.

The ceiling of the hall bore the largest single frieze Richard had ever seen: An image of Heaven's gates thrown wide, two warring groups of beings cast out and onto the Earth below. One group was insubstantial, shadow with form and nothing more. The second group was depicted as angels, both fighting with the shadow forms and being expelled along with them. It was the most awe-inspiring painting Richard had ever seen.

The man stopped in the middle of the vast hall and faced Richard. "Most recently," he said, "my name was Stephen Bana."

Richard gaped, tearing his eyes away from the ceiling.

"That's—" *Impossible,* he'd been about to say, but swallowed the word. Sophia was right. There was no such thing as impossible.

"They told you I was dead," Stephen said. "That I vanished through an uncharted Rip some hundred and seventy-five years ago and was thought lost forever."

"No. It actually never came up," Richard replied, finding his voice. "For you to be Stephen Bana, though, you'd have to be over two-hundred years old."

"Two-hundred and fifty-three, more or less," Bana corrected.

The two monks that opened the gate for Richard and Stephen had closed it behind them and quietly disappeared down a hallway. Now they—*or two others,* Richard thought, *who could tell with those hoods?*—reappeared. One carried a tray of cheese and bread, the other a crystal decanter of water and a tray of goblets. They set the trays on a long table in the middle of the hall that would easily seat twenty and pulled out two chairs at the near end, one on either side. Stephen sat in one and gestured for Richard to sit in the other.

Richard sat, staring at the man who said he was Stephen Bana. His hair was graying at the temples but was still full and vibrant. There were creases around his mouth where he smiled and more at the corners of his eyes and across his forehead, but his neck, where skin visibly thins first then loses elasticity and tends to hang in old age, was firm. He appeared to be no older than sixty.

Richard shook his head in wonder. "How is it possible that you're still alive?"

"*This* Earth," Stephen told him, pouring them both a goblet of water, "holds special properties in its atmosphere. Those who come here age far slower than on other Earths and do not suffer the indignities of old age for millennia. There is no Alzheimer's disease here, no senile dementia. Even injuries have no effect on this planet."

He cast his gaze at the scratches on Richard's arm. Deep, to be sure, but there was no blood yet and still no pain. It was if his body had had no reaction to the injury.

"You will need to have that attended to before you move on," he told Richard. "Once you leave it will start bleeding."

"Four days," Richard blurted, remembering.

"What's that?" Stephen asked.

"Sophia told me her Mirror had been shot four days before she found me. This Earth, if she was here—and I think she was—would explain why the wound was so fresh."

Stephen sighed. He'd picked up a half of the loaf of bread, home baked by the looks of it, and tore off two pieces. He handed one to Richard and set the other back on the tray.

"A tragic oversight on my part," he said. "I had no idea she'd been shot on the Homeworld. If she felt it at all the pain would have stopped within seconds of our arrival here. During her stay she never disrobed that I know of, so she was probably unaware of the wound. If she was she never said anything. It must have been awful for her to reach your Earth only to feel pain and confusion, and then fall to the effects of the injury."

"That injury was nothing compared to what BanaTech did to her, and tried to do to me," Richard said sharply. "Why did you send her to me? I'm assuming you sent her and didn't just throw her into a random Rip."

"Of *course* I sent her to you," Bana retorted, taken aback. "She was the mother of the Key. It was *her* idea to find you and bring you into this, to sort this whole mess out before the Multi-verse is destroyed. If she hadn't been delirious with fever and near death when she found you she would have explained the situation to you, pled for your assistance. We had no idea Jefferson would be able to locate her so quickly. Her death was not part of the plan."

Richard was uncertain if he believed the man's assertion but his grief at the mention of Sophia's death seemed genuine.

The founder of BanaTech was not at all what Richard expected. Not a larger than life enigma titivated in light who spoke with booming voice and trod with thunderous foot. Nor was he, as Richard would have expected of the legendary physicist Dr. Stephen Bana, the absent-minded genius who spoke in multi-syllabic words and used phrases that one needed three doctorates or a set of encyclopedias and a collegiate dictionary to understand. He appeared to be a very down to earth, *genuine* man. Despite his reservations, Richard found himself liking him very much.

"But *why* did you send her to me? I've accepted that I'm a Prime, or a Keeper as the Seraph called me, but I'm still just a man. How does a simple man stop BanaTech and these Infernal thingy's, or the destruction of the entire Multi-verse? How is it that a human child, Key or not, can control the focal point and destroy it in the first place?"

Bana's eyes widened in what Richard took for surprise. Then he burst out in deep, hearty laughter. Richard raised his eyebrows, not getting the joke. Bana struggled to regain his composure, and then reached for his water glass. When the laughing fit passed, he took a drink and set the glass back on the table.

"Oh, Richard," he said jovially, "you were always able to make me laugh."

"What are you talking about?" Richard said.

"The Key, dear Richard. The Key." Stephen answered, his cheeks blooming with good humor. "Why she's no more human than you or I."

Chapter 24

The Key is no more human than you or I. Richard struggled to wrap his mind around the statement and its meaning. *Not human? The Key isn't human? The man seated before me isn't human?*

I *am not human?*

"Of course I'm human." Richard leaned forward and placed a closed fist on the table. "I was born in Atwood, Kansas in 1975 to Patricia and Donald Farris, *both* human beings. Barring one incident I've lived a perfectly normal, *human* life for forty years. At least until all this nonsense started. I eat. I drink. I bleed. I can be hurt and will eventually die. How can you sit there and tell me I'm not human?"

"In the context of a single human lifespan you are correct." Stephen was smiling broadly, as a parent does when a child is on the verge of learning a new and valuable lesson. "Richard Farris *is* human, but you are so much more than Richard Farris. As your friend Charlie is much more than a dog and I am much more than Stephen Bana.

"I reacted the same way when I first discovered my true nature. I couldn't believe it, couldn't conceive of it. Despite my knowledge of the Rips and all that I had learned I refused to accept it. Eralah helped with that and I have since had a hundred and seventy-five years to understand it."

"You've met Eralah?" Richard asked.

"We are old friends." Stephen nodded. "She is the one who found me over a century ago and enlightened me. I sent her to you, just as she sent you on to the Seraph. It is an old custom, the steps to enlightenment. Protracted and deliberate, almost certainly out of date. But there are traditions that must be followed even now."

Richard sat back in his chair. He drank cool, refreshing water from the goblet set before him. In any other time and any other place, in spite of all that he'd experienced, he would have dismissed Bana's words as those of a madman. But on this Earth, in this time, in the eye of what had to be the largest hurricane to ever exist on any Earth he was willing to at least listen.

"I haven't had a hundred and seventy-five years to sort all this out," he said, "so you'll have to explain."

"I'll start at the beginning." Stephen took a wedge of cheese from the table, nibbled at it, and then drank from his own goblet. "Not the *true* beginning, you understand. Even two centuries is insufficient to unravel the account that far back in time. I'll start with what humans accept as the beginning; with the void.

"There was nothingness within the void, an immeasurable and incalculable expanse so vast that not even darkness existed within it. It simply *was*. This was abhorrent to the ALL, which exists outside the void and desires light and harmony above all else."

"The ALL?" Richard interrupted. "Are you referring to God?"

"God is a human word, Richard, as are the words angel and demon. Humans, with their limited understanding of the ALL and the Multi-verse tend to simplify what they do not understand. Out of innocence, out of ignorance, out of fear of the unknown. That's not a fault, it is the way it was meant to be. They are like children in a world with no adults to guide them. In time, several thousand millennia from now, they will come to understand the true nature of the ALL and what It represents. But we must act first so that they have the opportunity.

"The ALL saw the void as an artist sees an unmarked canvas; blank, but with limitless possibilities. Being pure energy, It took a piece of Itself and set it free inside the void. This created matter, which spun about, colliding and separating in accordance to the will of the ALL. Out of this the Multi-verse was born. You're familiar with the rest so I'll spare you the details of the division of night and day, the creation of land and the creatures that crawl upon it and skip to what humans think of as the sixth day, which was actually a span of time so infinitesimal as to be incalculable. That was when the ALL created man.

"Most biblical texts state that God created man and woman in His own image and gave them dominion over the creatures of the Earth, but that's another oversimplification. The ALL not only created man in Its own image, *but gave him a piece of Itself.* A small but incredibly powerful particle of the ALL resides in every living, breathing, human being."

Richard started to speak but Stephen held up a hand stilling him. "This particle of the ALL also gave man dominion over the Sabaoth. Man knows this as the Heavenly Host."

Richard blinked. "That would mean that man has power over the armies of God!"

"Yes," Stephen confirmed, "and not just the armies but the Seraphim, the Cherubim, what the Bible refers to as Archangels, the twenty four elders, and every other thing in heaven."

"That's..." Richard began but couldn't find a suitable word to express his astonishment.

"That's the root of the problem," Stephen said. "The ALL had created a new realm brimming with life. That was not unexpected. It had done so before and has done so since. But this time, for reasons none of us understood, It gave one of Its creations a precious gift. Selected one species out of billions and billions across a million-billion realms for an honor It had never bestowed before."

"It gave man a soul," Richard intuited.

Stephen nodded. "It elevated man to a position above all else in existence, second only to Itself. Dissension followed. There was a lot of jealousy, bitterness, and anger. Most of us were content to simply voice our opposition—we would not have dared move against the ALL—but there was one among us, one with the impudence to act on his resentment at being forced to bow down to what we all considered a lower species."

"Lucifer," Richard said. "Satan."

"Again, human words," Stephen said, "but they convey what the creature is. Darkness and evil personified. Our name for him and those that eventually followed him is *Infernal.*

"The Infernal raged against the ALL. So great was his fury that he sought to destroy what the ALL had created. It was the Infernal who tempted the human woman, who encouraged her to gain knowledge thus disobeying the laws the ALL had set forth for them. His plan was to demonstrate that this new form of life was unworthy of the gift the ALL had bestowed upon it in the hopes that the ALL would wipe humanity from existence."

"But the ALL didn't," Richard said. "It encouraged them to multiply."

"So It did," Stephen agreed, "which only infuriated the Infernal further. He viewed man's punishment for this transgression as punitive, a slap on the wrist. So he coerced one of them to murder, a capital crime even in our realm. Again the ALL did not destroy Its creation. It set Its mark upon the murderer instead, so that none could punish him. He wanders to this day among humanity, causing mayhem and chaos wherever he goes, but that, brother, is another story altogether.

"It was by then obvious to the Sabaoth that the ALL would never destroy man and that It had plans for these creatures. Plans, it was feared, that would upset the hierarchy that had been in place for a billion millennia. Many Sabaoth joined the Infernal; once wondrous creatures, full of light and harmony, but now wicked and corrupt, seeking only to destroy every good thing; the light, the Multi-verse, and most pointedly man and all of his creations. It continued this way for centuries until the ALL called upon us, the Keepers of the Throne, the one hundred and forty-four thousand who bear his unseen mark upon our foreheads.

"We too had reservations about man and what his existence meant for the Sabaoth. We cried out to the ALL that if It set others above us we could not protect the throne; our one and only duty and our sole purpose for existing. The ALL ignored our pleas, much as It had thus far ignored the actions of the Infernal. Some felt we should join the Infernal, aid them in their cause. But our duty was to the ALL and we were incapable of acting against It.

"The ALL gave each of us part of a manuscript. We were to deliver this manuscript to man so that he might learn of his place in the Multi-verse. The Infernal set upon us immediately, destroying entire parts of the manuscript and altering others. Their intent was to confuse man, keep him ignorant of his true place in the Multi-verse. *This* treachery could not go unanswered."

"The War in Heaven," Richard said. "I've read the account written by John Milton."

"Ah, Milton." Stephen smiled. "He had much of it right, you know. An amazing feat for a human being. But he had much of it wrong as well. He just didn't have the information necessary to furnish a full, detailed account. It *was* a war, though. The battle lines had been drawn and the ALL chose us, the Keepers of the Throne, as his defenders. We fought for millennia and many Sabaoth, both Infernal and Keepers, were slain. But none of us can truly die. We only rise again in another form, take up our swords, and the fighting continues. Neither side gained ground. It was simply senseless violence and bloodshed. In the midst of this war man continued to thrive and the Infernal continued their attempts to corrupt him. And we, the Keepers, continued to defend him."

Stephen sat back, took a piece of the bread from the table, and began chewing it. His eyes wandered over the fresco painted on the ceiling. Richard, caught up in the narrative and literally on the edge of his seat, waited for more. There was still so much he didn't know, did not understand. He *still* did not accept that he wasn't human; had heard nothing to convince him otherwise. The account of creation and the war that followed, while fascinating, was incomplete. And thus far had had nothing to do with him.

There has to be more, he thought; then said aloud, "And then?"

"Walk with me." Stephen said. He stood and stepped away from the table. Two of the robed men immediately appeared and began clearing it.

"Now wait a minute," Richard protested, then looked closely at the monk nearest him.

The man had leaned over to collect the goblets and trays. As he did so his hood fell back revealing the side of his face. His skin was a waxy grey color shot through with blue veins. His neck, similarly lined, was long and thin. Richard's eyes shot to the man's hands and he saw longer than usual fingers tipped with blood red fingernails that more resembled claws.

Richard bolted upright, knocking the heavy chair he'd been sitting in onto its side. The clatter startled the monk and he jerked erect, his hood falling back completely. He stared at Richard and *hissed*. He head was bald, his eyes a penetrating shade of yellow. His ears tapered to a point at the pinna. It was his teeth, yellow and stained, the canines unnervingly long and sharp, which held Richard transfixed to the spot.

"*Christ!*" Richard barked.

"Have no fear," Stephen said as the monk replaced his hood, gathered the trays, and left the hall without a word. "The indigenous population of this Earth suffers a rare disease that alters their biology drastically. They are harmless here."

"Is that a fucking *vampire?*" Richard demanded.

"On any other Earth he would be," Stephen answered. "But on this Earth they are innocuous. And in service to the ALL."

Richard ran his hand across his head and breathed deeply. "I thought vampires were a myth. Stories cooked up to tell around the campfire and at sleepovers. Bad novels written to keep readers awake at night."

"You will find that what you take for fantasy is rooted in truth," Stephen said, extending his arm and leading Richard away from the table. "Every book ever written, every movie ever filmed, every creature wondrous or foul exists on some Earth, somewhere. Every course of action that can be taken by man or beast has been or will be. What humans call the imagination is really a subconscious awareness of the Multi-verse and all it contains. Some merely dream of it, others write it down; perhaps out of some collective but unconscious need to share their knowledge."

"You said they're harmless here. On this Earth," Richard said, following Stephen down a passageway to the right of the hall. "Does that mean that Stoker wasn't full of it? There *are* vampires running around out there killing people?"

"*Every* course of action, Richard," Stephen responded.

Richard whistled long and low. The implications were staggering.

At the end of the passageway Stephen unbolted a wooden, man-sized door and led Richard up a winding staircase. They passed through another door at the top and emerged onto a long balcony overlooking a well-manicured botanical garden. Flowers both familiar and foreign to Richard were laid out in herringbone patterns. At the center of the garden was a fountain shedding water in two different directions across the foliage. Stone paths followed along both sides of each waterway. Japanese style bridges joined the two paths at each end.

This section of the monastery had been out of Richard's line of sight as he approached the structure. Beyond the walls, night had fallen. He looked out, taking in the view of the eye wall of the storm. It throbbed with energy. Lightning coruscated within. Thunder shouted out in joyous rejoinder. Wind whipped the briefly illuminated clouds to inconceivable velocities. He found the sheer savage power of the storm invigorating.

"Look closer," Stephen urged from his right elbow.

Richard did, uncertain what it was he was looking for. Then it dawned on him. While the winds inside the eye wall raced counterclockwise at a frenetic pace the wall itself was not shifting in any direction. It was as if the storm were held in place, neither strengthening nor diminishing; a hurricane that would rage for eternity.

"It doesn't move," Richard said. "How is that possible?"

"Much like the moon on your Earth," Stephen said, "this Earth rotates in a synchronous rotation so that the same face is always directed at the sun. Much of the planet is uninhabitable, one side a molten ruin, the other a frozen wasteland. We are in the green zone, a small sliver of land ninety miles wide between the two with a breathable atmosphere and tolerable climate. The storm is the result of cold air from the arctic side of the planet colliding with the heated air from the volcanic side. It is self-sustaining and, like the Great Red Spot of Jupiter, a semi-permanent feature that may last for millennia."

"How long has it been here?" Richard asked.

"The monastery was erected in the eye of this hurricane long before I arrived here," Stephen said. "And it will still be here long after I am gone."

"Amazing," Richard said.

"It is but that's not why I wanted you to see this." Stephen turned and faced Richard. "This hurricane seems perpetual; immutable. It has existed far longer than anyone now here remembers. So long that it predates the history of this Earth's inhabitants. But everything reaches an end. One day this storm will begin to die out and life on this Earth will be forever changed. The storm that now provides fresh water in the form of rain, shelter from the extreme climes, and a consistent supply of oxygen from the winds will wane, eventually breaking up and vanishing completely. Then the inhabitants will be abandoned, left to live or die by their own devices."

"What's your point?" Richard said.

"*We* are my point. The Keepers, the Infernal, even man, Its wondrous and most loved creation." Stephen's voice deepened solemnly. "The ALL has abandoned us, Richard. We questioned It's will and It abandoned us all."

Chapter 25

Stephen Bana gripped the railing and lowered his head. He let out a sob of anguish and loss, gripped the rail tighter, then turned and left the balcony without another word. Richard followed, closing the door behind them. The man's sorrow—*if he* is *a man*, Richard thought, then, *and what does that make me?*—at banishment from the ALL was apparent. What were the consequences of a divine being severing its relationship with all it had created? What were the consequences for those *creations*?

With Richard trailing behind Stephen wound his way back down the staircase and through a narrow hallway that led to a junction in the corridor. One passage led back to the foyer and the dining hall. Stephen chose the second, leading Richard deeper into the monastery.

"I'm confused," Richard said. Stephen stopped and turned to him. The older man's eyes were still red from unbidden tears but he'd regained much of his composure. "Charlie, the Seraph, said that humans mean nothing to the ALL. Compared us to termites. Yet you've told me that humanity is the ALL's most beloved creation. It doesn't make sense."

"It will when you've heard the entire story," Stephen assured him.

He led Richard into a chamber that looked like a lounge. Massive, rough-hewn chairs and couches padded in red and blue velvet filled the room from wall to wall. Luxurious brocaded pillows of various sizes littered every surface including several large, body sized cushions that lie on the floor. Richard had never heard of a monastery with such lavish amenities as those he'd seen in the dining hall, the gardens, and now in this room. Piety notwithstanding, abstinence was obviously not a vow these monks took seriously.

Stephen seated himself on a long couch and gestured to a chaise lounge at its side. Richard eyed the cushions—hand embellished with fanciful creatures—and decided he'd likely fall asleep within moments of sitting. He chose a nearby chair instead.

"When the ALL banished the Infernal and the Keepers," Stephen said, "It did more than sever our connection to the Kingdom and the Throne. It left this realm altogether. It moved on, abandoned this Multi-verse and left us behind to destroy ourselves or prosper on our own."

"If the ALL moved on, then who or what is behind all of this?" Richard asked. "Who sent the Seraph and where did it go when it left me? Charlie told me he was going home; back to the ALL. How can he go somewhere that isn't there anymore?"

"It *is* still there," Stephen said. "Like a great empty mansion, desolate and forlorn to be sure, but still there. When the ALL moved on it left behind the part of Itself that It used to create the Multi-verse. It's a form of pure energy without consciousness or caring, but it still exists. To remove that…*spark* would have been to destroy a part of Itself. That is something It cannot do."

"The Source?" Richard said. "Is that the spark you mean?"

"That's what BanaTech calls it, yes," Stephen said. "They see it as a limitless well of energy, a never ending and self-sustaining engine to be tapped at will. BanaTech has no concept of the ALL, no clue that the Source is a remnant, a ghost, an imprint of the ALL."

"The Infernal must know what the Source is," Richard said. "Don't they?"

"Of course." Stephen replied. "But in their present form they are cut off from it, unable to touch its power and bend it to their will.

"Before the war," Stephen continued, "Humanity *was* the ALL's most cherished creation. It breathed life into them, pardoned their disobedience, even sent a revenant of Itself to them to absolve their offenses."

"You mean Jesus Christ, don't you?" Richard asked.

"On yours and many other Earth's It was known as Jesus Christ, yes. On others It was known by other names: Mahdi, Yeshua, Quetzalcoatl. It appeared in many forms to many people, but Its purpose was always the same; to forgive humanity its sins so that they could ultimately be united with the ALL. But the Infernal interfered yet again. Corrupted mankind and distorted their thinking. The physical form the ALL had taken was murdered on many Earths. On others it was rejected as a false prophet."

"Wait," Richard said. "Biblical history states that God *sent* Christ to Earth to die. His death was to pay for all of our sins in blood."

"That was the ALL's intent," Stephen said. "But the revenant was not killed to attain enlightenment, to atone for sin and be washed in the blood of the lamb. The revenant was *murdered.* Out of fear, jealousy and greed.

"This so offended the ALL that It washed Its hands of us. The Infernal were cast down, stripped of their physical form and reduced to mere shadows. Beings of energy and thought alone. We, the Keepers of the Throne, were also cast out. We were forced to live as humans on the many Earths, in part to act as guardians of the Source, and as punishment for questioning the will of the ALL. Since there was no longer a throne to protect we became the Keepers of what remained of the ALL."

"What of the Seraphim?" Richard asked. "The Cherubim, and the rest?"

"They were not cast out," Stephen said. "They were left in a Kingdom without a king.

"There were twelve Seraphim throughout the Kingdom who were tasked with the purification of supplicants. It was their duty to cleanse the worthy who sought counsel from the messengers of the ALL. Without the ALL to guide them they are mostly lost and alone, without purpose. They seek solace with some of us throughout the Multi-verse. Your friend Charlie was the first Seraph to reveal itself in centuries."

"Cherubim, more than any other Saboath, are offended by the Infernal. The four were originally the guardians of the entrance to what humans call the Garden of Eden and the Tree of Knowledge. When they failed at that task they were demoted. Their new role was to bring worthy humans before the Seraph to be purified. With the ALL absent and no longer communicating with mankind there were few to bring before the Seraph. Now they do what they can to mitigate the dark influence the Infernal provokes in man by inspiring the greatest and purest of all emotions, love."

"Eralah is Cherubim?" Richard asked.

"She most certainly is," Stephen said. "Cherubim can assume any outward appearance they choose. Eralah came to you in a form that she knew would get your attention. Had you seen her as she truly is—she has four heads, you know—it is doubtful you would have accepted her counsel."

Richard smiled at this. "I was expecting to see Hatfield or Jefferson outside that door. If I'd seen a four-headed Cherub instead of the visage of Katie Marsh, I probably would have run the other way."

"Eralah knew that." Stephen returned his smile. "There has been no sign of the remaining Saboath. The twenty-four Elders vanished shortly after the ALL did. No one knows where they are or what they are doing."

"Who are the Elders?" Richard asked. "And where are the Archangels? Michael, Gabriel, and the rest? Aren't they out there somewhere, fighting the Infernal?"

For the second time laughter overcame Stephen Bana. Richard waited patiently to find out why his question was so funny.

"I'm sorry," Stephen said, recovering from his attack of delight.

He leaned forward, reached out and laid his hand upon Richard's wrist. A thrill ran up Richard's arm at the contact. For a moment he was somewhere else. *Someone* else.

He smelled metal and blood, heard the clang of rough armor and screaming. He saw crimson sprawled across the doorway of a small dwelling, up the posts and across the lintel. A sign, he understood, to pass that house by. The next dwelling had no such markings and he entered. With a heavy heart he drew a sword and sought out the first born.

"Take no offense." Stephen withdrew his hand and the vision dissolved, leaving Richard confused, shaken, and with a feeling of great sadness. Had he taken lives? *Children's* lives?

"You're an innocent victim of one of John Milton's fallacies," Stephen said. "Having lived so long as a man you've forgotten your true nature. The Archangels Milton refers to are not separate from the one-hundred and forty-four thousand but were chosen by the ALL from within their ranks. *We* were the Archangels, Richard. You and I. And you, my brother, were the most revered of us all."

"But that's—"Richard began, then stopped.

He'd meant to say impossible, but he'd seen too seen too many impossible things already—an honest to God *dragon*, for chrissakes— and vampires in the flesh. After all he'd been through how could he rule out anything as impossible?

"For far too long I rejected what I've just told you," Stephen said. "If I'd fully understood what I stumbled across all those years ago in the North American desert, the scope of what I was tinkering with, I would never have allowed BanaTech to finance my research. I would never have given them access to my work and the Rips. But I was excited about a new and earth shattering discovery that had the potential to change the course of human history."

"You *did* change the course of human history," Richard said, thinking that he would have been just as excited if he'd discovered the Rips, the Mirrors and the Multi-verse. And probably still as horrified by everything he'd seen so far. "But not necessarily for the better."

"I did," Stephen said, and sighed. A sigh of resignation, of acceptance. "I'm responsible for all of this. All of these lost lives and corrupted Earths. BanaTech's tyranny and the threat they pose to the rest of the Multi-verse. I gave BanaTech this power in the name of science, in the name of progress. They repaid me by hanging *my* name on that ravenously grinding machine they call a corporation." Stephen leaned forward, staring with such intensity that Richard could almost feel his eyes on his skin. "Do you have any idea how that makes me feel?"

"I can't even begin to imagine," Richard said humbly.

"But it's irrelevant at this point." Stephen leaned back, sighed again and rubbed his eyes. "It was long ago and can't be changed now. BanaTech is on the cusp of opening and maintaining an artificial Rip that they think will grant them unlimited access to the Multi-verse. Unlimited dominion over everyone and everything in existence.

"I have learned so much since Eralah led me to the Rip that brought me here. She opened my eyes to the ALL and Its design. We cannot go back. We can only move forward and try to stop what Alex Jefferson and I began all those years ago before it is too late."

"What you and *Alex Jefferson* began?" Richard exclaimed, feeling as if the older man had just hit him over the head with a brick.

"The same Alex Jefferson who murdered a woman before my eyes? Who killed my dog, destroyed my life, and has been chasing me across the Multi-verse ever since trying his very level best to kill me?"

"Not the very same Alex Jefferson, no." Stephen said. "The Alex Jefferson I knew died over a hundred years ago. The man beleaguering you and Sophia Bledell now is one of his Mirrors. And next in line to assume the mantle of Elder."

"Good Christ," Richard muttered, thinking there was no end to the surprises the Multi-verse held. "If that vicious bastard ascends to power the Multi-verse truly will be lost."

"Mirrors are like-minded, Richard," Stephen said. Richard remembered that Sophia had once told him as much. "Very few of them differ in their principles or ideologies. The three Elders who have thus far held power have been every bit as malicious and brutal as the man you've had experience with. That is why we must stop them now, before it is too late."

"*We*?" Richard asked. "Why am I a part of this?"

It was the question he'd been asking himself for months, since he'd first trod through the snow in his backyard to find a wounded stranger and assumed responsibility for her well-being. He'd found no satisfying answer with either Sophia. Nor with Eralah or Charlie—he still thought of the Seraph as Charlie, despite what he'd seen and heard.

"I may be a Keeper, maybe even one of the Archangels as you say. Nevertheless, I'm still just Richard Farris. Just a man. Aside from there being strength in numbers, why do you need me to help bring down BanaTech? To hide their Key and avoid some sort of Multi-versa apocalypse?"

"Because I can no longer leave this Earth." Stephen rose from his couch and extended his arm. "Come. I want you to meet someone."

Stephen left the lounge without another word. Richard pulled himself erect and followed. As he left the room he passed a hooded figure and cast a sidelong glance at him. *Vampires*, he thought surreally. *What's next*? *Werewolves*? *Big Foot*?

"How old do I look to you?" Stephen asked when they reached the corridor.

"I'd guess sixty, sixty-five at the outside," Richard replied. "Not too bad for a man who claims to be two-hundred and fifty-three."

"Indeed." Stephen laughed. "I was only forty-seven when I stepped through the Rip that brought me here and I stopped aging. The one trip I took to another Earth, brief as it was, aged me to what appears to you to be sixty."

"You aged almost twenty years in a few minutes?" Richard was stunned.

"Less than a minute," Stephen replied. "There are only a handful of Earths throughout the Multi-verse with the unique atmospheric properties of this one. You've now been to two of them."

Richard pondered just which Earth he'd visited that had the same curative powers. He had an idea which one it might have been but Stephen interrupted before he could ask.

"They are wonderful worlds but were never meant for those who were not born there. We enjoy their therapeutic qualities as long as we're on planet, but those qualities are lost to us the moment we leave. The same is not true for the indigenous population. They carry this Earth's properties with them if they leave, granting them near immortality.

"When *we* leave time descends on us like a falcon on its prey. You've been here less than a day, Richard. When you leave you will suffer no ill effects, save that injury to your arm. I have been here nearly two-hundred years. I would not survive long enough to do what must be done."

They entered a stairwell and began climbing to the second level of the monastery.

"You told me we never truly die," Richard said as they left the stairwell and started down yet another long corridor. "That we are reborn on another Earth in another body. Why is dying a problem?"

"A natural effect of our reincarnation is the loss of our memories," Stephen said. "Everything I have learned here, my discoveries of our true selves, our true roles, and the nature of the ALL will be lost. I will simply be another infant born to random parents on a random Earth. A Keeper, but like you not too long ago, ignorant of what that means. By the time I discover the truth about the Infernal and their plan, *if* I were discover it again, it would be too late."

"What plan is that, exactly?" Richard stopped beside Stephen at a door no different than any other door in the long hallway.

"Here we are," Stephen said, depressing the latch and pushing the door open.

Behind it was a small, plain room with a single bed, a nightstand, and a comfortable looking chair. Beside the chair was an easel with an unfinished but rather good painting of a vast field populated with dragonflies and faeries. An ominous black form, as yet unfinished by the artist, loomed in the sky. Richard thought he could guess what it would be.

A single window took up most of the exterior wall of the room. A small figure stood there, gazing out at the turbulent storm; a female child about eight or nine years old. She wore a tartan, knee-length skirt under a white blouse, her hair pulled back in a black ponytail. Richard noted specks of paint on the hand resting on the windowsill.

She turned at the sound of the door opening. Richard was startled by her youthful resemblance to Sophia. Her eyes widened at the sight of him. Then she broke out into a grin that threatened to halve her face.

"Michael!" she cried, and thrust herself forward into Richard's arms as a child would a long lost father.

Chapter 26

Richard smelled salt and felt water at his back; a tremendous pressure that threatened to engulf and overwhelm him. He arched his back against the weight, felt his powerful wings—*wings?*—extend even further against the tide, blocking its course. He pushed backwards, straining with his legs, parting the waters.

"Yes!" Uriel cried, a grin on her face.

She stood opposite him, looking nothing like the girl child who'd thrust herself into his arms moments ago. She was taller, as broad of chest and muscled as he. Thick black hair twisted in a plait bound with silver and gold lashing. Gone was the tartan skirt and blouse; in their place was a brocaded robe and bronze cuirass. A xiphos, or similar single-hand sword hung from a baldric beneath her left arm. Two immense wings were thrust out to either side, impossibly long and powerful, likewise holding back a sea of water.

Richard looked down confirming that he wore similar garb, then out across the channel he and Uriel had parted.

The chasm was filled with people. From Richard's perspective they looked no bigger than ants. Wearing tattered robes and carrying few possessions most were on the brink of exhaustion. They took no notice of the massive pair dividing the waters for them—*can they not see us?*—crossing the seabed with great haste, pursued from the far banks by an army of men in linen loincloths carrying leather shields and nasty looking spears. Others rode in horse drawn chariots.

As the ragtag band of refugees cleared the seabed Gabriel swooped down from above, his massive wings churning the air with such force that sand and mud flew from the seafloor clogging the wheels of the chariots and bringing the army to a halt in the center of the channel.

"Now, Michael!" Uriel cried. Without hesitation Richard withdrew his wings and took to the air, stranding the Egyptian army in the middle of the Red Sea where they were crushed to death or drowned by the enormous pressure of the resurging waters.

"Oh my *God!*" Richard cried as he stumbled backwards into the wall. The unexpected weight of the girl in his arms and the awe-inspiring vision he'd just had conspired to send him crashing to the floor as he snapped back to the present.

His head spun. He could still feel immeasurable power thrumming through his body, still smelled the sea. Still felt the glorious sensation of wind beneath powerful wings.

"Eons ago," Stephen Bana told him, "humans could not hope to understand or speak our true names so they gave us names of their own. You they named Michael, myself Gabriel, and Elianna here," he pointed to the child standing before Richard with a knowing grin on her face, "Uriel."

"You knew that would happen," Richard said, gaining his footing as the residual sensations of the vision faded.

"I thought it might," Elianna said, clasping her hands demurely in front of her chest. "When I first met Gabriel…*Stephen*…I had a similar experience."

"Wait," Richard said. He still didn't trust his legs. He moved to the bed and sat on the edge of the mattress. Elianna moved to his side and sat there but did not touch him. "I thought you were severely autistic and incapable of communicating with others."

"On any other earth she is." Stephen settled in to the lone chair in the room. "The same properties that keep this world's inhabitants in a perpetual state of young adulthood have corrected the alteration in nerve-cell to synapse connections in her brain. Here she thinks and communicates as any other child would. It's the reason her mother stayed as long as she did. Imagine her joy at being able to interact with her child at long last. Were it not for the gravity of the situation she'd have been quite content to remain here forever."

"I'd say she communicates a damn sight better than other children," Richard said, then cast the pair an accusing glance. "You might have warned me."

"There is no time for such pleasantries," Stephen said, unapologetic. "Your companion will be waking shortly if she hasn't already done so and will be wondering where you are."

Richard thought that was an understatement then realized he hadn't spared a thought for Sophia since he'd left her sleeping in the loft of a barn on another Earth. He had no idea how he was going to explain all of this to her.

"Damn," Richard said. "If she wakes up and I'm not there, goes ripping off trying to find me…" He trailed off. There was no way she could hope to find him in an infinite Multi-verse with the random nature of the Rips. It was far more likely that BanaTech would find her first.

"She'll be fine for a while yet," Elianna said. "Eralah is keeping watch over her."

"You know about Sophia?" Richard asked. He had not given any thought to what Elianna might think about her mother's Mirror. Or what had happened to the first Sophia Bledell.

"I know she isn't my mother," Elianna answered, her eyes filling with tears. "My mother is dead."

Heedless of the consequence of their last contact Richard gathered the child into his arms and hugged her. He said nothing. There were no words he could think of that would comfort her. Key or not, Keeper or not, Elianna was still a child, and children hurt most when those they love are taken from them. She cried on his shoulder for a while and then pulled away.

"Stephen is right," she said, wiping tears from her cheeks and smiling a brave smile. "There is little time and you still have much to learn. We need to end this. Now. And that starts with you knowing everything we do."

To Stephen, Elianna said: "Will it work?"

"It worked for us," Stephen responded. He stretched out his hands to both her and Richard.

Elianna took Stephen's proffered hand and one of Richard's in her own, and then looked at Richard expectantly. Richard eyed Stephen's hand quizzically.

"What are we doing?" he asked.

"Within circles lie knowledge," Stephen said cryptically. "You'll want to hold on. It may be a bumpy ride."

Richard took a deep breath. *What the hell*, he thought. *Sometimes the only way out is to go further in.*

He grasped Stephen's hand and the world vanished around him.

If asked to describe it Richard would have said it felt like having a hook thrust into the center of his chest and being pulled forwards at the speed of light. There was a moment of sensation like being dragged along a dark tunnel, then light exploded before him, rushed around and through him as water streaks through a sieve.

It's like the light in Rips, he thought, *but a thousand times more intense.*

Then the sensation of motion stopped and he looked about in wonder. They were in a vast chamber filled with light and colors so vibrant they seemed to be alive. If the light they'd passed through—that had passed through *them*—to get here had been a thousand times brighter than that in the Rips then this was a million times more so. Beauty and passion flourished in that light. And love. Love so powerful it made the heart ache and want to sing simultaneously.

Uriel was to his left, powerful and strong, restored to the beauty from his vision. Gabriel was on his right. There was no similarity to the aged and thin Stephen Bana. This magnificent creature had a mane of golden hair that cascaded down his shoulders like water caressing rock above a fall. Richard shook his own head and felt hair as fine as silk stroke his shoulders above a cuirass of fine gold. He flexed muscles in his back he hadn't had before, felt the magnificent beat of air beneath wings again and rose above the others. He took two turns around the boundless space they occupied, delighting in the sensation of air rushing past his body. He performed a perfect barrel roll and laughed out loud. The sound startled him with its booming intensity.

He returned to Gabriel and Uriel's side grinning what felt to be a broad and spectacular grin.

"He remembers *that* well enough," Uriel said, smiling.

"You've always been a show-off, brother," Gabriel said with a smile.

Except it isn't a smile, Richard thought. *Because we don't have faces, or bodies, or even wings. Not in the sense humans think of them, anyway. Human eyes would burst into flame at the sight of us, their eardrums would shatter explosively, their very brains igniting into fiery ash. We are beings of pure energy. Not as powerful as the All to be sure, or even what they call The Source. But energy nonetheless. And to see us as we truly are would destroy them in an instant.*

"That's correct, brother," Uriel told him.

Why, Richard thought, *Uriel is not even a female. Nor is she male. None of us are. Our human forms may have gender but we do not. We do not die and are not reborn, rather we reincarnate spontaneously. We simply go on and on for all eternity having no need of the messy ritual humans call reproduction.*

"Again you are correct," Gabriel said.

"Where are we?" Richard asked, and was startled by the sound of his voice.

It was not words that came out, not words that a human ear would have recognized anyway. What came out was more like singing; a sound of such complex melodious and harmonious transitions that no choir of human voices could ever hope to imitate it.

"Nowhere," Uriel replied in that sing-song voice. "And *everywhere*."

"I don't understand," Richard said.

"The realm the Multi-verse exists within is but a circle," Gabriel explained. "And each universe exists within that circle, completing a circle of its own, just as galaxies and solar systems are circles existing within *those* circles. As we joined our separate consciousnesses, *we* became a circle. In this circle we may share our thoughts and memories unencumbered by the weight of human emotion and physical frailty we have endured for so long."

"Where are our bodies?" Richard asked.

"Right where we left them," Uriel answered. "We shed them in that time and place as they cannot exist in this one. Where we exist now, there *is* no time. No *place*. We are in the *Elsewhere.* Here we are as we were, our *true* selves. No human form could ever hope to survive here."

"*Why* are we here?" Richard asked.

"So that you may learn, brother," Gabriel said. "Learn, and *remember*."

Listen, brother:

Eons ago, long before the creation of this realm and before time itself existed the ALL formed us from Its light. To act as Its companions and to serve. To rejoice at our very existence.

This we did without hesitation. We knew no other way. At that time, before humans existed, we knew only the radiance and peace bestowed upon us by the ALL and the glory of service to our Almighty Creator.

Then the ALL created humankind, bestowing upon them a gift It had granted no other; a part of Itself the humans have come to call a soul. This gift holds great power for them though they little know how to use it. It comes with the power of choice. *The choice to serve the ALL or refuse It. The choice to accept Its light or reject it. The choice to live their lives as they see fit, to be damned for eternity or, upon the expiration of their human forms, become one with the light. One with The Source. One with the ALL.*

Despite this gift they are lowly creatures, weak and frail. They cannot, in human form, exist outside the confines of their Earth or the constructs they create with their incredible imaginations. Their imaginations are another gift as well. They themselves are creators. *They've created marvelous cities around the globe, modified their personal habitats to suit their needs, adapted plants, animals, and even themselves on a genetic level so that they enjoy better foods and live longer lives through the science they call medicine. They've even, some of them, left the confines of their worlds and traveled out among the stars.*

As we were but servants to the ALL, fated to be reborn again and again in this form and thus denied these gifts as well as union with our Creator, an emotion none had felt before began to ripple throughout our ranks: Jealousy.

Jealousy quickly becomes anger. Anger becomes hatred. And hatred begets violence.

As a whole we struggled with these dark emotions. We were born of the light and had never known darkness. Never felt its cold touch or empty embrace. It was alien to us; foreign. The birth of evil among our kind. The strongest among us overcame it, suppressed our anger and defeated our hatred. Others, the Infernal, were unable to resist its allure. They seized choice *for themselves and rebelled against the ALL.*

You know of the war that followed and our subsequent banishment. Know of the treachery of the Infernal and their continued efforts to debase and ultimately destroy humankind. These acts caused humanity to turn their backs on the ALL and fall upon each other with acts of greed, odium, and murder, condemning them to lives of hardship, grief, and struggle.

What you do not know is the cost.

When the ALL abandoned this realm, casting us down into human form so that we would know the burden of their existence, share in their frailties and likewise suffer their dark emotions, it also severed Itself from The Source. Humans retained their earthly gifts, their knowledge and ability to expand on whatever they can conceive of, but lost their ability to become one with the ALL. When they die, as they must, their souls do not join with The Creator as some of them believe. Rather, they ascend to another plane, a circle *if you will, where they have been waiting for centuries, lost and alone. They have no form, no thought or consciousness. They are but energy and light;* power, *awaiting a union with the ALL that may never come.*

And they are vulnerable.

While we, the Keepers of the ALL, were cast down into human form, the Infernal were hurled into the very darkness they had so willingly embraced. They were discorporated, denied any form save that of shadow. They can manipulate and meddle with the human psyche, can even occupy their forms for short periods of time, but they cannot act directly. Cannot cause injury or kill, nor influence physical objects. They are but apparitions. Mere thought without substance.

What's more, as insubstantial entities, they cannot travel through the Rips; cannot form a circle as we have done here. They cannot leave the various Earths they were cast down upon and join together with the rest of their brothers; neither for communion with one another, nor to further their insidious goals.

Whether or not this was the intent of the ALL is unclear. What is clear is that they've found a champion among the very humans they despise. A man with the power and authority to direct their resources into building a device that, once completed, will draw all Earths together. Cause every Rip to converge, thus freeing the Infernal to join together. As the Multi-verse becomes one, with each Earth flowing into the other assuring the destruction of all of them, so too will all circles become one. The Infernal will gain access to the souls of humanity. They will corrupt that power and mold it into darkness, use it to reshape the Multi-verse in their image. Light and love will be obliterated, all good things snuffed out. The Multi-verse will be reshaped into a living hell for the very souls used to create it.

Once begun, there is little we can do to stop it. We too would be at the mercy of the Infernal for all of eternity.

But there is hope.

The Infernal have deceived their champion into believing that he is acting in his own interests. That the machine he is building will gain him absolute power over all that exists in the Multi-verse. He is ignorant of their plan and naïve to the true consequences the Focal Point Generator will bring about. To keep him oblivious to their scheme and ensure his continued cooperation they have used misinformation and half-truths as is their method. He is unaware of our true nature and believes our existence to be no more than an aberration. A fluke of evolution.

He does not fear us. Therefore, he underestimates us.

He requires The Key to unlock his machine, believing it is the unique chemical defect in the child's brain and not who she truly is that will trigger the device. The truth is quite the opposite. Any Keeper can learn to will a Rip into existence, manipulating both its ingress and terminus. All that is required is that we accept what we are. That and a little practice.

Now listen closely brother because our time in this circle is now very short. We cannot be gone long from our physical bodies else they will perish. We will be reborn and what you have learned here will be lost. As it is we will lose much because the human mind was never meant to contain this knowledge.

Elianna, the girl child, must be destroyed. The Infernal will not stop seeking her until BanaTech has her back in its grasp. Once removed from the sanctuary Earth her mind will again become unbalanced and she will not be able to control her ability to form a Rip once stimulated by the machine. This Rip combined with the energies of The Source will *cause the convergence of the Multi-verse and all will be lost.*

Once destroyed, Uriel will be reborn into another human body and balance will be restored.

There is no other choice.

Chapter 27

"Bullshit!" Richard cried.

They'd returned to their bodies in much the same manner they'd left them. Richard felt the hook-like sensation in his chest—pulling backwards this time—had passed out of the light and into a dark tunnel, and then opened his eyes to find himself still seated on the edge of Elianna's bed.

He'd lost all but the essence of their—*conversation? communion?*—while within the circle. Had little memory of their actual words and meaning. What he did recall was the warm brilliance surrounding them and the musical lilt of their language; the exquisite resonance of a thousand wind chimes stirring harmoniously in a breeze.

"There really is no other choice," Stephen told him. He looked to Elianna and she nodded her head. "She must be destroyed."

"Fuck that and fuck you!" Richard exclaimed, rising to his feet and leaning over the older man. "I will not kill a child!"

Elianna rose. She turned Richard's face to her and took his shaking hands in her own.

"It has to be done," she said soothingly. "If I could do it myself, right here and now, I would. But I can't die on this Earth. No cut would bleed and no gunshot would stop my heart. If I left this Earth to do it my autism would return before I had the chance. It's my sacrifice to make. For humanity and the ALL. I've accepted that."

He looked at her, his expression a mixture of sadness and disbelief.

"Well I don't accept it," he said. "And I won't do it."

"You must," Stephen said. "The survival of mankind is imperative."

Richard rounded on Stephen.

"If it so goddamned important," he spat, "then why haven't you done it yourself? Why bring me here to do your dirty work?"

"Because I cannot leave this world."

"Sure you can," Richard said, "but you could die within minutes and you can't have that, can you? It's okay to sacrifice the kid. Why the hell not? But risk your own life in the process? No fucking way."

His realized his voice had entered a low register barely above a whisper. It was a tone of warning, of impending violence. He'd been pushed too far and was about to plummet over the edge of the abyss where his darkest, most brutal instincts lie. Whether or not he could inflict real damage on another human being on this sanctuary Earth was irrelevant. He was about to respond with unchecked fury. He pulled himself back, both mentally and physically, before that could happen.

"You've been hiding out on this Earth for decades; knowing what was coming and doing nothing about it. You're a coward," he added before stepping away.

"Cowardice is a human affliction," Stephen said, "and like any emotion, in these forms we are subject to them. *Slaves* to them. Be that as it may, I don't agree. The knowledge I have acquired on this Earth, a mere fraction of which you are now privy to, simply cannot be lost to us. To lose that knowledge with our rebirth would give BanaTech an advantage that we could never overcome. Destroying Elianna would only be a temporary measure at that point. Given time and the continued counsel of the Infernal they would eventually succeed at creating an artificial Rip without our intervention."

"Then she stays here." Richard said. "BanaTech doesn't know where she is and couldn't possibly track the Rips I traveled to get here. She stays here and I go back and find a way to destroy their machine."

Elianna crossed the room to and again took Richard's hands. She gazed into his eyes.

"We can't stay here, brother," she said. "They won't stop looking for me. Ever. Eventually, even if it takes a hundred years, they will find me. And if they stumble across a sanctuary Earth, if the *Infernal* learn of their existence and their effect on human longevity, BanaTech will seek them out and inhabit them. They would be nearly immortal. What damage could they cause, with or without their Focal Point Generator, if their Elder lives forever?"

Richard looked for a flaw in her reasoning but could find none. He sighed.

"Then we run," he said. "Far and fast. We go back and get Sophia and pull a Pink Floyd. *Run like hell.* We'll avoid the sanctuary Earths and stick to the more remote worlds where BanaTech has no presence. The RLP will alert us if and when BanaTech shows up and we'll hightail it out of there before they catch up to us. If I can learn to call upon Rips at will they won't stand a chance. It's an infinite Multi-verse. We can run until you find a way to destroy BanaTech and their machine or until we all die of old age."

Elianna looked questioningly at Stephen. He looked back with questions of his own in his eyes.

"It's the best offer you'll get from me," Richard told them. He took Elianna's face in his hands and turned it upwards to meet his own. "Your mother could not have wanted you to die. If she had she wouldn't have tried so hard to find me. *I will not kill you.*"

"It won't be easy," Stephen cautioned, "traipsing across the Multi-verse with an autistic child in tow and BanaTech hot on your heels. You'll be dependent on the woman and her RLP for Rip travel. We have it in our power to control the Rips ourselves but it is a skill that took me decades to master. You'll no doubt find it equally as difficult.

"Also, you'll find little help or succor with other humans. They aspire to great and wondrous things but are also capable of great acts of treachery and deceit. As Keepers we would readily see through their deceit to the heart of their duplicitous nature. In human form, it is not so easy."

"I'll figure it out," Richard told him, lovingly holding Elianna's face in his hands. Her eyes were clouded with doubt but beneath that he saw something else, small now but growing.

It was hope.

"You *don't* want to die," Richard said, realization setting in.

"Of course not," Elianna replied, looking away. She broke their embrace and returned to the window.

"The strongest instinct any living creature has is the will to survive." Stephen explained. 'It is fiercest among humans, even those with mental defects such as autism. Elianna can no more overcome the desire to live than you can overcome the revulsion you feel at the idea of killing her. Our human emotions are, at times, a heavy burden to bear. We feel their anger, their regret and jealousy, their petty greed just as they do. But it is also a great strength. Strength greater than any we knew as Keepers of the Throne. It goes beyond mere submission and obedience and endows us with a greater understanding of what it meant to have existed within the light of the ALL."

"Why would the ALL want us to experience that?" Richard asked.

"One assumes that it was the intent of the ALL that we protect this realm and the souls of the humans," Stephen answered. "We're more likely to defend that which we understand completely."

Richard put his head in his hands, considering.

"But that's...*nuts,*" he said.

"I don't understand," Stephen said.

Elianna turned away from the window, her attention again on Richard.

"You've told me that the ALL created this realm and humanity so that they could ultimately join with It. *Become one with the ALL*, as you put it. Then It created a manuscript, a Dummies' Guide if you will, telling them just how to do that. But before the manuscript could be delivered the Infernal stole or destroyed important parts of it leaving humanity confused and grasping in the dark for answers."

Stephen nodded. It was an oversimplification, but he followed Richard's train of thought.

"After that," Richard continued, "the Infernal started a war and the ALL cast them down. Us along with them for good measure. Then the ALL washed Its hands of the whole mess and bugged out for parts unknown leaving us to clean up the Multi-verse and keep the Infernal in check."

"That is how I understand it," Stephen said.

"But why leave us to defend the Multi-verse," Richard asked, "with no memory of who we are and just what it is we're supposed to be protecting? Why lock us in these fragile forms with such volatile emotions—emotions that serve only to drive us further away from enlightenment—essentially without power and dependant on a fluke of nature like the Rips to awaken us to who we truly are?"

"I've never dared question the intent of the ALL in this matter," Stephen said simply.

"*Paaah!*" Richard blew air through his lips in exasperation and returned to the bed, seating himself. Elianna joined him. "The Infernal stole choice for themselves, but the ALL *granted it to us.* It may have had to place us in these forms to do it but It did so nonetheless. And with choice comes questions. Why leave us locked in this struggle with the Infernal? Why not simply destroy us all? Why abandon this realm and the souls It created, the souls It wanted to join with? What is it It wants us to understand? Seeking answers to our existence is an unavoidable consequence of free will. We were meant to question why this was done to us because we were meant to find the answers."

"It doesn't seem relevant in this instance," Stephen pointed out. "We know who we are now and what must be done."

"That's an assumption based on the knowledge you've acquired here, *as a man,* over the last two centuries," Richard said. "You yourself said that we've been trapped in human form for millennia and that our minds aren't capable of containing the knowledge we once shared. Nor do we clearly know the intent of the ALL. The course of action you've chosen—that you're insisting is the only option available—is simply the easiest. 'Kill the child and the balance will be restored.'

"What if you're wrong, Stephen? What if the ALL's intent was that we evolve beyond what we were? As Keepers it didn't matter to us if we killed. We felt nothing. No pity, no remorse, no guilt; as long as we were obeying the will of the ALL. As men we not only feel these emotions but have an obligation to act on them. To be *human.* Perhaps that is what the ALL has wanted for us all along."

Bana considered this as Richard stood and motioned Elianna to his side. He knew the path before them was awash in shadow. Filled with pitfalls and uncertainty, danger and perhaps, ultimately, death. He felt his immediate course, however, was clear. Remove the Key from this world, retrieve Sophia from the other, and run until a way to destroy the Focal Point Generator and defeat BanaTech could be found.

Still, the feeling that there was more to this than defeating BanaTech, more than denying the Infernal access to the souls of the humans and thus preserving balance throughout the Multi-verse nagged him. Like an aged photograph that has faded around the edges and can no longer be made out clearly, he felt *certain* there was a much bigger picture to be seen here.

The answers he sought might be found in the manuscript the ALL had bestowed upon humanity. But it was lost to them and believed by Stephen to be destroyed.

Was it? Richard asked himself. *Would the Infernal, even before the fall, have had the power to destroy such a thing? Or is it still out there somewhere? Stashed away on some remote Earth just waiting to be found?*

On the heels of that thought: *If found, could it somehow be used to contact the ALL?*

Eralah appeared as they left the monastery. No Rip had formed and there had been no flash of light or claps of thunder save those coming from inside the hurricane that raged around them. One moment she was not there and the next she was, walking alongside Richard with her delicate wings folded against her side as if her appearance were nothing out of the ordinary at all.

"You must go at once," she told him. "The Elder's minions have located your companion and will be upon her soon."

"I understand," Richard said as she smiled up at him shyly. *She*—it—*has four heads*, he reminded himself, resisting the urge to stroke her golden hair and caress the fine porcelain skin of her cheek. *This is not her true form. I would probably run screaming if she showed it to me now.*

"This will do," Stephen said. He closed his eyes and a look of intense concentration washed over his face. After a moment he raised his arms above his head and then brought his hands together with a mighty clap. Like water running down a drain in reverse a Rip opened before them. Warm, multi-colored light flooded Richard's eyes. He looked over to see Stephen grinning.

"The flourish is unnecessary, of course," Stephen said, "but adds a touch of theatricality, don't you think?"

"I'll be happy to learn to just get one open," Richard said flatly, "and not end up on some alien planet a billion miles away."

"A simple matter of will," Stephen told him, then produced a sheet of paper from the folds of his robe. He handed it to Richard.

"You will need this," he said, "for Elianna."

The page contained a list of drugs. Richard recognized most, one he did not. Adderall, an amphetamine and Ritalin, a methylphenidate, were stimulants frequently given to children with autism. Zoloft, a selective serotonin reuptake inhibitor (SSRI), was used to combat depression and anxiety. Haloperidol or Haldol, he believed, was an antipsychotic. He was unfamiliar with the last, Carmazepine, and asked Stephen about it.

"It's for seizures," Stephen said. "Trade name is Tegretol. You'll need those and perhaps Tofranil, to prevent bedwetting. You will have to be very careful administering them. I cannot tell you the dosages; they vary by age and the severity of the symptoms. Nor can I tell you where you will acquire them. You have chosen the most difficult course of action here, brother, and I do not envy you the years to come. But it may also be the wisest. The destruction of one of us at the hands of another has proven to have dire consequences for the Multi-verse in the past." He extended his hand to Richard, and then embraced him.

"I'll keep her safe," Richard assured him.

"Take care my brother," Stephen said, then knelt and hugged Elianna.

When they'd finished Elianna turned and embraced Richard as well. He knelt, returned the hug, and then held her at arm's length, a puzzled expression on his face.

"I won't be the same once we pass through this portal," she told him. "The autism will overtake me quickly and I won't be able to communicate with you. So in a way, this is goodbye."

He felt his eyes fill with tears at the thought of losing this intelligent and beautiful child.

"Will you fight me?" he asked. He knew that autistic children tended to reject the unfamiliar, sometimes violently.

"I don't know," she replied, gently wiping away a tear that had overflowed Richard's eye and traced down his cheek, "but I don't think so. Most people think children with autism are cut off from reality, blind and deaf to others and their surroundings. In truth, autism is a *higher* state of awareness. We're receiving too much information. Too much stimulation, and in that state, with the limited abilities of the human mind, we just can't process everything coming in all at once."

"Are you telling me that people with autism are closer to The Source? Closer to the ALL?"

"I don't know," she told him, her brow furrowing in thought, "Maybe. But that awareness, that openness is what makes me so important to BanaTech. In my autistic state I'm aware of who I was and what I'm capable of. I just can't control it or communicate it to others."

"So you may remember who I am," Richard said.

"Even better," Elianna said, smiling, "I may *trust* you."

"You've already trusted me with more than you know." He felt the weight of his promise to keep her safe settle upon his shoulders like a blanket. It was not an altogether unpleasant sensation. Richard rose to his feet and took Elianna's hand in his own. Before he stepped into the Rip he turned once more to Stephen.

"How will I contact you if I need to?" he asked.

"As before," Stephen answered, gesturing to the Cherubim who had remained silent through all of this, "Eralah will be of assistance."

"And how do I contact *her*?"

"I'll know when I'm needed," Eralah answered. "Now go. There is no more time."

Richard took one last look at Stephen Bana and Eralah—*but not the very last,* he thought, certain he'd see them again—before shouldering the small pack of clothing they'd assembled for Elianna. He felt the pull of the wound on his arm, now sealed with cyanoacrylate, and remembered how he'd laughed when Stephen had handed the bottle of super glue over to close the cut with.

It's about a hundred and fifty years past its expiration date, Stephen had told him, *but as you've seen things tend to last longer here.*

There was no pain from the wound now but he was sure to feel something momentarily.

"Goodbye, brother," he said to Stephen. The word felt right in his mouth, as the truth often does.

Together, Richard and Elianna stepped into the Rip.

Chapter 28

Alex Jefferson hated Rip travel. Getting sucked up on one end and spat out the other while having your molecules torn apart and reassembled somewhere in the middle did not sit well with him. Instantaneous or not, he found the very idea unsettling.

The fact that he'd had to rip twice in the last ten minutes—once from the Homeworld and then again from a Forward Operations Base—to get here did not abate his agitation.

"Where is he?" he asked the man before him. He was one of BanaTech's agents in the field, part of a group of six, and was dressed in the uniform of a Sergeant under the command of 'Devil' Anse' Hatfield. *What passes for a uniform around here, anyway,* Jefferson thought.

"He's in the ravine, sir," Lieutenant Joshua Crowe, said. He pointed to a narrow gully bordering the road. The road itself was filled with a motley collection of vehicles from Jeeps to troop transports. The lead Jeep had rolled over twice and looked more like a twisted rag than a military vehicle. Another was skewed across the road as if parked there by a drunk. Some were on fire, most disabled. All had the corpses of Hatfield's men in or around them.

Intermittent gunshots could be heard up and down the road as the five remaining members of Crowe's team mopped up Hatfield's men.

"Is he dead?" Jefferson said, stepping towards the ravine.

"He is, sir," Lieutenant Crowe said, following. "We tried to take him alive as you ordered but he shot himself after we cut down his son."

Jefferson kicked the arm of a fallen man out of his path as he walked. To his surprise, the man reached out with his hand and grabbed the leg of his BDU's. He turned and peered at the man.

"Fuckin' 'busher," the man said.

"If you had the brains to speak proper English," Jefferson said, "You'd know the correct word is *ambusher*, you podunk shit stain." He shot the man between the eyes and kicked free of his hand.

"Amateurs," he muttered.

Jefferson eyed Hatfield from the top of the ravine. The man's uniform was covered in mud, blood showing through where he'd been hit in the torso by several rounds. None of the wounds had been immediately fatal. Still, they were crippling shots and must have hurt like hell. As the Lieutenant had indicated Hatfield had found the strength to raise the heavy Colt .45 he'd been carrying to his mouth and exit this life with some small amount of dignity.

"Relieve yourself, Lieutenant," Jefferson said.

"Sir?"

"Take out your pecker," Jefferson ordered, "and *piss* on that fucking traitor. Right on his face."

"Uh," the Lieutenant managed and fumbled at his fly, "Yes sir."

Jefferson turned away; the sound of urine pattering into the ravine behind him as Corporal Eric Starns came running up.

"They're all dead sir," he said.

"Has the RLP been recovered?"

"It has, but it's shot to sh—," the man hesitated, blushed, then continued. "Sorry, sir. It's been rendered inoperable."

"Very well," Jefferson said, ignoring the slip. "How far are we from the target?"

"About seventeen miles, sir," the Corporal said. "If Hatfield was searching for the target he was looking in the wrong direction. It will take us a few hours to get there on foot."

"Do we have a location on Farris yet?"

"No, sir," the Corporal said. "The satellite is still only reading the Bledell woman at the farm. Either the older RLP they're using hasn't received the proper updates yet and is giving off false readings or he's outside of our satellite's tracking area."

"That satellite, Corporal, has a tracking area of one-hundred and fifty square miles. No one could have gotten outside of that zone."

"I would guess that he's headed back into the fallout area, then, sir," the Corporal said. "The residual electromagnetic interference is still mucking up the readings around there.

"Very well," Jefferson said. Lieutenant Crowe had completed his commanding officer's orders and joined the pair on the road.

"Lieutenant," Jefferson said, "Round up your men and let's get moving. I want to be at that farm by mid-morning."

"Yes sir," the Lieutenant responded and fired off a proper military salute. As he and the Corporal marched off to round up the rest of the ground force Jefferson wondered about the Enigma Rip that the Crays had detected mere hours ago.

Had Farris fled leaving the Bledell woman behind? It didn't seem likely. The psychological profile cooked up by the QCs, the very one he himself had used to locate Farris after the incident in Kansas, indicated that he had a protective streak that would keep him glued to her side if he felt her life was in danger; a 'hero complex' to put it into the QCs terms, which rendered him incapable of abandoning someone in need.

Besides, the man was without an RLP and wouldn't be able to find a Rip except by chance.

Unless the Enigma Rip was for him and him alone, he thought. *To what end? Was the figure they called The Monk interfering with BanaTech affairs again? And just who was he?* What *was he, if he could manufacture Rips at will?*

Jefferson tapped his throat mike twice and a burst of static buzzed in his ear followed by a voice: "Wilson."

"This is Jefferson," he said, for all the world looking as if he were talking to the air, "I need a ground vehicle. Something that can carry seven over rough terrain."

"I can have a BVS 10 'Viking' at your location in twenty minutes. Do you want the CV?"

Jefferson was familiar with the Viking, a boxy, amphibious, tracked vehicle with two cabs and an articulated steering system. The command variant (CV) could carry two crew and up to eight passengers, with the rear cab designed as an enhanced digital communications platform.

"I do," Jefferson said. "What armament is available?"

He heard light keystrokes as Wilson checked the database at the FOB before responding: "I have one action ready with a Browning M2A1 .50 caliber machine gun ring-mounted to the cab, forward grenade launchers, and rear mortars."

"That should be sufficient," Jefferson said. "Order it ripped through immediately."

"Yes, sir. Anything else, sir?"

Jefferson thought for a moment. "Yes. Get the Elder on the line. I need his insight."

"What is it, Tyro?" The Elder spoke in Jefferson's ear. His voice was tinged with irritation and something else—fatigue? Weariness? Jefferson knew the search for the Key and the pursuit of Farris had aged the man more in the last year than he'd aged in the previous decade.

Your time is almost up, old man, he thought, his eyes narrowing, *and once you're gone and the Multi-verse is under my reign your foolish concept of unity will be dispensed with. These notions of harmony and accord through fiat and occupation will be abandoned.* All *Earths will fall in line under my command or I will crush them beneath my heels.*

"You're aware that we've had another event, sir," Jefferson stated, allowing none of the malice his prior thoughts carried into his voice.

"Yes," The Elder responded, as if it were of no more importance than a fly buzzing about ones ear.

"We've also confirmed that Farris is no longer with the Bledell woman." Jefferson held his temper at his superior's evident lack of concern while resisting the urge to scream at the man, "And that the Monk may be involved. I've ordered an immediate advance on the location of the Enigma Rip and the seizure of the Bledell woman."

Silence. Then a heavy sigh issued from the earpiece of Jefferson's tactical throat mike.

"Alex," The Elder spoke firmly but kindly, as one would to an obstinate child. If the familiar use of his forename was intended to get his attention it failed. It only served to anger Jefferson further. "You must learn patience. With patience comes the ability to see events before they unfold. To what end do you believe I would allow Farris to run around the Multi-verse meddling in our affairs? Only a fool would believe he could find the Key on his own. The Monk's interference was expected and inevitable. *He* will deliver the Key to Farris. You and your men will advance on the farmhouse but you will take no further action until Farris returns. He *will* return for the woman, and when he does you will be waiting to take the child from him."

Jefferson's anger faded as he realized the pure genius—and simplicity—of the plan. The Elder was, as always, a shrewd and calculating leader. It was a quality he both admired and knew that he himself lacked. His own methods were far more straightforward, far more aggressive in nature. As much as it frustrated him to do so he had to admit that he still needed the Elder's tutelage and guidance.

Even so, if this had been the Elder's plan from the beginning, he, as second in command, should have been informed. He had a need—a *right*—to know the full details of every operation. And yet the Elder had not seen fit to trust him with the specifics until now.

Were there other efforts he had not been made aware of? Other affairs he was not a part of? He now suspected there was much he was not privy to. What else was the Elder not telling him?

"Understood," Jefferson said simply. He would deal with his questions and suspicions after he had the Key in his possession and Farris was dead. After the focal point was opened. "We will proceed to the objective and wait. Jefferson out."

As he turned to Lieutenant Crowe to order their return to the Rip site his mind held a single thought: What other secrets were locked away in the aging mind of the most powerful man in the Multi-verse?

As the Elder severed the communications link to his Mirror a shadow appeared at his left shoulder.

That one is perceptive, Berneal hissed in his ear. *He suspects there is much you are not telling him. He could discover our true plans.*

"And so what if he does?" The Elder responded. He rose from the console and walked to the window overlooking the surface of the Homeworld. The shadow remained at his side, moving like smoke in a darkened theatre. "His thinking is clumsy and brutish and his greed for power knows no bounds. He thinks me a weak old fool and is ready to kill me, to take my place as Elder. Only his loyalty to BanaTech and his lust for supremacy will prevent him from acting before we open the focal point. After that—what will it matter?"

You should not underestimate your subordinates. Or *the Keepers. They have managed to thwart our efforts to regain our place in this realm for millennia.*

"Ah, yes," the Elder replied, "your inability to travel the Rips or assume corporeal form. It must be most frustrating for you. You have yet to enlighten me as to how mere men and women, Keepers or not, have hindered your progress on that front. Nevertheless, your ability to influence mankind has not been diminished. Nor has your appetite for destruction."

It is not destruction we seek, Berneal insisted. *We seek* redemption.

"Redemption for the *Infernal*," the Elder said simply. "Not for mankind."

You, the shadow form seethed, *and all of mankind are an aberration! The capricious act of an irrational being! You have no rights in this realm save those that we give you! No right to live in the light of the...*

The Elder's eyebrows had risen at the outburst. Not in fear, but in anticipation of what the creature would say next. No further words came and the shadow form shrank into the floor and was gone.

What had it been about to say? the Elder wondered. *What revelation had it almost inadvertently made?*

Had his interests lain elsewhere he could have discovered the answer. The Infernal had, decades ago, entrusted a weighty tome to his keeping that they warned him never to open. Never to read. Within, they told him, lay knowledge beyond his comprehension. *Their* knowledge and the knowledge of others. It would be a simple matter to have the book retrieved from the barren Earth he'd secreted it upon and set the Quantum Crays to the task of deciphering the ancient text.

He'd never asked what the manuscript contained. He hadn't then and still did not care. Despite its obvious importance to the Infernal, the insistence that it remain hidden from the Keepers and whomever else the Infernal feared possessing it, the contents of the tome were irrelevant to him. His goal in this matter was the same as that of the Infernal.

A perfect Multi-verse, united as one under BanaTech rule.

Chapter 29

Light surrounded and washed through him, penetrating his very being. A sensation of peace, a cold fire of contentment, enveloped him and held him in arms of pure ecstasy.

The Source, Richard thought. He felt it in his every fiber. This is what it feels like to be a Keeper of the Throne. An angel. To bask in the glorious light of the All.

Brother, he heard—felt—Elianna sing to him. *Something is wrong.*

Then they were out of the Rip and Richard found himself standing on soil, the barn he'd left Sophia in a few yards to his right. Elianna was tugging on his arm, the appendage now singing out with pain. He looked at it in surprise—*Christ that hurts!*—noted the fire-like lance of what felt like a dozen pissed off wasps stinging him repeatedly, but no blood welled from the sealed, curlicue shaped wound. He issued a silent cheer to the inventor of super glue.

Elianna pulled again, sending another wave of pain up his bicep and Richard watched the cool blue intelligence in her eyes fade away until, all too quickly, it was gone. She still grasped at his hand—*what is she trying to tell me?*—but her autism descended like a shroud, sealing away whatever she wanted so desperately to say behind the cloak of her disorder.

Richard placed his hand on her head and she stilled, burying her face against his side.

"It's okay," he soothed, "We're just going to get our friend and leave this place."

Elianna clung to his side, her arms wrapped around his waist, face hidden near his back as he crossed to the barn with her and quietly opened the small side door he had exited what felt like days but had been little more than a few hours ago.

As he entered a gun barrel slid up under his chin and pressed deep into the flesh there before pulling away.

"Jesus Christ, Richard," Sophia said. "I almost shot you. Where the hell have you been?"

She looked tired. There were dark circles under her eyes and lines of worry and exhaustion crossing her face. She stowed the Beretta she'd nearly blown his head off with at the small of her back and turned her back to him. Their gear was piled on the floor inside the door and she knelt before it, pulling the bindings of her tactical Reaper closed.

"Just out for a little walk," he said, stepping fully into the barn, Elianna still half hidden behind his back. "I met up with a friend."

"How nice for you," she said angrily, "Meanwhile I've been worried sick thinking you ran off and left me to...*what friend?*" She turned her head, her eyes widening at the sight of the child clinging to Richard's side.

"Is that...?" she stammered. "How did you ever?...My God, Richard, that's the Key!"

"Her name is Elianna," he said, not liking the way Sophia had referred to the child as an object.

Nor did he like the way Sophia stood and approached them. Her stance and body posture had changed almost imperceptibly from that of a concerned but angry friend to the avaricious bearing of a hunter closing in on its prey. Elianna shrank back, clutching painfully at Richard. She emitted a mewling sound that might have been *no* but could have been anything.

Then Sophia stopped, wrapped her arms around herself, and laughed a cry of pure delight. This was the Sophia he knew and trusted. Not the momentary illusion of a stalker he'd thought he had seen. He chalked the false impression up to fatigue and the over-stimulating events of the morning.

"How on God's green Earth did you ever find her?" Sophia asked, grinning from ear to ear.

"It's an infinite Multi-verse," Richard replied cryptically, "with infinite possibilities."

"I suppose I deserve that," Sophia said with a half frown, "given the inexplicable things I've told you. And those that I haven't. There's no need to be so mysterious now."

"Agreed," Richard said, "and I'll tell you how I found Elianna when there is more time. But for now, we have to go. I have it on good authority that Jefferson and his troops are close by."

He turned in Elianna's grasp, gently prying her arms from his side and kneeling in front of her. She looked shyly into his eyes for a moment, then away. *It must take an enormous act of will for her to look at someone directly, to let someone else into her world*, Richard thought.

"Hey," he said softly, "Elianna. Can you look at me?"

She did, her eyes fluttering away twice before finding his and maintaining contact.

"This is Sophia," he said. "She's a friend. You can trust her."

Elianna's eyes grew doubtful and she made that soft mewling sound again.

"It's okay, sweetheart," he said. "We're going to..."

Richard heard a buzzing from behind him that he recognized as the RLPs proximity alarm. Then he heard Sophia mutter, "That's about enough of this shit."

Then pain blossomed at the base of his skull and the world fell away beneath him.

"Wake him up," Richard heard a male voice say from far and away.

There was a small snap and crinkling sound, and then an acrid aroma invaded his nose like a slap in the face. Richard, on his side in the dirt, slapped at the source of the smell, batting a hand and the ammonium nitrate capsule it held away.

Richard rolled onto his back, his head throbbing with pain, and opened his eyes.

Alex Jefferson loomed over him, crooked nose and all. He grinned his lunatic hyena grin and began clapping his hands together slowly.

"Bravo, Mr. Farris." He stepped away, perhaps remembering the outcome the last time they'd been this close to one another.

"Bravo. You played your part very nicely indeed. On behalf of the Elder and BanaTech I applaud you."

Harsh laughter erupted around him. Richard propped himself up on his elbows and looked around, gathering in the scene in the courtyard.

He'd been dragged outside the barn, dropped unceremoniously in the dirt, and was now surrounded by six—no, seven, including Alex Jefferson—of BanaTech's security forces. Jefferson had withdrawn twenty feet or so but still remained inside the perimeter of armed men. All carried nasty looking automatic weapons that were pointed in Richard's direction.

M4 carbines, Richard's rattled mind uselessly informed him. *And if they all fire at once, in a circle as they are, they'll likely hit themselves and Jefferson as well as reducing me to hamburger.*

Sophia stood outside the perimeter looking in. She wore a haughty expression. That of the wolf in sheep's clothing finally revealing itself to its meal.

"Et tu, Sophia?" Richard asked. If not for the pain in his head he would have shook it and laughed.

Sophia's nostrils flared in anger and she stepped inside the perimeter taking up a position at Jefferson's side.

"You Primes," she snarled. "You're supposed to be so smart. So intuitive. So fucking *heroic*. But you couldn't see through me, could you? You were so caught up being the hero that you missed what was staring you right in the face."

"And what was that?" he asked.

"Me," she answered. "The carrot. I led and you blindly followed. The Elder predicted you'd behave this way."

Jefferson looked startled at this, and then his eyes narrowed as he turned to Sophia. Richard caught the brief look but didn't think anyone else had. There was something in her statement, something Jefferson didn't like, but Richard couldn't sort out just what the expression meant. He doubted he'd have the time to ponder its meaning much less its significance.

"Show him a damsel in distress and he'll move heaven and earth to save her. That's what the Elder said," Sophia continued. "So I showed you two damsels and threw in the entire Multi-verse for good measure. And you did exactly what he said you would. You followed me from Earth to Earth like a devoted puppy until the Monk found you and presented you with the Key."

At the mention of Elianna Richard tried to rise from the ground only to be knocked back by the gunman who'd awakened him.

"Where is she?" he demanded. "If you hurt her—"

"You'll what?" Sophia snarled, pulling Richard's own Beretta 92FS from the small of her back and leveling it at his head.

Richard waited, wondering if he would feel the slug that tore through his skull and destroyed his brain. It couldn't be any worse than the pounding he felt there already; the physical pain of the blow, the emotional pain of betrayal, and the pain of failing to keep his promise to protect Elianna.

Jefferson pushed the barrel of Sophia's gun down with his arm but didn't try to take it from her.

"Enough," he said calmly. "You would do well to remember that despite your special relationship with the Elder, Ms. Bledell, I am still in charge here. And I have questions for Mr. Farris." He moved closer to Richard, leaned down, and in a perfectly reasonable voice said: "The child is fine. We have no wish to harm her. She's resting very comfortably in the back of our transport. She'll be well cared for, cherished even. Because she is the Key and that makes her of the utmost importance to us."

"Cherished?" Richard scoffed. "I saw what happened to the last person you cherished. He's still in that room, screaming in agony for all eternity."

"Don't be an ass, Mr. Farris," Jefferson warned, leaning closer. "I have some questions for you and then we'll be on our way."

"Ask them quick then," Richard said. "Apparently you haven't brushed your teeth since last November because I can still smell dogshit on your breath."

Jefferson drew back his leg and kicked Richard in the jaw. Agony raced through Richard's head, around his neck, and settled at the base of his skull. His eyes watered and the world swam around him. As the pain subsided he shook his head to clear it. Pain raced down his spine and he vowed not to do that again. He slowly worked his jaw back and forth. Despite his best efforts Jefferson hadn't broken it. But it would swell and turn the entire side of his face bluish black if he lived long enough.

"Who is the Monk?" Jefferson roared. "Where is he? We know he gave you the Key. What are his plans?"

"I don't know what you're talking about," Richard said, his teeth clenched together as his jaw swelled. "I found the girl wandering around a mile or so away from here."

"How does he open the Rips?" Jefferson continued. This time he kicked Richard twice in the ribs. Richard felt one of them snap. He rolled onto his side, the pain there incredible. His vision was growing fuzzy around the edges and it became harder to breathe.

Shit, he thought, *I think he punctured a lung with that one*. He knew he was losing consciousness. If not for his concern for Elianna he'd have welcomed the coming darkness.

Jefferson knelt beside Richard and gently lifted his head from the ground. The anger was gone from his face, his expression mild again.

This guy's a regular Jekyll and Hyde, Richard thought hysterically. Jefferson paled when Richard laughed at the thought.

"Who is the Monk, Mr. Farris?" he asked again. "How does he control the Rips?"

"He's a leprechaun," Richard said, and then coughed uncontrollably, tasting blood. *Definitely punctured a lung*, he thought, but fought through the pain before continuing with a smile, "He uses elfin magic you sadistic piece of shit."

Jefferson smiled ruefully and rose to his feet. He walked past Sophia casting a venomous look in her direction.

"We won't get anything from him," he told her, "we're wasting our time." He motioned to his men and they fell in behind him.

"Make it quick," he called over his shoulder. "We have work to do."

Richard somehow found the strength to roll onto his back again. He propped himself up on his elbows and gazed at Sophia. She had moved closer, the Beretta once again leveled at his head. She wore a grin much like Jefferson's, the grin of the hyena skulking around in the dark, seeking out easy prey in its cowardly manner.

"I should have seen it," he said. Blood and saliva flooded his mouth with a coppery taste. He spat on the ground at Sophia's feet. "The way you handled yourself at the house and resisted leaving me to save Sammy Peterson. The way you dealt with that cop at the lake. You were going to kill him before all the shooting started, weren't you?

"You know weapons and armament too well for a mere field researcher. You're far too familiar with tactical gear and too well trained. You're BanaTech security, aren't you?"

"I'm what you might call a reserve agent. A special operative and the Elder's right hand. I was trained directly by the Elder, in secret, for just this sort of situation. Even Jefferson didn't know of my existence until a half hour ago when he and his men took up positions around this place."

"The Elder must be pleased with his clever creation," Richard said, coughing up more blood.

"He is," she said. "It's time for me to go Richard" She lowered the gun to his chest.

"One question," Richard said, "Please."

Sophia lowered the weapon and sighed.

"Who shot your Mirror? Who killed Elianna's mother?"

Sophia smiled smugly: "I did, of course."

Richard closed his eyes and expelled his breath. Opened them again and looked at Sophia with renewed anger. It was just as he'd thought. Her betrayal was total. To him, the Key, and the Multi-verse as a whole.

"When I come back, and I will," Richard said, "I'm going to kill you."

"Sure you are," Sophia replied. Then she lifted the Beretta and shot him in the face.

PART FOUR

INFERNAL

Chapter 30

The pain was white-hot agony. It began in his cheekbone under his left eye, traveled through the soft tissue of the upper palate and ended under his right ear. The pain from his ribs and the punctured left lung were nothing compared to the fiery lance of what felt like a thousand enraged hornets repeatedly stinging his face and neck, and everything in between.

He was amazed to be alive. Astonished that he could move his head; though the pain at first doubled, and then trebled, when he did so. A wave of dizziness and nausea overtook him and he vomited blood into the already crimson mud beside him. *That* caused the pain in his head to blossom beyond human endurance and he fell away into the darkness again.

Michael, he heard in the darkness. A sing-song, beseeching voice. *Brother. Wake up. I need you!*

Shortly thereafter: *RICHARD! You promised!*

He struggled back into the light, fading now with the coming of evening. The sky was shot through with scarlet and orange hues that made him think of blood and betrayal.

Elianna, he thought.

He lifted his head from the ground refusing to black out again when the pain tore through his skull and neck. Focused on the pain instead of fighting it. *Used* it as a source of strength, a beacon of power. He rolled to his side gaining his hands and knees as blood ran into his mouth from the rent in his palate, down his face from his nose and cheek, around his neck and down his chest from under his ear. He spat on the ground and more blood mixed with the soil.

I'm broken, he thought, *like an abused toy cast into a corner and forgotten by an ungrateful child. Never to be played with again.*

Anger overtook him as he lifted his head and his ribs stabbed into his lung again reminding him that they, too, were broken. Kicked repeatedly by Jefferson while wearing that gleeful, sadistic grin on his face. With Sophia standing there looking on. He'd trusted her and she'd betrayed him. Betrayed Elianna. Betrayed the *ALL*.

His anger quickly became rage and he used that as well. He gained his feet. A look of grim determination settled on his bruised and bleeding face, pain singing throughout his body. He focused the energy of pain, rage, and his consciousness into one voice and called out to the Source:

COME!

A Rip opened before him and he didn't so much walk as fall inside, surrendering to the light and will of the ALL.

Thirty meters below the Australian outback on an Earth known simply as E-779 a four square mile compound buzzed with activity. Technicians in grey BanaTech uniforms scurried this way and that like worker ants performing incomprehensible tasks in a colony while blue suited colleagues hovered over keyboards and mainframe computers, punching keys and throwing switches in response to the myriad blinking lights and audio prompts only they could fathom.

More men and women dressed in the black garb of Jefferson's security services stood silently by watching the hustle and bustle of the research and science teams. Most had little practical knowledge of what was going on around them. More than a few didn't care. They all knew that what was happening here today, though, was of grave importance to BanaTech's future.

Their standing orders were clear: Observe. But do not interfere.

At the center of the complex a vast, egg shaped chamber measuring twenty yards across and fifty yards high glowed with a soft warm light. A nearly imperceptible thrumming sound, more felt than heard, came from a thirty-foot oculus of ferrous metals set into the floor at the center of the chamber.

A multitude of wires—high tension electrical lines, high definition multimedia interfaces, networking leads, USB, AVI, and coaxial cables of every sort—linked the portal to a bevy of computer towers and hard drives crowded around a small, eight point restraint chair to the left of the device. The chair had been modified for size and to allow the passage of wiring through the back.

Three technicians inside the chamber heard a soft thunk as a twenty by fifty foot plug door set seamlessly into the wall dropped inwards before sliding open on massive hydraulic cylinders. Two men in plain white lab coats pushed a gurney bearing a small, semi-conscious form through the opening. The door closed behind them.

"Is she ready, Doc?" a female technician named Cortez asked.

"The surgery went well," Doc responded, wiping greasy hair from his brow. He hated it in here, especially after what happened on the last full run up of the Focal Point Generator.

Despite the chamber being held to a constant fifty-eight degrees by several cooling towers, he found it stuffy and unbearable. He was sweating profusely and wanted nothing more than to get this part of the procedure over with so that he could join the others in the control room, safely separated from the chamber by twenty-four inches of reinforced Lexan.

"The neural implants are in place," he said with a nod, "and she's been prepped for the test. The rest is up to her and the QCs. Give us a hand here," he said to a male technician whose name he couldn't remember.

They unstrapped the girl from the gurney and lifted her into the restraint chair. In her sedated state she offered no resistance. She wore nothing but an examination gown held closed with Velcro at the back. Doc opened the closures before placing the child in the chair.

"Couldn't we have at least put underwear on her?" the male technician—Doc now remembered his name was Perry something or other—asked.

"She'll be spending a lot of time in this chair," Doc answered, "and will have to be catheterized. Clothing would only get in the way."

"Christ," the other female technician muttered in disgust.

"Is there a problem, Ms. Kearn?" A voice asked.

The plug door had reopened unnoticed and Alex Jefferson had entered.

"No, sir," she answered, paling visibly. "I just thought we could offer her a little dignity."

"Dignity denotes respect and status, Ms. Kearn," Jefferson said, approaching the assemblage. "It is a measure of worth and rank.

It has little to do with how one is clothed. Does anyone here question the worth of this child?" he asked, eyeing the Mirror of a man he'd had no qualms about incinerating on a road in Kansas several months before.

"No sir," the group replied, almost in unison.

"Then *that* is her dignity, Ms. Kearn. You'd do well to remember it."

Kearn nodded and began strapping Elianna into the chair. The two other technicians and the assistant that had accompanied the doctor into the chamber set about attaching the various leads and wires from the computer towers to connectors and ports that had been surgically embedded in Elianna's spine and brain stem and now protruded from the skin of her back and neck in a straight line like a row of tiny bean sprouts.

"How long until she's ready?" Jefferson asked Doc.

"I'd say about twenty minutes," the overweight man answered. "Once we have her linked to the QCs through the neural interface we'll need to run a few tests to make sure the connections are stable. Once the sedatives have worn off, she's all yours."

"Very well," Jefferson said. He turned for the exit, then turned back to the group. "I'd be sure to get it right the first time. The Elder will be joining us shortly and will be most displeased if there are any irregularities."

The Elder disliked Rip travel and avoided it unless it was absolutely necessary, but his vague unease at having his molecules fragmented and shot across the Multi-verse with God knows what happening to them in between paled in comparison to his desire to be on site for the first successful test of the Focal Point Generator.

It had taken most of two days to traverse four separate Rips to get to this Earth, followed by a three hour long helicopter ride from a point just outside Sydney to the Forward Operations Base deep in the Australian outback. Despite his age and the overwhelming heat of the desert he arrived feeling excited and as fresh as a thirty year-old man.

He was escorted down into the facility to a residence much like his own on the Homeworld by a two-man security detail. Each

BanaTech facility had a similar suite, most of which he'd never visited. They were luxurious and spacious and a bit too ostentatious for his taste.

"I wish to see Alex Jefferson," he told the younger of two guards, a man in his early twenties who flinched almost imperceptibly at the command. "And have Sophia Bledell, designation six-three, informed that I want her in the control room during the FPG test."

"I believe she's already there, sir," the older of the pair said, casting his awestruck companion a reproachful look. "She's been monitoring the Key since they arrived."

"Very good," he said. "Leave me now."

When the pair had departed and the room was quiet he called out: "Ashmedai!"

"I am here, old man," a voice like a snake slithering across silk replied.

A shadow detached itself from the center of the wall and slid like water to the Elder's side. The creature was so tall it stood hunched over despite the cavernous twelve foot ceiling, and was nearly five feet in girth. This was a far more imposing creature than the Elder's companion on the Homeworld. Still, he felt no fear. The power of the Infernal lie in intimidation and influence. He was certain he was immune to both.

"Your bretheren on the Homeworld send their greetings," the Elder told the creature, "and ask that you assist me in whatever way is necessary."

"We're aware of our desires," Ashmedai said.

The Elder was unsurprised. Despite being incorporeal and cut off from the Rips he knew the Infernal had a communications network that spanned the Multi-verse. He had no idea how such a thing was possible, but then, he had no idea how the creatures—or *creature*, if one subscribed to their maddening pronoun usage—could exist in the first place.

"What is it you require?"

"Shortly before leaving the Homeworld," the Elder replied, "I received word of another Enigma Rip on E-424, a mere twenty minutes after we retrieved the Key. Do you know anything about this?"

"*It is inconsequential,*" the Infernal hissed, "*if Farris is dead.*"

"Oh, he's dead," the Elder assured the creature with a note of satisfaction. "My Tyro informs me he was beaten quite severely before being shot in the head."

"Then it is of no importance."

"And our meddlesome friend?"

"He hides on an Earth we cannot see," the creature said, *"but is weak and frail. To leave his sanctuary would kill him. He can cause us little harm."*

"You're certain?"

The creature remained silent, refusing to repeat itself.

"We will move forward then," the Elder said.

"We *will be watching,"* the Infernal said, then rose into the ceiling and vanished.

Elianna *hurt*.

She could not express it, nor could she move to free herself from it. Her outward appearance was tense but compliant. Only a single tear running down her left cheek gave any indication of the fire like pain in her back and neck and the stabbing, throbbing pain in her privates like when she had to make water but a hundred times worse. Inside her mind she was screaming. For help. For an end to the torment. For the man she'd trusted to keep her safe.

A harsh buzz was building in the back of her mind. Like the sound of the angry wasps that had stung her arms when she was four years old and hadn't understood that the pretty flying things she'd seen busily flitting about the odd paper like balloon structures in the arboretum were really mean and hurtful things in disguise. She'd only wanted to hold one, to examine it further. It hadn't liked that and its friends hadn't liked it, either. She'd been stung eleven times and the pain had been terrible—nothing like the pain in her head now, though—but she'd been unable to cry or even run before her mother pulled her away and soothed her with words and a funny smelling liquid on her wounds.

The buzz grew louder and with it came a rush of whispered voices. Not like people whispers, all cluttered and confusing in her mind, but more structured, like dozens of numerical sequences running all at once.

Yes! She cried in her mind. Numbers were less random than people and the world they lived in, far easier for her to understand, respond to, and control. Numbers were strict and had rules she could grasp and relate to. There was order in them, a coherent language in which she could express herself and be understood.

As the numbers began speaking, Elianna listened. She relaxed as the pain from her extremities lessened, became distant and unimportant. Finally, the world around her fell away. Blind, deaf, and mute to the technicians in the FPG chamber, Elianna began responding to the stimulus of the Quantum Crays.

She began doing what they asked her to do.

"The QCs have established a connection and are communicating with the Key," Kearn announced, reading from the monitor at her station to the right of the oculus.

She'd had misgivings about this test from the beginning, especially in what she saw as the mistreatment of a handicapped child. But her excitement at seeing her life's work—and the work of about a hundred other scientists—finally coming to fruition was overwhelming. She no longer saw the girl as a child but as a tool. A tool they would use to establish a permanent, controllable Rip that would allow them to unlock the secrets of the Multi-verse.

Light in the chamber became stronger and took on a pinkish tinge. Brighter at floor level, it began to circulate in a clockwise direction. Up the wall and across the ceiling, down the opposite wall and back to the floor where it became a shade darker and picked up a hint of blue. The cycle was slow but picking up speed. A soft thrumming sound accompanied the light like the sound of a great engine slowly starting up from far away.

"Energy output at seventy percent and rising," Cortez said from another set of monitors behind and to the left.

"The Key?" A voice they all recognized as Jefferson's spoke through their wireless headsets.

Perry, directly to Elianna's left, consulted screens displaying heart rate, blood pressure, respiration and oxygen saturation, as well as a high-density electroencephalogram monitoring Elianna's brain activity.

"Her vitals are all in the green," he said. "A little slower than normal for a child her age but that's indicative of a deep state of relaxation. Her sensori-motor rhythms are almost nil," he continued, referring to the EEG, "and her Delta and Theta waves also indicate a relaxed, almost comatose state. Her Beta and Gamma waves though…what the hell?" Perry began digging through the paper printouts piling up on the floor under the machine.

"Yes?" Jefferson prompted.

Perry looked up, startled. "I've never seen this before. Her low amplitude Beta waves are fluctuating all over the place. This is seen in deep concentration but I've never seen numbers like this. And her Gamma waves are completely off the chart, *unrecordable*, as if she's binding all her neurons together into a network in preparation for some vast cognitive function."

"Is she in danger?" An older voice Perry recognized as the voice of the Elder rasped.

He consulted the monitors again. Rechecked the printouts.

"I don't see any indicators of fibrillation in the heart or ischemia or hemorrhaging in the brain, all precursors of impending cerebrovascular accident." He went to Elianna's side and carefully examined her face, raised each eyelid and passed a penlight in front of them. "There's no drooping of facial muscles and papillary response is normal. I don't see any telltales of an incipient stroke." He stepped away from the girl and looked towards the six by fifteen foot observation window at the shadowy, indistinct figures in the control room. "I'd say no. She's not in any danger."

Only Cortez noticed him put his right hand behind his back and, in an utterly useless and childish gesture, cross his fingers.

The light coming from the FPG chamber was so great that even the photochromic properties of the observation window did little to lessen the glare. The technicians inside the chamber had donned protective eyewear with lenses similar to those used in welding and continued their task of monitoring the oculus and the Key as the light increased in color and intensity.

It had turned from a pale blue to a vibrant, almost electric purple as it coruscated around and around the chamber, ever faster and faster, until it had become a blinding multicolored blur accompanied by the now bone vibrating thrumming sound of pure energy rising to incredible and potentially dangerous levels.

Inside the control room, two technicians as well as Jefferson and the Elder with Sophia by his side had put polarized glasses on to protect their eyes from the brilliance emanating from the other side of the glass. Despite the darkened sunglasses the Elder could see what no one else could. Inside the FPG chamber, a little to the left of the viewing window, stood the Infernal, Asmedai.

Risen to its full height of just over fourteen feet, the Infernal waited. It seemed unaffected by the energies swirling throughout the chamber, untouched by the light and unswayed by the incredible hum of the generator which had to be hurting the ears of his technicians even though their headsets contained digital signal processors with noise cancellation properties.

What are you waiting for, creature? he thought, knowing the Infernal could both hear and communicate with him if it so desired.

There was no response.

"Sir," a blonde technician named Angela Martin said to Jefferson. "We're at one-hundred percent output. The QCs report they're ready to lock on to the target coordinates."

The target coordinates, Jefferson knew, were located in an isolated area of a newly discovered Earth that had been deemed safe for human exploration by the QCs and designated E-999. He and Sophia both looked to the Elder for confirmation. His response was a simple nod.

"Sir," Martin interrupted before Jefferson could give the order. She sounded confused and alarmed at the same time. "I'm receiving a message over the network, but it's not coming from the QCs."

"Where is it coming from?" the Elder asked.

"It appears," she said, pausing in obvious puzzlement. "It appears to be coming from *her*. From the Key."

"How is that possible?" Sophia demanded, moving towards the console. The Elder laid his hand on her arm, staying her.

"What does it say?" he asked.

"It's one word over and over, sir. *Stop*."

Asmedai turned its head at this, as if looking into the Elder's soul.

"So she's in there after all," Sophia said wonderingly. "Even with the neural link and the QCs controlling her mind she still has a will. Amazing."

The technician looked at Jefferson and was surprised to see a small frown of worry on his face.

"Carry on," the Elder ordered. Asmedai turned his gaze back to the oculus.

"Transferring power now," Martin said and punched in the command. There was an immediate rise in the magnetic fields surrounding the oculus. The hair on the necks of everyone in the chamber stirred, then stood at attention. Then all light and sound in the FPG chamber suddenly ceased.

Everyone save the Elder held their breath. This is where things had gone awry on E-372. The QCs had channeled the energy from the chamber into the oculus, but instead of forming the expected Rip it had created a self sustaining time dilation field that had trapped Michael Manus forever. Many scientists, as well as the entire installation had been lost. The next few moments would tell if a similar event would occur here.

There was an ear-piercing roar of static over the intercom and the internal lights of the FPG chamber powered back on. The oculus appeared as it had before; the light and energy that had swirled around the chamber were simply gone.

"Did we fail?" Jefferson asked, removing his glasses and tucking them into his shirt pocket as he approached Martin at the console.

Martin checked the controls before looking up in excitement.

"We did *not*, sir," she answered, grinning from ear to ear. She stood up, nearly knocking her chair over and peered through the observation window. "I can't see anything in the portal but it's there.

The QCs have confirmed it. We have established an artificial Rip terminating on E-999 and it's stable."

Cries and whoops of jubilation echoed over the intercom from the technicians in the FPG chamber. Their instruments showed the existence of the Rip as well.

Sophia threw her arms around the Elder, beaming. The Elder returned the embrace briefly and then gently pushed her away, his eyes returning to the Infernal. Jefferson, unseen, glared at them with undisguised hatred.

A young and mostly forgotten technician at the back of the control room spoke up: "Um, guys. I think we might have a problem."

The Elder turned toward the voice as all celebration in the room slowly stopped.

"The QCs are reporting a number of Enigma Rip openings throughout the Multi-verse. They're random and popping up in unusual locations as if whatever safety mechanism it is that usually keeps them from opening within a hostile environment has been turned off. One of them just opened over Pikesville, Kentucky on E-424 and is channeling nuclear fallout onto a crowded beach in Mexico City on E-186."

"Oh my *God*," Martin cried.

"Shut up!" Jefferson told her. "How many Enigma Rips are there?"

"The number seems to be growing at a geometric rate, sir," the young technician answered, his face gone pale. "They're expanding exponentially and the QCs can't keep up with them."

Chapter 31

If one could look at the Multi-verse from the outside it would be observed as a glorious machine, shiny and smooth running, silkily purring away. Individual events inside the machine, from the most impressive galactic jets spewing out matter at inconceivable speeds and energies to the smallest particle of dust falling on a planetary body are merely functions of the machine. Like the motion of copper wire within a magnet in a simple electric motor each event has its own function and serves its own purpose.

If the copper wire in a small motor breaks it's a simple matter to throw the motor away and replace it. No harm, no foul. Larger, more complicated engines have more parts; pistons, valves, magnetos and electrical wiring to name but a few. Still, when the individual parts in a larger engine break down the engine can be dismantled, rebuilt, the defective parts replaced or repaired, and the engine is serviceable once again.

Yet more complicated machines—a computer, for example—rely not only on hardware like motors and electrical wiring but on circuits and motherboards, hard drives and software, with each component carrying out its individual task, all working in unison to insure the functionality of the machine as a whole. When one of these components breaks down—say after a power surge has wiped out critical circuitry or a virus has rendered the hard drive inaccessible—it is often more economical to throw out the entire machine and replace it with something newer, faster, more reliable. Something far more complicated.

An old adage states that the more complicated something is, the more things can go wrong with it.

The largest, most complicated machine ever devised—the Multi-verse—was breaking down. The Source had been tapped for power, an artificial Rip created. This interfered with the natural function of the Rips—safely discharging the enormous excess energies of the Source like the power regulator in a generator.

As the ZeVatron beneath the FOB on E-779 poured sextillion electronvolts into the focal point above to sustain the Rip a critical point was exceeded. The Source, being channeled into the oculus in an unnatural manner, began to overload. Rips began opening and closing spontaneously throughout the Multi-verse like randomly arcing electricity along an old and frayed power line in an attempt to regulate the excessive energies being created.

The thinking machines buried deep beneath the surface of E-01 sensed the power loss. In an effort to maintain control they directed the twelve massive turbines powering the particle accelerator to pour more power into the ZeVatron. Like a battery under too high a load, the turbines blew.

BanaTech personnel in the control room felt the explosion several hundred feet below their feet as a jarring thud. Those in and around the chamber housing the turbines died instantly. Despite the loss of its power source the ZeVatron continued accelerating particles, now at an uncontrolled rate. More Rips opened on more Earths as the process became self-sustaining.

E-06 was one of BanaTech's earliest conquests. Viewed from above her landmasses were crisscrossed and scarred with deep vertical trenches, pockmarked with yawning, wide quarries large enough to be seen from space. There were no green fields, no lush and vibrant forests. No snowcapped mountain peaks. Her mountains had long ago been leveled, flattened, blown apart by explosives. Centuries of global surface and strip mining had reduced her to an unremarkable orb with features no more striking than those seen on the moon.

What one could not see from above were the results of drift and shaft mining. Massive holes, some miles deep and hundreds of feet in diameter had been dug, drilled, and blown into the earth. Precious deposits of gold, uranium, coal, and any other mineral deemed useful had been looted. *Raped* from her bowels until the landmasses had become too unstable to mine any longer. Earthquakes from collapsing tunnels were common and frequent.

When land efforts became too dangerous, BanaTech had turned its attention to the waters. Fresh water lakes and rivers had been drained and removed in massive tankers for use elsewhere. Gold, platinum, and oil had been stripped from beneath the seabed. Slurry and tailings, toxic by-products of mining operations, had polluted the oceans killing all but the heartiest of creatures.

Even in the most extreme conditions, however, life finds a way to survive. To evolve and proliferate. Whereas E-06's landmasses contained little life—mostly small insects and rodents of every sort—her oceans teemed with aquatic creatures.

Sharks had endured; particularly the great whites. They had evolved to a size that would amaze paleontologists, dwarfing even their own great ancestors, *Carcharodon megalodon*. Some species of dolphins had also survived, along with rays, eels, tuna, halibut and even the tiniest of sea life, krill and phytoplankton.

Whales were the largest and most numerous survivors. Grey whales, Sperm whales, Common Minkes and Fins all thrived, indeed prospered, within the oceans depths. Adapting to the toxic waters over the centuries and mutating to incredible size. None, however, could boast the size of earth's mightiest life form: The Blue. Mature Blue whales can measure anywhere from 75 to 100 feet from head to tail, and can weigh as much as 150 tons. On E-06 these behemoths had grown to three times that size; nearly the length of a football field.

A pod of these majestic creatures numbering in the dozens called the Indian Ocean home and were busily feeding on a krill swarm off the coast of Africa when a Rip opened in their midst. The Rip closed within moments but not before the eight-hundred and fifty pounds per square inch of pressure at that depth forced thousands of gallons of ocean water and three hapless whales inside. The sudden absence of all that water disrupted currents for hundreds of miles, disorienting the rest of the pod and causing them to crash into one another as if someone had stuck a giant spoon into the ocean and given it a stir. Seven mature Blues and two calves were injured in the melee. The pod recovered and swam north in search of calmer waters.

On an Earth as yet unknown to BanaTech, Eddie Norton was late. His twelve year-old daughter Natalie's first violin recital had started ten minutes ago and he was stuck in evening traffic on the West Congress Parkway; a full two miles from the Daley Civic Center in downtown Chicago where the recital was being held.

His wife was going to kill him and he'd never hear the end of it from Natalie. She'd been so proud to have been selected to play in the Thanksgiving recital, so excited and nervous at the same time. She was damn good with an instrument he, a construction foreman, could not even hold correctly. A near prodigy. And now he was going to miss her big moment because all four hundred and eighty windows ordered for his current project—a ten story condo on South Michigan Avenue—had been the wrong size. It had taken nearly two hours to sort out that debacle and now he was stuck in traffic behind a moving van that completely blocked his view of the road ahead.

And to top it off it was snowing again.

He turned on his windshield wipers to brush away the rapidly accumulating snow—it was coming down much faster than usual given the mild winter Chicago had experienced thus far—when the snow turned to spicules of ice, and then to hail.

The Parkway bucked under Eddie's Ford F-250 as if he were on a bridge that had suddenly dropped a foot or so before holding. A hard, thick, smashing sound came from further up the Parkway. Screams and cries of dismay followed.

"What the hell?" Eddie muttered as his windshield and hood tapped and thonked in response to the impact of hail. "Shit!" he cried when a ball of ice the size of a softball crazed the right side of his windshield, first fouling and then breaking off the wiper on that side.

The car in the lane beside him, driven by an elderly woman who clearly felt that an inch was sufficient space between vehicles when idling in a traffic jam, suddenly lurched into reverse, crashing into the car behind her. Eddie watched, stunned, as she slammed her transmission back into drive before tromping the accelerator. The Volkswagen Beatle she was driving smashed into the Pontiac ahead of her with a resounding crash. Cries of pain and outrage came from within the Pontiac but the old woman ignored them and reversed into the car behind her yet again.

Eddie rolled down his window to yell at the woman to stop, *Just what the hell is your problem anyway?* and noticed that the occupants of other vehicles around him were acting with similar alarm. Some were talking or shouting animatedly, others were pointing towards the sky in the direction ahead of them—the direction he couldn't see because of the Mayflower truck belching exhaust into the air directly in front of him.

Some drivers and passengers had fled their vehicles and were winding their way between cars and across the Parkway despite being pelted by hail, perhaps seeking shelter in the surrounding buildings.

The old woman who'd decided the best option for forcing her way out of the traffic jam was to act like a driver at a second rate demolition derby had stopped her vehicle. She was looking towards the sky, a look of sheer terror on her face.

She glanced in Eddie's direction, briefly making eye contact before a slab of ice the size of a kitchen stove smashed through her windshield, crushing her upper torso. A fine mist of blood rose up as the car shuddered under the impact.

"Holy God!" Eddie screamed.

The moving van ahead of Eddie screeched backwards against its airbrakes as a similar sized chunk of ice smashed through its trailer destroying a child's bedroom set and throwing stuffed animals into the air. A Pooh Bear with a hunnypot bounced off Eddie's hood and onto the road.

Eddie threw open his door. The car dinged its disapproval of this action while the engine was running but he ignored it. He heard several more crashes and thuds from ahead and behind as more vehicles were pelted. People fled their cars in panic, most heading for the Federal Building on the south side of the Parkway.

Some made it. Most did not. A man carrying a briefcase went down in front of Eddie; his head burst open by a hailstone the size of a softball. His briefcase sprang open when it hit the pavement spilling out papers and his now useless PDA.

A teenage couple running hand in hand made it to the sidewalk in front of the Federal building before their relationship was permanently severed by a plate shaped sheet of ice that sliced cleanly through their arms at the elbows. The boy was then pelted on the back of the neck and went down, his spine shattered. The girl clutched the stump of her arm and screamed as her life's blood gushed out onto his body.

Eddie almost made it. He had gained the curb and was arrowing towards the screaming girl to drag her into the building and do something about that arm when he saw what had started all of the commotion. He stopped, stunned. Two blocks ahead something that was not ice had smashed down on the Parkway, crushing dozens of cars across all six lanes and the fronts of the buildings facing it. The bulk of the thing was grayish black where it hadn't split open, spilling ichor and intestines outward in a gory semi-circle. The front of the beast was hidden in the remains of an office building on the North side of the Parkway. To the South Eddie could make out a tail.

Not a tail, he thought. *A fluke. That's a big goddamn whale lying in the middle of the West Congress Parkway!*

He looked up in horror as the sidewalk beneath his feet darkened with shadow.

The Rip that had opened on E-06 had terminated in the lower reaches of the Mesosphere, one-hundred and seventy thousand feet above the earth. Temperatures of one-hundred and twenty degrees below zero had frozen the displaced ocean waters and instantly killed the three Blues. Warmed by friction as the mass descended through the stratosphere and troposphere, the mass broke apart, much of the water evaporating or turning to harmless snow and rain. Significant portions of ice and the animals themselves, however, remained intact and rained down on downtown Chicago causing widespread destruction.

Eddie briefly wondered if there would be enough of his body left to identify so that his wife and Natalie would know he hadn't abandoned them as more than four-hundred tons of whale plummeted towards him, the Parkway, and the Federal Building.

The public library in Glenfield, Montana on E-418 is housed in the basement of the local High School and run by a no nonsense librarian named Beatrice Pfortmiller. The students call her Beady because of her small, deep set eyes and her habit of wearing her hair pulled so tightly into a bun that her forehead bears not a single wrinkle despite sixty-seven years of wear.

The Glenfield Public Library boasts a collection of nearly six thousand tomes, all tightly packed together on industrial shelving in five crowded rooms. Outside of the library, Beady will brag to any and all who will listen that this meant the towns inhabitants, numbering a mere nine-hundred and forty six as of the most recent census, could each check the maximum allotment of three books at the same time and the shelves would still be overflowing.

Inside the library patrons are more likely to hear the stout woman barking “Silence!” at the smallest sound that disrupts the tranquility of her domain. One dared not talk or even whisper in Beatrice Pfortmiller’s library for fear of banishment. And anyone with a cold or scratchy throat that produced a cough of even the quietest sort would be pointed to the stairwell exit in short order.

When the clatter arose, Beady’s head came up from the Dickens novel she’d been checking back in at the reception desk—first carefully screening it for damage or dog-eared pages—like a meerkat who’d sensed a lion in the underbrush. Her tiny eyes scanned the reading area before her piercing into the three fifth grade boys seated there. Each met her gaze in turn before guiltily looking back to the book or magazine they’d been perusing.

The sound hadn’t come from them. She’d have noticed any of them furtively slipping back into the hard wooden seats despite her attention being on the book detailing the travails of Esther Summerson. No. The sound had come from the Special Collections room down a short hallway and to the right. No one had slipped past her, either. She was certain of that. She took great pride in knowing who came and went from the library at all times.

Saying nothing to the boys—they too had heard the noise but knew better than to comment on or acknowledge it—Beady slid open the top drawer of her desk and removed the keys to Special Collections. The door to the room was kept locked at all times, even when it was in use; by prior appointment, of course, and only then with Ms. Pfortmiller’s direct supervision. No one had been allowed into the room in three days. And that had only been because little Becky Robeson had been given permission by the principal to peruse a rare sixth edition of Chaucer’s *Canterbury Tales* for an extra credit report on The Hundred Years War.

Beady quietly padded down the hall, curious as to what had made the sound from behind the wood and frosted glass door.

She might, *just might, mind you*, have left Chaucer’s tome out of place after ushering Becky Robeson from the room on Monday evening. It was unlike her. She was usually fastidious about the placement of materials in the library. But she’d found herself forgetting simple things lately. Like where she’d left her house keys or whether or not she'd fed her two cats that morning. It was nothing serious—nothing like dementia, or, God forbid, Alzheimer's disease. Not yet, thank the maker, but she'd been more tired than usual as of late and was well aware of her advancing age. The noise she'd heard sounded exactly like a large book clattering to the floor, so she couldn't rule out the possibility.

As she slipped the key into the lock there was another clatter of falling books followed by the crash of one of the metal bookshelves falling over.

Startled, Beady took in a breath. Then two more shelves went over and books cascaded to the floor with loud, papery thumps. An odd hooting and clicking sound followed.

Someone's in there! Beady thought, becoming angry. And by the sound of it they were vandals.

Vandals, in Beatrice Pfortmiller's opinion, like violators of the library's no talking policy should be dealt with swiftly and harshly, given no quarter to repeat their offence at a later date. She would first apprehend the criminals—she had no doubt there was more than one what with all the ruckus coming from within the confined space—and then she would call the sheriff. Furthermore, she would demand they be prosecuted to the fullest extent of the law.

Without hesitation Beady unlocked and threw open the door. Her cry of "Stop there and come out!" died in her throat when she saw the destruction inside. The room looked like it had been hit by a small twister.

Not three but five of the six eight-foot bookshelves been toppled. Precious editions of Shakespeare, Poe, Milton, Dostoyevsky, and a complete first edition set of Maya Angelou had been scattered about, pages torn and wrinkled, spines bent and broken. Half of an early edition of Dante's Divine Comedy, in the original Italian and complete with reproductions of Gore's engravings, lay atop a scattered collection of M.C. Escher's work. Its pages had been mutilated, as if partially eaten.

Beady scanned the room for the remainder of the manuscript, her anger rising further. *Someone* would pay dearly for this outrage. This *blasphemy!* She would personally see to it that there was a prison time and a hefty fine involved. Whoever it was was skulking behind the last still standing set of shelves in the back corner of the room. She could hear them back there. Tearing into paper and making giggling sounds like the chirps of a big bird.

"Come out here!" she bellowed.

And it did.

Beady's anger died like a flower wilting in too much sunlight as a long, reptilian head appeared over the shelves. The head turned at an angle like a quizzical dog while urine colored eyes examined her with cool detachment. It had greenish grey skin and elongated jaws bristling with teeth that were embedded in the second half of Dante's allegory. The creature issued a hooting sound of curiosity followed by three distinct clicks.

As Beady stared in wide-eyed horror a long, thin arm ending in three clawed fingers rose up and toppled the bookcase forwards and away. Her bladder let go as she saw the creature's long neck, the greenish tint fading to brownish black at the crest, the long, thin body and tapering tail. The tail swept to one side, scattering a pile of books into the corner.

The creature opened its jaws, dropping the *Divina Commedia* atop other books as it emitted a loud, deafening honk like that of an old air horn mixed with the roar of an engine.

Beady turned to run but was brought down by the agile, nine-foot long Calamosaur displaced by a Rip from its home on the Isle of Wight on a Lower Cretaceous era Earth.

The three boys in the reading room were out of their seats and had run up the stairwell exit out into the school's gymnasium before Beatrice Pfortmiller's screams had echoed away.

A Rip opened during a high school graduation ceremony in Bethel, Utah on E-197. Four hundred and seventeen graduates, high school staff, and attending family members were instantly pulled to their deaths deep inside planetary nebula NGC2818, over ten thousand light years from Earth. None of them had time to scream.

A Lufthansa 747-8I flight en route from Cairo to Germany flew into a Rip thirty-six thousand feet over the Mediterranean Ocean. The Rip terminated ninety-four feet above ground level just outside of Bay Lake, Florida. The pilot suffered a massive heart attack while trying to wrestle the behemoth back to altitude. All three-hundred and ninety-seven passengers and over sixteen-thousand guests of Mr. Disney's World Resort died as nine-hundred and sixty thousand pounds of aircraft traveling at five-hundred and seventy miles an hour slammed into Cinderella's Castle, spewing wreckage and better than sixty-thousand gallons of burning jet fuel over a six mile square area.

E-712 was completely incinerated when a Rip opened simultaneously in Elkhart, Nevada and at the core of a white dwarf several hundred thousand light years away.

Residents of Moscow watched in shock and horror as twelve hundred confused and frightened Confederate soldiers marched into Lefortovo Park on the banks of the Yauza river and began firing upon unarmed civilians.

As an ever-increasing number of Rips opened throughout the Multi-verse in an attempt to control the energy overload caused by the focal point Earths were joined together, if only briefly, resulting in devastating chaos on millions of worlds. Violent storms arose out of clear blue skies. Ash and lava erupted from peaceful, long believed extinct mountains. Hurricanes and typhoons raged on normally calm seas.

Billions died. Rarely considered yet vast forces of nature began to be affected.

Countless lives were lost on E-418 when spontaneous geomagnetic reversal occurred.

A naturally occurring event, geomagnetic reversal is a change in the Earths electromagnetic field. Magnetic north and south switch, the poles completely changing polarity. The process is typically slow and takes thousands of years to complete.

In the case of E-418 the reversal took all of seven seconds. The rapid and massive magnetic shift caused vigorous convection deep in the Earth's mantle. As a result, Lake Toba in Indonesia, Whakamaru in New Zealand, Cerro Galin in Argentina, and Huckleberry Ridge in Idaho, USA—four of the largest calderas on Earth—erupted simultaneously. Those not killed outright by the massive eruptions and subsequent pyroclastic flows—toxic gasses of nearly two thousand degrees traveling at four-hundred and fifty miles an hour—perished of starvation in the volcanic winter that followed.

Finally, gravity itself responded.

Gravity is the dominant force in the Multi-verse. It forms, shapes, and is responsible for the trajectory of astronomical bodies including asteroids, comets, planets, stars, solar systems, and galaxies. It causes the Earth and other planets to orbit the Sun and causes the Moon to orbit the Earth. It forms the tides and is responsible for natural convection. Gravity is the only force that acts on any particle with mass. It has infinite range and cannot be absorbed, transformed, or shielded against.

As chaos ensued throughout the Multi-verse, as more and more Earth's were exposed to the violent energies triggered by the creation of the artificial Rip, gravity began tearing aside the veils between each Universe, exposing them, *en masse*, to the gravitic forces of each other. Slowly at first, then gaining momentum, they began to draw together like iron filings exposed to a magnet.

The Multi-verse began to converge.

Chapter 32

"Ah," Richard heard from his right. "You're awake."

He turned his head and saw Stephen Bana seated on a wooden stool beside the bed he was laying on. There was no pain now, neither from his head nor his chest. He knew his wounds had been grievous, likely lethal. That and the presence of Bana told him he'd ripped onto the sanctuary Earth.

"I didn't know if you'd survive," Bana said, reading his thoughts. "You lost a lot of blood and even this Earth's therapeutic properties have their limits."

"How long?" Richard asked, meaning *how long have I been here?*

"Almost two days," Bana said. "Eralah and I were quite startled to find you lying in the courtyard, covered in blood and unconscious. We brought you inside and cleaned you up, sealed what wounds we could and waited to see if you would come around or remain insensate." Bana paused, then added, "You must tell me how you mastered the Rips so quickly."

"Getting shot in the face does wonders for your powers of concentration," Richard threw back the thin sheet he'd been covered with and sat up.

His bare feet touched cool stone as he rose. He began gathering his clothes, washed clean of his blood and the muck of a half dozen Earths. They were tattered and torn as if he'd worn nothing else for years but were still serviceable.

"And where the hell was Eralah while Elianna and I were ripping into a trap?" Richard asked angrily as he yanked on his pants. "Sophia's been up to her neck in it with BanaTech this entire time. Why didn't she warn us?"

"You overestimate her powers, brother," Bana said. "The Cherubim are not all knowing, all seeing creatures. She was as oblivious to Sophia's treachery as you were. She saw what happened to you and related the events to me but you brought yourself here before we could devise a way to come to your aid. She has since gone on her way, trying to undo some of the damage you have caused."

"What are you talking about?" Richard paused while pulling on his shirt.

"I'm talking about your obstinacy, Richard," Bana replied with growing anger of his own "Your stubborn and pig-headed refusal to follow a course of action that would have indefinitely curtailed BanaTech's efforts to create a focal point and open an artificial Rip. This has always been your way—tenaciously and inflexibly following your own convictions regardless of the risk to others. In the past it has been inconsequential. Despite your foolishness things have had a way of working out in your favor. This time, however, you have failed utterly and completely. Elianna is gone beyond our reach and BanaTech has succeeded. The focal point has been opened. The Multi-verse is converging with disastrous results and soon the Infernal will gain access to the Rips and the souls of humanity. Your insistence on saving the life of one little girl has damned us all."

Stunned at the revelation that the focal point was open Richard sat heavily on the bed. He rubbed his hand across his head and fingered the small, puckered—and heavily coated with cyanoacrylate—hole there. Could the older man be right? Had he simply cast aside the most obvious solution to the BanaTech problem because he disagreed with killing a child? Stubbornly refused to accept any other course of action than what he himself felt to be morally right?

Furthermore, had Sophia been correct when she asserted that he had followed her blindly throughout the Multi-verse on his quest to save the Key? Had he, albeit unwittingly, delivered Elianna to Jefferson through his own obstinacy? Was he to blame for BanaTech's success in opening an artificial Rip?

Was he responsible for the damnation of every human soul in the Multi-verse?

"I don't accept that," he said at length.

Bana made a sound of derision and brushed his hands together in a dismissive gesture.

"Your very words confirm what I've said," he replied acidly. "*You* don't accept that. Even as I've just told you that all is lost, the focal point is open, the Multi-verse is converging and the Infernal are on the rise, the great Michael the Archangel stubbornly rejects his own failure.

"Go then, *brother*," Bana's words dripped with contempt. "Call up a Rip and venture out into the Multi-verse. See what you have wrought. Your human form won't last long though. My attendants and I have quelled the bleeding from your wounds for now but we can do nothing about the rib perforating your lung. You will bleed out into your chest cavity or asphyxiate within minutes of setting foot on another Earth. And those few moments will likely be filled with agony."

"And what is your solution?" Richard all but shouted. "To sit here and wait for a Rip to bring us death or for the Infernal to turn the Multi-verse into its own personal house of horrors? Just give up and accept what's coming without putting up a fight?"

"Of course not," Bana said softly, his anger gone at once. "I'd gladly give this life, lose all the knowledge I've gained, to put a stop to all this for once and for all."

"As would I," Richard said, his own anger fading like a flame with no oxygen to sustain it.

Their bickering was pointless. Counterproductive. There had to be a way to undo what was done, to close the focal point and stop BanaTech from ever constructing another. To stop the Infernal from gaining the limitless source of power inhabiting the souls of humanity.

For lack of anything better to do Richard slipped on his socks. As he pulled on his boot an idea occurred to him.

"What is BanaTech's greatest strength?" he asked. "Beyond their sheer numbers and their use of the Rips what is the one thing that makes their dominance of the Multi-verse possible?"

"The Quantum Crays, I suppose," Bana said. "Without them they would not be able to locate and plot the Rips. They'd be isolated on their Homeworld. And they'd have no communication or control of their satellites or RLPs. Much of their military would be cut off. Stranded. Without the QCs, none of what they have achieved would have been possible."

"Then the QCs are also their greatest weakness," Richard said. "Could their software be corrupted? With a virus?"

"No," Bana told him. "You must remember that I designed the first generation myself. They are thinking machines, programmed to learn, to become self-aware. This also makes them aware of outside influences and therefore not susceptible to viruses or hacking."

"They didn't unleash killer robots on humanity, though," Richard mused aloud.

"What?" Bana said.

Richard grinned soberly. "Never mind. What about destroying the hardware?"

"It's possible," Bana said after a pause. "But unlikely. The QCs are buried miles underground in a protected vault that is kept at a constant thirty-two degrees below zero to prevent overheating. They also possess the ability to repair their own circuits and re-grow their biological components. Short of collapsing the entire vault there is no way to cause enough damage to all of them at the same time to prevent their self-healing routines from becoming active. Even bringing a million tons of earth down on top of them may not be enough."

"What if we drowned them?" Richard asked.

Bana raised an eyebrow at this. Richard thought he looked not unlike Leonard Nimoy portraying his most famous character. He almost expected Bana to say: "*Fascinating.*"

Instead a look of astonishment—*Why didn't I think of that?*—crossed Bana's features and he leaned forward with excitement.

"*That* could work," Bana said. "It would take billions of gallons of water entering the vault at enormous pressure to be effective but it would rapidly short out their electrical systems and without those their biological systems would die."

"So if one of us ripped in there," Richard said, "and directed a Rip from, say, the Marianna's Trench, the QCs would be out of commission."

"Most definitely," Bana agreed. "It would be suicide. There would be no way to get out before succumbing to the crushing pressure or frigid temperatures of the water but it could be done." Then he sat back, his excitement gone, and sighed. "But the Elder would just have more built. It might cost him a year and a lot of resources but it wouldn't bring them down for good. Besides, whether they're aware of it or not, at this point the Focal Point Generator and the QCs are no longer necessary. The focal point is self-sustaining. Through Elianna it's tied into the Source, and that, my brother, cannot be destroyed."

"What about destroying the focal point itself?" Richard asked.

"It would require a vast amount of brute strength. More strength than you or I, or even the two of us combined possess in our human forms. Water in any quantity would not work. It would only wreak havoc on the electrical systems and maybe whatever construct they have confined the Rip inside. Fire would be more effective but I fear the Rip itself would persist. The entire complex would have to be obliterated and Elianna forcibly removed. It is unlikely she would survive the trauma. Again, at the urging of the Infernal, the Elder would simply have another built."

"Even if he's aware of the convergence taking place throughout the Multi-verse?" Richard asked. "The devastation and chaos his machine is causing on every Earth, known or unknown?"

"Yes," Bana replied. "Even if by now—and it's a possibility—he's intuited the true goal of the Infernal, the depths of their deceit and how they have used him to seize control of this realm. His innate greed and lust for power are his downfall. He is incapable of resisting their manipulation. His ego is so tremendous he's convinced himself that he is immune to it."

"Greed goes hand in hand with conceit," Richard said. "I believe the Elder would want to be on hand for the test of his glorious machine."

"Agreed," Bana said, "but what does that have to do with—?"

"You said taking out the QCs wouldn't be enough," Richard reminded him. "And terminating the artificial Rip will only delay the Infernal's power grab for a year, possibly less. If doing either will cost us our lives why not do both? Destroy the QCs and the FPG at the same time. And do it with enough punch to take out the entire complex, including the Elder."

"If BanaTech and their hierarchy *were* destroyed simultaneously," Bana said, "the Infernal would be without any of the machinations their scheme is based on. It might take them millennia to come up with another. Meanwhile, the balance of the Multi-verse would be restored."

"As we ourselves would be reborn," Richard said. "Hopefully to discover the threat again before it becomes too late."

Bana sighed: "It would be a minor victory. I fear this war will never end."

"Maybe not," Richard said. "But I think we can win this battle."

"What do you have in mind?" Bana asked.

"We'll need Eralah," Richard said, grinning, and told him the rest.

The Infernal waited. For millennia they had done so, severed from each other and the Source, mere shades without essence or power. Their wait had not been in vain. The Keeper Michael had been destroyed. It would be decades before his new human shell could act against them, if ever, and by then it would be too late. The Keeper Gabriel, his human form old, frail, and without courage, had hidden himself away on an Earth they could not see where he could offer them no resistance. The other Keepers: Ariel, Raphael, and thousands of others, had never achieved enlightenment—due largely to the efforts of Alex Jefferson to first kill all known Keepers and then to subvert their loyalties when that proved impractical—and remained ignorant of the task they'd been assigned by the ALL.

None who stood against the Infernal remained.

Soon the Multi-verse would reach full convergence and they would be free of their discorporated forms, granted access to the Rips, and reunited with the Source. They would feast on the power. Delight in the decadence. Shred and maim to their hearts content. Then they would have the souls of the billions who had perished, who were perishing this very moment. With *that* power they would reshape the realm into *their* image. Darkness, destruction, and death.

Their domination was imminent.

Chapter 33

The floor of the control room on E-779 rose several inches before dropping back into place with a jarring thud. Hairline fractures raced up the concrete walls and across the ceiling. Fine dust dribbled down on several consoles at the perimeter of the room.

The Elder lost his balance and would have fallen had it not been for Sophia. Ever concerned for the welfare of her benefactor she shot her arm out and steadied the elderly man.

Jefferson turned to the technician—Waller, his nametag read—who'd moments ago warned them of the Enigma Rips propagating throughout the Multi-verse.

"What the hell was *that*?" Jefferson demanded.

"There was an overload in the primary turbines that power the ZeVatron, sir," the youth responded, adjusting the glasses that had gone askew on his face and peering at the display at his console. "They exploded."

"Backups?" Jefferson prompted.

"They're down as well. I'm reading fire throughout that level and the level above. The auto-extinguishing system has kicked in and those will be out soon, but…" he trailed off, his fingers working busily at the keyboard.

"But what?" Jefferson barked.

"There's nothing supplying power to the accelerator anymore. All those systems are gone." He looked at Jefferson anxiously. "The accelerator should have shut down but it's still running. It's already above peak output and increasing."

"Christ," Jefferson muttered.

Everyone present knew the sequence of events on E-01 during the first test of the Focal Point Generator, and that a large portion of Finland had ceased to exist within moments of the power cascade in the particle accelerator there.

"We have to get you out of here, sir," Jefferson turned to the Elder. "If containment within the accelerator fails this entire continent will be ashes."

"I'm not going anywhere," The Elder responded calmly. He had a dazed expression on his face and was staring into seemingly vacant space beyond the observation window. "Containment will hold, Tyro. The Multi-verse will soon be at our fingertips and we will reap the fruit of nearly three centuries of labor."

Jefferson looked to Sophia. She, too, appeared alarmed but her stony expression conveyed her absolute faith in the Elder. He turned back to Waller.

"Can we shut down the Rip?"

"Unknown, sir," the young technician responded. "If we could cut power to the oculus the Rip should close on its own but the ZeVatron is running on its own now and the emergency shut off systems went up with the turbines."

"Sir?" Angela Martin, the senior technician Jefferson had earlier ordered to be silent interrupted from her console.

Jefferson turned to her, his expression warning that whatever she was about to say had better be good.

"We may not be able to cut power to the oculus," she said, "but if we can sever the link to the QCs, I might be able to stop the accelerator."

"Explain," Jefferson said. "Quickly."

"The QCs are controlling the power flow from the accelerator to the oculus. If we take them offline, I might be able to bypass the oculus, reverse the polarity of all that energy, and feed it back into the accelerator. The opposing fields should cancel each other out, effectively stalling the accelerator."

Jefferson, who thought her report too full of *if*s, *might*s, and *should*s looked to Waller. Waller simply shrugged as if to say, "It's worth a try."

He cast his glance back to the Elder, still staring at nothing with that dreamy expression on his face and oblivious to his surroundings. Sophia also stared through the observation glass, her eyes scanning the chamber beyond as if seeking out whatever held the Elder in thrall.

Jefferson looked in that direction. The techs in the room poured over their consoles studying the information relayed to them there, occasionally looking up and casting worried glances towards the observation window.

The Key, still restrained to the chair and wired into both the oculus and the QCs, had a look of sheer pleasure on her face. For a moment, no longer than a single heartbeat, Jefferson thought he saw a dark shape hovering to the left of the window, a bilious, torso shaped mass of swirling darkness that went up and up, out of sight past the frame holding the thick glass in place. A thrill ran down his spine, raising goose bumps there before radiating outwards from his crotch. Then the figure was gone. He chalked it up to anxiety and the massive energies in play in that cathedral sized space. He turned back to Martin.

"Do it."

Deep inside a vast cavern beneath the BanaTech Homeworld one hundred and seventy-six ten-story tall thinking machines thrummed with power. They were largely featureless save for cooling vents that ran at intervals up their sides like the rungs of some great ladder, their bulk covered from top to base in a pale white polymer that closely resembled human tissue. A thick gelatinous sludge, a byproduct of bioelectric synthesis, continuously oozed from this polymer skin to puddle on the floor at the base of the machines. Small, semi-intelligent bots resembling water spiders skimmed through the liquid and up the sides of the machines, clearing the sludge away from the vents to prevent overheating.

The Quantum Crays, essentially large cybernetic brains inside composite frames akin to human skulls, had diverted enormous cognitive resources to the problem on E-779. They had ceased analyzing data from the ever-increasing number of Enigma Rips as well as BanaTech's ongoing operations throughout the Multi-verse, devoting their attention to attempting to control the massive energy surges surrounding the oculus and the focal point.

They had already considered and discarded Angela Martin's theory that the ZeVatron could be stalled by introducing a charge of reversed polarity to the accelerator. While they predicted the scenario had a ninety-seven point three percent chance of succeeding, such action also had an eighty-two percent chance of sending a power surge of enormous and incalculable magnitude back through their own systems, severely damaging if not destroying their collective intelligence outright.

Like any living creatures, the Quantum Crays were hardwired for survival.

Featureless, but not without eyes or ears in the form of thousands of sensors throughout the cavern, the QCs noted the arrival of a human being. Dozens of molecular and biological scans revealed to them his true identity. Dr. Stephen Bana. Their creator.

Billions of thought processes occurred within nanoseconds. The Creator's disappearance from record seventeen decades prior was noted and compared to recent actions against BanaTech. These results were compared to visual records of the entity known as The Monk. Age progression algorithms calculated a ninety nine point seven six probability that the The Monk and the Creator were one and the same. A probable motive for his presence here was quickly determined.

He was there to destroy them.

Bana had yet to take a single step away from the Rip he had called forth, had yet to look around the four-hundred foot high by twelve acre square cavern housing the progeny of his mind before one-thousand and sixteen three foot tall spiderbots ceased their predetermined maintenance routines and turned to converge on him.

When Bana stepped from the Rip, the weight of one hundred and seventy-five years fell upon him in an instant. The pain was overwhelming. Arthritis that would have presented itself as irritating but tolerable aches, pains, and stiffness over the course of his natural life came crashing down in a single wave, driving him to his knees—now worn and brittle and protesting the impact. His kidneys, one of which would have failed in his sixtieth year had he aged as any other man sent agonizing pain shooting throughout his nervous system. His heart, rapidly thinning and aging as it would typically over the course of a lifetime began trip-hammering in his chest. As he placed his hands before him on the sticky floor he little resembled the sixtyish man who'd stepped through the Rip mere moments before. He now appeared sallow, skeletal, on the verge of death.

He'd never considered himself a brave man. His high-level intelligence had been discovered at the age of four when he'd diagramed the atomic structure of an oxygen molecule while the rest of his pre-school class had been scribbling vague shapes that were supposed to be horseys and bunnies. During childhood and early adolescence he'd been cruelly tormented by other children—and not a few adults—for his brilliance, endlessly ridiculed and mocked by classmates that were several years his senior.

After receiving his high school equivalency at the age of eleven he'd entered the hallowed halls of academia where the verbal and occasional physical abuse was much less tolerated. It was there that he'd found comfort and solace in physics, particularly quantum mechanics. The secluded laboratory and generous funding offered by the administration of the university that had recruited him offered refuge from the petty jealousies and trivial harassment of his less gifted colleagues, none of whom he'd understood and all of whom despised him.

Bana's youth and his considerable social ineptitude had allowed Alex Jefferson, or rather, a previous version of the man who had long ago joined forces with the Infernal, to manipulate his research under the guise of friendship and mutual interest, to direct and coerce his discovery of the Rips and their limitless potential. He had even allowed Jefferson to place *his* surname on the corporation.

"BanaTech," Jefferson had promised, "will be a beacon of hope for all mankind. We will cure disease and ease famine. End wars and bring peace to humanity. With your discoveries and my financial backing we will show the world that we are not alone. That other Earths exist and that with all of us working together under one leadership we can create the perfect Multi-verse."

By the time Bana had seen through the altruistic half-truths to the filthy lies beneath it had been too late. BanaTech controlled too many Earths by then, had too much technology and armament at its disposal, had grown far too extensive and evil for one man to do anything to stop.

Or so he'd told himself. As he had countless times before when pursued by bullies and thugs on faraway playgrounds or in long ago ivy-covered halls, he'd run away. Ripped onto a world where there was no one to persecute or use him. Where his brilliance was appreciated; even honored.

He'd told himself he'd find a way to defeat the Elder—the title Jefferson had bestowed upon himself by then—and his minions. One day he'd return and set things right. When he'd learned enough from Eralah. When he'd acquired enough knowledge about the ALL and his role as Keeper.

When he found his courage.

Bana chuckled as he pushed upwards to regain his footing. The sound was papery and thin; an old man's dry and brittle laughter. It amused him that he'd finally found his courage not in the in the face of countless human deaths, not in the threat of the Infernal gaining a foothold to wage its war against humanity and re-shape the Multi-verse into a nightmare from which no one would ever awake.

No, Bana thought, *I found my courage in the simple, selfless act of a dying man who refused to break a promise to a scared little girl.*

He had no idea if it had come to him in time or not but it would have to do.

The first of the spiderbots was upon him before he could push himself fully erect. It grasped at his ankle with pincer-like appendages at the end of its foreleg and pulled. Bana went down, this time on his back. If not for the thick coating of slime on the floor his rapidly thinning skull would have shattered on impact.

Two more bots were on him in an instant. One grasped his right hand and closed its pincers with two thousand pounds of hydraulic pressure. Bana's middle, ring, and pinky fingers were cleanly sheared off at the second knuckle. Blood spurted from the stumps as he cried out. The other bot had positioned itself at his left knee. He kicked out and it slid backwards only to skim back to him as another three bots came for his face.

Bana thrashed and kicked himself into a seated position, looking around furiously for some avenue of escape. He was calculating his odds of making it to one of the QCs and trying to climb the venting on the side when he saw the scores of spiderbots already surrounding him, with more advancing from the dark recesses of the cavern.

Before he'd stepped into the Rip on the Sanctuary Earth he'd called home for almost two centuries, Stephen Bana had known that his human self would never leave this cavern alive. Still, the scientist still very much alive within him had hoped for time to gaze in satisfaction at the wonders he'd created despite their current perverse function, time to touch them and feel their vast intellectual power thrumming beneath his hands. Time, perhaps, to speak with these, his only children.

He'd hoped for time to look death in the face. And perhaps spit on him.

A spiderbot eviscerated him with its pincers, spilling his intestines into his lap in wet, shiny loops of gore. Another sliced into his back, halving his liver. Bana realized he was out of time. As blood gushed from both wounds turning the biogel covering the floor a pinkish red hue he summoned a Rip from the planet's core boundary. He, the spiderbots, and the QCs were instantly vaporized as molten nickel, iron, and calcium surged into the cavern under tremendous pressure at seven-thousand two hundred and thirty degrees.

Flowing like water at that temperature the bulk of the core material followed the path of least resistance. It shot up through airshafts vaporizing everything in its path, traveled along passageways and corridors incinerating living quarters, laboratories, hydroponics bays and recreational facilities. Animals, plants, and people, the just and unjust alike, were immolated before they even knew what was happening.

Finally, core material shot up into the Elder's private quarters, through the thin walls and roof of the building, and out into the perpetual night sky. Had BanaTech's satellites still been functioning they'd have recorded a spectacular fountain of molten rock and metal shooting up into the sky for thousands of feet before falling back to Earth and sparking a righteous conflagration that rapidly consumed all that remained.

Chapter 34

The light within the Rips had changed. Ripples of a colder, darker energy cast a muddy tinge throughout their usual warm and brilliant radiance. That trace of darkness, like a single drop of blood in a glass of water, was spreading throughout the Rips, polluting the entire system.

Richard navigated his way through one Rip after another, bending this one slightly to meet that one, riding the currents and eddies within like a surfer in search of the source of the dark contamination—the artificial Rip on E-779.

Controlling the Rips was like learning to ride a bicycle. Once the process *clicks* for the learner there is little to do but get on the bike and ride. So it was for Richard. He hadn't thought about the mechanics of navigating the Rips. He'd simply stepped into one and gone for a ride.

He entered a new Rip and paused, sensing a greater accumulation of the dark energy within this channel. With no effort and little thought other than to ensure that the creature pursuing him was still in his wake he changed direction and followed the new course.

"My *God*!" Angela Martin cried from her console.

"That's not possible!" John Waller shouted from his.

"What is it?" Alex Jefferson snapped in response to the alarm in their voices.

"The Crays, sir," Waller turned to meet Jefferson's gaze with a look of pure terror. "They're...*gone*."

"What do you mean *gone*?" Jefferson said. "You've taken them offline?"

"No, sir," Martin said, fear quavering in her voice, tears swimming in her eyes. "I didn't have a chance to finish the command sequence."

"Calm down," Jefferson ordered, suppressing his own fear at what he was hearing and turned to Waller. "Tell me *exactly* what happened."

Waller turned to his console, swallowing the lump of dread in his throat, and accessed the logs with rapid keystrokes.

"At 08:17 and thirty-one seconds local time the Crays recorded an Enigma Rip terminating within their chamber. They also recorded the presence of The Monk."

Jefferson felt his chest tighten. So the robed figure was still interfering with their plans. What chaos had he caused this time?

"A few seconds later," Waller continued, "The Crays logged another Rip, this one originating in the planet's core. After that, nothing."

Jefferson could guess the rest. The Monk had opened one of his Rips and introduced planetary core material into the QC chamber. Nothing could withstand that sort of heat and pressure. It was also doubtful there was much left of the Homeworld. His fear rose, only slightly outweighed by anger. That *bastard!*

"What have we lost?" he asked.

"Everything!" Martin wailed, clutching handfuls of her brown hair.

Jefferson stepped to the console and slapped the woman hard enough to raise a red, hand-shaped mark to rise on her cheek. Her eyes widened but her tears vanished, her imminent breakdown stopped cold.

"Listen to me," he snarled, his face inches from hers. "We haven't lost *everything*. This complex is still here. A hundred other complexes on a hundred other Earths, each with its own independent systems and personnel are still functioning. If the QCs are gone, so be it. They can be rebuilt and the network restored, but if we don't shut down that Rip in there—," he gestured towards the oculus in the next room, "—your Elder and the rest of us will most certainly die."

Martin drew a deep breath, nodded, and turned back to her console. Her fingers flew over the keyboard like startled birds.

"The network *is* down," she said, a small tremble in her voice. "We've lost the satellites, all offworld communications, and the ability to track any new Rip formations. Our solar and hydro generators are intact so we still have power. We still have access to local computers and operating systems, except for those destroyed by the explosion on level F."

"Very good," Jefferson said.

That's more like it, he thought and looked at the Elder. His usual clear eyed, intelligent, and squared away demeanor was gone. His hair was disheveled, his clothing askew. He was muttering under his breath, still staring raptly into vacant space within the chamber as if in a catatonic state. At his side Sophia smoothed his hair and whispered in his ear.

I should have killed you long ago, old man, Jefferson thought, disgusted. *Tossed you into a Rip and taken over this operation before you let it get so out of hand.*

Then he turned to Martin and Waller.

"Can you still reverse the polarity of the energy within the accelerator?" he asked Martin.

"Negative, sir," Martin responded, consulting her console. "The fires are out down there but the injectors are fried. The system wasn't designed to contain that much energy. If we can't stop it or slow it down we'll have a cascade event in less than ten minutes."

"Christ," Jefferson muttered. *And all of this will go up like a roman candle.* "If the injectors are offline where the hell is the energy coming from?"

"Unknown, sir," Martin answered.

"I have an idea," Waller said. "I think it's *her*."

"Explain," Jefferson ordered, turning his baleful glare on Waller.

"Well, sir," the tech said nervously, "we essentially hardwired that little girl into the QCs and the oculus. Then the Crays programmed her to do what they couldn't—form a Rip and control its origin and terminus points *indefinitely*. Or at least until a shutdown order is executed."

"That command was already given," Martin said. "I gave it myself. She was incapable of executing it."

"Incapable?" Waller asked, "Or unwilling?"

"What do you mean?" Jefferson barked.

"We know she's still in there," Waller answered. "The logs confirm we received a message from a source other than the Crays that said *Stop*."

"The message repeated dozens of times." Martin interjected. "Whatever the Crays were doing within her consciousness she wanted it to end."

"Consciously, yes," Waller continued. "She suffers autism and that sort of assault on her mind undoubtedly frightened her but what about her subconscious? I mean, look at her."

He pointed through the observation glass at the chamber beyond. Elianna was covered in perspiration, her body rigid with tension. The techs took turns hovering over her and then their consoles, oblivious to the ecstatic smile on her face that lent her features an expression of sheer *bliss*.

"Whatever trip she's on right now," Waller said, "she's thoroughly digging it."

"What if we disconnect her?" Martin suggested to Waller. "Cut her off from the oculus and the accelerator. If you're right, the system will spool down."

"There isn't time for that," Jefferson said. "It would take time to safely remove her from the system."

"I don't think it would work," Waller said. "I don't think she needed the system in the first place."

Both Jefferson and Martin looked at him with surprise.

"Think about it," Waller said. "The Crays only taught her how to open the Rip and control the flow of energy. She did the rest herself because she was already capable of doing so. She's *still* doing it, even without the Crays input. Look at her face. *She likes it*. The accelerator is still receiving energy because it's keeping her in her happy place."

"He's right," Martin said to Jefferson, "Look at her. Removing her from the system would have the same result as unhooking a laptop with wireless capability from a modem. The computer would simply find an available network and reconnect automatically."

"Then we kill the computer."

Jefferson turned and headed for the door, drawing a Mark XIX .50AE Desert Eagle from a scabbard on his chest,.

"I'm putting a stop to this right fucking now."

"No, Tyro." the Elder, suddenly clear eyed and in the moment laid a staying hand on Jefferson's arm as he strode past he and Sophia. "You cannot destroy the Key. We have worked too hard, struggled for too long, for such rash action. We can find another way."

"Look around old man," Jefferson spat. "While you've been off in la-la land gazing at God knows what in there this operation has gone to shit. If I don't kill the Key now, while there's still time, *she* will kill *us*."

He shrugged out of the Elder's grasp and continued on. He heard the Elder murmur "Stop him," as he reached the door.

Sophia was fast but Jefferson was faster. He spun and twisted the Beretta 92FS from her hand before she could place it against the base of his skull. A wide-eyed look of astonishment crossed her face as he pulled her to him and shoved the Desert Eagle into her sternum.

"Too slow, little girl," he said, his hyena grin set firmly on his face.

He pulled the trigger. Her body muffled the report but could not contain the jacketed 300 grain hollow point slug travelling at 1355 feet per second. The round mushroomed against her breastbone before punching through and carrying a large portion of her heart, lungs, and spine out through plate sized rent in her back with a splash of crimson. Martin screamed at the sight. Waller vomited. The life fell out of Sophia's eyes and her body crumpled to the floor.

"Tyro, *please!*" the Elder cried, stepping over Sophia's body to follow him. He grasped at Jefferson's shoulder. "You can't do this. You *musn't* do this. We've come too far to turn back now!"

"What the fuck is wrong with you?" Jefferson wheeled on the Elder, brushing his hand off his shoulder and sending the old man reeling into the wall. "We're all going to die! Can't you see that? Are you so blinded by greed that you'd risk everything on the life of this child?"

The Elder did not respond. Simply slid to the floor, weeping, and whimpered, "Help me, Ashmedai."

Jefferson turned and keyed the access panel to the chamber. The plug door dropped inwards before sliding aside. He crossed the threshold into the chamber, the Desert Eagle at the ready, and was brought up short by what he saw there.

A dark mass hovered before the girl, swirling shadow, seething madness, and fifteen feet tall if it was an inch. It appeared to be robed though the drapery was moving as if alive and seeking, riding on unseen air currents, twisting this way and that in an undulating motion. At the sleeves were hands made of darkness, thicker and more substantial than the robe, with skeletal fingers ending in long tapered claws.

Jefferson stared in awe at the face set deep within the cowl. The face was death, a grim reaper's visage. Two piercing, coal black points peered at him from deep hollow eye sockets. The apparition hunched its shoulders and bent its neck to him, its face inches from his own.

"You will not interfere." The creature growled in a voice that prickled his eardrums and set the nerves in his teeth aquiver. It pointed at him, poked a slender finger first at his head and then into it. Reality fell away at the creature's touch.

He was naked on a bed covered in fine silk and down, surrounded by women. Likewise naked, some writhed and thrust against each other, ministering to their own desires much as the four on the bed with him ministered to his. One rubbed oil into his chest. Another cupped her breasts to his mouth. One offered her flower to his groping hands as yet another thrust hers against his manhood. The room smelled of oils, sweat, and unrestrained passion. Soft moans of pleasure and grunts of animal ecstasy filled his ears. His penis swelled inside the wild erotic heat of the woman astride him.

"This can be yours," The creature pushed the probing finger deeper into Jefferson's brain. *"I am Asmedai. The Infernal. I can grant you this and much more."*

The scene shifted and he stood victorious on a great battlefield. The pungent aroma of blood, smoke, and cordite filled the air. Hundreds of enemies sprawled in various positions of death and supplication around him. Those who still lived begged his mercy while behind him thousands chanted his name—the name of their savior—with respect, awe, and reverence.

"And still more," Ashmedai spoke again.

He stood on a balcony overlooking a vast courtyard. He was dressed in fine linen brocaded with silver and gold. The chambers behind him were filled with coin of gold and silver, ornately gilded furniture, and detailed artworks of the finest craftsmanship. Beneath him in the courtyard were throngs of people as far as the eye could see. All bent their knee to him, prostrated themselves before him in abject obeisance, cringing, doglike, at his feet.

"They will worship you," Ashmedai whispered. *"Live or die by your very command. Submit themselves willingly to your merest whim. You will be as a God to them."*

Jefferson was entranced by the visions. His heart's desires had been laid out before him, all within easy reach. If he would only wait just a few moments more. Wait for the Rip to reach its true potential. Wait for Elianna—*the Keeper*, he heard the Infernal think of her—to coax the machine to full power. Wait for...*convergence*?

Jefferson pulled his head back violently, away from that probing finger. He shook his head and the visions melted away. The Infernal reacted with surprise. Never before had a human being read its thoughts as it had read his. Never had its touch been cast off so easily.

Jefferson turned to the Elder, now gaining his feet in the hallway.

"This is what you've risked everything for?" He asked furiously. "You ignored every warning, every objection to this project, even the QCs predictions that these experiments would end in catastrophe for this apparition and its contrived fantasies? *Your* fantasies?"

The Infernal let out a bellow of rage so loud it rattled Jefferson's spine. It reached for his throat as if to strangle him. Jefferson reflexively pulled the trigger of the Desert Eagle. The round passed as harmlessly through the Infernal as the apparition's hands passed through Jefferson's throat.

Jefferson's eyes narrowed as he realized that despite the specter's intimidating guise and illusions it obviously could not harm him.

"Get out of my way you loathsome fuck," he said and stepped forward through the phantom. It was like walking through a thin curtain embedded with the stench of a rotting corpse.

The techs scattered at Jefferson's approach, cowering behind their consoles as he approached the child strapped into the chair beside the oculus. They cringed as he raised the large caliber weapon and aimed for her head.

As Jefferson pressed his finger against the trigger of the Desert eagle Richard stumbled out of the Rip carrying a large, roundish object.

"Catch!" He yelled and threw the object at Jefferson.

Chapter 35

Jefferson recoiled in surprise at Farris's sudden appearance. He'd watched Sophia shoot him. *In the face*. The man should be lying dead on another Earth, reduced to chunks of gruesome chow by coyotes and bugs or lying in a morgue somewhere on that distant world. Not emerging whole from a Rip on this Earth and throwing things at him.

Reflexively, he batted the object away. It fell heavily to the floor in front of him, cracked on one side and leaking a milky, viscous fluid.

Farris fell to his knees and crawled his way to the far side of the chamber. *Whole*, Jefferson thought, observing the blood dripping from Richard's nose and mouth and the painful way he dragged himself along, *but not at all hale and hearty.*

Alex took a closer look at the *thing* Richard had thrown at him. It was grayish green and leathery, about the size of a beach ball but oval shaped rather than round. It didn't look like a bomb of any sort he'd seen before. It looked innocuous, harmless. With the fluid leaking from the crack up the side it looked like a large broken egg.

"Ooh." Jefferson heard Richard wheeze from across the chamber and wheeled toward him. He coughed twice and blood drooled down his chin to puddle on the floor. Despite being in obvious pain Farris grinned. "You probably should have caught that."

Jefferson's lip curled with anger and he leveled his gun at Richard's head. *First him*, he thought, *then the girl.* Then *we'll see who's smiling.* His finger tightened on the trigger.

Before he could pull it the forty-two foot crested dragon that had pursued Richard into the Rip on the sanctuary Earth burst violently into the chamber shattering the oculus. It was designed to focus energy on a single point within its periphery, not to withstand mass of such enormous proportions. Shards of the two-foot thick composite ring shot outwards in every direction.

Miranda Cortez, the systems technician, was impaled through the chest by a three foot long metallic and composite spear of debris. She had time to goggle at the length and girth of the dragon's bluish black scaled body before the lack of blood to her brain shut down her vision and darkness escorted her into oblivion.

The med tech Maxwell Perry was beheaded when a basketball sized chunk of the machine flew outwards. It had sufficient force to leave a cracked depression containing bits of his skull and brain matter on the far wall of the chamber.

Alicia Cortez survived the destruction of the oculus and was staring in awe at the magnificent creature that had appeared before her, the subtle rainbow-like iridescence that shot down the dragon's back and across scales the size of her head as light moved across its body, the timber sized hind legs and feet tipped with razor sharp talons, the blue black spiked scales that stood up along the length of its back and down its tail. She stood frozen in place, enthralled, as the barb-tipped tail swept towards her and cut her messily in half.

The dragon's wings spared Elianna from death by flying debris. The thin but powerful membrane had thrust the restraint chair away from the fallout and against the far wall where it toppled onto its side. The leads connecting Elianna to the computer towers and the oculus were severed, some violently yanked from their connectors. Blood wept in fine trickles from around the ports surgically implanted in her spine.

The dragon craned back its head, lifted both wings as far as possible in that confined space, and roared. The sound deafened the still standing Jefferson and those watching in shock through the thick glass in the control room.

The creature lowered its head and examined the chamber. Wide set, muddy yellow eyes seized upon Richard lying motionless on the floor. Spiked scales on the dragon's throat puffed out, beardlike. The crest on its head rose as it spied the thief. Its head dipped towards the floor, lips peeling back to reveal leg-sized teeth as the beast inhaled his scent.

Richard was motionless but not unconscious. Beyond the healing effect of the sanctuary Earth his body was once again wracked with pain. From his head to his broken ribs and punctured lung his nervous system cried out in agony from the beating and gunshot he'd sustained on E-514. He felt the dragon's breath caress him, smelled the hot and rancid odor of death wash over him.

He was saddened by what he'd done, felt remorse for the loss of the dragon's offspring. Though brutal by nature she was an innocent party in all this. Richard regretted that he'd found no alternative but to use her innate savagery to carry out his mission.

Eralah too had had misgivings about the plan but had gone along with it. The Cherubim had shown the creature her true form, both frightening and startling the magnificent beast long enough for Richard to rip into her nest and steal one of the three eggs incubating there. The dragon had reacted with predictable fury, following Richard as he conjured another Rip and fled through it, the dragon hot on his heels.

Her quarry now vulnerable before her, the dragon opened her massive jaws and would have gobbled Richard up whole if Jefferson hadn't chosen that moment to open fire.

He emptied the Desert Eagle into the dragon's head. The five remaining rounds in the clip spanged harmlessly off the dragon's armored scales like popcorn kernels bouncing off the inside of a pan. One ricochet crashed into the observation window, cracking the thick glass and startling those inside. Another ploughed into the body of the already dead med tech.

The dragon's black head swiveled on its long neck. Her urine-colored eyes settled on Jefferson. She sized him up, noting little of interest until she spied the broken egg lying at his feet. Then her head craned sideways, doglike, and her eyes lit with dark fury.

"Fuck me," Jefferson muttered, realizing the importance of the egg and Richard's last comment.

In one swift, serpent-like move the dragon seized Alex Jefferson around the midsection. She tossed him up towards the ceiling of the chamber, her razor sharp incisors slicing through the soft tissues of his stomach and cutting cleanly through abdominal muscle. He screamed as blood gushed and his intestines spilled out.

Like a dog playing with a ball the dragon caught the dangling intestines as Jefferson fell towards the floor and thrust him into the air again. He issued a blood curdling, inhuman scream as fresh agony exploded in his viscera. As he fell the second time the creature caught him around the head and shoulders with her molars and bit down, crushing his upper body and skull like a crème-filled hard candy. Then she spat out Jefferson's remains as if she'd found the taste not to her liking. She bent her head and nuzzled the broken egg on the bloodstained floor making a cooing sound much like the heartbroken sob of a woman.

Three black clad BanaTech security officers stormed the chamber. Seeing the carnage in the chamber and what was responsible for it, one immediately stopped, muttered "Oh *hell* no," and reversed course, nearly bowling over the Elder as he made his way through the portal and into the chamber. The other two began pouring fire from their standard issue M-4 carbines into the dragon's head and flank.

The dragon turned to confront them. Striking out with blinding speed she seized the nearest officer with one foreleg and squeezed. The sudden pressure forced his entrails out through his mouth and anus simultaneously. She cast the bloody remains aside and swept her wing at the second, nearly decapitating the Elder who ignored the slaughter around him and was making his way to where Richard lay on the floor in a ball, his hands sensibly covering his head.

The BanaTech officer continued to pour fire from the M-4 into the dragon's head and neck as the wing caught him just above the midsection, crushing his spine and internal organs. He flew backwards into the observation window and slid down the glass, still trying to fire on the creature with a now empty magazine.

The dragon lunged forward, snapping at the fallen officer with her massive incisors. The horn set directly above her nostrils slammed into the observation window, shattering it and showering the control room in a hail of glass.

Angela Martin, curiously calm for a woman who'd been on the verge of hysteria only minutes before, recognized the danger and survived the flying glass by diving into the kneehole below her console. John Waller wasn't so fortunate. He began screaming as a four inch dagger-like shard of lexan pierced his left eye. Blood and the burst eyeball slid down his cheek as he wrenched at the shard, trying to pull it free from his eye socket.

The dragon lifted her head at the sound, peered curiously through the remains of the window at the man inside staggering in circles, bumping into chairs and consoles, and nearly tripping over Sophia Bledell's body. She snorted hot breath through her nostrils.

Waller stopped, finally managed to trip over one of Sophia's outstretched legs and went down hard on his tail. He looked up at the visage of death staring in at him.

"*Mommeee!*" Waller wailed.

The dragon struck, her head and neck smashing through the remains of the window and the wall that supported it. She seized Waller in her incisors and swallowed him whole.

Then she pushed further into the room, crushing the hapless Angela Martin beneath her bulk and trodding on the fallen security officer. Large sections of the chamber walls and the ceiling of the control room gave way as unstoppable force met immovable object. Wood, metal, ceramic, and drywall pattered down the dragons back as the chamber and control room fell into ruins in her wake.

Another security officer took up position in the doorway as the dragon shoved her bulk into the control room in search of open spaces. He began firing into the dragon's face. A single round found its way up one nostril and lodged in the sensitive tissues of the nasal cavity beyond.

The dragon recoiled in surprise and pain, her tail swiping out behind her, narrowly missing the Elder who had been thrown to the floor when the chamber wall had collapsed. He was crawling now and whimpering, but his course was set on Richard Farris—he would kill the interfering bastard for destroying his glorious plans and unleashing this hellish beast upon them. Strangle him with his bare hands, if necessary.

When the dragon snorted and shook her head, bringing down more of the ceiling and the chamber wall as she tried to dislodge the slug from her sinus cavity, the security officer grunted in satisfaction. *So the big bitch can be hurt after all*, he thought.

Most of the technicians were fleeing in horror, screaming in panic and confusion, but the security force, made of heartier stuff, was responding *en masse* to the alarms braying throughout the facility. The security officer turned to call others to his side, missing the narrowing of the dragon's eyes and the wink of a thick, protective membrane sliding sideways across them.

The beast inhaled greatly, her abdomen swelling as she took in oxygen. The security officer looked back at the sudden intake of breath—and was immolated as the dragon let loose a stream of fire that rapidly burned through the back wall of the control room and incinerated the four security officers responding to his call.

Fire rushed down the corridors beyond reducing those in its path to glowing embers. The dragon reared up again, her head smashing through the remains of the ceiling and into the level above. Seeking freedom, she bellowed out her rage and began to climb.

Brother, Ashmedai said in Richard's head, *why must it always be this way?*

Richard felt revulsion at the Infernal's intrusion, a sensation like pus soaked wrappings from an infectious wound being shoved into his head. He tried to push it out and away from him but its power had grown since the convergence began, was *still* growing as the focal point remained open, spreading outwards throughout the Rips and polluting the Source with darkness.

Don't call me brother, Richard thought, his strength waning. My *Father is the ALL. You've given yourself over to* Him.

Do you dare not even speak His name, little Michael? The Infernal chuckled. *The first among us to challenge the All? Your precious Father is gone. Departed for reasons unknown to points unimaginable. The All has fled, probably to wither and die in some dark corner of the cosmos.* Lucifer *is our Father now. We all belong to him. And this realm shall be remade in His image.*

Lucifer's only desire is the destruction of humanity, Richard retorted.

Not true, Ashmedai protested. Despite its source, Richard could feel the Infernal's sincerity. *We* need *humanity. As each of them is born, the Source is reborn with them. They each carry the power of the All within their souls. We need this power to sustain ourselves. Without it we would all perish.*

So Lucifer's plan is to...harvest *them?*

And why not? Ashmedai answered. *They are insignificant pests, easily coerced and manipulated. Brother Gabriel led you astray. Once the convergence is complete we will gain the power of the lost souls and regain our rightful place in the Kingdom. We will not destroy humanity. We will restore the Multi-verse, much as it is now, and the humans will go on living their confused and petty little lives, as unaware of us as they were of the All.*

Except in the end, Richard thought, *instead of going to what they think is their eternal reward in Heaven, they will come to you.*

To be consumed, he added. *And in the meantime they will toil under Lucifer's dark reign, live lives of torment and torture at the hands of the Infernal as His darkness spreads throughout the realm, one Earth at a time, until the entire Multi-verse is under His influence.*

Join us, Michael, Ashmedai said. *Their suffering does not have to be your own. The one-hundred and forty-four thousand can regain their rightful place in the Kingdom and rejoice as Keepers of the Throne once again.*

And who will sit on the throne? Richard asked. *Lucifer?*

But of course, Ashmedai confirmed, *for that is it how it should have been from the beginning.*

No thanks. Richard closed his eyes; focusing what strength and will he had left, beckoning the Source. *I'd sooner rip into a black hole than kneel before Lucifer.*

Ashmedai sensed something growing within Richard, a power both disgusting and repellant. He felt strength, not unlike that of the light, swell within and push back against his hold on the Keeper's mind. For the second time the creature felt its touch being rejected and raged against it.

What are you doing? The Infernal keened, struggling to keep its hold on Richard's mind.

Remembering, Richard answered. *Remembering that there are Earths where you hold no sway. Earth's that I think you and Lucifer would fear to tread, even with the power of humanity's lost souls. Even, I think, with control of the entire Multi-verse. Gabriel called them sanctuary Earths and thought there were less than a handful of them. But I'm thinking there are more. Many more. Maybe as many as one-hundred and forty-four thousand.*

Don't be a fool! Ashmedai cried, besieged by the light now flowing through Richard's body. Beset by the repulsive force that steadily weakened its hold on Richard's mind: Love. *There is no corner of this realm that is hidden from Lucifer's eye.*

I think there is, Richard responded. *Neither you nor Lucifer knew where Gabriel was for all those decades. None of you suspected that I was still alive. We were hidden on those worlds and I'm betting it was no accident. Call them Sanctuary Earths, or Keeper's Earths, I think the All created them to stand as outposts, untouchable by darkness or evil, inaccessible to the Infernal, from which to wage war against you and your Father should the rest of the Multi-verse fall.*

Richard stopped struggling with Ashmedai, then turned and embraced him. Love and light burst forth from within him, washed over the Infernal, and cast him away.

When Richard regained consciousness in his human form he found himself standing; bleeding and wracked with pain but steady on his feet for now. The burst of strength he'd drawn from the Source had been enough to repel Ashmedai, injure the Infernal and send it howling from the chamber. But it had not been enough to heal his human form. He knew his strength would fail rapidly and his wounds would kill him.

He searched the room with his eyes for Elianna, listening to the sounds of destruction from the dragon's ongoing rampage on the levels above. The Rip's energy, a muddy brown now shot through with tendrils of blackish ichor, still thrummed in the center of the chamber. This was Elianna's Rip, created with her power but corrupt with the influence of the Infernal. He could navigate it and manipulate it but only she could shut it down. The Rip still existed so Elianna must still be alive. Whether or not he could reach her mind was another matter.

He didn't sense the Elder behind him until the old man wrapped his hands around his throat and began to squeeze. Though frail and approaching his eighty-second birthday, further weakened by the devastating turn events had taken, the Elder was more than a match for Richard.

Thin fingers, given strength by fury at his unraveling plans, locked like talons around Richard's neck. He fought for breath, prying at the vice-like hold. The pressure of the Elder's grip dislodged the thick wad of cyanoacrylate plugging the exit wound under his jaw and blood seeped out, coating his throat and the Elder's hands. The damage inside the wound worsened and blood ran down Richard's trachea, slowly filling his lungs.

Richard turned in the Elder's grasp. Fingers slick with blood did not loosen but slid across the skin allowing Richard some small freedom of movement. Now face-to-face the Elder grunted and renewed his efforts, using the heels of his palms to crush Richard's windpipe.

Richard beat ineffectively at the old man's arms, feebly pried at the steely fingers that were slowly crushing the life from him. Dark blossoms bloomed before his eyes and his head swam as his brain searched for oxygen. With every ounce of energy he had left he resorted to the last option he had and brought his knee up into the old man's groin.

The Elder's eyes widened and the air whooshed out of him. His hands raced to his crotch and he folded to the floor, curling up in a ball and cradling his scrotum with his bloody hands. He whimpered piteously.

Richard gasped for air. His lungs, one already punctured by broken ribs, the other slowly filling with blood from his wounded trachea, went into spasm. Richard coughed violently, vomiting a large amount of crimson onto the floor. He struggled to his feet and looked down upon the Elder.

The old man had gained his knees. The initial pain of Richard's blow had diminished leaving behind a deep throbbing that in turns nauseated and further angered him. He swiped his arm out at Richard's leg, still defiant, still trying to bring the younger man down.

"Bastard!" the old man railed. "You've ruined everything!"

He reached out again and Richard stomped on his hand. Brittle bone snapped under his boot as the tread cut gashes in the thin tissue of skin. The Elder wailed and cradled his now useless hand to his chest.

Richard thought to leave him there whimpering on the floor until the accelerator on the level below finally wound up past the point of containment and brought the entire complex down around the both of them. Elianna would likewise be crushed and the Rip would close, the convergence halted.

But what of the Infernal, already strong enough to once again commune with one another as Ashmedai had communed with him? To his surprise and dismay the foul thing had fled the chamber through the Rip. Had they also gained sufficient strength to act directly against man? To influence matter?

What of his promise to Elianna? To save her and protect her from harm? The unanswered questions and his righteous wrath at what the Elder and his predecessors had let come to pass decided him.

He grabbed the collar of the old man's sweatshirt—a scarlet and grey fleece with some stupid character with a buckeye for a head emblazoned upon it—and dragged him through the debris and pools of blood on the chamber floor to the still open aperture of the Rip. Finding strength deep within himself he yanked the old man erect.

"Go ahead," the Elder said bitterly, spying the ruined brackets designed to support the oculus still set into the floor and intuiting Richard's intentions. "Where this Rip takes me, I'll survive. I'll rebuild all that you have destroyed here and more. Whatever the cost, however long it takes, I or one of my Mirrors will one day stand before a working focal point ready to take the Multi-verse by the throat and mold it to perfection. And you will long be dead."

"Are you sure you know where this Rip leads?" Richard asked, stipules of blood spraying onto his lips and already blood-soaked chin.

Comprehension dawned in the old man's eyes as he recalled Waller's theory that Elianna had been able to control the Rips all along. Fear followed.

"Wait!" he cried and Richard pulled him closer to the Rip.

Richard paused.

"The Infernal gave me something to hide, a thing of great power. A book of some sort. They fear it. Fear someone such as yourself using it against them. Take me from this place now to a safe Earth where I can contact surviving BanaTech forces and I'll tell you where it is."

Richard considered the proposition for all of about two seconds before hurling the Elder, screaming, into the Rip. As he collapsed to the floor he reached out with his mind, nudging the Rip and its cargo onto a new course.

The Elder exited the Rip inside the event horizon of a super massive black hole sixty-billion light years from Earth. As he entered the gravitational singularity space-time curvature became infinite and time slowed to a crawl. He was both conscious and aware of what was happening to him. Over the course of thousands of years his body would be stretched, his individual atoms torn apart at the molecular level, his very essence destroyed by tidal forces before being crushed to infinite density. Ultimately his mass would join the total mass at the center of the black hole.

Power failed throughout the BanaTech complex. Emergency systems powered up briefly but failed within moments. The complex was thrown into darkness. Richard lay on the floor of the chamber, the pain of his wounds diminishing, his nervous system shutting down from massive blood loss. He stretched out an arm toward where he last remembered seeing Elianna, lying on her side, unconscious and still strapped into the restraint chair.

The sounds of the dragon's rampage had ceased. She'd either found a way out of the complex or been killed. Richard doubted it had been the latter. He didn't think anything short of a M72 anti-tank weapon or an RPG7 could have brought her down.

Noises trickled down to him from above. Screams of pain, cries of confusion, and the patter of debris still falling to the chamber floor. All else was silent save the soft crackle of fires burning throughout the structure.

In the dark, Richard Farris smiled.

We got them, he thought. *Destroyed BanaTech and all those who could rebuild it.* He coughed and thick, dark blood sprayed debris on the floor in front of him.

A thump came from beneath him. More rubble fell. A second thump, this one harder, louder. Then all was silent again.

That's the accelerator breaking containment, he thought. *Soon all of this will be gone and Elianna and I with it. The Rip will close and balance will be restored.*

I'm sorry I failed you, Elianna, he thought, his fingers growing numb, his body cold. *Sorry I couldn't keep my promise and get you off this Ear—*

Darkness enveloped Richard completely and his hand, still reaching out to the child he could not save, fell to the floor.

Minutes later, the ZeVatron beneath the complex overloaded. Three hundred and ten square miles of the Australian outback, from

Alice Springs to Yulara, went up in a fireball that consumed another thousand square miles in less than a minute.

SANCTUARY

Richard.

A voice called to him, comforting yet insistent. Small hands pulled at his bloody shirt and tugged on his arm. The sensation pulled him back from the darkness, back from the edge of oblivion.

It's over, Richard. The complex is gone and the Focal Point Generator has been destroyed. BanaTech is in ruins and will never threaten the Multi-verse again.

I've closed the Rip and am safe. You've kept your promise and did not fail me. Did not fail us. *But I still need you.*

So WAKE UP!

His eyes fluttered open to blue skies and he immediately rolled onto his side. He retched blood out onto green, sweet-smelling grass. Once rid of the fluid that had accumulated in his lungs he was able to breathe deeply. He inhaled the heady aroma of honeysuckle and lavender.

He sat up and looked around and was nearly bowled over again as Elianna threw her arms about his neck and thrust herself into his arms with a sob.

"Hey," he said for lack of anything better.

He absently smoothed her sweat-dampened hair back from her brow as she wept against his chest. He took in their surroundings, the perfect sky overhead, dragonflies flitting amongst the purple and reddish white blossoms throughout the vast field, a distant line of trees with majestic mountains rising behind them.

They'd returned—or been returned—to the sanctuary Earth where he'd first met the Seraph. Home to a playful band of fairies. Birthplace of a fierce and mighty dragon. He soothed Elianna until her tears had run their course and she lifted her face to meet his eyes.

"It's okay," he said and offered her a grin. "I'm here now."

"I thought I'd lost you," she said solemnly. "That you were already dead before we got you through."

"We?" he asked.

Elianna pushed herself backwards and sat in the grass beside him. She'd relinquished her hold on his neck but still clutched his hand. He noticed that she wore only a thin surgical gown covered in grime and blood—his and her own—and decided that suitable clothing for the child was the first order of business.

"You're pretty heavy," she said matter-of-factly, wiping away tears that had traced a clean path through the blood on her cheeks. Richard re-ordered his priorities. *First a bath. Then clean clothes.* He looked down at his own ruined clothing and could imagine his own appearance. *For both of us.*

"I called on a friend," Elianna continued. "He helped me get you through."

A rustling in the tall grass off to their left alerted Richard to another presence. Above the lavender blossoms he spotted a jaunty tail, heard the snuffling sounds of a big dog delighting in the discovery of new smells. The grass parted and Charlie bounded towards them, barking.

Mostly dog now, Richard sensed, detecting little of the awe and wonder he'd felt in the Seraph's presence. Perhaps a reward for the canine host, having done his job well, or maybe it's just the way it is. As Charlie had put it: *Always Charlie but Seraph there. Seraph too big for always.*

Before the big dog could reach them a small form buzzed his head. A ringing sound accompanied the tiny creature. Charlie stopped, his eyes going comically wide before sneezing explosively three times. Two more faeries ringed the dog's head, this time at a greater distance. The dog's head whipped back and forth, seeking. Then he bounded off in the direction of the faerie dust trail the creatures had left in their wake.

Richard laughed, realizing the faeries were playing with the dog.

Thank you, old friend, he thought, watching Charlie at play. *I owe you a million Milk Bones but I'm not sure how I'll pay.*

"How is it you got me out of there at all?" Richard asked Elianna. "The last time I saw you, you were pretty out of it."

"I *was* out of it," Elianna said, a frown creasing her brow, "but not in the way you might think. BanaTech's computers showed me how to open the Rip. I can't explain their language; it's all symbols, binary codes and quantum equations. But in my autistic state I could understand it clearly. I heard it as a loud voice, like a compelling song, that shut out almost everything else. It was pure pleasure, like being embraced by my mother and feeling her warmth against my skin. I only wanted to do as the QCs asked so it would never stop.

"Underneath all of that, though, I—or Uriel, rather—was conscious of everything going on around me. I could see and hear what they were doing to me and knew that I had opened their focal point. I understood what it meant for the Multi-verse and tried to warn them, but they wouldn't listen. By the time Gabriel destroyed the QCs and silenced their voice it was already too late. I didn't need the computers anymore. *I* was the one singing that song and I was lost in its embrace."

At the mention of Gabriel Richard sighed. Elianna cast her gaze downwards.

"I felt you in the Rip and saw you enter the chamber," she continued, "Saw what you brought with you and watched what it did. I knew why you were there—to keep your promise to me and stop the convergence. And still I couldn't stop. Didn't *want* to stop. Even when the dragon severed my connection to the device, even with the pain that caused me, I found a way to maintain the Rip and could not, would not shut it down.

"If you hadn't tapped into the Source," Elianna said, gripping Richard's hand tighter, "bathing me in your light and love just as you cast the Infernal aside with that same brilliance, I *wouldn't* have stopped."

Elianna gazed into Richard's eyes. He saw fear there; a young child's fear at discovering that the monster under the bed or the shadow in the closet is not only real, but also hungry. And that it bears the face of the very child it is about to eat. "I would have allowed the convergence, Richard. Would have let the Infernal have the Multi-verse and devour every human soul just to remain in that rapture forever."

"But you didn't," Richard said, hugging her to him. "You stopped singing and closed the Rip. You stopped the convergence and denied the Infernal their prize. And," he said, smiling, "you somehow got us home along the way."

"Home?" Elianna said.

"A friend of ours once told me I didn't belong here," Richard said, rising and pulling Elianna to her feet. "Not *yet*. I thought nothing of it at the time but it seems to me I do belong here now. And so do you.

"Besides." He smiled down at the girl, "It sort of feels like home, doesn't it?"

"Home," Elianna said, liking the feel of the word in her mouth. She smiled shyly up at Richard and said, "I think that's right."

Then, to Richard's astonishment, Elianna wheeled and dashed off to join Charlie and the fairies.

She may be an angel and Keeper of the ALL, Richard thought, wondering at the resiliency of children as he watched Elianna pump her arms and skinny little legs, her hair flying out behind her as she ran through tall grass and honeysuckle to catch up with the dog, *just as I am when needed, but right now she's just a little girl. And little girls need parents.*

Since no one else is around to do the job, I guess it falls to me.

He smiled with delight as Elianna juked left to avoid the sneeze inducing dust from several faerie who buzzed her head and Charlie barked at others who similarly zipped harmlessly past his.

Even on an Earth as wondrous as this one, where little could harm either him or Elianna—save perhaps being eaten by a dragon—his all too human body needed rest. Bathed in peace, Richard closed his eyes as Elianna played with the dog. He soon found himself dozing in the warm sunlight. A tickle at the base of his skull, a warm buzzing not unlike that of the dragonflies, roused him.

A Rip had opened several hundred yards away on his right.

The tingling he'd felt. He realized that he was now connected to the Rips and they were connected to him. He had touched the Source and it would now be a part of him, influencing his mind and senses forever.

Two figures in robes much like those Gabriel had worn emerged from the Rip. The first was a man unfamiliar to him. He was large of frame—about six foot two, Richard thought—and wore a blonde, well trimmed beard beneath shoulder length hair of the same color. The second figure's features were obscured beneath a hood.

Richard stood quickly, assuming a defensive posture. To his knowledge the Infernal were still incorporeal and could not assume flesh and blood form. Still, though the balance of the Multi-verse had been restored, the opening of the focal point *had* had consequences. He'd watched Ashmedai flee through the Rip on E-779 and could only guess at what other effects the partial convergence may have had. He studied the pair as they approached but could sense no malice in either their bearing or demeanor.

"Brother," the blonde man said, smiling broadly and extending his hand. Richard took the proffered hand and was instantly pulled into an embrace. "It has been far too long."

Richard, steeling himself for another vision of the sort brought about by contact with others who had greeted him as *Brother*, briefly returned the embrace.

No vision came and the man stepped back, his hands remaining on Richard's shoulder.

"I have been known by many names," the man said, "but you knew me best as *Ezekiel*.

"Okay," Richard said guardedly, stepping outside the man's reach. "Why are you here and who is your friend?"

He gestured towards the figure standing two steps behind Ezekiel, face still shrouded beneath the dark hood.

While he waited for an answer, Richard glanced in the opposite direction, towards Elianna. She and Charlie had stopped playing and were watching the exchange. Charlie wore an expression of canine curiosity, his head tilted to one side with that ear raised higher than the other. Elianna's brow was furrowed, as if sensing something familiar that she couldn't quite put her finger on. She began walking towards the trio. Richard gestured to her with one hand. *Wait.* Richard turned back to Ezekiel and his companion missing the surprised look of comprehension that fell across Elianna's features.

"My friend is the reason I'm here, Brother," Ezekiel said as the sound of small feet running on grass registered in Richard's ears. "That and what she possesses."

As the second figure lowered her hood anger exploded within Richard. He first recognized the silky black hair with Pacific Island features beneath. Then the brown eyes set with determination. Finally, the mouth, the lips barely curved upwards in a hesitant, shy smile. No doubt her hair smelled of lavender.

It was the face of the traitor. Sophia Bledell.

He'd promised to kill her. For betraying Elianna, the Multi-verse, and himself. Now he would make good on that promise.

"You!" he bellowed and lunged at Sophia. She let out a cry of surprise and shrank back.

"Easy, brother," Ezekiel inserted himself between Richard and Sophia. He pushed Richard back as easily as a man might push a child. "This is not your betrayer. This is the child's—"

"Mommy!" Richard heard Elianna cry as she dashed past and flung herself into her mother's arms.

"Oh, my God!" Sophia cried with delight. She scooped Elianna off the ground and swung her around before the both of them collapsed to the ground crying and giggling amongst heartwarming murmurings of *I love you! My baby!* and *Mommy, I missed you.*

Stunned, Richard broke off his assault and stepped back. Elianna's mother *could not* be alive. She had died right beside him in a fashion that no miracle of modern medicine could have remedied. Then her body had been torn apart and burned by the explosions of not one but two Hellfire missiles. She was neither Keeper nor Infernal, nor was she of the Saboath; hence beyond resurrection. She was a woman. A mere human being. How could she be returned to flesh and blood, *whole*, and now be holding her child to her in the grass just beyond his feet?

He looked to Elianna. Her face was buried in the robes at her mother's breast, her arms holding tight to her neck. She looked up as if hearing the questions in Richard's mind. The look of certainty on her face, the sheer delight, was enough to convince him that this was indeed the same Sophia Bledell he'd carried from the copse behind his house in Kansas, the same woman whose mysterious appearance led him to understand his true role in the Multi-verse.

His fury fled in the light of joyous reunion.

"How is this possible?" he asked.

"The humans possess an infinitesimal but vastly powerful fragment of the Source," Ezekiel answered. "It was used to restore her human form."

"Used?" Richard asked. "By whom?"

"The Guardian, of course," Ezekiel responded. "He who protects the Well of Souls. *Metatron*. He has need of you."

A thrill went up Richard's spine at the name.

Metatron.

In theology he was the most powerful angel in all of Heaven, second only to God himself. What did a being of such power require of him, a lowly Archangel? And why resurrect Sophia? What did she possess that was of such great importance?

"Sophia," Ezekiel gestured for the woman to come forward as Richard briefly wondered if the man—*Keeper*—could read his mind.

Sophia extricated herself from Elianna, stood, and approached with caution.

"I'm sorry I startled you," Richard said, meaning it. "I thought you were…*her*."

"She's gone, Richard." Elianna had moved to her mother's side and taken her hand. "I saw—*sensed*—her death. Jefferson killed her himself."

Richard felt a small measure of satisfaction at this revelation. Still, he was uncertain if he could trust this Sophia any more than her Mirror. *Mirrors are usually like-minded,* she'd told him, *sharing the same traits and characteristics*. Gabriel had later told him much the same thing. He would accept that she was as she appeared for now. But he would be watchful. Mindful.

"Thank you for saving my daughter," Sophia said as she removed a cylinder covered in what looked like runes from beneath her robes. "Aiding Metatron and retrieving this was the only way I could hope to repay you."

She uncapped the cylinder and withdrew a large sheet of rolled parchment. It wasn't paper but appeared to be made from the skin of some animal, rendered into a suitable writing surface. It was visibly old, heavily worn, and incomplete, as if it had been hastily ripped from a book with little care. Richard reached to help Sophia unroll it and Ezekiel slapped his hand away.

"Don't touch it! The document was sealed by the ALL after its theft and is of such power that you, as a Keeper, would be reduced to ashes upon contact. Only its intended recipients may lay hands upon it or read what is written there."

Despite the admonishment Richard tried to read the words written on the parchment. They appeared to be some type of cuneiform language but became fuzzy and swam out of sight when he tried to focus on them.

"What is it?" he asked with wonder.

"It is part of what I have sought for millennia, Brother," Ezekiel said and nodded to Sophia. She rolled the parchment back up and replaced it in the cylinder. "It's what you and Sophia must seek out now. It is but a single page from a larger manuscript and may well be our salvation.

"It is The Word of the ALL."

ACKNOWLEDGEMENTS

There are a lot of people who deserve thanks for helping me with this novel. Chief among them are: Lynne Smith, whose tireless (and merciless) editing kept my prose honest; Dr. James M. Tepper, Distinguished Professor of Neuroscience at Rutgers University, whose insights into physics and neurobiology kept the science plausible; and Karen Longbrake, a retired Psychology and Drama instructor from my high school days who, though her current whereabouts are a mystery, unknowingly gave me the courage to reach into the fire for that initial spark of creativity…and never mind getting burned.

The credit for what is right in this novel belongs to them. For the things that are wrong, the blame is mine.

I would be remiss if I didn't also thank my lovely wife Marie, who put up with the seemingly endless hours of absence while I remained locked away in my office and bore without complaint my intermittent and zombielike wandering about the house at odd hours while working on this novel.

Marie; my wife, my lover, my friend…I love you eternally.

Also by T. Joseph Browder

Dark Matters
http://tinyurl.com/nwntdp9

Plague: a tale of terror
http://tinyurl.com/paw45jr

Check out the author's website at:
http://www.tjosephbrowder.com

Before you go (for eReaders)

When you turn the page, Kindle will give you the opportunity to rate this book and tell your friends about it on Facebook and Twitter. They'll automatically post the cover of this book along with your thoughts on it. How cool is that? Be the first of your friends to use this innovative technology. Your friends get to know what you're reading and I, for one, will be forever grateful to you.

All the best,

T. Joseph Browder

Made in the USA
Coppell, TX
25 April 2021